12 12/30/58

388324A

Happy Birthday to the
"Ghoul of My Dreams"

B.J.

A CHOICE
of MURDERS

23 stories BY MEMBERS OF THE
MYSTERY WRITERS
OF AMERICA

EDITED BY *Dorothy Salisbury Davis*

NEW YORK

CHARLES SCRIBNER'S SONS

ACKNOWLEDGMENTS

The authors of the stories in this collection have kindly granted special permission to the editor and the Mystery Writers of America to include them in the book. Grateful acknowledgment is made to the authors and also to the copyright holders, magazines, publishers, and agents named below.

All rights reserved. Inquiries about film, television, anthology, and other special rights in the individual stories should be sent to the Mystery Writers of America, Inc., 228 West 24th Street, New York 11, N. Y. who will refer them to the proper sources.

"The Glass Bridge" by Robert Arthur, Copyright 1957 by H. S. D. Publications, Inc. Reprinted by permission of the author and *Alfred Hitchcock's Mystery Magazine;* "The Girl with the Burgundy Lips" by Lawrence G. Blochman, Copyright 1952 by Lawrence G. Blochman. Reprinted by permission of the author; "A Matter of Scholarship" by Anthony Boucher, Copyright 1955 by Anthony Boucher. Reprinted by permission of the author and Willis Kingsley Wing; "Mr. Nobody" by Wenzell Brown, Copyright 1957 by *Male.* Reprinted by permission of the author. This story was first published in the magazine under the title "Anonymous Fame"; "Mr. Wickwire's 'Gun Moll'" by Mignon G. Eberhart, Copyright 1956 by Mignon G. Eberhart. Reprinted by permission of the author; "The Blessington Method" by Stanley Ellin, Copyright 1956 by Davis Publications, Inc. (Formerly Mercury Publications, Inc.). Reprinted by permission of the author and *Ellery Queen's Mystery Magazine;* "The Man Who Wasn't Scared" by Andrew Garve, Copyright 1957 by Davis Publications, Inc. (Formerly Mercury Publications, Inc.). Reprinted by permission of the author and *Ellery Queen's Mystery Magazine;* "Blood Will Tell" by Anthony Gilbert, Copyright 1958 by Mystery Writers of America, Inc. Reprinted by permission of the author; "Snap Shot" by Michael Gilbert, Copyright 1957 by Davis Publications, Inc. (Formerly Mercury Publications, Inc.). Reprinted by permission of the author and *Ellery Queen's Mystery Magazine;* "The Night the Stairs Creaked" by Ryerson Johnson, Copyright 1958 by Mystery Writers of America, Inc. Reprinted by permission of the author; "Nonie" by Helen Kasson, Copyright 1958 by Mystery Writers of America, Inc. Reprinted by permission of the author; "The Stranger on Horseback" by James A. Kirch, Copyright 1947 by James A. Kirch. Reprinted by permission of the author; "Guilt-Edged Blonde" by Ross Macdonald, Copyright 1953 by Flying Eagle Publications, Inc. Reprinted by permission of the author and Flying Eagle Publications, Inc.; "A Decidedly Innocent Man" by Margaret Manners, Copyright 1957 by H. S. D. Publications, Inc. Reprinted by permission of the author and *Alfred Hitchcock's Mystery Magazine;* "The Shill" by Stephen Marlowe, Copyright 1955 by Star Publications, Inc. Reprinted by permission of the author and the author's agents, Scott Meredith Literary Agency, Inc.; "The Couple Next Door" by Margaret Millar, Copyright 1954 by Davis Publications, Inc. (Formerly Mercury Publications, Inc.). Reprinted by permission of the author and *Ellery Queen's Mystery Magazine;* "Future Imperfect" by Stuart Palmer, Copyright 1957 by *Mystery Digest.* Reprinted by permission of the author and *Mystery Digest;* "Murder for Fine Art" by John Basye Price, Copyright 1958 by Mystery Writers of America, Inc. Reprinted by permission of the author; "The Inner Circle" by Ellery Queen, Copyright 1946 by Little, Brown and Company. Reprinted by permission of the author and *Ellery Queen's Mystery Magazine,* First published as "The Adventure of the Inner Circle"; "Theresa" by Marc Seymour, Copyright 1957 by H. S. D. Publications, Inc. Reprinted by permission of the author and *Alfred Hitchcock's Mystery Magazine;* "Cover Her Face" by Ruthven Todd, Copyright 1957 by King-Size Publications, Inc. Reprinted by permission of the author and King-Size Publications, Inc.; "Justice Magnifique" by Lawrence Treat, Copyright 1958 by H. S. D. Publications, Inc. Reprinted by permission of the author and *Alfred Hitchcock's Mystery Magazine.* This story first appeared in the magazine under the title "The French Touch"; "11 O'Clock Bulletin" by Robert Turner, Copyright 1955 by McCall Corporation. Reprinted by permission of the author and the author's agents, Scott Meredith Literary Agency, Inc.

CONTENTS

CONTENTS

INTRODUCTION

ONE hesitates to worry the mystery these days with either praise or reappraisal. It is as often and as agonizingly re-examined as, say, our foreign policy, or as a small boy's ears.

Everybody is doing it.

Its fanciers do it. Its foes do it. Its own craftsmen, even its hacks do it, but the only galling meddlers really, to my mind, are those lugubrious friends of the family who come to it as to a wake, mouthing pious laments for the good old days.

Those were the days, as I understand them, when a detective couldn't see an ankle for counting the buttons that led up to it, when science was something he could put in his eye, or at least to his eye, and thereby have his logic confirmed, never confounded, when all policemen were gentlemen, polite however stupid, all scoundrels villainous from the nursery to the noose.

Well, the old days, good or bad, are gone. The mourners say the detective story has gone with them. Perhaps it has. I don't think so. I have a feeling that so long as a contemplative man walks the city streets, the country roads, musing on the ways and wonders of his fellows, seeking the predicate in that which was unpredictable but happened nonetheless, so long as there is surprise in love, joy in discovery, fear in the unknown, honor in courage and humor in the ironic, so long will the detective story discover man for man.

No, I don't really think the detective story has run out on us. Rather, I think we may sometimes—readers and writers—run out on it, naturally, properly, healthily, and only to return with the heart absence is presumed to make grow fonder.

No doubt the detective story has changed. As science has opened up so much that is new in so many endeavors, how reactionary to

vi

expect the story of detection or crime to stand still! Is the thriller less thrilling for the dagger's being in the mind instead of the body? Is the discovery of how it got there less a detective story in one instance than in the other?

The greatest change, however, is in the company a detective story must keep these days: where once it dominated crime fiction, today it must stand muster with numerous and distinguished fellow thrillers. Just how diverse a company they are, this collection of stories by members of The Mystery Writers of America may illustrate.

We chose as theme "Contrasts in Murder," seeking tales almost tender—in a deadly way, of course—and we have interspersed them with the hard, smashing lore of violent crime. Some are detective stories in what the purists would call the classic tradition.

I cannot be held solely responsible for these Murders: accessories-before-the-fact Jean Potts and Jerome Barry of MWA and accessory-after-the-fact Burroughs Mitchell of Charles Scribner's Sons are quite as deeply implicated. Scarcely less so, for having so willingly aided and abetted us, is Catherine Barth, MWA executive secretary.

And none of us would be in this predicament at all were it not for the generous connivance of more than a hundred MWA authors, twenty-three of whom now come forth.

DOROTHY SALISBURY DAVIS

Piermont, New York
April 14, 1958

The Blessington Method

MR. Treadwell was a small, likeable man who worked for a prosperous company in New York City, and whose position with the company entitled him to an office of his own. Late one afternoon of a fine day in June a visitor entered this office. The visitor was stout, well-dressed, and imposing. His complexion was smooth and pink, his small, near-sighted eyes shone cheerfully behind heavy, horn-rimmed eyeglasses.

"My name," he said, after laying aside a bulky portfolio and shaking Mr. Treadwell's hand with a crushing grip, "is Bunce, and I am a representative of the Society for Gerontology. I am here to help you with your problem, Mr. Treadwell."

Mr. Treadwell sighed. "Since you are a total stranger to me, my friend," he said, "and since I have never heard of the outfit you claim to represent, and, above all, since I have no problem which could possibly concern you, I am sorry to say that I am not in the market for whatever you are peddling. Now, if you don't mind—"

"Mind?" said Bunce. "Of course, I mind. The Society for Gerontology does not try to sell anything to anybody, Mr. Treadwell. Its interests are purely philanthropic. It examines case histories, draws up reports, works toward the solution of one of the most tragic situations we face in modern society."

"Which is?"

"That should have been made obvious by the title of the organization, Mr. Treadwell. Gerontology is the study of old age and the problems concerning it. Do not confuse it with geriatrics, please. Geriatrics is concerned with the diseases of old age. Gerontology deals with old age as the problem itself."

"I'll try to keep that in mind," Mr. Treadwell said impatiently.

1

"Meanwhile, I suppose, a small donation is in order? Five dollars, say?"

"No, no, Mr. Treadwell, not a penny, not a red cent. I quite understand that this is the traditional way of dealing with various philanthropic organizations, but the Society for Gerontology works in a different way entirely. Our objective is to help you with your problem first. Only then would we feel we have the right to make any claim on you."

"Fine," said Mr. Treadwell more amiably. "That leaves us all even. I have no problem, so you get no donation. Unless you'd rather reconsider?"

"Reconsider?" said Bunce in a pained voice. "It is you, Mr. Treadwell, and not I who must reconsider. Some of the most pitiful cases the Society deals with are those of people who have long refused to recognize or admit their problem. I have worked months on your case, Mr. Treadwell. I never dreamed you would fall into that category."

Mr. Treadwell took a deep breath. "Would you mind telling me just what you mean by that nonsense about working on my case? I was never a case for any damned society or organization in the book!"

It was the work of a moment for Bunce to whip open his portfolio and extract several sheets of paper from it.

"If you will bear with me," he said, "I should like to sum up the gist of these reports. You are forty-seven years old and in excellent health. You own a home in East Sconsett, Long Island, on which there are nine years of mortgage payments still due, and you also own a late-model car on which eighteen monthly payments are yet to be made. However, due to an excellent salary you are in prosperous circumstances. Am I correct?"

"As correct as the credit agency which gave you that report," said Mr. Treadwell.

Bunce chose to overlook this. "We will now come to the point. You have been happily married for twenty-three years, and have one daughter who was married last year and now lives with her husband in Chicago. Upon her departure from your home your father-in-law, a widower and somewhat crotchety gentleman, moved into the house and now resides with you and your wife."

Bunce's voice dropped to a low, impressive note. "He is seventy-two years old, and, outside of a touch of bursitis in his right shoulder, admits to exceptional health for his age. He has stated on several occasions that he hopes to live another twenty years, and according to actuarial statistics which my Society has on file *he has every chance of achieving this.* Now do you understand, Mr. Treadwell?"

It took a long time for the answer to come. "Yes," said Mr. Treadwell at last, almost in a whisper. "Now I understand."

"Good," said Bunce sympathetically. "Very good. The first step is always a hard one—the admission that there *is* a problem hovering over you, clouding every day that passes. Nor is there any need to ask why you make efforts to conceal it even from yourself. You wish to spare Mrs. Treadwell your unhappiness, don't you?"

Mr. Treadwell nodded.

"Would it make you feel better," asked Bunce, "if I told you that Mrs. Treadwell shared your own feelings? That she, too, feels her father's presence in her home as a burden which grows heavier each day?"

"But she can't!" said Mr. Treadwell in dismay. "She was the one who wanted him to live with us in the first place, after Sylvia got married, and we had a spare room. She pointed out how much he had done for us when we first got started, and how easy he was to get along with, and how little expense it would be—it was she who sold me on the idea. I can't believe she didn't mean it!"

"Of course, she meant it. She knew all the traditional emotions at the thought of her old father living alone somewhere, and offered all the traditional arguments on his behalf, and was sincere every moment. The trap she led you both into was the pitfall that awaits anyone who indulges in murky, sentimental thinking. Yes, indeed, I'm sometimes inclined to believe that Eve ate the apple just to make the serpent happy," said Bunce, and shook his head grimly at the thought.

"Poor Carol," groaned Mr. Treadwell. "If I had only known that she felt as miserable about this as I did—"

"Yes?" said Bunce. "What would you have done?"

Mr. Treadwell frowned. "I don't know. But there must have been something we could have figured out if we put our heads together."

"What?" Bunce asked. "Drive the man out of the house?"

"Oh, I don't mean exactly that."

"What then?" persisted Bunce. "Send him to an institution? There are some extremely luxurious institutions for the purpose. You'd have to consider one of them, since he could not possibly be regarded as a charity case; nor, for that matter, could I imagine him taking kindly to the idea of going to a public institution."

"Who would?" said Mr. Treadwell. "And as for the expensive kind, well, I did look into the idea once, but when I found out what they'd cost I knew it was out. It would take a fortune."

"Perhaps," suggested Bunce, "he could be given an apartment of his own—a small, inexpensive place with someone to take care of him."

"As it happens, that's what he moved out of to come to live with us. And on that business of someone taking care of him—you'd never believe what it costs. That is, even allowing we could find someone to suit him."

"Right" Bunce said, and struck the desk sharply with his fist. "Right in every respect, Mr. Treadwell."

Mr. Treadwell looked at him angrily. "What do you mean—right? I had the idea you wanted to help me with this business, but you haven't come up with a thing yet. On top of that you make it sound as if we're making great progress."

"We are, Mr. Treadwell, we are. Although you weren't aware

of it we have just completed the second step to your solution. The first step was the admission that there was a problem; the second step was the realization that no matter which way you turn there seems to be no logical or practical solution to the problem. In this way you are not only witnessing, you are actually participating in the marvelous operation of The Blessington Method which, in the end, places the one possible solution squarely in your hands."

"The Blessington Method?"

"Forgive me," said Bunce. "In my enthusiasm I used a term not yet in scientific vogue. I must explain, therefore, that The Blessington Method is the term my co-workers at the Society for Gerontology have given to its course of procedure. It is so titled in honor of J. G. Blessington, the Society's founder, and one of the great men of our era. He has not achieved his proper acclaim yet, but he will. Mark my words, Mr. Treadwell, some day his name will resound louder than that of Malthus."

"Funny I never heard of him," reflected Mr. Treadwell. "Usually I keep up with the newspapers. And another thing," he added, eyeing Bunce narrowly, "we never did get around to clearing up just how you happened to list me as one of your cases, and how you managed to turn up so much about me."

Bunce laughed delightedly. "It does sound mysterious when you put it like that, doesn't it? Well, there's really no mystery to it at all. You see, Mr. Treadwell, the Society has hundreds of investigators scouting this great land of ours from coast to coast, although the public at large is not aware of this. It is against the rules of the Society for any employee to reveal that he is a professional investigator—he would immediately lose effectiveness.

"Nor do the investigators start off with some specific person as their subject. Their interest lies in *any* aged person who is willing to talk about himself, and you would be astonished, at how garrulous most aged people are about their most intimate affairs. That is, of course, as long as they are among strangers.

"These subjects are met at random on park benches, in saloons, in libraries—in any place conducive to comfort and conversation. The investigator befriends the subjects, draws them out—seeks, especially, to learn all he can about the younger people on whom they are dependent."

"You mean," said Mr. Treadwell with growing interest, "the people who support them."

"No, no," said Bunce. "You are making the common error of equating *dependence* and *finances*. In many cases, of course, there is a financial dependence, but that is a minor part of the picture. The important factor is that there is always an *emotional* dependence. Even where a physical distance may separate the older person from the younger, that emotional dependence is always present. It is like a current passing between them. The younger person by the mere realization that the aged exist is burdened by guilt and anger. It was his personal experience with this tragic dilemma of our times that led J. G. Blessington to his great work."

"In other words," said Mr. Treadwell, "you mean that even if the old man were not living with us, things would be just as bad for Carol and me?"

"You seem to doubt that, Mr. Treadwell. But tell me, what makes things bad for you now, to use your own phrase?"

Mr. Treadwell thought this over. "Well," he said, "I suppose it's just a case of having a third person around all the time. It gets on your nerves after a while."

"But your daughter lived as a third person in your home for over twenty years," pointed out Bunce. "Yet, I am sure you didn't have the same reaction to her."

"But that's different," Mr. Treadwell protested. "You can have fun with a kid, play with her, watch her growing up—"

"Stop right there!" said Bunce. "Now you are hitting the mark. All the years your daughter lived with you you could take pleasure in watching her grow, flower like an exciting plant, take form as an adult being. But the old man in your house can only wither and decline now, and watching that process casts a shadow on your life. Isn't that the case?"

"I suppose it is."

"In that case, do you suppose it would make any difference if he lived elsewhere? Would you be any less aware that he was withering and declining and looking wistfully in your direction from a distance?"

"Of course not. Carol probably wouldn't sleep half the night worrying about him, and I'd have him on my mind all the time because of her. That's perfectly natural, isn't it?"

"It is, indeed, and, I am pleased to say, your recognition of that completes the third step of The Blessington Method. You now realize that it is not the *presence* of the aged subject which creates the problem, but his *existence*."

Mr. Treadwell pursed his lips thoughtfully. "I don't like the sound of that."

"Why not? It merely states the fact, doesn't it?"

"Maybe it does. But there's something about it that leaves a bad taste in the mouth. It's like saying that the only way Carol and I can have our troubles settled is by the old man's dying."

"Yes," Bunce said gravely, "it is like saying that."

"Well, I don't like it—not one bit. Thinking you'd like to see somebody dead can make you feel pretty mean, and as far as I know it's never killed anybody yet."

Bunce smiled. "Hasn't it?" he said gently.

He and Mr. Treadwell studied each other in silence. Then Mr. Treadwell pulled a handkerchief from his pocket with nerveless fingers and patted his forehead with it.

"You," he said with deliberation, "are either a lunatic or a practical joker. Either way, I'd like you to clear out of here. That's fair warning."

Bunce's face was all sympathetic concern. "Mr. Treadwell," he cried, "don't you realize you were on the verge of the fourth step? Don't you see how close you were to your solution?"

Mr. Treadwell pointed to the door. "Out—before I call the police."

The expression on Bunce's face changed from concern to disgust. "Oh, come, Mr. Treadwell, you don't believe anybody would pay attention to whatever garbled and incredible story you'd concoct out of this. Please think it over carefully before you do anything rash, now or later. If the exact nature of our talk were even mentioned, you would be the only one to suffer, believe me. Meanwhile, I'll leave you my card. Anytime you wish to call on me I will be ready to serve you."

"And why should I ever want to call on you?" demanded the white-faced Mr. Treadwell.

"There are various reasons," said Bunce, "but one above all." He gathered his belongings and moved to the door. "Consider, Mr. Treadwell: anyone who has mounted the first three steps of The Blessington Method inevitably mounts the fourth. You have made remarkable progress in a short time, Mr. Treadwell—you should be calling soon."

"I'll see you in hell first," said Mr. Treadwell.

Despite this parting shot, the time that followed was a bad one for Mr. Treadwell. The trouble was that having been introduced to The Blessington Method he couldn't seem to get it out of his mind. It incited thoughts that he had to keep thrusting away with an effort, and it certainly colored his relationship with his father-in-law in an unpleasant way.

Never before had the old man seemed so obtrusive, so much in the way, and so capable of always doing or saying the thing most calculated to stir annoyance. It especially outraged Mr. Treadwell to think of this intruder in his home babbling his private affairs to perfect strangers, eagerly spilling out details of his family life to paid investigators who were only out to make trouble. And, to Mr. Treadwell in his heated state of mind, the fact that the investigators could not be identified as such did not serve as any excuse.

Within very few days, Mr. Treadwell, who prided himself on being a sane and level-headed businessman, had to admit he was in a bad way. He began to see evidences of a fantastic conspiracy on every hand. He could visualize hundreds—no, thousands—of

Bunces swarming into offices just like his all over the country. He could feel cold sweat starting on his forehead at the thought.

But, he told himself, the whole thing was *too* fantastic. He could prove this to himself by merely reviewing his discussion with Bunce, and so he did, dozens of times. After all, it was no more than an objective look at a social problem. Had anything been said that a *really* intelligent man should shy away from? Not at all. If he had drawn some shocking inferences, it was because the ideas were already in his mind looking for an outlet.

On the other hand—

It was with a vast relief that Mr. Treadwell finally decided to pay a visit to the Society for Gerontology. He knew what he would find there: a dingy room or two, a couple of underpaid clerical workers, the musty odor of a piddling charity operation—all of which would restore matters to their proper perspective again. He went so strongly imbued with this picture that he almost walked past the gigantic glass and aluminum tower which was the address of the Society, rode its softly humming elevator in confusion, and emerged in the ante-room of the Main Office in a daze.

And it was still in a daze that he was ushered through a vast and seemingly endless labyrinth of rooms by a sleek, long-legged young woman, and saw, as he passed, hosts of other young women, no less sleek and long-legged, multitudes of brisk, square-shouldered young men, rows of streamlined machinery clicking and chuckling in electronic glee, mountains of stainless-steel card indexes, and, over all, the bland reflection of modern indirect lighting on plastic and metal—until finally he was led into the presence of Bunce himself, and the door closed behind him.

"Impressive, isn't it?" said Bunce, obviously relishing the sight of Mr. Treadwell's stupefaction.

"Impressive?" croaked Mr. Treadwell hoarsely. "Why, I've never seen anything like it. It's a ten-million-dollar outfit!"

"And why not? Science is working day and night like some Frankenstein, Mr. Treadwell, to increase longevity past all sane limits. There are fourteen million people over sixty-five in this country right now. In twenty years their number will be increased to twenty-one million. Beyond that no one can even estimate what the figures will rise to!

"But the one bright note is that each of these aged people is surrounded by many young donors or potential donors to our Society. As the tide rises higher, we, too, flourish and grow stronger to withstand it."

Mr. Treadwell felt a chill of horror penetrate him. "Then it's true, isn't it?"

"I beg your pardon?"

"This Blessington Method you're always talking about," said Mr. Treadwell wildly. "The whole idea is just to settle things by getting rid of old people!"

"Right!" said Bunce. "That is the exact idea. And not even J. G. Blessington himself ever phrased it better. You have a way with words, Mr. Treadwell. I always admire a man who can come to the point without sentimental twaddle."

"But you can't get away with it!" said Mr. Treadwell incredulously. "You don't really believe you can get away with it, do you?"

Bunce gestured toward the expanses beyond the closed door. "Isn't that sufficient evidence of the Society's success?"

"But all those people out there! Do they realize what's going on?"

"Like all well-trained personnel, Mr. Treadwell," said Bunce reproachfully, "they know only their own duties. What you and I are discussing here happens to be upper echelon."

Mr. Treadwell's shoulders drooped. "It's impossible," he said weakly. "It can't work."

"Come, come," Bunce said not unkindly, "you mustn't let yourself be overwhelmed. I imagine that what disturbs you most is what J. G. Blessington sometimes referred to as the Safety Factor. But look at it this way, Mr. Treadwell: isn't it perfectly natural for old people to die? Well, our Society guarantees that the deaths will appear natural. Investigations are rare—not one has ever caused us any trouble.

"More than that, you would be impressed by many of the names on our list of donors. People powerful in the political world as well as the financial world have been flocking to us. One and all, they could give glowing testimonials as to our efficiency. And remember that such important people make the Society for Gerontology invulnerable, no matter at what point it may be attacked, Mr. Treadwell. And such invulnerability extends to every single one of our sponsors, including you, should you choose to place your problem in our hands."

"But I don't have the right," Mr. Treadwell protested despairingly. "Even if I wanted to, who am I to settle things this way for anybody?"

"Aha." Bunce leaned forward intently. "But you do want to settle things?"

"Not this way."

"Can you suggest any other way?" Mr. Treadwell was silent.

"You see," Bunce said with satisfaction, "The Society for Gerontology offers the one practical answer to the problem. Do you still reject it, Mr. Treadwell?"

"I can't see it," Mr. Treadwell said stubbornly. "It's just not right."

"Are you sure of that?"

"Of course I am!" snapped Mr. Treadwell. "Are you going to tell me that it's right and proper to go around killing people just because they're old?"

"I am telling you that very thing, Mr. Treadwell, and I ask you to look at it this way. We are living today in a world of progress, a world of producers and consumers, all doing their best to improve our common lot. The old are neither producers nor consumers, so they are only barriers to our continued progress.

"If we want to take a brief, sentimental look into the pastoral haze of yesterday we may find that once they did serve a function. While the young were out tilling the fields, the old could tend to the household. But even that function is gone today. We have a hundred better devices for tending the household, and they come far cheaper. Can you dispute that?"

"I don't know," Mr. Treadwell said doggedly. "You're arguing that people are machines, and I don't go along with that at all."

"Good heavens," said Bunce, "don't tell me that you see them as anything else! Of course, we are machines, Mr. Treadwell, all of us. Unique and wonderful machines, I grant, but machines nevertheless. Why, look at the world around you. It is a vast organism made up of replaceable parts, all striving to produce and consume, produce and consume until worn out. Should one permit the worn-out part to remain where it is? Of course not! It must be cast aside so that the organism will not be made inefficient. It is the whole organism that counts, Mr. Treadwell, not any of its individual parts. Can't you understand that?"

"I don't know," said Mr. Treadwell uncertainly. "I've never thought of it that way. It's hard to take in all at once."

"I realize that, Mr. Treadwell, but it is part of The Blessington Method that the sponsor fully appreciate the great value of his contribution in all ways—not only as it benefits him, but also in the way it benefits the entire social organism. In signing a pledge to our Society a man is truly performing the most noble act of his life."

"Pledge?" said Mr. Treadwell. "What kind of pledge?"

Bunce removed a printed form from a drawer of his desk and laid it out carefully for Mr. Treadwell's inspection. Mr. Treadwell read it and sat up sharply.

"Why, this says that I'm promising to pay you two thousand dollars a month from now. You never said anything about that kind of money!"

"There has never been any occasion to raise the subject before this," Bunce replied. "But for some time now a committee of the Society has been examining your financial standing, and it reports that you can pay this sum without stress or strain."

"What do you mean, stress or strain?" Mr. Treadwell retorted.

"Two thousand dollars is a lot of money, no matter how you look at it."

Bunce shrugged. "Every pledge is arranged in terms of the sponsor's ability to pay, Mr. Treadwell. Remember, what may seem expensive to you would certainly seem cheap to many other sponsors I have dealt with."

"And what do I get for this?"

"Within one month after you sign the pledge, the affair of your father-in-law will be disposed of. Immediately after that you will be expected to pay the pledge in full. Your name is then enrolled on our list of sponsors, and that is all there is to it."

"I don't like the idea of my name being enrolled on anything."

"I can appreciate that," said Bunce. "But may I remind you that a donation to a charitable organization such as the Society for Gerontology is tax-deductible?"

Mr. Treadwell's fingers rested lightly on the pledge. "Now just for the sake of argument," he said, "suppose someone signs one of these things and then doesn't pay up. I guess you know that a pledge like this isn't collectible under law, don't you?"

"Yes," Bunce smiled, "and I know that a great many organizations cannot redeem pledges made to them in apparently good faith. But the Society for Gerontology has never met that difficulty. We avoid it by reminding all sponsors that the young, if they are careless, may die as unexpectedly as the old . . . No, no," he said, steadying the paper, "just your signature at the bottom will do."

When Mr. Treadwell's father-in-law was found drowned off the foot of East Sconsett pier three weeks later (the old man fished from the pier regularly although he had often been told by various local authorities that the fishing was poor there), the event was duly entered into the East Sconsett records as Death by Accidental Submersion, and Mr. Treadwell himself made the arrangements for an exceptionally elaborate funeral. And it was at the funeral that Mr. Treadwell first had the Thought. It was a fleeting and unpleasant thought, just disturbing enough to make him miss a step as he entered the church. In all the confusion of the moment, however, it was not too difficult to put aside.

A few days later, when he was back at his familiar desk, the Thought suddenly returned. This time it was not to be put aside so easily. It grew steadily larger and larger in his mind, until his waking hours were terrifyingly full of it, and his sleep a series of shuddering nightmares.

There was only one man who could clear up the matter for him, he knew; so he appeared at the offices of the Society for Gerontology burning with anxiety to have Bunce do so. He was hardly aware of handing over his check to Bunce and pocketing the receipt.

"There's something that's been worrying me," said Mr. Treadwell, coming straight to the point.

"Yes?"

"Well, do you remember telling me how many old people there would be around in twenty years?"

"Of course."

Mr. Treadwell loosened his collar to ease the constriction around his throat. "But don't you see? I'm going to be one of them!"

Bunce nodded. "If you take reasonably good care of yourself there's no reason why you shouldn't be," he pointed out.

"You don't get the idea," Mr. Treadwell said urgently. "I'll be in a spot then where I'll have to worry all the time about someone from this Society coming in and giving my daughter or my son-in-law ideas! That's a terrible thing to have to worry about all the rest of your life."

Bunce shook his head slowly. "You can't mean that, Mr. Treadwell."

"And why can't I?"

"Why? Well, think of your daughter, Mr. Treadwell. Are you thinking of her?"

"Yes."

"Do you see her as the lovely child who poured out her love to you in exchange for yours? The fine young woman who has just stepped over the threshold of marriage, but is always eager to visit you, eager to let you know the affection she feels for you?"

"I know that."

"And can you see in your mind's eye that manly young fellow who is her husband? Can you feel the warmth of his handclasp as he greets you? Do you know his gratitude for the financial help you give him regularly?"

"I suppose so."

"Now, honestly, Mr. Treadwell, can you imagine either of these affectionate and devoted youngsters doing a single thing—the slightest thing—to harm you?"

The constriction around Mr. Treadwell's throat miraculously eased; the chill around his heart departed.

"No," he said with conviction, "I can't."

"Splendid," said Bunce. He leaned far back in his chair and smiled with a kindly wisdom. "Hold on to that thought, Mr. Treadwell. Cherish it and keep it close at all times. It will be a solace and comfort to the very end."

AUTHOR'S POSTSCRIPT: I understand that since the publication of the story a society much like the Blessington-Bunce outfit *has* been set up in an aluminum and glass tower on Madison Avenue, and even in these Recession days is prospering mightily. If you want the address just call on me. I get ten percent.

EDITOR'S NOTE: *The Blessington Method* won for Stanley Ellin the MWA Edgar for the best mystery short story published in 1956.

11 O'clock Bulletin

THERE was the kind of heat where you lie on your back and don't move—hardly breathe, even—and still you sweat. I was in my room just lying there, staring at the ceiling and listening to the old lady clanking pots and pans around out in the kitchen when the thing began to slip up on me again. It was like a pulse beating in my mind: *Tonight,* it said, *Tonight, Tonight, Tonight.*

Lying around doing nothing wasn't any good.

I got up and walked to the dresser mirror and looked into it. I wanted to make sure I didn't look sick or nervous or anything—I didn't want to get the old lady upset. It was bad enough for her.

It seemed I looked a little bit older than 18 tonight, but maybe it was because I always tried to look tough and tense when I looked into a mirror and because I had a pretty heavy beard for my age; I'd started shaving when I was 15. But I didn't look sick or nothing. I looked all right.

Out in the kitchen there was the smell of something baking. It smelled good but at the same time it made me a little upset in the stomach. The old lady was hunkered in front of the oven and she was pulling a pie out of the thing. The crust was crinkled around the edges and nicely browned. She looked up at me and poked out her lower lip and blew at a wisp of hair over her sweat-beaded forehead.

"Apple, Davie," she said. "It came out nice, too. Your favorite, a nice apple pie."

"Hey, that's swell," I told her. I guess maybe I didn't sound too enthusiastic, though, because she flashed me a funny look.

"You want to set the table, we're ready to eat," she said.

I got out the silver and stuff and set it around and sat down and she put a big dish of franks and beans on the table. I got a knot in my stomach, looking at them. I got kind of like a sore throat. I looked up at the clock and saw that it was 7:30. I didn't mean to do that because I'd promised myself I wouldn't look at any clocks, but I just sort of did without thinking.

Then I got up from the table and walked out of the kitchen. I went over by the window in the living room and looked down onto the street. It was summer and still light out. The window was open and I could hear as well as see the little kids playing stickball down on the street. They ran around like crazy down there and there didn't seem to be any pattern to it but there was, of course. I knew that. I used to do it myself, over in the old neighborhood where we lived. Only remembering it, it seemed as though it wasn't really me but somebody else way back then.

When I looked up, I saw Mary Polaff in a window across the street, leaning out and looking over here. She's only a kid but she's got a shape on her already. I started to wave and yell something when I saw her quickly draw back out of the window. She thought I couldn't see her and she turned and called to somebody back in the room behind her and then her fat old lady came over to her and the two of them stood back a little from the window, looking out over here, and they probably thought I couldn't see them there, but I could.

I knew what they were staring at, what they were talking about. I shouldn't have done it but I got sore; you know how it comes over you quick and later you get ashamed but at the time you don't even know its happening. I leaned out the window and I could feel veins bulging at my neck and temples. I yelled:

"What the hell are you peekin' at, nosy? Go ahead and look! Take a good look, why don't you?"

Then I pulled back in and turned around and the old lady had come out of the kitchen. She looked like she wanted to cry but couldn't, and she said: "Davie! Please, Davie, please, darling!"

I turned away from her and stood there feeling dopey and weak with the anger gone out of me. She came over and put her arm around my shoulders. She said: "Come on out and eat, Davie.

Please. We've got to keep control, son. Remember what we decided. We aren't going to think about it. Please."

"Yeah," I said. "Only what the hell were they lookin' at? Do I look like I'm different from anybody else, a freak or something?"

I pulled out from under her arm. I said: "I guess I ain't hungry. I forgot to tell you, I had a hamburger late this afternoon, so I don't want anything right now. I'll see you later."

I walked toward the door and she sounded sort of panicky as she called: "Where are you going, son? What are you going to do?"

"I don't know," I said. "Going for a walk, maybe. I don't know."

She didn't say anything else but I knew she wanted to. She wanted to ask me what about the movie we were going to see, the musical down at the Parkside, the nice dopey musical that wouldn't have any crime stuff in it or anything, that she thought would be nice if we could see, but she didn't do that.

I felt pretty sorry for the old lady. I felt lousy walking out on her, but she was going to get on my nerves bad if I stuck around and I'd end up saying something to hurt her. So I got out. Maybe I'd get a grip on myself later and come back. I didn't know.

Outside on the street the heat was still coming up from the pavement and bouncing off the apartment houses even though the sun was almost gone down. I felt like I was going to suffocate. I walked fast away from the house, not looking at the people sitting out on the stoops. Some of the kids playing stickball yelled something at me but I didn't hear what it was and I didn't pay any attention.

After awhile I was at the 181st Street IRT subway entrance and without thinking about it or why or where I was going, I went in and downstairs. It should have been cool down there but it wasn't. It was hotter than the street. I took a downtown express. Those big crazy overhead fans in the subway car whirled and made a wind that mussed your hair up and all and blew pieces of newspaper around but they didn't make you any cooler. I sat right under one. There was about a dozen people in the car with me. It seemed every time I looked at one of them they were staring at me with a funny look but that wasn't really so; I knew I just thought that.

When we got to Times Square I got out and went upstairs. Broadway was jammed with people walking around, looking in windows and yammering at one another the way it always is on a hot summer night in New York. Up near the top of that screwy little triangle-shaped Times Tower building electric bulbs blinked out the time: 8:32 P.M.

I swore at the clock and at myself for looking at it and my throat began to hurt again. I couldn't seem to swallow at all for a few moments.

The first bar I came to, I turned in. I started to go right out again when I saw it was mobbed with service guys, Army guys and sailors in summer whites and a couple of Air Force guys, but then I figured maybe it'd do me good to get into a fight. Maybe knocking the crap out of some guy or vice versa, would help. So I went in and pushed into the bar between a sailor whose whites were too tight across his big can and a stocky-looking paratrooper. I didn't beg anybody's pardon for crowding in. They both turned too quick and looked at me but they didn't say anything. They just made room for me.

The back-bar mirror had a fishnet draped across it, supposed to make the place look cooler or something and when you saw yourself through the holes in the net you looked at one feature at a time. I saw I had a pretty big nose and I had one eyebrow higher than the other. I always thought I looked like Jeff Chandler, a little, only I didn't tonight. Not through that fishnet. I just looked like some ordinary jerk who was mad about something.

I had $3.50 in my pocket. I had a shot and a beer chaser and that was half a buck, so I knew I was good for seven rounds, anyhow.

It was a noisy place, with all the service guys talking it up and the juke box turned up loud so you could hear it out on the street and running without stopping. But nobody knew me here; nobody paid any attention. After a couple of drinks I got to kind of like it.

I didn't hardly feel the first three drinks at all or at least I didn't notice it, but then something happened, I knew I was getting a little tight. I don't get a muscle on over nothing at all until I'm a little greased.

The big swabbie next to me asked the bartender what time it was and the bartender turned and looked up at an electric clock on the wall down at the end of the bar. I hadn't noticed it before. I hadn't thought about the time since I'd come into the place; I swear I hadn't. But now I looked up at the clock, too, and it was 9:30 already and now it was only an hour-and-a-half off and I guess suddenly realizing it was that close, I got kind of uncorked. I turned to the sailor.

"If the time means so much to you, why don't you buy yourself a damned watch? They pay you in the Navy, don't they?"

As soon as I said it I knew I was going to get broken in half. The guy was big enough to do that. But I didn't care. It wasn't that I was brave or tough or anything; it just didn't seem to matter. But the Navy guy just turned around, looking kind of surprised. He said, quietly:

"You ought to take it easy, Mac. What's eatin' on you, anyhow?" He had one of those slow Southern accents.

I told him it wasn't any of his business what was eating on me and he looked me over carefully and shook his head sadly and said it was too bad he had a date and he was so late already. I agreed with him but he just looked back at the clock again and left the bar. I felt funny about that—kind of let-down, like; kind of disappointed. I looked both ways along the bar, waiting for somebody else to have something to say but nobody was paying any attention.

I had one more drink and then a blowzy old blonde hustler came in with some guy who wasn't so stiff he couldn't navigate but he must've been pretty well laced to be giving this bag any time at all. It was plain she was mining him and making time like anything. As soon as they got into a booth they started smooching it up. It was kind of disgusting at their age.

I was standing sideways to the bar, with my back turned to that clock at the other end, and I couldn't help watching this pair. Then, I don't know whether it was the drinks or what, but the blonde bindle began to look like my old lady. I mean like the old lady might look in a few years, maybe 10, if she dyed her hair. It was crazy and I don't know what it was about the blonde that reminded me of the old lady because she didn't really *look* like her, but it was something. It got me. It made me think about the old lady and what the hell good was I doing her or myself, even, laying one on like this, feeling sorry for myself. I thought that it still wasn't too late to take her to the show.

So I left the place. It was dark out now—as dark as it ever gets in Times Square, that is—and a little cooler. You come out onto Broadway at night and it kind of shocks you no matter how used to it you are. There's something about it. Like a world where nothing's real and you forget everything except you want to have a big time, a hell of a time; and if you're alone or even with some guys, you want a girl bad, real bad. It was like that with me, tonight.

It felt so good I walked down to 42nd and then up to 50th, stalling off going home for awhile, and then walked over to Eighth Avenue to take the Independent subway up to Washington Heights.

That was a bad deal. Eight Avenue was empty and sad even though it, too, was all lit up. There's something about Eighth Avenue; it'll never get anywhere. In some other town it'd be the big deal, the Main Drag. But it's too close to Times Square, here. It's like a dirty, beat-up old floozy walking beside a pretty young showgirl and they're both dressed the same but that's the end of it. It gave me the real glooms.

It made the thing I'd been trying not to think about all night, all day, being to press on my mind again like a thumb in a wound.

I couldn't let it. Once I let go and really thought about it I wouldn't be able to stop. I all at once felt all alone, walking along Eighth there, like that, and about four inches high and trembling scared and I had to do something fast. I went into another creep joint.

This one was bird. I hadn't noticed the name of it but the minute I went in I knew it was called Paddy's Shamrock Bar or something. It was one of those saloons that cater to professional Irishmen. They had a raft of crazy-shaped shillelaghs hanging back of the bar and some brown derbys and they still had dirty green bunting and decorations from St. Patrick's Day draped across the mirror here in August, for crying out loud. But it wasn't very crowded and they had a big 30-inch TV set going and I didn't see any clock in the place. So I bellied up to the bar, like they say in the Westerns.

The TV had one of those situation-comedy things on, all about a dumb blonde and her roommate, only the blonde's dumbness didn't get on your nerves because she was kind of cute about it and what she had in front, it didn't make much difference how dumb she was. It didn't break me up or give me convulsions or anything but it was something to watch that put you in a kind of vacuum and the dozen or so Countycorkmen in the joint got such a root out of it, it was contagious. I even laughed, once.

I had two more boilermakers while this was on and was on the seventh, the last one I could pay for, when the thing ended. The stuff had taken hold by this time, too, though not as good as I wanted. All I had was a kind of loose, tingle-fingered, putty-like looseness all over and everything was too sharply focused like in 3-D or something. I knew it was one of those times like I'd heard older guys talk about where no matter how much you lapped up, you didn't get really drunk.

While I sipped the last drink the commercial came and the guys at the bar stopped staring at the TV like they'd never seen one before and got back to doing some serious drinking and talking.

It was one of those places where everybody knew everybody else and calls them by the first name and everybody pleasantly insults everybody else and calls them gutter names and nobody gets sore. Nobody paid any attention to me. I began to feel like the invisible man from Mars. That was all right. That was about like I wanted it.

Then a big beetle-browed guy with a soup-bowl haircut that looked as if he gave it to himself and with his blue workshirt sleeves rolled up over arms that were big as my thighs, started *shushing* everybody, trying to stop the talk that had busted out along the bar.

As it quieted down I heard him say: "Shhhhh, shut up, now, and be listenin' to the news. The news! The news!" He kept saying that one word over and over.

I looked up at the TV and there was a serious-faced college-grad type sitting behind a desk with a globe map on it and a can of motor oil and he was yakking at us with his very sincere, serious voice.

As though the big guy had waved a magic wand, everybody in the joint shut up now and went back to staring at the TV. I heard the newscaster say: "—but first, the eleven o'clock local news, straight from the wire services of the . . . ."

I didn't hear the rest of it. All I heard was somewhere in my mind, the guy's voice saying over and over again, "The news! The news!" and the announcer's voice saying, "the eleven o'clock . . . . the eleven o'clock . . . . the eleven o'clock . . . ." like a record that had broke and stuck there.

Eleven o'clock. In another three minutes. . . .

What I should have done was get out of there. I didn't have to listen to the newscast. The part I didn't want to hear would not come on until near the end, anyhow, maybe in a special bulletin or something, if they put it out over this one at all. I had plenty of time. I didn't have to hear it. But I didn't even think about that, then. I didn't think about anything.

I kept looking at the newscaster's sincere, serious face in closeup now, filling the whole screen and listening to the even, cultured tone of his voice and I could feel my fingers squeezing the heavy-bottomed shot glass on the bar in front of me until I thought I'd never get them unstuck.

I heard myself saying like it was somebody else, very loud, almost hysterical: "Shut it off! Shut that thing off!"

All the heads along the bar swung around toward me as though they were on a wire. They looked at me like I'd suddenly cursed aloud in the middle of Mass. I didn't care. That voice was going on and on and it was going to say something I didn't want to hear.

"Are you going to shut that damn guy off?" I shouted.

They weren't. I could tell. I knew. But I couldn't let him keep talking up there. I probably couldn't have done it again in a million years if I'd wanted to, if I tried, but this time it was easy. I picked up the shot glass. It was at least 40 feet down to that TV set and it was on a shelf 10 feet from the floor but I hit the screen dead center and the glass went right through the picture tube and one second there was this big bright shot of the newscaster and the sound of his voice and then there was nothing but some jagged glass in the front of the seat and the most silence you ever heard.

I saw the big shave-necked Irishman coming toward me. His face was the color of the bricks he probably laid all day and his eyes were too little and too bright, way back in his head. But I couldn't seem to move.

"And why did you do that?" He sounded hurt. He didn't sound mad at all. "Have you gone daft, boy? Why did you do that?"

He didn't wait for me to answer even if I could have. He started slapping me and I can't stand anyone slapping me and I guess that was when you could say I flipped a little. There was still some beer in my big glass and it splashed back on me when I swung it off the bar and hit him in the forehead with it. It was good glass. It didn't break even when it slipped from my hand and fell to the floor. Then I hit him in the belly with my fist.

The rest of it's not too clear. It seemed like a hundred guys came at me all at once only it couldn't have been because there was only a dozen or so in the place. And that was all right with me. I wanted them to. The bartender, who looked too fat to move if his pants were on fire, came over the bar like a gazelle. He had a big knobby-looking blackthorn shillelagh in his fist.

It was a ball for awhile because they all tried to get to me at once and were like a herd of hogs trying to squeeze through a narrow gate. They were climbing all over each other to get to me, and I kept pumping punches fast as I could move my arms and I hit the first three flush in the face. I felt the gristle of somebody's nose go. I felt the sickening shifting softness of an eyeball under my fist. Then something hit me in the cheek and it didn't hurt too bad but it made my ears ache and somebody grabbed my arm and took it and twisted it some crazy way and I felt something snap and I screamed. Then it was like a brick wall falling down on me and wouldn't ever stop, even after I was all covered with it so that I couldn't see and everything was dark. . . .

I was in an ambulance, only it took me awhile to figure that out, even though the sound of the whining siren was right in my ears and I saw two guys in white jackets and the cop, sitting across from me. My face didn't feel like a face. It felt like one of those big throbbing, slithering masses of goo that comes out of the sea to invade the earth like in horror stories. I moved and that made my arm one big electric shock that hurt like hell. That reminded me.

I said: "What time is it?"

The cop and the two ambulance guys just sat there and looked at me. I had the crazy notion that they hadn't heard me, that no matter how loud I talked they wouldn't ever hear me; they'd just sit there like that forever, staring at me.

Then the baldheaded ambulance guy looked at a wrist-watch and said: "Eleven-twenty." He had a funny voice, sort of thick and gargly.

I lay there and didn't move any more on account of my arm and I began to think and now there didn't seem to be any reason not to do that. What harm could it do, now? It was over. It was forever over and 17 minutes ago they'd shot the big juice through him and he'd jumped and strained against the strap like I'd heard that they do but the lights didn't dim all over the place at the time because I'd heard that didn't really happen any more. And then maybe three, four or was it five minutes and he'd been still. He hadn't moved any more.

Even though they'd had his head covered I could see what he looked like. He had that same expression on his face I'd seen once when I was about 10 and he took me on a hike over to the Palisades and a copperhead bit his leg. He sat right down and lit a match to my Boy Scout knife and after tying a handkerchief real tight above it, bled the wound. He was awful pale and looking the closest to crying I'd ever seen him but looking more mad than hurt and his big, even white teeth showing in a grin or a grimace or something.

That's what he'd looked like tonight when they did that to him, I knew.

I don't know how long I'd been crying before I realized it, but I was really tearing it off. Bawling like a baby. I thought: *But it isn't for you, up there, you hear that? I wouldn't cry for you or be sorry for you for no money, because you stopped being my old man five years ago when you ran off with her and left me and the old lady. Because when we knew you weren't coming back we agreed to pretend like you were dead and never talk about you and we did that; it wasn't so hard after awhile. And I ain't crying for me and the old lady because we got along all right. We both work and we've done all right.*

Only why did you have to catch the lousy little tramp with somebody else, finally, and kill her and make all that big stink in the newspapers and the trial and all and they had to execute you tonight at eleven-o-three? Pop, why did you have to do that?

And I thought: *So to hell with you, it ain't because of you I'm bawling, it's because of this arm, the way it's killing me, hurting. That's all. You understand that?*

Then I must have tried to get up because the two ambulance guys and cops pounced on me and held me down and one of them stuck a needle into my good arm and that was all I knew. . . .

AUTHOR'S POSTSCRIPT: In hearing about executions, I've often considered how horrible it must be for someone near and dear to the doomed—figuring that everyone—even the most vicious killer, has had somebody who loved him—his mother, etc., etc. Yet this aspect of an execution has never been touched in newspapers or anywhere—so far as I know. The original title of the yarn, *Ricochet,* meant to bear out that theme—that an execution indirectly hits others than the actual victim.

The Shill

Eddie gawked and gawked. The crowd came slowly but steadily. They didn't know they were watching Eddie gawk. That's what made a good shill, a professional shill.

He was, naturally, dressed like all the local thistle chins. He wore an old threadbare several years out of date glen plaid suit, double-breasted and rumpled-looking. He wore a dreary not quite white shirt open at the collar without a tie. And he gawked.

He had big round deepset eyes set in patches of blue-black on either side of his long narrow bridged nose. His lower lip hung slack with innocent wonder. He had not shaved in twenty-four hours. He looked exactly as if he had just come, stiff and bone weary and in need of entertainment, off the assembly line of the tractor plant down the road at Twin Falls. He stared in big eyed open mouthed wonder at Bart Taylor, the talker for the sideshow, as Bart expostulated and cajoled, declaimed and promised the good-sized scuff of townsfolk who had been drawn consciously by Bart Taylor's talking and unconsciously by Eddie's gawking.

He was a magnificent shill and he knew it and Bart Taylor knew it and not only the people at the Worlds of Wonder sideshow knew it but all the folks from the other carnival tents as well, so that when business was slow they sometimes came over just to watch Eddie gawk and summon the crowd with his gawking and they knew, without having studied psychology, as Eddie knew, that there was something unscientifically magnetic about a splendid shill like Eddie.

They used to call Eddie the Judas Ram (cynically, because the thistle chins were being led to financial slaughter) and the Pied Piper (because the thistle chins followed like naive children the unheard music of his wondering eyes and gaping mouth). But all that was before Eddie fell in love with Alana the houri from

Turkestan who did her dance of the veils at the Worlds of Wonder, Alana who was from Baltimore and whose real name was Maggie O'Hara and who, one fine night when she first joined the carnival at a small town outside of Houston, Texas, stole Eddie's heart completely and for all time. After that Eddie was so sad, his eyes so filled with longing, that they didn't call him anything and didn't talk to him much and just let him do his work, which was shilling.

From the beginning, Eddie didn't stand a chance. He was a shill. He was in love with Alana, who was pale, delicate and beautiful, and everyone knew at once he was in love with her. In a week, all the men in the carnival were interested in Alana, whom nobody called Maggie. In a month, they all loved Alana, each in his own way, and each not because Alana had dunned them but because Eddie was a shill. It was as simple as that. Alana, however, for her own reasons remained aloof from all their advances. And the worst smitten of all was Bart Taylor, the talker and owner of Worlds of Wonder.

Now Bart finished his dunning and Eddie stepped up to the stand, shy and uncertain looking, to buy the first ticket. Bart took off his straw hat and wiped the sweat from the sweat band and sold Eddie a ticket. A good part of the scuff of thistle chins formed a line behind Eddie and bought tickets too. They always did.

Inside, Eddie watched the show dutifully, watched Fawzia the Fat Lady parade her mountains of flesh, watched Herko the Strong Man who actually had been a weight lifter, watched the trick mirror Turtle Girl, who came from Brooklyn but had lost her freshness in Coney Island and now was on the road, and the others, the Leopard Man and the Flame Swallower who could also crunch and apparently swallow discarded light bulbs and razor blades, Dame Misteria who was on loan from the Mitt camp down the midway to read fortunes at Worlds of Wonder and Sligo, a sweating red-faced escape artist who used trick handcuffs to do what Houdini had done with real ones.

But there was no Alana. Eddie waited eagerly for her act of the dancing veils, which was the finale of the show, but instead, the evening's organized entertainment concluded with Sligo. After that, the booths and stalls inside the enormous tent would remain in operation although the central stage was dark. The thistle chins, wandering about listlessly under the sagging canvas both because it was hot and because they too sensed something was missing from the show, had left the expected debris, peanut bags and soft drink bottles and crumpled sandwich wrappers, in the narrow aisles among the wooden folding chairs in front of the stage.

Eddie found Bart Taylor outside in his trailer, spilling the contents of his chamois pouch on a table and counting the take. "Two and a half bills," Bart said. "Not bad."

"How come Alana didn't dance?" Eddie wanted to know.

"Maybe she's sick or something."

"Didn't she tell you?"

"I haven't seen her," Bart Taylor said, stacking the bills and change in neat piles on the table in front of him. He was wearing a lightweight loud plaid jacket with high wide peaked lapels of a thinner material. One of the lapels was torn, a small jagged piece missing from it right under the wilted red carnation Bart Taylor wore. The carnation looked as if it had lost half its petals too.

"Well, I'll go over to her trailer," Eddie said.

"I wouldn't."

Eddie looked at him in surprise. "Any reason why not?"

"No," Bart said quickly. "Maybe she's sick and sleeping or something. You wouldn't want to disturb her."

"Well, I'll go and see."

A shovel and a pick-ax were under the table in Bart Taylor's trailer. Eddie hadn't seen them before. "Don't," Bart said, and stood up. His heavy shoe made a loud scraping sound against the shovel. He was a big man, much bigger than Eddie and sometimes when the carnival was on a real bloomer with no money coming in they all would horse around some like in a muscle camp, and Bart could even throw Herko the Strong Man, who had been a weight-lifter.

"O.K.," Eddie said, but didn't mean it. He went outside and the air was very hot and laden with moisture. He looked up but couldn't see any stars. He wondered what was wrong with Bart Taylor, to act like that. He walked along the still crowded midway to the other group of trailers on the far side of the carnival, past the lead joint where the local puddle-jumpers were having a go at the ducks and candle flames and big swinging gong with .22 ammo, past the ball pitching stand where shelves of cheap slum were waiting for the winners, past the chandy who was fixing some of the wiring in the merry-go-round. For some reason, Eddie was frightened. He almost never sweated, no matter how hot it was. A shill looked too obviously enthusiastic if he sweated. But now he could feel the sweat beading his forehead and trickling down his sides from his armpits. He wasn't warm, though. He was very cold.

There was no light coming through the windows of Alana's trailer. The do not disturb sign was hanging from the door-knob. The noise from the midway was muted and far away, except for the explosive staccato from the lead joint. Eddie knocked on the aluminum door and called softly, "Alana? Alana, it's Eddie."

No answer. Eddie lit a cigaret, but it tasted like straw. His wet fingers discolored the paper. He threw the cigaret away and tried the door. It wasn't locked.

Inside, Eddie could see nothing in the darkness. His hand groped for the light switch. The generator was weak: the overhead light flickered pale yellow and made a faint sizzling sound.

Alana was there. Alana was sprawled on the floor, wearing her six filmy veils. In the yellow light, her long limbs were like gold under the veils. Eddie knelt by her side. He was crying softly before his knees touched the floor. Alana's eyes were opened but unseeing. Her face was bloated, the tongue protruding. From the neck down she was beautiful. From the neck up, it made Eddie sick to look at her.

She had been strangled.

He let his head fall on her breast. There was no heart beat. The body had not yet stiffened.

He stood up and lurched about the interior of the small trailer. He didn't know how long he remained there. He was sick on the floor of the trailer. He went back to the body finally. In her right hand Alana clutched a jagged strip of plaid cloth. Red carnation petals like drops of blood were strewn over the floor of the trailer.

"All right, Eddie," Bart Taylor said softly. "Don't move."

Eddie turned around slowly. He had not heard the door open. He looked at Bart Taylor, who held a gun in his hand, pointing it unwaveringly at Eddie.

"You killed her," Eddie said.

"*You* killed her," Bart Taylor said. "My word against yours. I own this show. Who are you, a nobody. A shill. My word against yours."

"Why did you do it?"

"She wouldn't look at me. I loved her. I said I would marry her, even. She hated me. I couldn't stand her hating me. But I didn't mean to kill her."

"What are you going to do?" Eddie said.

"Jeep's outside. Tools. We'll take her off a ways and bury her."

"Not me," Eddie said.

"I need help. You'll help me. A shill. A nobody. They all know how you were carrying a torch for her. You better help me."

"Your jacket," Eddie said. "The carnation. They'll know it was you."

"Not if we bury her."

"Not me," Eddie said again.

"It's late. There are maybe thirty, forty people left on the midway. We've got to chance it now. It looks like rain. Won't be able to do it in the rain. Let's get her out to the jeep now, Eddie."

"No," Eddie said. He wasn't crying now, but his eyes were red.

Bart came over to him. Eddie thought he was going to bend over the body, but instead he lashed out with the gun in his hand, raking the front sight across Eddie's cheek. Eddie fell down, just missing Alana's body.

"Get up," Bart said. "You'll do it. I swear I'll kill you if you don't."

Eddie sat there. Blood on his cheek. The light, yellow, buzzing. Bart towering over him, gigantic, menacing. Alana, dead. Dead.

"On your feet," Bart said. "Before it starts raining."

When Eddie stood up, Bart hit him again with the gun. Eddie would have fallen down again, but Bart held him under his arms. "You'll do it," Bart said. "I can't do it alone."

"O.K.," Eddie said. "I feel sick. I need some air."

"You'll get it in the jeep."

"No. Please. I couldn't help you. Like this. Air first. Outside. All right?"

Bart studied him, then nodded. "I'll be watching you," he said. "Don't try to run. I'll catch you. I have the gun. I'll kill you if I have to."

"I won't try to run," Eddie promised. He went outside slowly and stood in front of the trailer. He took long deep breaths and waited.

Eddie gawked at the trailer. It was like magic, they always said. It had nothing to do with seeing or smelling or any of the senses, not really. You didn't only gawk with your eyes. Not a professional shill. Not the best. You gawked with every straining minuteness of your body. And they came. The thistle chins. The townsfolk. Like iron filings and a magnet. They came slowly, not knowing why they had come, not knowing what power had summoned them. They came to gawk with you. They came, all right. You've been doing this for years. They always came.

You could sense them coming, Eddie thought. You didn't have to look. In fact, you shouldn't. Just gawk, at the trailer. Shuffling of feet behind you. A stir. Whispering. What am I doing here? Who is this guy?

Presently there were half a dozen of them. Then an even dozen. Drawn by Eddie, the magnificent shill.

There were too many of them for Bart to use his gun. They crowded around the trailer's only entrance. They waited there with Eddie. Unafraid now, but lonely, infinitely lonely, Eddie led them inside.

They found Bart Taylor trying to stuff carnation petals down his throat.

AUTHOR'S POSTSCRIPT: There are shills in carnivals and along mid-ways everywhere—like music they know no national boundaries ... I've seen shills in Coney Island and in Rockaway Park, and I've seen them in the Prater in Vienna and along the Boulevard St. Michel in Paris' St. Germaine, and wherever I've seen them their soft-lure of the paying customers is uncanny. For *The Shill*, then, it only remained to carry a professional shill's skill to the ultimate: the soft-lure not to gaming but to revenge.

MIGNON G. EBERHART

Mr. Wickwire's "Gun Moll"

SHE was a singularly attractive lady with a singularly unattractive dog, and I had no idea, naturally, that either of them was involved in murder. While the dog looked capable of any perfidious crime, the lady did not. She was fresh as a rose.

A rather full-blown rose it is true, slightly middle-aged, but charming; a delightful perfume drifted from her corner. I sat opposite her; we were both waiting for the vet to return to his office; it was about seven o'clock of a rainy spring night. I held my dog Happy firmly by the leash and eyed the lady. She held her dog absently and eyed the door to the street. Her bare wrists were round and white; her hand wore no wedding ring, which pleased me.

Now I do not wish to give a wrong impression; I am and intend to remain a bachelor; my name is James Wickwire. I am rather on the elderly side, being a senior vice-president of a bank. Since my duties include the care of various estates, those duties have also included the task of dissuading some of my clients from diving into capital in order to finance sundry get-rich-quick schemes—those particular clients being, all too frequently, widows. This is merely a professional hazard; I only say that, in consequence, the absence of a wedding ring on the lady's hand rather pleased me. I had no thought of amorous dalliance.

It was different with Happy; amorous dalliance was pre-eminent in his mind; he had taken one look at the lady's dog and fallen in love. He gave a frenzied lunge in her direction and I pulled him back hard. The lady said absently, "Down, Lola," and watched the door.

Lola did not obey; she flopped an ungainly paw in a lumberingly coquettish gesture which appeared to drive Happy out of his few wits with delight. I restrained him and glanced at my watch; it was twelve minutes after seven. I said politely to the lady, "Dr. Sherman was called on an emergency just as I arrived. He said he'd be right back."

She nodded. "It's twelve minutes after seven," she said and watched the door anxiously.

I supposed her anxiety concerned Lola, although I have never seen so revolting a creature; she was a brown, ungainly animal, a veritable Jukes of a mongrel, with the nose of a terrier and the ears of a German shepherd except that one of them slanted backward while the other slanted forward in an indescribably raffish way. However, there is no accounting for the vagaries of human affection. I said, "Dr. Sherman is an extremely fine vet. I'm sure he'll see to your dog. . . ."

She gave me a surprised glance. "Oh, I'm only going to board Lola here. She's not got anything wrong with her."

There was, of course, everything wrong with her. My own dog, Happy, is a gigantic, liver-colored creature, predominantly Great Dane, although I have suspected a touch of the husky, in his pedigree; but he is a prince of dogs compared to Lola. I winced as I watched Lola rolling a waggish eye at Happy. He made another lunge at her and the door opened and a man came in.

It was not the vet. He was a small, thin man in a raincoat with a Lady's handbag, bright red, under his arm. I had a swift impression that he did not see me, for my chair was behind a large filing cabinet, and in the same instant it occurred to me that the lady herself carried no handbag at all. And then a number of things happened.

He said, "I want to talk to you," and seized the lady's arm. She sprang up and cried, "No! No!" Happy conceived one of his whimsical dislikes and surged the length of his leash at the man, who jerked around with a look of surprise and alarm.

I do not think that Happy would in fact dismember anybody, but occasionally he gives the impression of so intending. Lola instantly joined in the fray and got her teeth in the man's trouser leg. He dropped the red handbag, which fell open, and it was stuffed with money.

I had a flashing but unmistakable glimpse of a huge roll of bills. The lady made a quick dive at the handbag, the man gripped her and seemed to be trying to pull her toward the street; she resisted violently and, while I do not believe that I dropped Happy's leash intentionally, still Happy did get away from me. The man saw him coming, kicked Lola to free himself, released the lady and scooped up the handbag full of money all in one motion, and made it to the door, closing it behind him just as Happy thudded against it.

The door quivered; the man disappeared into the rainy night. I snatched up Happy's leash. Lola licked her chops and the lady turned breathlessly to me.

"What is your name? Please . . ."

I replied automatically, "Wickwire. James—"

"Thank you," she said and to my dismay thrust Lola's leash into my hand and whipped out the door herself, leaving nothing of her presence save a fragrance of flowers. And Lola. The dogs lolloped wildly around my legs and, as I was endeavoring to disengage myself from the tangle of leashes, a sudden crash of sound from the street outside froze the dogs, and me, too, for it was undeniably a gun shot.

Immediately the door was flung open again. Dr. Sherman dashed in, shouted, "There's a man shot!" and dashed wildly out again. He left the door open and, as Happy is devoted to the vet, Happy shot out after him. Happy being a very vigorous dog, willy-nilly Lola and I were forced to follow. A little crowd had already collected in the street about thirty feet away. It parted as Happy thundered upon it. I had a swift glimpse of the little dark man in the raincoat, huddled now in the gutter.

The street light shone down brightly through silver slivers of rain. There was no red handbag anywhere. The lady, like the handbag, was nowhere to be seen.

I am strongly opposed to murder; I exerted all my influence over Happy and got him—and Lola, like the end of a remarkably animated kite—back into the vet's office. And presently the vet returned. "Guy's dead," he said. "Patrolman on the job. Squad car on the way—now, then, what's Happy eaten this time?"

I was listening to the shriek of the approaching squad car, thinking of a lady who refused to take a handbag stuffed with money, ran into the street scarcely a moment before the murder, and left her dog. I replied that a box of carpet tacks had disappeared in Happy's immediate vicinity and the vet saw Lola and put a hand to his head. *"What's that?"*

I replied that to the best of my belief it was a dog.

"Your dog?" The vet pointed an outraged finger at Lola, who grinned cozily at him. "Mr. Wickwire, have you gone out of your head?"

"Certainly not," I snapped and described the lady, the incident, and then made the mistake of trying to put the leash in the vet's hand.

"No!" he cried in a voice of anguish. "A thousand times no! I never saw that creature before. I don't know who the lady was. And I'm not going to keep that dog here!"

I daresay a career of inducing dogs with gleaming white teeth to swallow pills they do not wish to swallow develops a certain iron in a man's nature; an hour later when I went home, I took Lola with me. It was an hour not without incident, for we had scarcely got Happy under the fluoroscope—which revealed no carpet tacks in his capacious interior—when the police arrived to inquire if either of us had seen or knew anything of the murder.

It was a triumph of my civic nature that I conquered a sneaking reluctance to do so and told them all about the lady, the handbag and the dog. Lola wore no tags, as a reasonable and law-abiding dog would do, and there was no possible way of identifying the lady. After taking various notes the police went away. And so did I—taking, as I've said, Lola with me; it was that or the pound for

Lola, owing to the lack of tags and the vet's intransigence. Besides, the lady had asked me for my name.

I pass over the greeting Wilkins, my only servant, gave Lola; she was unaffected by it save to give him a nip in the calf as he passed the soup, which then spilled over on Lola's head. Lola screamed pettishly and made a fretful dash at Wilkins, who displayed a feat of remarkable agility in ascending to the table top from whence he bitterly remarked that either he or Lola would depart from the house immediately.

In the end we shut Lola in a bathroom and Happy in my bedroom. After dinner I endeavored to ignore the sound of howls, moans, thuds, and at ten o'clock I turned on the radio and heard the news. The murdered man's name was Sol Brunk. And Sol Brunk together with one or two confederates—the police were uncertain about this—had held up a pay-roll messenger at six o'clock that evening and got away with what I believed is called the swag, amounting in this instance to fifty thousand dollars. One of Brunk's confederates had shot the messenger, who had, however, lived long enough to identify a photograph of Sol Brunk, which not remarkably the police had on file. It had been Sol Brunk who assailed the messenger directly, but the messenger had been shot from behind; So Sol Brunk was not his murderer.

The murderer of Sol Brunk was not known. The accomplice—or accomplices—had escaped. It was known that on occasion a woman, a gun moll so to speak, accompanied Sol Brunk on his nefarious excursions.

There was no description of the gun moll. There was no mention at all of a red handbag stuffed with money. There was no mention of the dog Lola.

After some thought only one conclusion emerged: the lady had made one half-hearted grab for the handbag, and the money; she had also strongly opposed Sol Brunk's company. But she had then hurried out into the street and disappeared altogether too coincidentally with murder. And thieves have been known to fall out.

It depressed me. Such white little hands and wrists to aim a revolver so very efficiently!

Wilkins set out my mild evening highball in a foreboding manner and went to bed. And it was about then that it struck me that there was something odd about the lady's—or rather the gun moll's—pretty white wrists, something inconsistent yet puzzling. I could not pin it down and analyze it.

In fact, as the clock ticked on I fell into a curious sort of reverie in which blossoms of some kind formed a very agreeable background, not orange blossoms exactly but blossoms and sunlit paths and most delightful company; the company was not precisely identifiable either, except that it was not that of a gun moll.

Indeed, the faint ting of a distant bell blended so suggestively with my dream that for some time I did not rouse to the fact that it was not, say, something resembling a wedding bell but the ting of the back door bell, touched lightly but repeatedly. I hurried back through the dining room and opened the kitchen door.

The lady flung herself into my arms. The scent of flowers surrounded me most delectably; a soft strand of her hair brushed my cheek. "Somebody's trying to kill me," she cried.

Since it seemed rather more than likely that she had killed somebody herself, I steeled myself against the kitten warmth and softness of her clinging figure. "Where have you been?" I demanded sternly.

"Riding the subways. I had some change in my pocket. Then I looked up your name in a phone booth and had just enough money for a taxi here. If you'll loan me taxi fare and give me Lola—"

"You can have Lola and welcome," I said austerely. "But I'd like to know. . . ."

Her blue eyes were amazingly candid. "Well, you see I left my handbag in the bar Lola likes."

Nothing in the way of dissolute behaviour on Lola's part could surprise me. I said, frostily, I fear, "Indeed."

"But then, you see, the bartender didn't give her peanuts and then they saw me, so I had to get away. And they'll not take Lola in a hotel; at least, they'll not keep her," she said candidly. "I don't suppose you'd see to her for a few days, Mr. Wickwire?"

This really horrendous request brought me to my senses like an electric shock, with the result that I shortly extracted the story—or *a* story, at least. According to the lady, at one time she had visited a bar not far from the vet's—"with friends," she said hastily, fluttering her eyelashes—and the bartender had had the shocking lack of foresight to give Lola peanuts. The lady had been walking Lola the evening of the murder and had tried to lead her past the bar; Lola, however, wanted more peanuts; quite logically they had entered the bar and settled themselves in a booth.

Her blue eyes widened; she said, "And you see there are high partitions, between the booths. Nobody can see you unless they pass right by." And at six-thirty she saw two men enter and settle themselves in the next booth to hers and Lola's.

They had talked in low but, to the lady, audible voices about their successful coup in robbing a pay-roll messenger; they were concerned not about shooting the messenger but about establishing an alibi for themselves, which they believed they had done by coming into the bar. "And I was terrified!" she cried, opening her blue eyes still wider. "I didn't know what to do. And then they saw me."

It developed that Lola had grown impatient as no peanuts were forthcoming and made shrill and penetrating complaint. So the men had peered over the partition anxiously and the lady had seized Lola's leash and run out of the bar, forgetting her red handbag.

"I'd seen the vet's sign; it wasn't far away. So I thought I'd leave Lola there and then go to a hotel and phone the police. I'm afraid to go home because my name—charge tags, club cards, everything —is in my handbag. They knew I had heard them. They couldn't let me get away. And one of them followed me, you saw him, so I had to hurry and you have such a kind face I knew you'd see to Lola and—"

"The man who followed you was shot."

"Oh, yes, I know. I was hurrying for the subway. I heard the shot behind me. I turned and saw him on the sidewalk and all the people running and . . ."

"Who shot him?"

"Why, the other robber, of course," she said simply.

"In the booth they were quarreling about the—the loot. One of them insisted on—I think it was two thirds but the other one kept saying, no, it was just fifty-fifty. Really it was dreadful.

"Just then they heard Lola and saw me. I think both of them followed me out of the bar and one waited in the street while the other followed me into the vet's. After the dogs scared him out, the other robber shot him, grabbed my handbag and then saw me. He had to get away fast but he had to get rid of me, too! So he followed me. In the subways. Took every train I took. Brown coat and hat. Young. Nice looking, really—but dreadful! Of course there were always people around. He couldn't do anything. But he's outside now."

I may have uttered a startled word. She nodded firmly. "Another taxi was behind the one I took. So then I ran around to the back door of your house."

I told myself to count ten. When I got to three I said, "How do you know that the men were in the bar at—you said they came into it at six-thirty. Was there a clock? How could they expect to establish an alibi?"

"Oh, that was easy. There's a clock near the door, set rather low. One of them must have turned it back while the other talked to the bartender. And then you see they must have intended to set it up again, the same way when they left. I saw the clock as I ran out of the bar and it was half an hour slow."

"Did you—*see* him turn the clock back?"

"Oh, no. It wasn't necessary to see it. I knew. I have a perfect sense of time. It's like perfect pitch. I always know exactly what time it is. Like—like dogs, you know, when it's dinner time. I knew that it was six-thirty when they came into the bar."

This, to speak bluntly, finished me; being a banker, approached in the course of duty for loans, I have listened to some preposterous stories but none as preposterous as this. I said sternly, "What about all that money in your handbag? There was at least five thousand dollars—"

"Twenty," she said. "It's mine, and I want it!"

The story was preposterous—a perfect sense of time indeed! And why was she carrying about twenty thousand dollars? There was no accounting for her motive in telling me such nonsense unless, in a confused way, it was intended to enlist my sympathy. There was clearly only one thing for me to do and that was call the police. I started for the kitchen telephone and someone knocked at the back door.

"No, no!" she cried, but I opened the door.

A man came in swiftly; he wore a brown hat and coat; he was young, handsome, slick and polite.

"Oh, there you are, Aunt Maisie," he said. "I've come to take you home. I'm sorry if she's troubled you, sir. She's quite all right, really, doesn't need to be in a sanitarium. But she does let her fancy run away with her—"

"You've been listening at the door," the lady—and almost certainly the gun moll—cried with unexpected spirit. "You're the other robber! You shot the man with my handbag!"

And he had told a good story, too, I reflected skeptically; a story that was almost certain to get his accomplice out of my house. There must be wheels within wheels, a complex situation between the two of them to which I had no key, except my previous conclusion that thieves do fall out.

"Come now, Aunt Maisie," the young man said and advanced upon us. The lady clutched my arm practically to the bone and cried, "He's got a gun!" I looked down, naturally, to see if she had broken my arm, saw her white bare wrist—and suddenly saw the truth.

And there wasn't anything I could do about it. Undoubtedly he did have a gun. The telephone was at least five feet away. Wilkins was asleep on the third floor. And at that point the lady gave a piercing shriek. *"Lola,"* she shrieked. *"Lola . . . . ."*

I have read the words, "pandemonium broke loose"; I never comprehended their meaning until the house rocked with it. Howls, yells, thuds and the rending crash of doors broke out from above; somewhere there were many madly running feet. I thrust the lady under the kitchen table and, since I am not a brave man, ducked under it myself. Happy hurtled through the kitchen door, swinging it back against the murderer, who went skittering across the floor. Lola flashed into view and into the corner from whence savage growls, thumps and curses arose; and suddenly two revolver shots crashed through the melee.

Peering out from under the table I perceived a ghostly figure in white in the doorway, which proved to Wilkins in a night shirt, who shouted in a quivering voice, "I borrowed your gun, Mr. Wickwire. Shall I shoot to kill or merely attempt to maim him?"

A panting, hoarse voice from the corner replied. "Don't shoot— don't shoot! Get these damned dogs off me!"

Well, since we had the young man so to speak, at a disadvantage, Wilkins and I trussed him up with roller towels before we tied up the dogs, too, and called the police. He did have a gun, which he had had no opportunity to use, being otherwise occupied. He also had the lady's handbag under his coat. He turned sullen and stubborn about confessing, but he still had the pay-roll, a sizeable wedge, in his pocket; and the police felt sure that his gun was that which had killed Sol Brunk.

It developed, too, in the course of conversation that Sol Brunk's girl friend was serving a term in jail.

They departed, police, murderer and all, some time later. Lola rolled a complacent eye at Happy, who was still, however, a little upset and snuffling at the back door in a menacing manner. Wilkins, the hero of the incident, draped a blanket modestly around him, made coffee for us and went back to bed. The lady said softly, "It was so sweet of you to believe me, Mr. Wickwire. About my sense of time, I mean. Some people don't."

I glanced at her white wrists, neither of which wore a watch. "Oh, yes," I said. "When we were at the vet's you said it was twelve minutes after seven. I had looked at my watch. I knew that you were right. But there was no clock in the vet's office, and you didn't wear a watch." I didn't add that I had not believed her until I remembered that small fact, and that its oddity had nudged at me earlier in the evening without making itself clear. I said instead, "It's a very unusual gift."

"Ah, well, it's only one of those things," she said and sighed. "Somehow it rather annoyed my late husband—"

"*Your late*—" I swallowed hard. During the chat with the police I had of course learned her name, which was Maisie Blane. But that was all.

"I'm a widow," she said. "That's why it was so hard to know what to do. A man's advice especially about investments—why, what's the matter, Mr. Wickwire?"

"Nothing," I said. "A slight touch of vertigo."

"Oh—that money, Mr. Wickwire, that twenty thousand. You see, I'm going to buy an oil well—that is, there's no oil discovered there yet but I feel sure there will be. And my banker opposed it so strongly that I just drew out the cash. But I'd like your opinion —Mr. Wickwire, really you look quite ill."

"Not at all. I'm sure you're right about the well," I lied and controlled a shudder. But I was conscious of a kind of emptiness within me as a pleasant little dream of blossoms whisked itself away.

I took her—and Lola—home. And she is an utterly delightful woman. She is also now a very rich woman as not one but two oil wells came in on the land she bought.

But the fragrant little dream of unidentifiable blossoms has never returned. Besides, there is Lola. I really cannot permit Happy to make so shocking a mesalliance.

AUTHOR'S POSTSCRIPT: I rather think that my point of departure for this story was observing my dogs who seem to have little, accurate, inner clocks, and thinking that humans have them too, when we care to listen to their ticking. Who has not said to himself on going to sleep, "I'll wake and get to the typewriter at eight in the morning?" One does wake at eight; I'm not sure that one does get to the typewriter so promptly, at least I don't.

ROSS MACDONALD

Guilt-Edged Blonde

A MAN was waiting for me at the gate at the edge of the runway. He didn't look like the man I expected to meet. He wore a stained tan windbreaker, baggy slacks, a hat as squashed and dubious as his face. He must have been forty years old, to judge by the gray in his hair and the lines around his eyes. His eyes were dark and evasive, moving here and there as if to avoid getting hurt. He had been hurt often and badly, I guessed.

"You Archer?"

I said I was. I offered him my hand. He didn't know what to do with it. He regarded it suspiciously, as if I was planning to try a Judo hold on him. He kept his hands in the pockets of his windbreaker.

"I'm Harry Nemo." His voice was a grudging whine. It cost him an effort to give his name away. "My brother told me to come and pick you up. You ready to go?"

"As soon as I get my luggage."

I collected my overnight bag at the counter in the empty waiting room. The bag was very heavy for its size. It contained, besides a toothbrush and spare linen, two guns and the ammunition for them. A .38 special for sudden work, and a .32 automatic as a spare.

Harry Nemo took me outside to his car. It was a new seven-passenger custom job, as long and black as death. The windshield and side windows were very thick, and they had the yellowish tinge of bullet-proof glass.

"Are you expecting to be shot at?"

"Not me." His smile was dismal. "This is Nick's car."

"Why didn't Nick come himself?"

He looked around the deserted field. The plane I had arrived on was a flashing speck in the sky above the red sun. The only human being in sight was the operator in the control tower. But

Nemo leaned towards me in the seat, and spoke in a whisper:

"Nick's a scared pigeon. He's scared to leave the house. Ever since this morning."

"What happened this morning?"

"Didn't he tell you? You talked to him on the phone."

"He didn't say very much. He told me he wanted to hire a body-guard for six days, until his boat sails. He didn't tell me why."

"They're gunning for him, that's why. He went to the beach this morning. He has a private beach along the back of his ranch, and he went down there by himself for his morning dip. Somebody took a shot at him from the top of the bluff. Five or six shots. He was in the water, see, with no gun handy. He told me the slugs were splashing around him like hailstones. He ducked and swam under water out to sea. Lucky for him he's a good swimmer, or he wouldn't of got away. It's no wonder he's scared. It means they caught up with him, see."

"Who are 'they,' or is that a family secret?"

Nemo turned from the wheel to peer into my face. His breath was sour, his look incredulous. "Christ, don't you know who Nick is? Didn't he tell you?"

"He's a lemon-grower, isn't he?"

"He is now."

"What did he used to be?"

The bitter beaten face closed on itself. "I oughtn't to be flap-ping at the mouth. He can tell you himself if he wants to."

Two hundred horses yanked us away from the curb. I rode with my heavy leather bag on my knees. Nemo drove as if driving was the one thing in life he enjoyed, rapt in silent communion with the engine. It whisked us along the highway, then down a gradual incline between geometrically planted lemon groves. The sunset sea glimmered red at the foot of the slope.

Before we reached it, we turned off the blacktop into a private lane which ran like a straight hair-parting between the dark green trees. Straight for half a mile or more to a low house in a clearing.

The house was flat-roofed, made of concrete and fieldstone, with an attached garage. All of its windows were blinded with heavy draperies. It was surrounded with well-kept shrubbery and lawn, the lawn with a ten-foot wire fence surmounted by barbed wire.

Nemo stopped in front of the closed and padlocked gate, and honked the horn. There was no response. He honked the horn again.

About halfway between the house and the gate, a crawling thing came out of the shrubbery. It was a man, moving very slowly on hands and knees. His head hung down almost to the ground. One side of his head was bright red, as if he had fallen in paint. He left a jagged red trail in the gravel of the driveway.

Harry Nemo said, "Nick!" He scrambled out of the car. "What happened, Nick?"

The crawling man lifted his heavy head and looked at us. Cumbrously, he rose to his feet. He came forward with his legs spraddled and loose, like a huge infant learning to walk. He breathed loudly and horribly, looking at us with a dreadful hopefulness. Then he died on his feet, still walking. I saw the change in his face before it struck the gravel.

Harry Nemo went over the fence like a weary monkey, snagging his slacks on the barbed wire. He knelt beside his brother and turned him over and palmed his chest. He stood up shaking his head.

I had my bag unzipped and my hand on the revolver. I went to the gate, "Open up, Harry."

Harry was saying, "They got him," over and over. He crossed himself several times. "The dirty bastards."

"Open up," I said.

He found a key ring in the dead man's pocket and opened the padlocked gate. Our dragging footsteps crunched the gravel. I looked down at the specks of gravel in Nicky Nemo's eyes, the bullet hole in his temple.

"Who got him, Harry?"

"I dunno. Fats Jordan, or Artie Castola, or Faronese. It must have been one of them."

"The Purple Gang."

"You called it. Nicky was their treasurer back in the thirties. He was the one that didn't get into the papers. He handled the payoff, see. When the heat went on and the gang got busted up, he had some money in a safe deposit box. He was the only one that got away."

"How much money?"

"Nicky never told me. All I know, he come out here before the war and bought a thousand acres of lemon land. It took them fifteen years to catch up with him. He always knew they were gonna, though. He knew it."

Artie Castola got off the Rock last spring."

"You're telling me. That's when Nicky bought himself the bullet-proof car and put up the fence."

"Are they gunning for you?"

He looked around at the darkening groves and the sky. The sky was streaked with running red, as if the sun had died a violent death.

"I dunno," he answered nervously. "They got no reason to. I'm as clean as soap. I never been in the rackets. Not since I was young, anyway. The wife made me go straight, see?"

I said: "We better get into the house and call the police."

The front door was standing a few inches ajar. I could see at the edge that it was sheathed with quarter-inch steel plate. Harry put my thoughts into words.

"Why in hell would he go outside? He was safe as houses as long as he stayed inside."

"Did he live alone?"

"More or less alone."

"What does that mean?"

He pretended not to hear me, but I got some kind of an answer. Looking through the doorless arch into the living room, I saw a leopardskin coat folded across the back of the chesterfield. There were red-tipped cigarette butts mingled with cigar butts in the ashtrays.

"Nicky was married?"

"Not exactly."

"You know the woman?"

"Naw." But he was lying.

Somewhere behind the thick walls of the house, there was a creak of springs, a crashing bump, the broken roar of a cold engine, grinding of tires in gravel. I got to the door in time to see a cerise convertible hurtling down the driveway. The top was down, and a yellow-haired girl was small and intent at the wheel. She swerved around Nick's body and got through the gate somehow, with her tires screaming. I aimed at the right rear tire, and missed. Harry came up behind me. He pushed my gun-arm down before I could fire again. The convertible disappeared in the direction of the highway.

"Let her go," he said.

"Who is she?"

He thought about it, his slow brain clicking almost audibly. "I dunno. Some pig that Nicky picked up some place. Her name is Flossie or Florrie or something. She didn't shoot him, if that's what you're worried about."

"You know her pretty well, do you?"

"The hell I do. I don't mess with Nicky's dames." He tried to work up a rage to go with the strong words, but he didn't have the makings. The best he could produce was petulance: "Listen, mister, why should you hang around? The guy that hired you is dead."

"I haven't been paid, for one thing."

"I'll fix that."

He trotted across the lawn to the body and came back with an alligator billfold. It was thick with money.

"How much?"

"A hundred will do it."

He handed me a hundred-dollar bill. "Now how about you amscray, bud, before the law gets here?"

"I need transportation."

"Take Nicky's car. He won't be using it. You can park it at the airport and leave the key with the agent."

"I can, eh?"

"Sure. I'm telling you you can."

"Aren't you getting a little free with your brother's property?"

"It's my property now, bud." A bright thought struck him, disorganizing his face. "Incidentally, how would you like to get off of my land?"

"I'm staying, Harry. I like this place. I always say it's people that make a place."

The gun was still in my hand. He looked down at it.

"Get on the telephone, Harry. Call the police."

"Who do you think you are, ordering me around? I took my last order from anybody, see?" He glanced over his shoulder at the dark and shapeless object on the gravel, and spat venomously.

"I'm a citizen, working for Nicky. Not for you."

He changed his tune very suddenly. "How much to go to work for me?"

"Depends on the line of work."

He manipulated the alligator wallet. "Here's another hundred. If you got to hang around, keep the lip buttoned down about the dame, eh? Is it a deal?"

I didn't answer, but I took the money. I put it in a separate pocket by itself. Harry telephoned the county sheriff.

He emptied the ash trays before the sheriff's men arrived, and stuffed the leopardskin coat into the woodbox. I sat and watched him.

We spent the next two hours with loud-mouthed deputies. They were angry with the dead man for having the kind of past that attracted bullets. They were angry with Harry for being his brother. They were secretly angry with themselves for being inexperienced and incompetent. They didn't uncover the leopard-skin coat.

Harry Nemo left the courthouse first. I waited for him to leave, and tailed him home, on foot.

Where a leaning palm tree reared its ragged head above the pavements, there was a court lined with jerry-built frame cottages. Harry turned up the walk between them and entered the first cottage. Light flashed on his face from inside. I heard a woman's voice say something to him. Then light and sound were cut off by the closing door.

An old gabled house with boarded-up windows stood opposite the court. I crossed the street and settled down in the shadows of its veranda to watch Harry Nemo's cottage. Three cigarettes later, a tall woman in a dark hat and a light coat came out of the cottage and walked briskly to the corner and out of sight. Two cigarettes after that, she reappeared at the corner on my side of the street, still walking briskly. I noticed that she had a large straw handbag under her arm. Her face was long and stony under the streetlight.

Leaving the street, she marched up the broken sidewalk to the veranda where I was leaning against the shadowed wall. The stairs groaned under her decisive footsteps. I put my hand on the gun in my pocket, and waited. With the rigid assurance of a WAC corporal marching at the head of her platoon, she crossed the veranda to me, a thin high-shouldered silhouette against the light from the corner. Her hand was in her straw bag, and the end of the bag was pointed at my stomach. Her shadowed face was a gleam of eyes, a glint of teeth.

"I wouldn't try it if I were you," she said. "I have a gun here, and the safety is off, and I know how to shoot it, mister."

"Congratulations."

"I'm not joking." Her deep contralto rose a notch. "Rapid fire used to be my specialty. So you better take your hands out of your pockets."

I showed her my hands, empty. Moving very quickly, she re-

lieved my pocket of the weight of my gun, and frisked me for
other weapons.

"Who are you, mister?" she said as she stepped back. "You
can't be Arturo Castola, you're not old enough."

"Are you a policewoman?"

"I'll ask the questions. What are you doing here?"

"Waiting for a friend."

"You're a liar. You've been watching my house for an hour and
a half. I tabbed you through the window."

"So you went and bought yourself a gun?"

"I did. You followed Harry home. I'm Mrs. Nemo, and I want
to know why."

"Harry's the friend I'm waiting for."

"You're a double liar. Harry's afraid of you. You're no friend
of his."

"That depends on Harry. I'm a detective."

She snorted. "Very likely. Where's your buzzer?"

"I'm a private detective," I said. "I have identification in my
wallet."

"Show me. And don't try any tricks."

I produced my photostat. She held it up to the light from the
street, and handed it back to me. "So you're a detective. You better
do something about your tailing technique. It's obvious."

"I didn't know I was dealing with a cop."

"I was a cop," she said. "Not any more."

"Then give me back my .38. It cost me seventy dollars."

"First tell me, what's your interest in my husband? Who
hired you?"

"Nick, your brother-in-law. He called me in Los Angeles today,
said he needed a bodyguard for a week. Didn't Harry tell you?"

She didn't answer.

"By the time I got to Nick, he didn't need a bodyguard, or anything. But I thought I'd stick around and see what I could find out
about his death. He was a client, after all."

"You should pick your clients more carefully."

"What about picking brothers-in-law?"

She shook her head stiffly. The hair that escaped from under her hat was almost white. "I'm not responsible for Nick or anything about him. Harry is my responsibility. I met him in line of duty and I straightened him out, understand? I tore him loose from Detroit and the rackets, and I brought him out here. I couldn't cut him off from his brother entirely. But he hasn't been in trouble since I married him. Not once."

"Until now."

"Harry isn't in trouble now."

"Not yet. Not officially."

"What do you mean?"

"Give me my gun, and put yours down. I can't talk into iron."

She hesitated, a grim and anxious woman under pressure. I wondered what quirk of fate or psychology had married her to a hood, and decided it must have been love. Only love would send a woman across a dark street to face down an unknown gunman. Mrs. Nemo was horsefaced and aging and not pretty, but she had courage.

She handed me my gun. Its butt was soothing to the palm of my hand. I dropped it into my pocket. A gang of Negro boys at loose ends went by in the street, hooting and whistling purposelessly.

She leaned towards me, almost as tall as I was. Her voice was a low sibilance forced between her teeth:

"Harry had nothing to do with his brother's death. You're crazy if you think so."

"What makes you so sure, Mrs. Nemo?"

"Harry couldn't, that's all. I know Harry, I can read him like a book. Even if he had the guts, which he hasn't, he wouldn't dare to think of killing Nick. Nick was his older brother, understand, the successful one in the family." Her voice rasped contemptuously. "In spite of everything I could do or say, Harry worshiped Nick right up to the end."

"Those brotherly feelings sometimes cut two ways. And Harry had a lot to gain."

"Not a cent. Nothing."

"He's Nick's heir, isn't he?"

"Not as long as he stays married to me. I wouldn't let him touch a cent of Nick Nemo's filthy money. Is that clear?"

"It's clear to me. But is it clear to Harry?"

"I made it clear to him, many times. Anyway, this is ridiculous. Harry wouldn't lay a finger on that precious brother of his."

"Maybe he didn't do it himself. He could have had it done for him. I know he's covering for somebody."

"Who?"

"A blonde girl left the house after we arrived. She got away in a cherry-colored convertible. Harry recognized her."

"A cherry-colored convertible?"

"Yes. Does that mean something to you?"

"No. Nothing in particular. She must have been one of Nick's girls. He always had girls."

"Why would Harry cover for her?"

"What do you mean, cover for her?"

"She left a leopardskin coat behind. Harry hid it, and paid me not to tell the police."

"Harry did that?"

"Unless I'm having delusions."

"Maybe you are at that. If you think that Harry paid that girl to shoot Nick, or had anything—"

"I know. Don't say it. I'm crazy."

Mrs. Nemo laid a thin hand on my arm. "Anyway, lay off Harry. Please. I have a hard enough time handling him as it is. He's worse than my first husband. The first one was a drunk, believe it or not." She glanced at the lighted cottage across the street, and I saw one half of her bitter smile. "I wonder what makes a woman go for the lame ducks the way I did."

"I wouldn't know, Mrs. Nemo. Okay, I lay off Harry."

But I had no intention of laying off Harry. When she went back to her cottage, I walked around three-quarters of the block and took up a new position in the doorway of a dry-cleaning establishment. This time I didn't smoke. I didn't even move, except to look at my watch from time to time.

Around eleven o'clock, the lights went out behind the blinds in the Nemo cottage. Shortly before midnight the front door opened and Harry slipped out. He looked up and down the street and began to walk. He passed within six feet of my dark doorway, hustling along in a kind of furtive shuffle.

Working very cautiously, at a distance, I tailed him downtown. He disappeared into a lighted cavern of an all night garage. He came out of the garage a few minutes later, driving a prewar Chevrolet.

My money also talked to the attendant. I drew a prewar Buick which would still do seventy-five. I proved that it would, as soon as I hit the highway. I reached the entrance to Nick Nemo's private lane in time to see Harry's lights approaching the dark ranch house.

I cut my lights and parked at the roadside a hundred years below the entrance to the lane, and facing it. The Chevrolet reappeared in a few minutes. Harry was still alone in the front seat. I followed it blind as far as the highway before I risked my lights. Then down the highway to the edge of town.

In the middle of the motel and drive-in district he turned off onto a side road and in under a neon sign which spelled out TRAILER COURT across the darkness. The trailers stood along the bank of a dry creek. The Chevrolet stopped in front of one of them, which had a light in the window. Harry got out with a spotted bundle under his arm. He knocked on the door of the trailer.

I U-turned at the next corner and put in more waiting time. The Chevrolet rolled out under the neon sign and turned towards the highway. I let go.

Leaving my car, I walked along the creek bank to the lighted trailer. The windows were curtained. The cerise convertible was parked on its far side. I tapped on the aluminum door.

"Harry?" a girl's voice said. "Is that you, Harry?"

I muttered something indistinguishable. The door opened, and the yellow-haired girl looked out. She was very young, but her round blue eyes were heavy and sick with hangover, or remorse. She had on a nylon slip, nothing else.

"What is this?"

She tried to shut the door. I held it open.

"Get away from here. Leave me alone. I'll scream."

"All right. Scream."

She opened her mouth. No sound came out. She closed her mouth again. It was small and fleshy and defiant. "Who are you? Law?"

"Close enough. I'm coming in."

"Come in then, damn you. I got nothing to hide."

"I can see that."

I brushed in past her. There were dead Martinis on her breath. The little room was a jumble of feminine clothes, silk and cashmere and tweed and gossamer nylon, some of them flung on the floor, others hung up to dry. The leopardskin coat lay on the bunk bed, staring with innumerable bold eyes. She picked it up and covered her shoulders with it. Unconsciously, her nervous hands began to pick the wood-chips out of the fur. I said:

"Harry did you a favor, didn't he?"

"Maybe he did."

"Have you been doing any favors for Harry?"

"Such as?"

"Such as knocking off his brother."

"You're way off the beam, mister. I was very fond of Uncle Nick."

"Why run out on the killing then?"

"I panicked," she said. "It would happen to any girl. I was asleep when he got it, see, passed out if you want the truth. I heard the gun go off. It woke me up, but it took me quite a while to bring myself to and sober up enough to put my clothes on. By the time I made it to the bedroom window, Harry was back, with some guy." She peered into my face. "Were you the guy?"

I nodded.

"I thought so. I thought you were law at the time. I saw Nick lying there in the driveway, all bloody, and I put two and two together and got trouble. Bad trouble for me, unless I got out. So I got out. It wasn't nice to do, after what Nick meant to me, but it was the only sensible thing. I got my career to think of."

"What career is that?"

"Modeling. Acting. Nick was gonna send me to school."

"Unless you talk, you'll finish your education at Corona. Who shot Nick?"

A thin edge of terror entered her voice. "I don't know, I tell you. I was passed out in the bedroom. I didn't see nothing."

"Why did Harry bring you your coat?"

"He didn't want me to get involved. He's my father, after all."

"Harry Nemo is your father?"

"Yes."

"You'll have to do better than that. What's your name?"

"Jeannine. Jeannine Larue."

"Why isn't your name Nemo if Harry is your father? Why do you call him Harry?"

"He's my stepfather, I mean."

"Sure," I said. "And Nick was really your uncle, and you were having a family reunion with him."

"He wasn't any blood relation to me. I always called him uncle, though."

"If Harry's your father, why don't you live with him?"

"I used to. Honest. This is the truth I'm telling you. I had to

get out on account of the old lady. The old lady hates my guts.
She's a real creep, a square. She can't stand for a girl to have any
fun. Just because my old man was a rummy—"

"What's your idea of fun, Jeannine?"

She shook her feathercut hair at me. It exhaled a heavy perfume which was worth its weight in blood. She bared one pearly
shoulder and smiled an artificial hustler's smile. "What's yours?
Maybe we can get together."

"You mean the way you got together with Nick?"

"You're prettier than him."

"I'm also smarter, I hope. Is Harry really your stepfather?"

"Ask him if you don't believe me. Ask him. He lives in a place
on Tule Street—I don't remember the number."

"I know where he lives."

But Harry wasn't at home. I knocked on the door of the frame
cottage and got no answer. I turned the knob, and found that the
door was unlocked. There was a light behind it. The other cottages in the court were dark. It was long past midnight, and the
street was deserted. I went into the cottage, preceded by my gun.

A ceiling bulb glared down on sparse and threadbare furniture,
a time-eaten rug. Besides the living room, the house contained a
cubbyhole of a bedroom and a closet kitchenette. Everything in
the poverty-stricken place was pathetically clean. There were
moral mottoes on the walls, and one picture. It was a photograph
of a towheaded girl in a teen-age party dress. Jeannine, before she
learned that a pretty face and a sleek body could buy her things
she wanted. The things she thought she wanted.

For some reason, I felt sick. I went outside. Somewhere out of
sight, an old car-engine muttered. Its muttering grew on the
night. Harry Nemo's rented Chevrolet turned the corner under
the streetlight. Its front wheels were weaving. One of the wheels
climbed the curb in front of the cottage. The Chevrolet came to a
halt at a drunken angle.

I crossed the sidewalk and opened the car door. Harry was at the wheel, clinging to it desperately as if he needed it to hold him up. His chest was bloody. His mouth was bright with blood. He spoke through it thickly:

"She got me."

"Who got you, Harry? Jeannine?"

"No. Not her. She was the reason for it, though. We had it coming."

Those were his final words. I caught his body as it fell sideways out of the seat. Laid it out on the sidewalk and left it for the cop on the beat to find.

I drove across town to the trailer court. Jeannine's trailer still had light in it, filtered through the curtains over the windows. I pushed the door open.

The girl was packing a suitcase on the bunk bed. She looked at me over her shoulder, and froze. Her blonde head was cocked like a frightened bird's, hypnotized by my gun.

"Where are you off to, kid?"

"Out of this town. I'm getting out."

"You have some talking to do first."

She straightened up. "I told you all I know. You didn't believe me. What's the matter, didn't you get to see Harry?"

"I saw him. Harry's dead. Your whole family is dying like flies."

She half-turned and sat down limply on the disordered bed. "Dead? You think I did it?"

"I think you know who did. Harry said before he died that you were the reason for it all."

"Me the reason for it?" Her eyes widened in false naïveté, but there was thought behind them, quick and desperate thought. "You mean Harry got killed on account of me?"

"Harry and Nick both. It was a woman who shot them."

"God," she said. The desperate thought behind her eyes crystallized into knowledge. Which I shared.

The aching silence was broken by a big diesel rolling by on the highway. She said above its roar:

"That crazy old bat. So *she* killed Nick."

"You're talking about your mother. Mrs. Nemo."

"Yeah."

"Did you see her shoot him?"

"No. I was blotto like I told you. But I saw her out there this week, keeping an eye on the house. She's always watched me like a hawk."

"Is that why you were getting out of town? Because you knew she killed Nick?"

"Maybe it was. I don't know. I wouldn't let myself think about it."

Her blue gaze shifted from my face to something behind me. I turned. Mrs. Nemo was in the doorway. She was hugging the straw bag to her thin chest.

Her right hand dove into the bag. I shot her in the right arm. She leaned against the doorframe and held her dangling arm with her left hand. Her face was granite in whose crevices her eyes were like live things caught.

The gun she dropped was a cheap .32 revolver, its nickel plating worn and corroded. I spun the cylinder. One shot had been fired from it.

"This accounts for Harry," I said. "You didn't shoot Nick with this gun, not at that distance."

"No." She was looking down at her dripping hand. "I used my old police gun on Nick Nemo. After I killed him, I threw the gun into the sea. I didn't know I'd have further use for a gun. I bought that little suicide gun tonight."

"To use on Harry?"

"To use on you. I thought you were on to me. I didn't know until you told me that Harry knew about Nick and Jeannine."

"Jeannine is your daughter by your first husband?"

"My only daughter." She said to the girl: "I did it for you, Jeannine. I've seen too much—the awful things that can happen."

The girl didn't answer. I said:

"I can understand why you shot Nick. But why did Harry have to die?"

"Nick paid him," she said. "Nick paid him for Jeannine. I found Harry in a bar an hour ago, and he admitted it. I hope I killed him."

"You killed him, Mrs. Nemo. What brought you here? Was Jeannine the third on your list?"

"No. No. She's my own girl. I came to tell her what I did for her. I wanted her to know."

She looked at the girl on the bed. Her eyes were terrible with pain and love. The girl said in a stunned voice:

"Mother. You're hurt. I'm sorry."

Let's go, Mrs. Nemo," I said.

AUTHOR'S POSTSCRIPT: Most of my Archer stories come out of some emotional sense of conflict which is even vaguer than a plot idea. I try to find a situation for it. The characters tend to invent themselves; I disclaim responsibility for them; the working-out of the plot is my conscious problem. I suppose that this one got its start in a story told me about a gangster who checked into a hospital in fear of his life, and kept a gun with him in bed.

JOHN BASYE PRICE

Murder for Fine Art

MY DEAR NIECE,

Now that I have reached the age of more than threescore, and my life draws to a close, I think it only right that you should know the real truth about my trouble with Pompeo—trouble that put me in the gravest danger of my life and nearly ended my career thirty years ago. Do not show this letter to anyone, but do not destroy it! Instead, wall it up in the new hall now being built at your convent, so that it may be found only after the building falls to ruins many hundred years hence.

It was in Rome in 1534, shortly after I had lost my position as Director of the Mint, that Pompeo approached me. I had known him for some time as a jeweller from Milan. He thought himself clever, but I regarded him as a pompous windbag, and (although he did not know it) as a secret enemy. However, I greeted him politely, and asked what he wanted.

"You would not call me an artist, would you?" he surprised me by asking.

"Well, hardly," I replied.

"And yet in half an hour I can make a better picture than the greatest artist can paint in a week."

"I have no time for jokes," I said, turning away in disgust.

He clutched my arm and took something out of his pouch. "Look at this!" he said

I stared in amazement at a piece of parchment he held in his hand. On it was a picture of the Coliseum, but such a picture as I had never dreamed of. Except that the picture was in black and white, it was exactly as if an image from a mirror had been miraculously transferred to the parchment.

"Did *you* make this?" I gasped.

"I did, in half an hour, yesterday morning."

I looked and looked at the picture. I could not imagine what medium had been used. The picture had not been drawn by pencil or pen, nor painted with oil-paint or water-colours.

Pompeo stood by, with a smirk on his face, watching my perplexity and wonder. Finally, I turned to him and asked, "But why do you show this to me, Pompeo?"

"The truth is," he said, "I need your help."

"*My* help?"

"Yes. I know that you are making some medals for Pope Clement (VII) and see him often. If you can get me an audience with his Holiness and will help persuade him to grant me a large reward for my new method of making pictures, it will make the fortunes of both of us, for I will give you one-tenth of all he gives me."

"But, Pompeo, you are closely related to Messer Trajano, the Pope's favourite servant. Why don't you approach his Holiness through him?"

"Unfortunately, an estrangement has arisen between us." This (I learned later) was true, and for a reason most discreditable to Pompeo. Under the circumstances I, of course, agreed to Pompeo's conditions. After he had sworn me to secrecy, he took me to his shop and revealed his secret.

No doubt you know, my dear niece, that with the right kind of lens it is possible to project a picture of the view outside on the wall of a darkened room. This is called a camera lucida. In brief, what Pompeo had done was to take a thick lens and place it at one end of a closed box, which thus acted as a small camera lucida. At the other end of the box he placed a plate of thin isinglass treated with chemicals (which I shall not name). The light of the image so affected the chemicals that they reproduced the outside scene on the isinglass in reversed black and white. Pompeo explained that it was necessary to fix the image by soaking the isinglass in other chemicals in a dark room to make the image permanent. Then with this plate exposed to sunlight he transferred the picture to chemically treated parchment.

I congratulated Pompeo on this great discovery, and told him to bring his sun-camera and chemicals to my house the next morning, from whence we would take them to show to the Pope.

I slept but ill that night, turning over and over in my mind two questions: first, where had Pompeo learned the secret of the sun-camera (for I was convinced that he was not capable of inventing such a thing by himself); and secondly, what was I to do in regard to the matter? It was not until the early hours that I reached an answer and a decision.

In the morning, Pompeo came to my house as arranged, but I greeted him with a long face. "I am sorry, Pompeo," I said, "but I have just heard that his Holiness was taken ill last night, and can see no one today. Let us hope that he will be recovered by tomorrow."

"I hadn't heard that," he said. (Neither had I, as a matter of fact, but I was determined that Pompeo should not see the Pope.)

I continued: "The news has just reached me; but come, it is too fine a day to sit here repining. I have a new gun, and the marshes are full of ducks and other fowl. Let's get on our horses and go out for a day of sport. Come, let us start."

"But what of the sun-camera and chemicals? I must take them home first."

"Not a bit of it!" I replied. "We can lock them up in my strong-box and they will be perfectly safe."

This was done, and we started off for the marshes. I was careful to find the most deserted spot imaginable. We tied our horses, and as we advanced towards the water I was holding the gun. It crossed my mind that anything falling into one of the nearby bogs would never be seen again. I looked all round, but no one was in sight, then I turned to Pompeo and said, "Now we are alone. Suppose this time you tell me the truth about the sun-camera. Who really discovered it?"

"As I told you before, I did."

"Oh, no Pompeo, you will never make me believe that a donkey like you could invent such a thing as the sun-camera . . . but never mind, I already know the answer. There is only one man who ever lived who was capable of making a discovery like that."

"Who do you mean?"

"That great artist, poet and scientist—Leonardo da Vinci."

"But, man—Leonardo has been dead for fifteen years!"

"Yes, but I was born in Florence myself, and I have heard that he left many unpublished note-books. You were in Florence a few months ago; no doubt you read them and stole the idea of the sun-camera."

"You are dreaming," said Pompeo; "but even if all that were true, what difference would it make? Leonardo is dead, and I have the sun-camera."

"No, you are wrong."

"What do you mean?"

"*I* have the sun-camera, Pompeo, locked up safe in my strong-box!"

"For the love of God, what's the matter with you? Surely you are not a thief? I thought you were my friend."

"You are no friend of mine, Pompeo. I know perfectly well that it was you, acting through Messer Trajano, who persuaded the Pope to deprive me of my position as Director of the Mint and to give the post to Fagiuolo instead."

"But that is an old story, why bring it up now?"

"Do you not understand, even yet? Here we are entirely alone; over there is a deep bog that would hide a body for ever; I am armed and you are not. In short, I am going to kill you, Pompeo!"

So saying, I cocked my gun. I had expected that he would attack me, but instead, he turned to run. Aiming the arquebus directly at him, I pulled the trigger; but by cursed ill-luck the gun misfired.

Dropping the gun, I drew my dagger and started after Pompeo. But in all my life, before or since, I have never seen anyone run as fast as he did. Fat as he was, he reached the horses first, flung himself astride, and galloped off as if the Devil were after him.

By chance or design Pompeo had taken the faster horse, but he weighed much more than I, so I had every prospect of overtaking him before we reached the city. But I lost him when he turned and took a short-cut through a field.

I set off for the city as fast as I could. By good luck I reached my house in time; I opened the strong-box and took out the sun-camera and the chemicals and hurried to the house of my best friend, Albertaccio del Bene, whom I knew I could trust. I left them with him for safe keeping and started back to my own house.

When I came in sight of it, as I had expected, I saw Pompeo in front of my door, and with him was the Bargello (sheriff) with his constables, some armed with pikes, some with arquebuses, and some with two-handed swords.

I approached and called out, "Pompeo, are you feeling better now?"

He was taken back for an instant, and then shouted at the Bargello, "Arrest that man; he tried to kill me!"

"Kill you, my dear fellow!" I exclaimed in a tone of amazement. "Your mind is more disturbed than I thought."

Turning to the Bargello, I said, "Pompeo's mind has been affected for some time; and this morning, when he came to see me, it was evidently much worse. He talked in such a wild way that I tried to soothe him by taking him for a day's shooting in the marshes. But as soon as we got there, he lost his reason altogether. He screamed that he saw the Devil coming after him and galloped off. I followed as fast as I could, for I feared that in his state he would do himself some injury. I have just arrived."

"Lies, lies, lies!" screamed Pompeo; "I tell you, he tried to shoot me, and would have, but his gun misfired!"

"But, Pompeo, calm yourself; why should I want to kill you?"

"You know why; you want to steal my invention—my sun-camera."

"Sun-camera! What on earth do you mean? I never heard of such a thing."

This enraged Pompeo so much that he forgot his need for secrecy. Turning to the Bargello, he said, "I have invented a machine that can make a better picture in half an hour than the best artist can draw in a week."

"Do you mean that *you* can draw a picture in half an hour that is better than one made by a trained artist?" the Bargello asked in astonishment.

"No, *I* don't draw the picture myself. With my machine the sun makes the picture for me. Just as if an image from a mirror had been transferred to parchment."

At this reply the Bargello's whole attitude changed. Turning to me, he said, "I beg your pardon for doubting you for a moment. You are right, Pompeo has gone mad. There can be no doubt that he is insane."

"No, no, no!" screamed Pompeo, "I'm *not* crazy. I don't care, now, whether the Pope gives me a reward or not. I'll show you my sun-camera and you can see for yourself." Pointing at me he said. "He locked it in his strong-box this morning. Have him open it and I will prove it to you."

In silence I handed my keys to the Bargello, and we three entered my house. The Bargello opened my strong-box, but, naturally, there was nothing inside.

"There you are," I said. "I am very sorry for Pompeo; I happen to have a medicine which is very useful in cases of this kind. Let me give Pompeo a few drops and soon, no doubt, he will be more quiet."

"For the love of God, no!" screamed Pompeo. "He's trying to poison me!" He was so worked up that he foamed at the mouth and acted in such a manner that if the Bargello had had any remaining doubts they would have been dispelled. He and his constables marched Pompeo away and locked him up.

The next day I was summoned by Pope Clement, for the Bargello had reported the matter to him. In answer to his questions, I told him that there was no doubt that Pompeo was dangerously insane. Others had reported the same thing, so the Pope ordered Pompeo to be confined in an asylum until he should recover his wits.

If Pompeo had been at all clever he would have calmed down and stated that he now realized that his tale of a sun-camera was a delusion, and that his mind was now recovered. But, like the donkey he was, he kept insisting that everything he had said was true. (As a matter of fact it was, but only I knew that.)

For a time everything went well with me. The Pope was very pleased with some gold medals I had made for him, and promised me enough new work to make my fortune. Everything seemed to be going my way, with the Pope my patron and Pompeo in the insane asylum. But suddenly the Pope was taken ill. I had finished another medal, and took it to him; he was in bed and unable to see the medal clearly, even with his spectacles. Three days later Pope Clement died.

I knew I must be careful, for anything can happen in the anarchy which occurs after one Pope dies and before the new Pope is elected. On Clement's death, his order confining Pompeo to the asylum was annulled.

I learned this unexpectedly. I was sitting in the street with several friends watching the great commotion which always follows the death of a Pope, when a group of ten Neapolitan soldiers, very well armed, came up and stopped just opposite us. The ranks opened, and Pompeo stepped out from the centre of the group and hailed me.

"So, Pompeo," I said, "I am happy to see that you have recovered your wits again. Or have you? I see that you have hired these ten men as a bodyguard. No doubt to protect you from some fancied danger?"

Pompeo replied with a torrent of abuse, and called me every vile name he could think of. My companions expected me to draw my sword against him, but I saw that was just what Pompeo wanted. If I drew my sword it would give his hired soldiers an excuse to kill me. My friends and I were armed, but were out-numbered. And so I said in a loud voice to Albertaccio del Bene, at my side, "If any sane man were to talk to me like that it would be the last thing he would ever do on this earth; but poor Pompeo has not yet recovered from his madness, so I will just ignore him."

This was too much for any of Pompeo's remaining caution, and he shouted when he should have kept silent. "We will see if I am crazy or not! Tomorrow, I will have another sun-camera ready; and this time the Bargello will believe *me*." So saying, Pompeo and his body-guard marched off slowly towards the Chiavica.

Although I did not show it, Pompeo's last words had given me a tremendous shock. I had supposed that it would take him weeks to grind a new lens for the sun-camera (for an ordinary spectacle lens will not do). Was it possible that he had already made another lens beforehand? Pompeo was a liar and a boaster, but this time he might be telling the truth. I wished then that I had drawn my sword and led my friends against him, but it was too late now. How could I ask them to attack a man who I had just stated was not responsible for his actions?

Very uneasy, I followed Pompeo's party alone, taking care to keep out of his sight. When the group reached the corner of Chiavica, all my fears were confirmed, for Pompeo entered an apothecary's shop while his guards remained at the door. He had told me that he always bought fresh chemicals from this shop just before making a sun-picture.

I saw all my plans in ruins about me, and knew that I had not an instant to lose. Pompeo came out of the shop, and his soldiers opened their ranks and received him in their midst. Nerving my-self, I drew my dagger, and taking everyone completely by sur-prise, I pushed into the midst of the group. Before they could draw their swords I seized Pompeo with my left hand and with the dagger in my other hand struck at his head. (I have always maintained, since, that I only meant to wound him, but this is not true.) I tried to kill him, and I did kill him, for as he turned away in fright, my dagger stabbed him just behind the ear and he fell stone-dead in the street.

Shifting the dagger to my left hand, I drew my sword to defend myself against odds of ten to one. However, these soldiers were so taken by surprise that they all ran to lift up the corpse, and before they could recover their wits and attack me, I had escaped alone through Strada Giulia.

You already know, my dear niece, what deadly danger I went through after the death of Pompeo. I had to go in hiding from the Bargello, who had orders to take me dead or alive. Worse still, Pompeo's family hired assassins with promises of great rewards if they would slay me. I had several very narrow escapes from being killed. Finally, I had to flee from Rome and take refuge in my native city of Florence.

After almost a year, my friends in Rome persuaded the new Pope Paul (III) to grant me the pardon of Our Lady's Feast in mid-August. I went to Rome under a safe-conduct, and presented myself to the Pope, who signed the pardon and had it registered at the Capitol. On the day appointed, I walked in penance in the procession, and so got clear of the murder at last.

And now, my dear niece, no doubt you are wondering why you have never heard anything about the sun-camera and its marvellous pictures. You will wonder why I did not use the invention and make a great fortune with it. To explain: Pompeo was wrong, that day on the marshes, when he thought that I wanted to steal the sun-camera for my own advantage. Murderer I have been, but never a thief. When I first realized that the discovery could only have been made by Leonardo da Vinci, I asked myself, "Why had not Leonardo given his discovery to the world?"

A little thought gave me the answer. Leonardo knew that artistic creation is the greatest glory of our human race. The past century has given us many great artists, and doubtless the next century will give us as many more. But suppose the secret of the sun-camera became known. Anyone and everyone, from Emperors down to common ploughboys, could make as accurate pictures as now only the greatest artists can make. Real artists no longer would be able to obtain patrons to order portraits, and would either starve or be forced into common labour. All the great artists of the future would be stifled in their youth. And artistic creation would be extinct.

And another matter. No doubt some artists with private means would continue painting for pure love of the work. But I fear that a group of quacks and charlatans without any artistic ability at all would paint pictures distorting things as they really are just for an effect of novelty. They might cover canvases with meaningless daubs of colour, and then try to persuade the ignorant and gullible that they were great pictures that common people couldn't understand.

Perhaps these "new artists" might even sneer at genuine artists doing honest painting, and say that their pictures only represented things as they are and were no better than sun-pictures.

The artists of centuries to come would thank me if they could know what I have done for them, even though it was necessary for me to murder my enemy, that thief Pompeo, to accomplish it.

I threw the camera into the Tiber, and I pray the Good Lord it may be three hundred years before someone else rediscovers its secret.

Your devoted uncle,
BENEVENUTO CELLINI

AUTHOR'S POSTSCRIPT: Every spring the Stanford University Art Department's water color class spends an afternoon in the lane in back of my home, painting pictures of the trees, garages, and garbage cans. Some of the work seems very good, but I found on talking to the students that not one intended to make art his, or her, profession. They explained that there is little demand now for the artist who paints things as they are . . . The thought came to me: how different plans of some of these students might have been if photography had never been discovered.

The Inner Circle

IF you are an Eastern alumnus who has not been to New York since last year's All-University Dinner, you will be astounded to learn that the famous pickled-pine door directly opposite the elevators on the thirteenth floor of your Alumni Club in Murray Hill is now inscribed: LINEN ROOM.

Visit The Alumni Club on your next trip to Manhattan and see for yourself. On the door now consigned to napery, in the area where the stainless steel medallion of Janus glistened for so long, you will detect a ghostly circumference some nine inches in diameter—all that is left of The Januarians. Your first thought will of course be that they have moved to more splendid quarters. Undeceive yourself. You may search from cellar to sundeck and you will find no crumb's trace of either Janus or his disciples.

Hasten to the Steward for an explanation and he will give you one as plausible as it will be false.

And you will do no better elsewhere.

The fact is, only a very few share the secret of The Januarians' obliteration, and these have taken a vow of silence. And why? Because Eastern is a young—a very young—temple of learning, and there are calamities only age can weather. There is more to it than even that. The cataclysm of events struck at the handiwork of the Architects themselves, that legendary band who builded the tabernacle and created the holy canons. So Eastern's shame is kept steadfastly covered with silence; and if we uncover its bloody stones here, it is only because the very first word on the great seal of Eastern University is: *Veritas.*

To a Harvard man, "Harvard '13" means little more than "Harvard '06" or "Harvard '79," unless "Harvard '13" happens to be his own graduating class. But to an Eastern man, of whatever vintage, "Eastern '13" is *sui generis*. Their names bite deep into

75

the strong marble of The Alumni Club lobby. A member of the Class is traditionally The Honorable Mr. Honorary President of The Eastern Alumni Association. To the last man they carry gold, lifetime, non-cancelable passes to Eastern football games. At the All-University Dinner, Eastern '13 shares the Chancellor's parsley-decked table. The twined-elbow Rite of the Original Libation, drunk in foaming beer (the second most sacred canon), is dedicated to that Class and no other.

One may well ask why this exaltation of Eastern '13 as against, for example, Eastern '12, or Eastern '98? The answer is that there was no Eastern '12, and Eastern '98 never existed. For Eastern U. was not incorporated under the laws of the state of New York until A.D. 1909, from which it solemnly follows that Eastern '13 was the university's very first graduating class.

It was Charlie Mason who said they must be gods, and it was Charlie Mason who gave them Janus. Charlie was destined to forge a chain of one hundred and twenty-three movie houses which bring Abbott and Costello to millions; but in those days Charlie was a lean weaver of dreams, the Class Poet, an antiquarian with a passion for classical allusion. Eastern '13 met on the eve of graduation in the Private Party Room of McElvy's Brauhaus in Riverdale, and the air was boiling with pipe smoke, malt fumes, and motions when Charlie rose to make his historic speech.

"Mr. Chairman," he said to Bill Updike, who occupied the Temporary Chair. "Fellows," he said to the nine others. And he paused.

Then he said: *"We are the First Alumni."*

He paused again.

"The eyes of the future are on us." (Stan Jones was taking notes, as Recording Secretary of the Evening, and we have Charlie's address verbatim. You have seen it in The Alumni Club lobby, under glass. Brace yourself: It, too, has vanished.)

"What we do here tonight, therefore, will initiate a whole codex of Eastern tradition."

And now, the Record records, there was nothing to be heard in that smoky room but the whizz of the electric fan over the lithograph of Woodrow Wilson.

"I have no hesitation in saying—out loud!—that we men in this room, tonight . . . that we're . . . Significant. Not as individuals! But as the Class of '13." And then Charlie drew himself up and said quietly: *"They will remember us and we must give them something to remember"* (the third sacred canon).

"Such as?" said Morry Green, who was to die in a French ditch five years later.

"A sign," said Charlie. "A symbol, Morry—a symbol of our Firstness."

Eddie Temple, who was graduating eleventh in the Class, exhibited his tongue and blew a coarse, fluttery blast.

"That may be the sign *you* want to be remembered by, Ed," began Charlie crossly . . .

"Shut up, Temple!" growled Vern Hamisher.

"Read that bird out of the party!" yelled Ziss Brown, who was suspected of holding radical views because his father had stumped for Teddy Roosevelt in '12.

"Sounds good," said Bill Updike, scowling. "Go on, Charlie."

"What sign?" demanded Rod Black.

"Anything specific in mind?" called Johnnie Cudwise.

Charlie said one word.

"Janus."

And he paused.

"Janus," they muttered, considering him.

"Yes, Janus," said Charlie. "The god of good beginnings—"

"Well, we're beginning," said Morry Green.

"Guaranteed to result in good endings—"

"It certainly applies," nodded Bill Updike.

"Yeah," said Bob Smith. "Eastern's sure on its way to big things."

"Janus of the two faces," cried Charlie Mason mystically. "I wish to point out that he looks in opposite directions!"

"Say, that's right—"

"The past and the future—"

"Smart stuff—"

"Go on, Charlie!"

"Janus," cried Charlie—"Janus, who was invoked by the Romans before any other god at the beginning of an important undertaking!"

"Wow!"

"*This* is certainly important!"

"The beginning of the day, month, and year was sacred to him! *Janus was the god of doorways!*"

"*JANUS!*" they shouted, leaping to their feet; and they raised their tankards and drank deep.

And so from that night forward the annual meeting of the Class of '13 was held on Janus's Day, the first day of January; and the class of '13 adopted, by unanimous vote, the praenomen of The Januarians. Thus the double-visaged god became patron of Eastern's posterity, and that is why until recently Eastern official stationery was impressed with his two-bearded profiles. It is also why the phrase "to be two-faced," when uttered by Columbia or N.Y.U. men, usually means "to be a student at, or a graduate of, Eastern U."—a development unfortunately not contemplated by Charlie Mason on that historic eve; at least, not consciously.

But let us leave the profounder explorations to psychiatry. Here it is sufficient to record that something more than thirty years later the phrase took on a grim verisimilitude; and The Januarians thereupon laid it, so to speak, on the doorstep of one well acquainted with changelings of chance.

For it was during Christmas week of last year that Bill Updike came—stealthily—to see Ellery. He did not come as young Billy who had presided at the beery board in the Private Party Room of

McElvy's Brauhaus on that June night in 1913. He came, bald, portly, and opulently engraved upon a card: Mr. William Updike, President of The Brokers National Bank of New York, residence Dike Hollow, Scarsdale; and he looked exactly as worried as bankers are supposed to look and rarely do.

"Business, business," said Nikki Porter, shaking her yuletide permanent. "It's Christmas week, Mr. Updike. I'm sure Mr. Queen wouldn't consider taking—"

But at that moment Mr. Queen emerged from his sanctum to give his secretary the lie.

"Nikki holds to the old-fashioned idea about holidays, Mr. Updike," said Ellery, shaking Bill's hand. "Ah, The Januarians. Isn't your annual meeting a few days from now—on New Year's Day?"

"How did you know—?" began the bank president.

"I could reply, in the manner of the Old Master," said Ellery with a chuckle, "that I've made an intensive study of lapel buttons, but truth compels me to admit that one of my best friends is Eastern '28 and he's described that little emblem on your coat so often I couldn't help but recognize it at once." The banker fingered the disk on his lapel nervously. It was of platinum, ringed with tiny garnets, and the gleaming circle enclosed the two faces of Janus. "What's the matter—is someone robbing your bank?"

"It's worse than that."

"Worse . . .?"

"Murder."

Nikki glared at Mr. Updike. Any hope of keeping Ellery's nose off the grindstone until January second was now merely a memory. But out of duty she began: "Ellery . . ."

"At least," said Bill Updike tensely, "I *think* it's murder."

Nikki gave up. Ellery's nose was noticeably honed.

"Who . . .?"

"It's sort of complicated," muttered the banker, and he began to fidget before Ellery's fire. "I suppose you know, Queen, that The Januarians began with only eleven men."

Ellery nodded. "The total graduating class of Eastern '13."

"It seems silly now, with Eastern's classes of three and four thousand, but in those days we thought it was all pretty important—"

"Manifest destiny."

"We were young. Anyway, World War I came along and we lost two of our boys right away—Morry Green and Buster Selby. So at our New Year's Day meeting in 1920 we were only nine. Then in the market collapse of '29 Vern Hamisher blew the top of his head off, and in 1930 John Cudwise, who was serving his first term in Congress, was killed in a plane crash on his way to Washington— you probably remember. So we've been just seven for many years now."

"And awfully close friends you must be," said Nikki, curiosity conquering pique.

"Well . . ." began Updike, and he stopped, to begin over again. "For a long time now we've all thought it was sort of juvenile, but we've kept coming back to these damned New Year's Day meetings out of habit or—or something. No, that's not true. It isn't just habit. It's because . . . it's *expected* of us." He flushed. "I don't know—they've—well—deified us." He looked bellicose, and Nikki swallowed a giggle hastily. "It's got on our nerves. I mean—well, damn it all, we're not exactly the 'close' friends you'd think!" He stopped again, then resumed in a sort of desperation: "See here, Queen, I've got to confess something. There's been a clique of us within The Januarians for years. We've called ourselves . . . The Inner Circle."

"The what!" gasped Nikki.

The banker mopped his neck, avoiding their eyes. The Inner Circle, he explained, had begun with one of those dully devious phenomena of modern life known as a "business opportunity"—a business opportunity which Mr. Updike, a considerably younger Mr. Updike, had found himself unable to grasp for lack of some essential element, unnamed. Whatever it was that Mr. Updike had required, four other men could supply it: whereupon, in the flush of an earlier camaraderie, Updike had taken four of his six fellow-deities into his confidence, and the result of this was a partnership of five of the existing seven Januarians.

"There were certain business reasons why we didn't want our er . . . names associated with the ah . . . enterprise. So we organized a dummy corporation and agreed to keep our names out of it and the whole thing absolutely secret, even from our—from the re-maining two Januarians. It's a secret from them to this day."

"Club within a club," said Nikki. "I think that's cute."

"All five of you in this—hrm!—Inner Circle," inquired Ellery politely, "are alive?"

"We were last New Year's Day. But since the last meeting of The Januarians . . ." the banker glanced at Ellery's harmless win-dows furtively, "three of us have died. *Three of The Inner Circle.*"

"And you suspect that they were murdered?"

"Yes. Yes, I do!"

"For what motive?"

The banker launched into a very involved and—to Nikki, who was thinking wistfully of New Year's Eve—tiresome explanation. It had something to do with some special fund or other, which seemed to have no connection with the commercial aspects of The Inner Circle's activities—a substantial fund by this time, since each year the five partners put a fixed percentage of their incomes from the dummy corporation into it. Nikki dreamed of balloons and noisemakers. "—now equals a reserve of around $200,000 worth of negotiable securities." Nikki stopped dreaming with a bump.

"What's the purpose of this fund, Mr. Updike?" Ellery was say-ing sharply. "What happens to it? When?"

"Well, er . . . that's just it, Queen," said the banker. "Oh, I know what you'll think . . ."

"Don't tell me," said Ellery in a terrible voice, "it's a form of tontine insurance plan, Updike—*last survivor takes all?*"

"Yes," whispered William Updike, looking for the moment like Billy Updike.

"I knew it!" Ellery jumped out of his fireside chair. "Haven't I told you repeatedly, Nikki, there's no fool like a banker? The financial mentality rarely rises above the age of eight, when life's biggest thrill is to pay five pins for admission to a magic-lantern show in Stinky's cellar. This hard-eyed man of money, whose business it is to deal in safe investments, becomes party to a melodramatic scheme whereby the only way you can recoup your ante is to slit the throats of your four partners. Inner Circles! Januarians!" Ellery threw himself back in his chair. "Where's this silly invitation to murder cached, Updike?"

"In a safe-deposit box at The Brokers National," muttered the banker.

"Your own bank. Very cosy for *you*," said Ellery.

"No, no, Mr. Queen, all five of us have keys to the box—"

"What happened to the keys of the three Inner Circleites who died this year?"

"By agreement, dead members' keys are destroyed in the presence of the survivors—"

"Then there are only two keys to that safe-deposit box now in existence; yours and the key in the possession of the only other living Inner Circular?"

"Yes—"

"And you're afraid said sole-surviving associate murdered the deceased trio of your absurd quintet and has his beady eye on you, Updike?—so that as the last man alive of The Inner Circle he would fall heir to the entire $200,000 boodle?"

"What else can I think of?" cried the banker.

"The obvious," retorted Ellery, "which is that your three pals traveled the natural route of all flesh. Is this $200,000 still in the box?"

"Yes. I looked just before coming here today."

"You want me to investigate."

"Yes, yes—"

"Very well. What's the name of this surviving fellow-conspirator of yours in The Inner Circle?"

"No," said Bill Updike.

"I beg pardon?"

"Suppose I'm wrong? If they *were* ordinary deaths. I'd have dragged someone I've known a hell of a long time into a mess. No, you investigate first, Mr. Queen. Find evidence of murder, and I'll go all the way."

"You won't tell me his name?"

"No."

The ghost of New Year's Eve stirred. But then Ellery grinned, and it settled back in the grave. Nikki sighed and reached for her notebook.

"All right, Mr. Updike. Who were the three Inner Circlovians who died this year?"

"Robert Carlton Smith, J. Stanford Jones, and Ziss Brown— Peter Zissing Brown."

"Their occupations?"

"Bob Smith was head of the Kradle Kap Baby Foods Korporation. Stan Jones was top man of Jones-Jones-Mallison-Jones, the ad agency. Ziss Brown was retired."

"From what?"

Updike said stiffly: "Brassières."

"I suppose they do pall. Leave me the addresses of the executors, please, and any other data you think might be helpful."

When the banker had gone, Ellery reached for the telephone.

"Oh, dear," said Nikki. "You're not calling . . . Club Bongo?"

"What?"

"You know? New Year's Eve?"

"Heavens, no. My pal Eastern '28. Cully? . . . The same to you. Cully, who are the four Januarians? Nikki, take this down . . . William Updike—yes? . . . Charles Mason? Oh, yes, the god who fashioned Olympus . . . Rodney Black, Junior—um-hm . . . and Edward I. Temple? Thanks, Cully. And now forget I called." Ellery hung up. "Black, Mason, and Temple, Nikki. The only Januarians alive outside of Updike. Consequently one of those three is Updike's last associate in The Inner Circle."

"And the question is which one."

"Bright girl. But first let's dig into the deaths of Smith, Jones, and Brown. Who knows? Maybe Updike's got something."

It took exactly forty-eight hours to determine that Updike had nothing at all. The deaths of Januarians-Inner Circlers Smith, Jones, and Brown were impeccable.

"Give it to him, Velie," said Inspector Queen at Headquarters the second morning after the banker's visit to the Queen apartment.

Sergeant Velie cleared his massive throat. "The Kradle Kap Baby Foods character—"

"Robert Carlton Smith."

"Rheumatic heart for years. Died in an oxygen tent after the third heart attack in eighteen hours, with three fancy medics in attendance and a secretary who was there to take down his last words."

"Which were probably 'Free Enterprise,' " said the Inspector. "Go on, Sergeant!"

"J. Stanford Jones, the huckster. Gassed in World War I, in recent years developed t.b. And that's what he died of. Want the sanitarium affidavits, Maestro? I had photostats telephotoed from Arizona."

"Thorough little man, aren't you?" growled Ellery. "And Peter Zissing Brown, retired from brassières?"

"Kidneys and gall-bladder. Brown died on the operatin' table."

"Wait till you see what I'm wearing tonight," said Nikki. "Apricot taffeta—"

"Nikki, get Updike on the phone," said Ellery absently. "Brokers National."

"He's not there, Ellery," said Nikki, when she had put down the Inspector's phone. "Hasn't come into his bank this morning. It has the darlingest bouffant skirt—"

"Try his home."

"Dike Hollow, Scarsdale, wasn't it? With the new back, and a neckline that—Hello?" And after a while the three men heard Nikki say in a strange voice: *"What?"* and then: "Oh," faintly. She thrust the phone at Ellery. "You'd better take it."

"What's the matter? Hello? Ellery Queen. Updike there?"

A bass voice said, "Well—no, Mr. Queen. He's been in an accident."

"Accident! Who's this speaking?"

"Captain Rosewater of the Highway Police. Mr. Updike ran his car into a ravine near his home here some time last night. We just found him."

"I hope he's all right!"

"He's dead."

"Four!" Ellery was mumbling as Sergeant Velie drove the Inspector's car up into Westchester. "Four in one year!"

"Coincidence," said Nikki desperately, thinking of the festivities on the agenda for that evening.

"All I know is that forty-eight hours after Updike asks me to find out if his three cronies of The Inner Circle who died this year hadn't been murdered, he himself is found lying in a gully with four thousand pounds of used car on top of him."

"Accidents," began Sergeant Velie, "will hap—"

"I want to see that 'accident'!"

A State trooper flagged them on the Parkway near a cutoff and sent them down the side road. This road, it appeared, was a shortcut to Dike Hollow which Updike habitually used in driving home from the City; his house lay some two miles from the Parkway. They found the evidence of his last drive about midway. The narrow blacktop road twisted sharply to the left at this point, but Bill Updike had failed to twist with it. He had driven straight ahead and through a matchstick guardrail into the ravine. As it plunged over, the car had struck the bole of a big old oak. The shock catapulted the banker through his windshield and he had landed at the bottom of the ravine just before his vehicle.

"We're still trying to figure out a way of lifting that junk off him," said Captain Rosewater when they joined him forty feet below the road.

The ravine narrowed in a V here and the car lay in its crotch upside down. Men were swarming around it with crowbars, chains, and acetylene torches. "We've uncovered enough to show us he's mashed flat."

"His face, too, Captain?" asked Ellery suddenly.

"No, his face wasn't touched. We're trying to get the rest of him presentable enough so we can let his widow identify him." The trooper nodded toward a flat rock twenty yards down the ravine on which sat a small woman in a mink coat. She wore no hat and her smart gray hair was whipping in the Christmas wind. A woman in a cloth coat, wearing a nurse's cap, stood over her.

Ellery said, "Excuse me," and strode away. When Nikki caught up with him he was already talking to Mrs. Updike. She was drawn up on the rock like a caterpillar.

"He had a directors' meeting at the bank last night. I phoned one of his associates about 2 A.M. He said the meeting had broken up at eleven and Bill had left to drive home." Her glance strayed up the ravine. "At four-thirty this morning I phoned the police."

"Did you know your husband had come to see me, Mrs. Updike —two mornings ago?"

"Who are you?"

"Ellery Queen."

"No." She did not seem surprised, or frightened, or anything.

"Did you know Robert Carlton Smith, J. Stanford Jones, Peter Zissing Brown?"

"Bill's classmates? They passed away. This year," she added suddenly. "This year," she repeated. And then she laughed. "I thought the gods were immortal."

"Did you know that your husband, Smith, Jones, and Brown were an 'inner circle' in The Januarians?"

"Inner Circle." She frowned. "Oh, yes. Bill mentioned it occasionally. No, I didn't know they were in it."

Ellery leaned forward in the wind.

"Was Edward I. Temple in it, Mrs. Updike? Rodney Black, Junior? Charlie Mason?"

"I don't know. Why are you questioning me? Why—?" Her voice was rising now, and Ellery murmured something placative as Captain Rosewater hurried up and said: "Mrs. Updike. If you'd be good enough . . ."

She jumped off the rock. "*Now?*"

"Please."

The trooper captain took one arm, the nurse the other, and between them they half-carried William Updike's widow up the ravine toward the overturned car.

Nikki found it necessary to spend some moments with her handkerchief.

When she looked up, Ellery had disappeared.

She found him with his father and Sergeant Velie on the road above the ravine. They were standing before a large maple looking at a road-sign. Studded lettering on the yellow sign spelled out *Sharp Curve Ahead,* and there was an elbow-like illustration.

"No lights on this road," the Inspector was saying as Nikki hurried up, "so he must have had his brights on—"

"And they'd sure enough light up this reflector sign. I don't get it, Inspector," complained Sergeant Velie. "Unless his lights just weren't workin'."

"More likely fell asleep over the wheel, Velie."

"No," said Ellery.

"What, Ellery?"

"Updike's lights were all right, and he didn't doze off."

"I don't impress when I'm c-cold," Nikki said, shivering. "But just the same, how do you know, Ellery?"

Ellery pointed to two neat holes in the maple bark, very close to the edge of the sign.

"Woodpeckers?" said Nikki. But the air was gray and sharp as steel, and it was hard to forget Mrs. Updike's look.

"This bird, I'm afraid," drawled Ellery, "had no feathers. Velie, borrow something we can pry this sign off with."

When Velie returned with some tools, he was mopping his face. "She just identified him," he said. "Gettin' warmer, ain't it?"

"What d'ye expect to find, Ellery?" demanded the Inspector.

"Two full sets of rivet-holes."

Sergeant Velie said: "Bong," as the road-sign came away from the tree.

"I'll be damned," said Inspector Queen softly. "Somebody removed these rivets last night, and after Updike crashed into the ravine—"

"Riveted the warning sign back on," cried Nikki, "only he got careless and didn't use the same holes!"

"Murder," said Ellery. "Smith, Jones, and Brown died of natural causes. But three of the five co-owners of that fund dying in a single year—"

"Gave Number 5 an idea!"

"If Updike died, too, the $200,000 in securities would . . . Ellery!" roared his father. "Where are you running to?"

"There's a poetic beauty about this case," Ellery was saying restlessly to Nikki as they waited in the underground vaults of The Brokers National Bank. "Janus was the god of entrances. Keys were among his trappings of office. In fact, he was sometimes known as *Patulcius*—'opener.' Opener! I knew at once we were too late."

"You knew, you knew," said Nikki peevishly. "And New Year's Eve only hours away! You can be wrong."

"Not this time. Why else was Updike murdered last night in such a way as to make it appear an accident? Our mysterious Januarians hotfooted it down here first thing this morning and cleaned out that safe-deposit box belonging to The Inner Circle. The securities are gone, Nikki."

Within an hour, Ellery's prophecy was historical fact.

The box was opened with Bill Updike's key. It was empty.

And of *Patulcius,* no trace. It quite upset the Inspector. For it appeared that The Inner Circle had contrived a remarkable arrangement for access to their safe-deposit box. It was gained, not by the customary signature on an admission slip, but through the presentation of a talisman. The talisman was quite unlike the lapel button of The Januarians. It was a golden key, and on the key was incised the two-faced god, within concentric circles. The outer circle was of Januarian garnets, the inner of diamonds. A control had been deposited in the files of the vault company. Anyone presenting a replica of it was to be admitted to The Inner Circle's repository by order of no less a personage, the vault manager informed them, than the late President Updike himself—who, Inspector Queen remarked with bitterness, had been more suited by temperament to preside over the Delancey Street Junior Spies.

"Anyone remember admitting a man this morning who flashed one of these doojiggers?"

An employee was found who duly remembered, but when he described the vault visitor as great-coated and muffled to the eyes, wearing dark glasses, walking with a great limp, and speaking in a laryngitical whisper, Ellery said wearily: "Tomorrow's the annual meeting of The Januarians, Dad, and *Patulcius* won't dare not show up. We'd better try to clean it up there."

These, then, were the curious events preceding the final meeting of The Januarians in the thirteenth-floor sanctuary of The Eastern Alumni Club, beyond the door bearing the stainless steel medallion of the god Janus.

We have no apocryphal writings to reveal what self-adoring mysteries were performed in that room on other New Year's Days; but on January the first of this year, The Januarians held a most unorthodox service, in that two lay figures—the Queens, *pater et filius*—moved in and administered some rather heretical sacraments; so there is a full record of the last rites.

It began with Sergeant Velie knocking thrice upon the steel

faces of Janus at five minutes past two o'clock on the afternoon of the first of January, and a thoroughly startled voice from within the holy of holies calling: "Who's there?" The Sergeant muttered an *Ave* and put his shoulder to the door. Three amazed, elderly male faces appeared. The heretics entered and the service began.

It is a temptation to describe in loving detail, for the satisfaction of the curious, the interior of the tabernacle—its stern steel furniture seizing the New Year's Day sun and tossing it back in the form of imperious light, the four-legged altar, the sacred vessels in the shape of beakers, the esoteric brown waters, and so on—but there has been enough of profanation, and besides the service is more to to our point.

It was chiefly catechistical, proceeding in this wise:

INSPECTOR: Gentlemen, my name is Inspector Queen. I'm from Police Headquarters, this is my son Ellery, and the big mugg on the door is Sergeant Velie of my staff.

BLACK: Police? Ed, do you know anything about—?

TEMPLE: Not me, Rodney. Maybe Charlie, ha-ha . . .?

MASON: What is it, Inspector? This is a private clubroom—

INSPECTOR. Which one are *you?*

MASON: Charles Mason—Mason's Theater Chain, Inc. But—

INSPECTOR: The long drink of water—what's *your* name?

TEMPLE: Me? Edward I. Temple. Attorney. What's the meaning—?

INSPECTOR: I guess, Tubby, that makes you Rodney Black, Junior of Wall Street.

BLACK: Sir—!

ELLERY: Which one of you gentlemen belonged to The Inner Circle of The Januarians?

MASON: Inner what, what?

BLACK: Circle, I think he said, Charlie.

TEMPLE: Inner Circle? What's that?

SERGEANT: One of 'em's a John Barrymore, Maestro.

BLACK: See here, we're three-fourths of what's left of the Class of Eastern '13 . . .

ELLERY: Ah, then you gentlemen don't know that Bill Updike is dead?

ALL: Dead! *Bill?*

INSPECTOR: Tell 'em the whole story, Ellery.

And so, patiently, Ellery recounted the story of The Inner Circle, William Updike's murder, and the vanished $200,000 in negotiable securities. And as he told this story, the old gentleman from Center Street and his sergeant studied the three elderly faces; and the theater magnate, the lawyer, and the broker gave stare for stare; and when Ellery had finished they turned to one another and gave stare for stare once more.

And finally Charlie Mason said: "My hands are clean, Ed. How about yours?"

"What do you take me for, Charlie?" said Temple in a flat and chilling voice. And they both looked at Black, who squeaked: "Don't try to make *me* out the one, you traitors!"

Whereupon, as if there were nothing more to be said, the three divinities turned and gazed bleakly upon the iconoclasts.

And the catechism resumed:

ELLERY: Mr. Temple, where were you night before last between 11 P.M. and midnight?

TEMPLE: Let me see. Night before last . . . That was the night before New Year's Eve. I went to bed at 10 o'clock.

ELLERY: You're a bachelor, I believe. Do you employ a domestic?

TEMPLE: My man.

ELLERY: Was he—?

TEMPLE: He sleeps out.

SERGEANT: No alibi!

INSPECTOR: How about you, Mr. Black?

BLACK: Well, the fact is . . . I'd gone to see a musical in town . . . and between 11 and 12 I was driving home . . . to White Plains . . .

SERGEANT: Ha! White Plains!

ELLERY: Alone, Mr. Black?

BLACK: Well . . . yes. The family's all away over the holidays . . .

INSPECTOR: No alibi. Mr. Mason?

MASON: Go to hell. (*There is a knock on the door.*)

SERGEANT: Now who would that be?

TEMPLE: The ghost of Bill?

BLACK: You're not funny, Ed!

ELLERY: Come in. (*The door opens. Enter Nikki Porter.*)

NIKKI: I'm sorry to interrupt, but she came looking for you, Ellery. She was terribly insistent. Said she'd just recalled something about The Inner Circle, and—

ELLERY: She?

NIKKI: Come in, Mrs. Updike.

"They're here," said Mrs. Updike. "I'm glad. I wanted to look at their faces."

"I've told Mrs. Updike the whole thing," said Nikki defiantly.

And Inspector Queen said in a soft tone: "Velie, shut the door."

But this case was not to be solved by a guilty look. Black, Mason, and Temple said quick ineffectual things, surrounding the widow and spending their nervousness in little gestures and rustlings until finally silence fell and she said helplessly. "Oh, I don't know, I don't know," and dropped into a chair to weep.

And Black stared out the window, and Mason looked green, and Temple compressed his lips.

Then Ellery went to the widow and put his hand on her shoulder. "You recall something about The Inner Circle, Mrs. Updike?"

She stopped weeping and folded her hands, resting them in her lap and looking straight ahead.

"Was it the names of the five?"

"No. Bill never told me their names. But I remember Bill's saying to me once: 'Mary, I'll give you a hint.' "

"Hint?"

"Bill said that he once realized there was something funny about the names of the five men in The Inner Circle."

"Funny?" said Ellery sharply. "About their *names?*"

"He said by coincidence all five names had one thing in common."

"In common?"

"And he laughed." Mrs. Updike paused. "He laughed, and he said: 'That is, Mary, if you remember that I'm a married man.' I remember saying: 'Bill, stop talking in riddles. What do you mean?' And he laughed again and said: 'Well, you see, Mary, *you're in it, too.*' "

"You're in it, too," said Nikki blankly.

"I have no idea what he meant, but that's what Bill said, word for word." And now she looked up at Ellery and asked, with a sort of ferocious zest: "Does any of this help, Mr. Queen?"

"Oh, yes," said Ellery gently. "All of it, Mrs. Updike." And he turned to the three silent Januarians and said: "Would any of you gentlemen like to try your wits against this riddle?"

But the gentlemen remained silent.

"The reply appears to be no," Ellery said. "Very well; let's work it out *en masse.* Robert Carlton Smith, J. Stanford Jones, Peter Zissing Brown, William Updike. Those four names, according to Bill Updike, have one thing in common. What?"

"Smith," said the Inspector.

"Jones," said the Sergeant.

"Brown," said Nikki.

"Updike!" said the Inspector. "Boy, you've got me."

"Include me in, Maestro."

"Ellery, please!"

"Each of the four names," said Ellery, "has in it, somewhere, the name of a well-known college or university."

And there was another mute communion.

"Robert—Carlton—Smith," said the Inspector, doubtfully.

"Smith!" cried Nikki. "*Smith College,* in Massachusetts!"

The Inspector looked startled. "J. Stanford Jones.—That California university, *Stanford!*"

"Hey," said Sergeant Velie. "Brown. *Brown University*, in Rhode Island!"

"Updike," said Nikki, then stopped. "Updike? There's no college called Updike, Ellery."

"William Updike was his full name, Nikki."

"You mean the 'William' part? There's a Williams, with an *s*, but no William."

"What did Updike tell Mrs. Updike? 'Mary, you're in it, too.' William Updike was in it, and Mary Updike was in it . . ."

"*William and Mary College!*" roared the Inspector.

"So the college denominator checks for all four of the known names. But since Updike told his wife the fifth name had the same thing in common, all we have to do now is test the names of these three gentlemen to see if one of them is the name of a college or university—and we'll have the scoundrel who murdered Bill Updike for The Inner Circle's fortune in securities."

"Black," babbled Rodney Black, Junior. "Rodney Black, Junior. Find me a college in that, sir!"

"Charles Mason," said Charles Mason unsteadily. "Charles? Mason? You see!"

"That," said Ellery, "sort of hangs it around your neck, Mr. Temple."

"Temple!"

"*Temple University* in Pennsylvania!"

Of course, it was all absurd. Grown men who played at godhead with emblems and talismans, like boys conspiring in a cave, and a murder case which was solved by a trick of nomenclature. Eastern University is too large for that sort of childishness. And it is old enough, we submit, to know the truth:

Item: Edward I. Temple, Class of Eastern '13, did not "fall" from the thirteenth floor of The Eastern Alumni Club on New Year's Day this year. He jumped.

Item: The Patulcius Chair of Classics, founded this year, was not endowed by a wealthy alumnus from Oil City who modestly chose anonymity. It came into existence through the contents of The Inner Circle's safe-deposit box, said contents having been re-covered from another safe-deposit box rented by said Temple in another bank on the afternoon of December thirty-first under a false name.

Item: The Januarian room was not converted to the storage of linen because of the expanding housekeeping needs of The Eastern Alumni Club. It was ordered so that the very name of the Society of the Two-Faced God should be expunged from Eastern's halls; and as for the stainless steel medallion of Janus which had hung on the door, the Chancellor of Eastern University himself scaled it into the Hudson River from the George Washington Bridge, during a sleet storm, one hideous night this January.

EDITOR'S POSTSCRIPT: Ellery Queen, who has had so many elo-quent things to say about the other writers and their stories, had nothing to say about *The Inner Circle*. The story came when it was ready; it was written. Classically simple? The story itself is in the classic tradition, though far from simple—a diminishing list of likely suspects, from out the last of which the detective names, un-waveringly, the murderer, and proceeds by his powers of observa-tion and deduction, to prove it forthwith.

Cover Her Face

So you think I'll make a good figure in one of your stories, do you? Well, let me tell you straight, I won't. You'll never get it across. *You* could never know what this place feels like and if you did, you'd never be able to write it down. Oh, I know they do their best to make it comfortable, but—think, man, think—only tomorrow morning they'll wake me early—if I have slept at all.

Yes, they'll give me my choice for breakfast. Civilized of them, isn't it? I guess I'll have kidneys and bacon, and I'll wash them down with a pint of beer. I always was a great one for my beer. Do you remember Kipling, the old Blimp?

I haven't read him since I left school, but for days it's been running in my head. I can't get it quite right. "He's drinking bitter beer today, but he's drinking it alone." It comes from a poem called *Danny Deever*.

Oh, so that's the way it goes, does it? Thanks. You've helped put that one out of my mind.

There are four paces this way and three, that. Have you ever lived in a room like this? Perhaps, eh? Yes, maybe, but *you* could go out for a walk when the walls started pressing in your head. *I* can't get out. They take me round the yard, but that's worse than useless.

It's only a short walk, they tell me, and a short flight of steps. They think this'll comfort me. But it'll be the last walk I'll ever take—forever and ever.

Well, what was it you wanted of me? What did you want to know? Of course, you're my cousin and that's why they let you in. Ghoulish, though, I call it, making copy out of my misfortunes. You just wanted to hear me speak, eh? Well, you've heard me speak. Why don't you go away?

I don't know why I did it myself—so *I* can't tell you. Eleven and a half hours from now—Oh, don't go—I don't mind talking. It'll take up some of the time and stop me thinking. Have you ever *heard* time walking past? It goes slowly—there's all eternity between each footstep—but you count them up and before you know it another hour has gone forever. One hour nearer the end —and I like being alive.

Oh, yes, I know you'll say she liked being alive, too. But that was different. She hadn't got my appreciation of life. She really didn't know *what* it was to be alive.

Listen, man! Can't you hear time roaring past? Oh, it's just my pulse that's beating in my ears, is it? But that's time too—that's one pulse-beat I'll never hear again. No, I don't think I'll crack up. I'll walk these last few steps just as if I was going to the corner for a packet of cigarettes. But don't go away—please! Just having you here is something—if not much.

It only goes to show that it's a mistake to go after a girl beneath you. She lacked the finer sensibilities which I myself have. Of course, she *was* pretty—if you like that kind of prettiness. I used to think I liked it myself, until I found out there was more to life than a pretty face and a fine figure.

It's odd, isn't it, to think I'm going to die because of someone who was so completely trivial. It isn't what you might call a death in the grand manner. They'll take me out of this cell and they'll hang me by the neck until I'm dead—dead—dead! Dead—just like any little vulgarian who had killed his girl. What a waste of all my gifts—gifts that might have been so useful to humanity.

You know I was clever. You see—I'm already talking of myself in the past tense? I *am* clever. I got through all my exams with flying colors. They said I'd a brilliant future. There was nothing I might not have done. And now this—all because of someone so utterly unimportant.

I was drunk when I met her. I'd gone to the Palais with a lot of chaps from the University. She looked so gay as she danced that I thought it would be fun to take her away from the clod who was her companion. Of course, I can now see that she was in her proper element. You know—water finding its own level and so on.

It wasn't difficult. I danced with her once or twice and then suggested we go for a drink. She said the pubs were shut, but I pointed out that I'd got some liquor in my flat. I can still remember the way she looked at me. Her big brown eyes were excited. It was a big adventure for her to go to a man's flat for a drink. Poor little thing.

To my offer of brandy, she said she'd rather have gin. I should have been warned then. Anyone who would prefer gin to brandy was obviously lacking in these points of sensibility which would make for a happy relationship with a man like me.

Yes, she was pretty, and even through the bad lines of her cheap frock I could see she'd a decent figure. It's funny how Kipling keeps coming back to me. Somewhere he refers to a woman who "looked like Old Greece and talked like the Old Kent Road." That just fits René.

Of course, I knew all along that wasn't her right name. She'd been christened plain Agnes, and her parents, of course, called her Aggie. I don't blame her for changing it, but she showed her lack of taste in the name she chose, and of education in the way she spelled it.

I don't like rushing things, so I didn't try anything that night. She told me afterwards she found this attractive in me. When I think of the clumsy pawing of clods, I shudder. And yet, that was what she'd been brought up to, and what she'd expected. She called me a gentleman and, though I'm no snob, I can't but say she was right. For me a gentleman is one who realizes that there's a time and a place for everything. I knew that evening was not the time.

Looking back on it now—God! how the time goes by—I can see that her little efforts at gentility fascinated me. I liked the silly way she lengthened her "a" and sometimes gave it a flavor of "e." Living at Davidson's Mains, I'd never met any girl but those in my own walk of life. You know the kind? Friendly, and honest, and terribly good at tennis or hockey. About as exciting as boiled puddings.

René was exciting. She walked as if she was alive, and not as if she was worrying about the respectability of her figure. There was none of that feeling of armor-plating I got when I danced with these honest burghers' daughters. You know what I mean? Your fingers counting the vertical ridges of whalebone or whatnot, or silk-sheathed rubber, instead of the nice hard knobs of the spine.

These girls were so afraid of the fact that they'd got figures that they hid them behind walls. You might almost say that the corset and the girdle were the modern chastity-belts, eh?

I'm glad you came, old man. You see I've just made a joke, and I haven't felt like doing that in a long time. Not a very good joke, perhaps, but still a joke.

René was plump where she was meant to be plump, and slim too in the right places. She didn't need a girdle to give her a hard, flat little belly.

Before she left that night, I'd found out where she lived and what she did. She worked in a shop at Tollcross, and lived with her people near Haymarket.

I made a date to meet her the next night. Even then I had the feeling she didn't quite belong, because, instead of asking her to meet me at the Café Royal or the Three Tuns, where the rest of the fellows went, I suggested Hughie's, in Rose Street—tough, you know, and free from my own crowd.

Of course, she was late. I drank a couple of pints waiting for her. I even looked at my watch several times. That wasn't like me. I'm usually capable of controlling my feelings. I don't believe in displaying my emotions. I told myself that she'd thought of her inferiority, and had decided she was not the sort of person for a chap like me.

All the same, I must give myself *some* credit. Thinking it over, I'm sure I chose Hughie's because it was the sort of place where she'd feel at home. Perhaps I'm doing myself less than justice when I talk to you? All the same, old man, it is good to have someone to speak to—it passes the *time*.

When she came into the bar, perky as a bird, turning her head this way and that, my heart bumped inside me. Of course, physiologically that's a misstatement, but you know what I mean? There was that feeling of a lump in my throat which I felt again when the judge put on that silly little square of silk. I'm sure I don't know why they call it a black cap. It's just a scrap of black silk.

I was flattered to notice she'd had her hair done. I suppose she'd felt her inferiority beside me, and felt that her dress from the Guinea Shop didn't quite go with my suit from Anderson & Sheppard. She'd felt she had to make an effort. So, as she couldn't afford more, she'd gone to one of those cheap hairdressers near Tollcross and had spent her few shillings on having her hair fluffed up.

When I rose to greet her, I got the impression that she wasn't used to having chaps rise for her. It seemed that, just by accident of my breeding, I was going the right way about impressing her. It's funny the way things work out, isn't it? Here I was, more or less slumming, just for the fun of it, and look where it's landed me!

All along I knew there was no future in it. I did my best to teach her to pronounce her words correctly, but when she got excited that dreadful Morningside accent crept out and grated on my ear.

I could, though, forgive her a lot for the sake of her face and her body. These were perfect. God! if she'd only had the mind to go with them, it might have worked!

But her mind was as empty as a blown eggshell. She'd filled it with bits from the movies and pieces from her favorite papers— *Pug's Paper, Red Letter* and so on. Her conversation was of "boys" —I, just imagine it, was her "boy"! And, when she forgot, she called me a "gent"—just as if I had to do with the natural functions of the body.

Yes, I suppose she *did* love me, in her shallow way. But what do we know of the feelings of those impulses and actions that are motivated by pure instinct? I flattered her pretty, petty little ego. I was a capture beyond her dreams. Soon I'd be a qualified doctor, and she'd be my wife. It was a true story from her pitiful reading—millgirl to duchess, eh?

You know how it is? A person of my sensitivity can always sense the dreams and motives of those he comes across. She was already seeing herself as "the doctor's wife," sitting in a drawing-room with etchings by D. Y. Cameron and Van Gogh's *Sunflowers* from the Medici Society, pouring out tea, drinking it with the little finger nicely crooked, and speaking in refined accents of her husband—"The Doctor."

Oh, yes, I knew her dreams. But I was brilliant and I could not see her as my wife, or as the lady to my knighthood. She would never have learned all the common decencies of life. She would never have shed all those little tricks which grated. Can you blame me?

In my mind, I can still dwell on the one visit I paid her parents. The only one—thank God! A four-roomed cottage, tumble-down and cramped, with a never-used parlor. You know the kind of place? I was given tea in the parlor, among the photographs of old football teams and the dusty castor-oil plants. You might say they were honest and simple working-people. I could not envisage them as my parents-in-law. I'll admit, however, that I preferred their Edinburgh accents to René's version of Murrayfield or Morningside.

Still, I *was* the victim of her fascination, of her simple pride in her body and face. It lasted a long time, but I always knew it couldn't go on forever. These things don't.

Yes, she *was* generous with herself, and in her naiveté she thought I was equally generous and meant everything I said to her. I daresay that, in the heat of the bed, I did promise her marriage. God! it's strange to think of it now, with the time running out like this.

Oh, if she'd been a little more sensitive and a little more receptive, I might even have risked it. But, the way things were, I couldn't gum up my career at the very start by marrying René. She'd have been a burden which even I couldn't have carried.

It was then I met Caroline. Yes, she's everything that I've always disliked about the Edinburgh girl. But her father's a brilliant surgeon. It wouldn't have been at all bad to be a rising young man with Sir John Bowditch as my father-in-law. I saw it all so clearly. I may flatter myself that I have a gift for seeing things clearly.

Besides, though I may be harsh about Caroline now, there was always the point that she was my own kind. She knew the people I knew, *and* she spoke the same kind of language. Oh, God, yes, I'd have got tired of her in a month or two, but the marriage would have gone on. I'd have established myself as one of the most brilliant of the younger men. Also, if I was careful, I was sure I would be able to find compensations for my family life. I don't think Caroline would ever have been suspicious of me. She'd have taken my exemplary behavior for granted—or, at least, would have expected me to be discreet.

I saw quite clearly, too, that I'd have to drop René. That was the trouble. She wouldn't be *dropped*. I suppose she saw her dreams fading, and was fighting for them. I tried to avoid seeing her, but she took to accosting me in the street. It really was *too* embarrassing.

I realized that the continued importunities might endanger my future, and I knew there'd have to be a show-down.

I want you to understand that I'd no thoughts of killing her. When I asked her to come round to my flat that Saturday afternoon, I merely wanted to tell her that it was all over between us. Of course, I'll admit I was a moral coward. I should've done it before. But you know how things are? I saw I'd have to get it over, whether I liked it or not.

There was something about the way she looked at me. So trusting. It made me feel crueler than I was. I told myself I was doing her a kindness. She'd never have fitted into my circle. Her shallow little mind could never have grasped the complexities of mine. Oh, I don't suppose Caroline would have got them either, but *she'd* have been content to be my wife without trying to intrude on my ideas.

I began gently. I was prepared for tears and, perhaps, even for some hysteria. I wasn't prepared for the transformation of the gentle René into a virago. She stormed at me and as she did so I was interested to notice that she shed the affectations of her speech and lapsed into her native Scots. Listening to her rage, I told myself I was well out of it.

I let her finish and got up to pour myself a drink. I measured a good four fingers of whiskey into the glass and took up the soda-siphon.

Then she spoke, quite softly, "David, you'll *have* to marry me. I'm going to have a baby."

I saw it. I was trapped. My brilliance would count for nothing tied to this vulgar little baggage. And I'd be tied for life. I knew it would be no use suggesting that anything could be done about it. She'd never have agreed. Although René wasn't a Catholic herself, her parents were and she'd imbibed enough of the doctrine to make *that* impossible.

Oh, yes, she'd got me neatly by the short hairs. I don't know why I did it, but in a sudden flush of rage—like a beast cornered—I swung the siphon at her. I don't think I meant to hit her with it, but she moved toward me just at that moment. Her lips were parted as though in readiness for a kiss, as though what she had said had made everything all right between us once more.

I felt rather than saw the heavy glass crash against the side of her head.

Then I was suddenly cool again. She lay crumpled on the floor. I bent down over her and realized she was dead. There was nothing I could do about it.

For about half an hour I walked up and down the room—just as these last weeks I've been walking up and down this cell. I thought I might explain it as an accident—for, damn it all, it was that and nothing more. I hadn't meant to kill her. I might have got away with that. She *could* have hit her head on the cast-iron fender.

But then I realized how that would involve me. I'd need to think of a way out which wouldn't blacken me in the eyes of Caroline's people. Sir John is an awful old stuffed shirt. You'd never dream he'd ever been young himself. No, it was clear I couldn't call the police and say there'd been an accident.

There was only one way out for me. That was to cut her up and dispose of the body. It was fortunate, I told myself, that I was such a brilliant hand at dissection. I took a piece of oilcloth and laid it on the table in the kitchen. I bent to pick her up. She wasn't heavy.

The siphon hadn't damaged her looks at all. She was still lovely. I laid a handkerchief over her face. I don't know what it was, but I couldn't bear to look at her. Do you remember from school—"Cover her face, mine eyes dazzle, she died young"? Yes? Well, I suppose it was something like that.

I don't suppose you want to hear about the next hours? I don't much like remembering them myself. The knife exploring where the loving hands had been. I was steady, though, and I made an excellent job of it.

There was, however, one point where I nearly lost control of myself. That was when I discovered she'd lied to me about her condition. But even that didn't make me wish to mar her face. Somehow I couldn't do it.

You know—everyone knows—how I strewed the minute particles of flesh and bone about The Meadows. It might have seemed a stupid move, but I'd often watched the dogs rioting about there, and I knew that, cut sufficiently small, these fragments would soon disappear. The trouble was her head.

When I'd finished my work I think I was pretty drunk. At any rate the whiskey bottle was empty and I was more than halfway through the brandy. I took them neat, for somehow I just couldn't use the soda-siphon.

You know the way things go? I was not alarmed when a police-man came to my flat one evening to ask if I'd seen her. I avoided the common error of saying I thought she'd gone off with another man. I don't say I didn't think of that, but I realized it might involve me. It might suggest that I'd been intimate with her. I managed to get it across that, while I'd certainly been friendly with the girl, I knew nothing of her love-life. That policeman went away satisfied.

What I hadn't counted on was her girl-friend in the shop where she'd worked. If I'd had any sense I'd have realized she couldn't keep a *romance,* as she'd have called it, like hers a secret. It was too like the stories in her pathetic papers. I'd represented her possi-bility of escape from trivial drudgery and her rise in the social scale.

The next time they came there were two of them. A constable and a fellow in plain-clothes. They were polite, I will say *that* for them. But the man in plain-clothes said, "I don't suppose you mind if we take a look round?" And, of course, I couldn't refuse.

All the time I was in Sauchiehall Prison, waiting for the trial, Caroline never came near me once. I felt annoyed by this. It showed a lack of trust in me. I never anticipated any trouble. Of course, I knew I shouldn't have cut up her body and disposed of it the way I'd done. But, then, a chap in my position couldn't afford to be mixed up in a thing like that. Of course, too, it was different now. The whole story would have to come out. I supposed that having a trial was just a formality.

It was so patently absurd to suppose that a man of my attain-ments would actually have murdered a shop-girl. To my surprise, I found that my lawyer didn't think it was as simple as I did. That's one of the troubles about living in a place like Edinburgh. All these old family lawyers are more dead than alive. Of course, they're all right on matters of property and so on—but they know nothing of the real facts of life.

The court was crowded. Looking along the public benches I

saw many of my friends. You were there, too, weren't you? I thought I saw you. I also saw René's parents. They looked old and shrunken. It was absurd that they should've been so upset over the death of such an unimportant person.

I realized quickly that I was the only person in court who had any real philosophical grasp of the meaning of civilization. Here I was, a potential benefactor of humanity, suffering the indignity of being tried for my life—*for my life,* mind you—all because of the death of one who had nothing to give to the people among whom she lived.

Nonsense, old boy, nonsense. That's rubbish. Beauty is an accident and the world could get along nicely without beautiful women. "Beauty is but a flower which wrinkles will devour." It couldn't get along without doctors.

My lawyer didn't want me to go into the witness-box. I had to insist. His account of what had happened was so garbled I felt I had to get it straight, in justice—that's a funny word—to myself. After all, I'd been there myself and I alone knew just what had happened.

I pointed out, rightly, that René was a person of no importance. It only goes to show that crass sentimentality is not quite dead. When I spoke some people on the public-benches hissed. I'm glad to say the judge made short work of them. He told them, more or less, to shut up or get out. I suffered no further interruptions.

One of the advantages of a training like mine is that you learn to tell a story briefly, without inessentials.

Of course, the other side did their best to blacken my character. They said I'd been trifling with the girl's affections and that I'd seen a personal advantage in a marriage with Caroline. This was nonsense. I was going to marry Caroline because she was the same kind of person as myself, with the same background. I'd sufficient faith in my own abilities to know that I didn't need to be helped to success. Then, too, they tried to make capital out of the way in which I'd disposed of the body. A set of sentimental slobs, they could not realize that my actions had been entirely logical.

The judge was a little man with a little dried-up face. He shuffled his notes slowly before he spoke to the jury. He reminded them that there were three verdicts in Scotland—Guilty, Not Guilty and Not Proven. He made some remarks about the jury's not being influenced by any personal distaste for the prisoner. I supposed he meant well, but I couldn't for the life of me see why he said it, unless he was trying to protect a man of his own level of intelligence against the malignancy of the unlettered mob.

I had little doubt about the verdict. They might not go all the way to saying I wasn't guilty, but I blessed my lucky stars that the trial was in Scotland, with that providential third verdict. Of course, I myself knew I wasn't guilty, but I couldn't vouch for what was going on in the minds of a lot of small tradesmen.

I may say that when the jury came back after only ten minutes and said I was guilty I nearly laughed. I thought the judge would send them back to reconsider the verdict, but he just nodded his little bird-like head.

I scarcely heard what he said to me. He said something about agreeing with the jury which showed me I'd been wrong in my estimate of him. He was a man utterly lacking in the finer points of sensibility. You might have expected a man in his position to realize that an educated man like myself could not set about murdering a shop-girl, for that was all she was. He asked me if I'd anything to say before he pronounced sentence.

I certainly had. I pointed out that the trial had been badly mismanaged and that it was ridiculous to think of punishing a man of my gifts—gifts of incomparable value to humanity—just because he had failed to make the true story acceptable to a bunch of clods. I indicated the jury. Further, I thought it was my duty to point out that the world was no poorer for René's death, whereas it would be a great deal poorer for mine. I thought I made the position clear.

Then he put on that silly little bit of black silk and, playing with a little nosegay of herbs, told me I would be hanged by the neck until I was dead. It was so farcial I could scarcely believe it myself.

However, I had little doubt that a higher court would see there'd been a gross miscarriage of justice, so I didn't worry. It's all so obviously absurd. The law is corrupt. My appeal was rejected and they tell me now there's no hope of a reprieve.

In a little more than ten hours the chaplain will come in and ask me to say my prayers. Why should I pray? It won't do *me* any good. Then they'll tie my hands behind my back and I'll go for that short walk. I don't think I'll break down. I still can't quite believe it's me in this cell. No—I mustn't think of it.

Thanks for coming, old fellow. You can make what use you like of what I've told you. You will make it clear that I'm suffering unjustly, won't you? It's destroyed all my faith in the infallibility of British justice. It's a travesty, that's what it is!

The whole situation is too ridiculous for words. If I'd been a little less sensitive than I am, I wouldn't be here now. They could never have proved it against me. It was all circumstantial evidence but for that one thing. I just couldn't bring myself to cut it up, so there it was in the kitchen cupboard—René's head in a jar of formalin.

EDITOR'S POSTSCRIPT: At lock-up time or bed-time, however it is called, I have had no word from Ruthven on what set him off on this tale. He is reading poetry somewhere on the West Coast, his own and other people's. By which I mean he is giving poetry readings, presumably for love and money. But I thought about the story and decided that if it's anyone we know in there, we don't want to look anyway, do we?

MARGARET MILLAR

The Couple Next Door

IT was by accident that they lived next door to each other, but by design that they became neighbors—Mr. Sands, who had retired to California after a life of crime investigation, and the Rackhams, Charles and Alma. Rackham was a big, innocent-looking man in his fifties. Except for the accumulation of a great deal of money, nothing much had ever happened to Rackham, and he liked to listen to Sands talk, while Alma sat with her knitting, plump and contented, unimpressed by any tale that had no direct bearing on her own life. She was half Rackham's age, but the fullness of her figure, and her air of having withdrawn from life quietly and without fuss, gave her the stamp of middle-age.

Two or three times a week Sands crossed the concrete driveway, skirted the eugenia hedge, and pressed the Rackhams' door chime. He stayed for tea or for dinner, to play gin or scrabble, or just to talk. "That reminds me of a case I had in Toronto," Sands would say, and Rackham would produce martinis and an expression of intense interest, and Alma would smile tolerantly, as if she didn't really believe a single thing Sands, or anyone else, ever said.

They made good neighbors: the Rackhams, Charles younger than his years, and Alma older than hers, and Sands who could be any age at all . . .

It was the last evening of August and through the open window of Sands' study came the scent of jasmine and the sound of a woman's harsh, wild weeping.

He thought at first that the Rackhams had a guest, a woman on a crying jag, perhaps, after a quarrel with her husband.

He went out into the front yard to listen, and Rackman came around the hedge, dressed in a bathrobe.

He said, sounding very surprised, "Alma's crying."

"I heard."

"I asked her to stop. I begged her. She won't tell me what's the matter."

"Women have cried before."

"Not Alma." Rackham stood on the damp grass, shivering, his forehead streaked with sweat. "What do you think we should do about it?"

The *I* had become *we*, because they were good neighbors, and along with the games and the dinners and the scent of jasmine, they shared the sound of a woman's grief.

"Perhaps you could talk to her," Rackham said.

"I'll try."

"I don't think there is anything physically the matter with her. We both had a check-up at the Tracy clinic last week. George Tracy is a good friend of mine—he'd have told me if there was anything wrong."

"I'm sure he would."

"If anything ever happened to Alma I'd kill myself."

Alma was crouched in a corner of the davenport in the living room, weeping rhythmically, methodically, as if she had accumulated a hoard of tears and must now spend them all in one night. Her fair skin was blotched with patches of red, like strawberry birthmarks, and her eyelids were blistered from the heat of her tears. She looked like a stranger to Sands, who had never seen her display any emotion stronger than ladylike distress over a broken teacup.

Rackham went over and stroked her hair. "Alma, dear. What is the matter?"

"Nothing . . . nothing . . ."

"Mr. Sands is here, Alma. I thought he might be able—we might be able—"

But no one was able. With a long shuddering sob, Alma got up and lurched across the room, hiding her blotched face with her hands. They heard her stumble up the stairs.

Sands said, "I'd better be going."

"No, please don't. I—the fact is, I'm scared. I'm scared stiff. Alma's always been so quiet."

"I know that."

"You don't suppose—there's no chance she's losing her mind?"

If they had not been good neighbors Sands might have remarked that Alma had little mind to lose. As it was, he said cautiously, "She might have had bad news, family trouble of some kind."

"She has no family except me."

"If you're worried, perhaps you'd better call your doctor."

"I think I will."

George Tracy arrived within half an hour, a slight, fair-haired man in his early thirties, with a smooth unhurried manner that imparted confidence. He talked slowly, moved slowly, as if there was all the time in the world to minister to desperate women.

Rackham chafed with impatience while Tracy removed his coat, placed it carefully across the back of the chair, and discussed the weather with Sands.

"It's a beautiful evening," Tracy said, and Alma's moans sliding down the stairs distorted his words, altered their meaning: *a terrible evening, an awful evening.* "There's a touch of fall in the air. You live in these parts, Mr. Sands?"

"Next door."

"For heaven's sake, George," Rackham said, "will you hurry up? For all you know, Alma might be dying."

"That I doubt. People don't die as easily as you might imagine. She's in her room?"

"Yes. Now will you *please*—"

"Take it easy, old man."

Tracy picked up his medical bag and went towards the stairs, leisurely, benign.

"He's always like that." Rackham turned to Sands, scowling. "Exasperating son-of-a-gun. You can bet that if he had a wife in Alma's condition he'd be taking those steps three at a time."

"Who knows?—perhaps he has."

"*I* know," Rackham said crisply. "He's not even married. Never had time for it, he told me. He doesn't look it but he's very ambitious."

"Most doctors are."

"Tracy is, anyway."

Rackham mixed a pitcher of martinis, and the two men sat in front of the unlit fire, waiting and listening. The noises from upstairs gradually ceased, and pretty soon the doctor came down again.

Rackham rushed across the room to meet him. "How is she?"

"Sleeping. I gave her a hypo."

"Did you talk to her? Did you ask her what was the matter?"

"She was in no condition to answer questions."

"Did you find anything wrong with her?"

"Not physically. She's a healthy young woman."

"Not *physically*. Does that mean—?"

"Take it easy, old man."

Rackham was too concerned with Alma to notice Tracy's choice of words, but Sands noticed, and wondered if it had been conscious or unconscious: Alma's a healthy young woman . . . Take it easy, old man.

"If she's still depressed in the morning," Tracy said, "bring her down to the clinic with you when you come in for your X-rays. We have a good neurologist on our staff." He reached for his coat and hat. "By the way, I hope you followed the instructions."

Rackham looked at him stupidly. "What instructions?"

"Before we can take specific X-rays, certain medication is necessary."

"I don't know what you're talking about."

"I made it very clear to Alma," Tracy said, sounding annoyed. "You were to take one ounce of sodium phosphate after dinner tonight, and report to the X-ray department at 8 o'clock tomorrow morning without breakfast."

"She didn't tell me."

"Oh."

"It must have slipped her mind."

"Yes. Obviously. Well, it's too late now." He put on his coat, moving quickly for the first time, as if he were in a rush to get away. The change made Sands curious. He wondered why Tracy was suddenly so anxious to leave, and whether there was any connection between Alma's hysteria and her lapse of memory about Rackham's X-rays. He looked at Rackham and guessed, from his pallor and his worried eyes, that Rackham had already made a connection in his mind.

"I understood," Rackham said carefully, "that I was all through at the clinic. My heart, lungs, metabolism—everything fit as a fiddle."

"People," Tracy said, "are not fiddles. Their tone doesn't improve with age. I will make another appointment for you and send you specific instructions by mail. Is that all right with you?"

"I guess it will have to be."

"Well, good night, Mr. Sands, pleasant meeting you." And to Rackham, "Good night, old man."

When he had gone, Rackham leaned against the wall, breathing hard. Sweat crawled down the sides of his face like worms and hid in the collar of his bathrobe. "You'll have to forgive me, Sands. I feel—I'm not feeling very well."

"Is there anything I can do?"

"Yes," Rackham said. "Turn back the clock."

"Beyond my powers, I'm afraid."

"Yes . . . Yes, I'm afraid."

"Good night, Rackham." *Good night, old man.*

"Good night, Sands." *Good night old man to you, too.*

Sands shuffled across the concrete driveway, his head bent. It was a dark night, with no moon at all.

From his study Sands could see the lighted windows of Rackham's bedroom. Rackham's shadow moved back and forth behind the blinds as if seeking escape from the very light that gave it existence. Back and forth, in search of nirvana.

Sands read until far into the night. It was one of the solaces of growing old—if the hours were numbered, at least fewer of them need be wasted in sleep. When he went to bed, Rackham's bedroom light was still on.

They had become good neighbors by design; now, also by design, they became strangers. Whose design it was, Alma's or Rackham's, Sands didn't know.

There was no definite break, no unpleasantness. But the eugenia hedge seemed to have grown taller and thicker, and the concrete driveway a mile away. He saw the Rackhams occasionally; they waved or smiled or said, "Lovely weather," over the backyard fence. But Rackham's smile was thin and painful, Alma waved with a leaden arm, and neither of them cared about the weather. They stayed indoors most of the time, and when they did come out they were always together, arm in arm, walking slowly and in step. It was impossible to tell whose step led, and whose followed.

At the end of the first week in September, Sands met Alma by accident in a drug store downtown. It was the first time since the night of the doctor's visit that he'd seen either of the Rackhams alone.

She was waiting at the prescription counter wearing a flowery print dress that emphasized the fullness of her figure and the bovine expression of her face. A drug-store length away, she looked like a rather dull, badly dressed young woman with a passion for starchy foods, and it was hard to understand what Rackham had seen in her. But then Rackham had never stood a drug-store length away from Alma; he saw her only in close-up, the surprising, intense blue of her eyes, and the color and texture of her skin, like whipped cream. Sands wondered whether it was her skin and eyes, or her quality of serenity which had appealed most to Rackham, who was quick and nervous and excitable.

She said, placidly, "Why, hello there."

"Hello, Alma."

"Lovely weather, isn't it?"

"Yes. . . . How is Charles?"

"You must come over for dinner one of these nights."

"I'd like to."

"Next week, perhaps. I'll give you a call—I must run now. Charles is waiting for me. See you next week."

But she did not run, she walked; and Charles was not waiting for her, he was waiting for Sands. He had let himself into Sands' house and was pacing the floor of the study, smoking a cigarette. His color was bad, and he had lost weight, but he seemed to have acquired an inner calm. Sands could not tell whether it was the calm of a man who had come to an important decision, or that of a man who had reached the end of his rope and had stopped struggling.

They shook hands, firmly, pressing the past week back into shape.

Rackham said, "Nice to see you again, old man."

"I've been here all along."

"Yes. Yes, I know. . . . I had things to do, a lot of thinking to do."

"Sit down. I'll make you a drink."

"No, thanks. Alma will be home shortly, I must be there."

Like a Siamese twin, Sands thought, *separated by a miracle, but returning voluntarily to the fusion—because the fusion was in a vital organ.*

"I understand," Sands said.

Rackham shook his head. "No one can understand, really, but you come very close sometimes, Sands. Very close." His cheeks flushed, like a boy's. "I'm not good at words or expressing my emotions, but I wanted to thank you before we leave, and tell you how much Alma and I have enjoyed your companionship."

"You're taking a trip?"

"Yes. Quite a long one."

"When are you leaving?"

"Today."

"You must let me see you off at the station."

"No, no," Rackham said quickly. "I couldn't think of it. I hate last-minute depot farewells. That's why I came over this afternoon to say goodbye."

"Tell me something of your plans."

"I would if I had any. Everything is rather indefinite. I'm not sure where we'll end up."

"I'd like to hear from you now and then."

"Oh, you'll hear from me, of course." Rackham turned away with an impatient twitch of his shoulders as if he was anxious to leave, anxious to start the trip right now before anything happened to prevent it.

"I'll miss you both," Sands said. We've had a lot of laughs together."

Rackham scowled out of the window. "Please, no farewell speeches. They might shake my decision. My mind is already made up, I want no second thoughts."

"Very well."

"I must go now. Alma will be wondering—"

"I saw Alma earlier this afternoon," Sands said.

"Oh?"

"She invited me for dinner next week."

Outside the open window two hummingbirds fought and fussed, darting with crazy accuracy in and out of the bougainvillea vine.

"Alma," Rackham said carefully, "can be very forgetful sometimes."

"Not that forgetful. She doesn't know about this trip you've planned, does she? . . . Does she, Rackham?"

"I wanted it to be a surprise. She's always had a desire to see the world. She's still young enough to believe that one place is different from any other place. . . . You and I know better."

"Do we?"

"Good bye, Sands."

At the front door they shook hands again, and Rackham again promised to write, and Sands promised to answer his letters. Then Rackham crossed the lawn and the concrete driveway, head bent, shoulders hunched. He didn't look back as he turned the corner of the eugenia hedge.

Sands went over to his desk, looked up a number in the telephone directory, and dialed.

A girl's voice answered, "Tracy clinic, X-ray department."

"This is Charles Rackham," Sands said.

"Yes, Mr. Rackham."

"I'm leaving town unexpectedly. If you'll tell me the amount of my bill I'll send you a check before I go."

"The bill hasn't gone through, but the standard price for a lower gastro-intestinal is twenty-five dollars."

"Let's see, I had that done on the—"

"The fifth. Yesterday."

"But my original appointment was for the first, wasn't it?"

The girl gave a does-it-really-matter sigh. "Just a minute, sir, and I'll check." Half a minute later she was back on the line. "We have no record of an appointment for you on the first, sir."

"You're sure of that?"

"Even without the record book, I'd be sure. The first was a Monday. We do only gall bladders on Monday."

"Oh. Thank you."

Sands went out and got into his car. Before he pulled away from the curb he looked over at Rackham's house and saw Rackham pacing up and down the veranda, waiting for Alma.

The Tracy clinic was less impressive than Sands had expected, a converted two-story stucco house with a red tile roof. Some of the tiles were broken and the whole building needed paint, but the furnishings inside were smart and expensive.

At the reception desk a nurse wearing a crew cut and a professional smile told Sands that Dr. Tracy was booked solid for the entire afternoon. The only chance of seeing him was to sit in the second-floor waiting room and catch him between patients.

Sands went upstairs and took a chair in a little alcove at the end of the hall, near Tracy's door. He sat with his face half hidden behind an open magazine. After a while the door of Tracy's office opened and over the top of his magazine Sands saw a woman silhouetted in the door frame—a plump, fair-haired young woman in a flowery print dress.

Tracy followed her into the hall and the two of them stood looking at each other in silence. Then Alma turned and walked away, passing Sands without seeing him because her eyes were blind with tears.

Sands stood up. "Dr. Tracy?"

Tracy turned sharply, surprise and annoyance pinching the corners of his mouth. "Well? Oh, it's Mr. Sands."

"May I see you a moment?"

"I have quite a full schedule this afternoon."

"This is an emergency."

"Very well. Come in."

They sat facing each other across Tracy's desk.

"You look pretty fit," Tracy said with a wry smile, "for an emergency case."

"The emergency is not mine. It may be yours."

"If it's mine, I'll handle it alone, without the help of a poli—I'll handle it myself."

Sands leaned forward. "Alma has told you, then, that I used to be a policeman."

"She mentioned it in passing."

"I saw Alma leave a few minutes ago. . . . She'd be quite a nice-looking woman if she learned to dress properly."

"Clothes are not important in a woman," Tracy said, with a slight flush. "Besides, I don't care to discuss my patients."

"Alma is a patient of yours?"

"Yes."

"Since the night Rackham called you when she was having hysterics?"

"Before then."

Sands got up, went to the window, and looked down at the street.

People were passing, children were playing on the sidewalk, the sun shone, the palm trees rustled with wind—everything outside seemed normal and human and real. By contrast, the shape of the idea that was forming in the back of his mind was so grotesque and ugly that he wanted to run out of the office, to join the normal people passing on the street below. But he knew he could not escape by running. The idea would follow him, pursue him until he turned around and faced it.

It moved inside his brain like a vast wheel, and in the middle of the wheel, impassive, immobile, was Alma.

Tracy's harsh voice interrupted the turning of the wheel. "Did you come here to inspect my view, Mr. Sands?"

"Let's say, instead, your viewpoint."

"I'm a busy man. You're wasting my time."

"No. I'm giving you time."

"To do what?"

"Think things over."

"If you don't leave my office immediately, I'll have you thrown out." Tracy glanced at the telephone but he didn't reach for it, and there was no conviction in his voice.

"Perhaps you shouldn't have let me in. Why did you?"

"I thought you might make a fuss if I didn't."

"Fusses aren't in my line." Sands turned from the window. "Liars are, though."

"What are you implying?"

"I've thought a great deal about that night you came to the Rackhams' house. In retrospect, the whole thing appeared too pat; too contrived: Alma had hysterics and you were called to treat her. Natural enough, so far."

Tracy stirred but didn't speak.

"The interesting part came later. You mentioned casually to Rackham that he had an appointment for some X-rays to be taken the following day, September the first. It was assumed that Alma had forgotten to tell him. Only Alma *hadn't* forgotten. There was nothing to forget. I checked with your X-ray department half an hour ago. They have no record of any appointment for Rackham on September the first.

"Records get lost."

"This record wasn't lost. It never existed. You lied to Rackham. The lie itself wasn't important, it was the *kind* of lie. I could have understood a lie of vanity, or one to avoid punishment or to gain profit. But this seemed such a silly, senseless, little lie. It worried me. I began to wonder about Alma's part in the scene that night. Her crying was most unusual for a woman of Alma's inert nature. What if her crying was also a lie? And what was to be gained by it?"

"Nothing," Tracy said wearily. "Nothing was gained."

"But something was *intended*—and I think I know what it was. The scene was played to worry Rackham, to set him up for an even bigger scene. If that next scene has already been played, I am wasting my time here. Has it?"

"You have a vivid imagination."

"No. The plan was yours—I only figured it out."

"Very poor figuring, Mr. Sands." But Tracy's face was gray, as if mold had grown over his skin.

"I wish it were. I had become quite fond of the Rackhams."

He looked down at the street again, seeing nothing but the wheel turning inside his head. Alma was no longer in the middle of the wheel, passive and immobile; she was revolving with the others—Alma and Tracy and Rackham, turning as the wheel turned, clinging to its perimeter.

Alma, devoted wife, a little on the dull side. . . . What sudden passion of hate or love had made her capable of such consummate deceit? Sands imagined the scene the morning after Tracy's visit to the house. Rackham, worried and exhausted after a sleepless night: *"Are you feeling better now, Alma?"*

"Yes."

"What made you cry like that?"

"I was worried."

"About me?"

"Yes."

"Why didn't you tell me about my X-ray appointment?"

"I couldn't. I was frightened. I was afraid they would discover something serious the matter with you."

"Did Tracy give you any reason to think that?"

"He mentioned something about a blockage. Oh, Charles, I'm scared! If anything ever happened to you, I'd die. I couldn't live without you!"

For an emotional and sensitive man like Rackman, it was a perfect set-up: his devoted wife was frightened to the point of hysterics, his good friend and physician had given her reason to be frightened. Rackham was ready for the next step. . . .

"According to the records in your X-ray department," Sands said, "Rackham had a lower gastrointestinal X-ray yesterday morning. What was the result?"

"Medical ethics forbid me to—"

"You can't hide behind a wall of medical ethics that's already full of holes. What was the result?"

There was a long silence before Tracy spoke. "Nothing."

"You found nothing the matter with him?"

"That's right."

"Have you told Rackham that?"

"He came in earlier this afternoon, alone.

"Why alone?"

"I didn't want Alma to hear what I had to say."

"Very considerate of you."

"No, it was not considerate," Tracy said dully. "I had decided to back out of our—our agreement—and I didn't want her to know just yet."

"The agreement was to lie to Rackham, convince him that he had a fatal disease?"

"Yes."

"Did you?"

"No. I showed him the X-rays, I made it clear that there was nothing wrong with him. . . . I tried. I tried my best. It was no use."

"What do you mean?"

"He wouldn't believe me! He thought I was trying to keep the real truth from him." Tracy drew in his breath sharply. "It's funny, isn't it?—after days of indecision and torment I made up my mind to do the right thing. But it was too late. Alma had played her role too well. She's the only one Rackham will believe."

The telephone on Tracy's desk began to ring but he made no move to answer it, and pretty soon the ringing stopped and the room was quiet again.

Sands said, "Have you asked Alma to tell him the truth?"

"Yes, just before you came in."

"She refused?"

Tracy didn't answer.

"She wants him to think he is fatally ill?"

"I—yes."

"In the hope that he'll kill himself, perhaps?"

Once again Tracy was silent. But no reply was necessary.

"I think Alma miscalculated," Sands said quietly. Instead of planning suicide, Rackham is planning a trip. But before he leaves, he's going to hear the truth—from you and from Alma." Sands went towards the door. "Come on, Tracy. You have a house call to make."

"No. I can't." Tracy grasped the desk with both hands, like a child resisting the physical force of removal by a parent. "I won't go."

"You have to."

"No! Rackham will ruin me if he finds out. That's how this whole thing started. We were afraid, Alma and I, afraid of what Rackham would do if she asked him for a divorce. He's crazy in love with her, he's obsessed!"

"And so are you?"

"Not the way he is. Alma and I both want the same things—a little peace, a little quiet together. We are alike in many ways."

"That I can believe," Sands said grimly. "You want the same things, a little peace, a little quiet—and a little of Rackham's money?"

"The money was secondary."

"A very close second. How did you plan on getting it?"

Tracy shook his head from side to side, like an animal in pain. "You keep referring to plans, ideas, schemes. We didn't start out with plans or schemes. We just fell in love. We've been in love for nearly a year, not daring to do anything about it because I knew how Rackham would react if we told him. I have worked hard to build up this clinic; Rackham could destroy it, and me, within a month."

"That's a chance you'll have to take. Come on, Tracy."

Sands opened the door and the two men walked down the hall, slowly and in step, as if they were handcuffed together.

A nurse in uniform met them at the top of the stairs. "Dr. Tracy, are you ready for your next—"?

"Cancel all my appointments, Miss Leroy."

"But that's imposs—"

"I have a very important house call to make."

"Will it take long?"

"I don't know."

The two men went down the stairs, past the reception desk, and out into the summer afternoon. Before he got into Sands' car, Tracy looked back at the clinic, as if he never expected to see it again.

Sands turned on the ignition and the car sprang forward.

After a time Tracy said, "Of all the people in the world who could have been at the Rackham's that night, it had to be an ex-policeman."

"It's lucky for you that I was."

"Lucky." Tracy let out a harsh little laugh. "What's lucky about financial ruin?"

"It's better than some other kinds of ruin. If your plan had gone through, you could never have felt like a decent man again."

"You think I will anyway?"

"Perhaps, as the years go by."

"The years." Tracy turned, with a sigh. "What are you going to tell Rackham?"

"Nothing. You will tell him yourself."

"I can't. You don't understand, I'm quite fond of Rackham, and so is Alma. We—it's hard to explain."

"Even harder to understand." Sands thought back to all the times he had seen the Rackhams together and envied their companionship, their mutual devotion. Never, by the slightest glance or gesture of impatience or slip of the tongue, had Alma indicated that she was passionately in love with another man. He recalled the games of scrabble, the dinners, the endless conversations with Rackham, while Alma sat with her knitting, her face reposeful, content. Rackham would ask, "Don't you want to play too, Alma?" And she would reply, "No, thank you, dear, I'm quite happy with my thoughts."

Alma, happy with her thoughts of violent delights and violent ends.

Sands said, "Alma is equally in love with you?"

"Yes." He sounded absolutely convinced. "No matter what Rackham says or does, we intend to have each other."

"I see."

The blinds of the Rackham house were closed against the sun. Sands led the way up the veranda steps and pressed the door chime, while Tracy stood, stony-faced and erect, like a bill collector or a process server.

Sands could hear the chimes pealing inside the house and feel their vibrations beating under his feet.

He said, "They may have gone already."

"Gone where?"

"Rackham wouldn't tell me. He just said he was planning the trip as a surprise for Alma."

"He can't take her away! He can't force her to leave if she doesn't want to go!"

Sands pressed the door chime again, and called out, "Rackham? Alma?" But there was no response.

He wiped the sudden moisture off his forehead with his coat sleeve. "I'm going in."

"I'm coming with you."

"No."

The door was unlocked. He stepped into the empty hall and shouted up the staircase, "Alma? Rackham? Are you there?"

The echo of his voice teased him from the dim corners.

Tracy had come into the hall. "They've left, then?"

"Perhaps not. They might have just gone out for a drive. It's a nice day for a drive."

"Is it?"

"Go around to the back and see if their car's in the garage."

When Tracy had gone, Sands closed the door behind him and shot the bolt. He stood for a moment listening to Tracy's nervous footsteps on the concrete driveway. Then he turned and walked slowly into the living room, knowing the car would be in the garage, no matter how nice a day it was for a drive.

The drapes were pulled tight across the windows and the room was cool and dark, but alive with images and noisy with the past:

"I wanted to thank you before we leave, Sands."

"You're taking a trip?"

"Yes, quite a long one."

"When are you leaving?"

"Today."

"You must let me see you off at the station. . . ."

But no station had been necessary for Rackham's trip. He lay in front of the fireplace in a pool of blood, and beside him was his companion on the journey, her left arm curving around his waist.

Rackham had kept his promise to write. The note was on the mantel, addressed not to Sands, but to Tracy.

"Dear George:

You did your best to fool me but I got the truth from Alma. She could never hide anything from me, we are too close to each other. This is the easiest way out. I am sorry that I must take Alma along, but she has told me so often that she could not live without me. I cannot leave her behind to grieve.

Think of us now and then, and try not to judge me too harshly.

Charles Rackham."

Sands put the note back on the mantel. He stood quietly, his heart pierced by the final splinter of irony: before Rackham had used the gun on himself, he had lain down on the floor beside Alma and placed her dead arm lovingly around his waist.

From outside came the sound of Tracy's footsteps and then the pounding of his fists on the front door.

"Sands, I'm locked out. Open the door. Let me in! Sands, do you hear me? Open this door!"

Sands went and opened the door.

AUTHOR'S POSTSCRIPT, OR STRICTLY SPEAKING, AUTHOR'S HUSBAND'S POSTSCRIPT—ROSS MACDONALD, SPEAKING OF HIS WORK, AND OF MARGARET MILLAR'S: "Most fiction, especially our sort of fiction, seems to be based on unconscious fantasies which the conscious plotting mind tries to rationalize and generalize, both for itself and the reader. We all have the same unconscious, as a friend of mine once said, but writers are more aware of it." Inspector Sands, after appearing in several of Margaret Millar's Canadian novels, was transplanted to California with this story. He seems to have rooted well there.

Anonymous Fame

JAMES HARRIS sat bolt upright in the rocking subway train. He was squeezed in so tightly between the fat man on his right and the woman reading a newspaper on his left, that he couldn't have leaned back even if he'd wanted to. This was the way he liked it. There was nothing to interfere with his watching the woman.

She was sitting halfway down the car on the opposite side, her purse and four or five packages piled on her lap. She was a dish, Harris thought, a real prize-winning baby, the kind who wouldn't give a guy like him as much as the time of day.

The thought made him angry. This dame had everything—looks, money, fame of a sort. And what did Harris have? Nothing. He wet his lips with the tip of his tongue and let his anger rise up against her. If things went right this afternoon, he'd more than even up the whole bloody score with her.

He ought not to be staring so hard, he warned himself. Then he grinned. Who noticed him? Especially with a looker like Mabel Kent close at hand.

Harris couldn't have torn his eyes away from her if he wanted to. Something about her got through to him, made his pulse race, scooped out a hollow place at the pit of his stomach so that he felt almost as though he were falling. She was a doll, all right. A bit on the flashy side; platinum blonde hair, smooth pink skin and over-full crimson lips made her so. She wore a lot of jewelry, too much perfume and her bottle-green dress stretched too tightly across her bosom. The arrogant way in which she walked and held her head showed that she knew what she had. But she wouldn't give it out easy. To get close to Mabel Kent, you'd need plenty of folding stuff in your pockets.

Harris had been following her for more than three weeks. But he was willing to bet that he could walk right up and speak to her and she wouldn't remember ever having seen him before. That burned him, yet it gave him a sense of power too. Almost as though he were an invisible man.

That's the way it had always been with him ever since he was a kid. In the crowded schoolrooms, in the teeming slums where he was raised, he was a complete nobody, the little guy who wasn't there. Nobody bothered him; they just left him alone. He had been an ordinary kid, shorter than most, with a pale face, undistinguished features, hair of an indeterminate brown and eyes that were a watery gray. Even his name was commonplace. Few people ever bothered to remember it. He'd never had a nickname either. He wasn't that important to anybody.

Harris had lived alone with his mother, a vague, defeated little woman who subsisted on relief checks. He never got close to anyone. No girl friends, not even a buddy. There'd been a time when he'd tried to change things, work his way into the gang that hung around the corner drug store. It hadn't panned out. They beat him up and once they'd beaten him, they forgot all about him, never bothered him again.

Next he'd tried wearing flashy clothes, talking loud, hammering metal cleats on his shoes so that he made a lot of noise when he walked. Now and then he'd draw a snicker but that was about all. Nobody noticed him unless he thrust himself upon them, and then something unpleasant always happened. So pretty soon he'd given it up. That was when he'd learned the advantages of being a nobody.

He'd discovered this hidden gift almost by accident. One day he'd walked into the drug store with a nickle to buy a candy bar. But the girl behind the counter had been too busy yacking with a couple of sharpie kids to pay him any mind. He tapped the nickle on the glass but all she did was turn her head and throw him a pained look.

He picked up a candy bar and thrust it in his pocket, then another and another until his pockets were bulging. He tossed the

nickle down on the counter and walked out. He was all shaky inside and sweat had sprouted out across his forehead and the back
of his hands. He expected to be grabbed and dragged down to the
police station. But nothing happened—nothing at all. And when
he finally gathered up enough nerve to go back to the drug store,
the fat girl's eyes slid across his face as though she'd never seen him
before. That's when he knew.

What he had, a real gift of being inconspicuous, was one that
almost amounted to genius. His worries were over. He'd never
starve or have to do menial work. He could take anything he
wanted and no one would ever see him do it.

He quit school and started drifting. At first he filched in the
five-and-ten-cent stores, the cheap, crowded markets, picking up
anything that struck his fancy.

His fingers grew nimble but he knew that wasn't the secret of his
success.

He could wander in and out of bars, hotel lobbies, restaurants,
snatching up a purse, a wallet or a loose bill. Nobody noticed him
while he was around; nobody missed him when he was gone. Instead of fighting against his nondescript appearance, Harris began
to cultivate it. Even when he had money, he wore a plain blue
serge suit, a white shirt, and plain tie.

But even while he practiced being inconspicuous, he couldn't
hold down a dream that haunted him. Some day James Harris
would be a big shot, famous, the talk of him on everybody's lips.

But until that time, the years rolled by and Harris remained
simply a petty thief. Now and then he got a job, always a piddling
little one that he hated, like being a stock clerk or a packer. After a
few weeks he'd drift away.

Harris knew he wasn't going to be president, not even a senator
or a representative. He wasn't going to be a moving picture star
or a great novelist. But somehow there had to be a short cut to
fame. Some of the kids he'd known in the slums had made the
headlines. How had they done it. Rackets. A big score. Killed

somebody. But they'd all been sent up the river or taken the hot squat in Sing Sing, too. It was the same story: you made a name for yourself, then you traded your name for a number. That was strictly for the birds, not for a hep guy like James Harris.

All the same if you were smart enough you could get away with murder. The word murder touched off something inside of him. There were plenty of murderers who never got caught. And they didn't have half the equipment Harris had. Like the Black Dahlia case out in California. Like Jack the Ripper.

Anonymous fame—that was the ticket. It suited Harris to a T.

He started reading books about criminals. Most of these guys were pikers. That was why they landed up on the gallows or in the electric chair. Come to think about it, even Jack the Ripper wasn't so hot. All his victims were street women, derelicts, drabs. Harris could shoot a lot higher—society women, actresses, the rich and famous. He could make them all shudder at the thought of him. They'd lock themselves up at night, be afraid to walk the streets even in daylight.

At first it was all a dream. Then Harris began to plan. He wouldn't need a weapon. A gun was noisy and a knife wasn't quick enough.

His hands! He knew how strong they were in spite of his appearance of weakness. They were all he would need—except a victim.

He wasn't in any hurry. When he slept, he'd feel his hands encircling smooth, warm flesh and he'd press harder and harder until he woke up. He'd be covered with perspiration and so excited he couldn't go back to sleep again. Still he bided his time. It couldn't be just any woman.

Then he saw Mabel Kent and he knew in a flash that she was the woman. He didn't know her name or who she was, but he recognized instinctively that she was the target for the homicidal drives that racked his days. She was the enemy, the personification of all the women who wouldn't give themselves to little men like

James Harris. He'd never win from her more than a glance of contempt, a faint expression of derision or distaste.

He'd seen her leaning over the perfume counter in a Fifth Avenue shop. He couldn't see her face, only the sensual lines of her figure and the contours of her rounded arm and neck. Her legs were nice, a little heavy at the calves, tapering down to slim ankles, the kind Harris liked.

She completed her purchase and turned, her eyes sweeping over him. He started before he remembered he didn't have to worry. Her gaze went on past him. He studied her face. It was just the way he'd pictured it in his dreams, fine-boned and firm-fleshed. Her cheek bones were wide, giving a depth to her cool blue eyes. He hadn't made any mistake. This was the woman, all right.

She was moving out of the shop onto the crowded avenue. He stood still until the crowd closed in around her. Suddenly a wave of panic hit him. He should have stayed close, not taking any chances on losing her. He darted forward, sweat pouring from his face, his hands trembling. He needn't have worried. You couldn't lose a dame like this. She stood out like a neon sign in a dark alley.

After that he stuck close behind her, never more than a few feet away. Other men turned to stare at her. Harris cast baleful glances at them. Couldn't they see he'd staked this dame off? He was surprised when she turned in at a subway kiosk. You'd expect a fancy frill like this to ride around in a Caddy. Or a taxi. But the subway made the chase easy. So why should he kick?

He tailed her to an apartment house on the West Side, just off Riverside Drive. He was right there on the steps when she dug out the key from her purse and opened the mailbox. After she'd gone in, he'd read her name on the mail-box. Mabel Kent—that was all.

He'd been disappointed in the place where she lived. He'd expected a plushy backdrop for a dame as smooth as this one. He looked the house over. A shabby old brownstone with an ornate glass door in front, four stories high with only apartments on each floor. Then it dawned on him. She'd like things cosy and private so that no one could stick his nose into her business. It confirmed his earlier impression of her. His lips formed a thin disapproving line. He'd picked the right woman. She had plenty coming to her.

Mabel Kent—the name suddenly rang a bell. He was an avid reader of the scandal sheets that gave the "inside dope" on the famous and near famous. He dredged his memory for the details of the stories about Mabel Kent. She had been a show girl who'd married a wealthy playboy. She'd ditched him to run off with a band leader. A couple of divorces. A role in a Broadway musical. Some TV appearances. Kent had never been tops, but she'd never been bottom either.

He stood in the doorway opposite the brownstone, thinking. She didn't know it but pretty soon she'd be on the front pages. Harris would do that for her. He'd give her more fame than she'd ever had. He looked down at his hands, flexing the strong fingers.

After that there was no room in his life for anything but Mabel Kent. He learned all about her habits, her foibles, how she spent each hour of the day. She rose late, never before two or three. Harris was always there, idling on the corner, lounging in a doorway, ready to pick up her trail. He never, never spoke to her, but he was never far away. Sometimes he took the table next to hers in a restaurant, the seat opposite on a bus. If she had ever smiled, nodded, even drawn away, his resolve might have been weakened. But she was oblivious to his presence.

She slept on the third floor front, her bed not far from the dormer window. He could glimpse her sometimes when she got up, her blonde hair disheveled, her face a little pouchy without makeup. But by the time she hit the street, she'd look like a million dollars again. He'd feel a welling of pride inside himself. This was the babe he'd picked, the one to share the big adventure with him.

Most of her afternoons she spent by herself. She didn't have any women friends. But the evenings were different. She never spent a night alone. There were plenty of men in her life. A different guy almost every night. But they all ran to type. Big, beefy studs with a lot of flash to them. Clothes made to order, fancy cars, free spenders.

He'd wander often to the block where Kent lived, haunting the place like a shadow, waiting for her to come home. He even rented a furnished room only a few blocks away so he'd never be far from her. He was always there when she showed up. He'd watch while her friend of the evening helped her out of the car. Watch while they ascended the stone steps together. The next few minutes would be terrible ones. They'd be climbing the stairs and he couldn't see them. When the lights clicked on in the third floor front, he'd let out his breath but he wouldn't move away. Not for a long time.

The pictures which formed in his mind created an exquisite torture within him, a compound of hate, pain, pleasure, envy, excitation and frustration. Sometimes he'd want to rush up the stairs, kick down the door, confront Mabel Kent with her duplicity. Couldn't she understand? She belonged to him, James Harris. Nobody else had a right to her.

He'd check the mad impulse. After all, all he had to do was wait. These lovers of hers were men of straw, shadows, unreal. They could never know, never experience the final intimate rapture that was to exist between himself and this woman. At times, he could almost bring himself to pity them.

After the first week or so there was no reason to wait. He could strike at any time and be sure of success. But that would bring the game to a close before he had fully tasted its savor. He thought up excuses to procrastinate, set imaginary obstacles in his own path.

Hanging around the block day after day was dangerous, but he couldn't bring himself to make the final play. Not without a sign. Not without a word from her. But that afternoon the sign had come. He'd followed her downtown while she shopped, trailed her from one shop to another.

She'd been leaving Spicer's when her high heel had slipped on the polished floor. She caught herself in time to prevent a fall, but some of her packages fell from her arm. One of them slithered to within a few inches of Harris' feet. He picked it up and handed it to her.

She'd said, "Thanks. Thanks a lot," smiling automatically as she would to any stranger. Her eyes had remained blank, unseeing. Then she had turned away limping a little, not even glancing back at him.

He wanted to rush after her, pull her around, make her look at him. He wanted to shout, "Can't you see me? Don't you know I'm alive?" But he held his tongue. There'd be time for that later. He stood still, hating her, yet wanting her too.

This was the day. He wouldn't wait any longer. He and Mabel Kent would be joined together in a relationship more intimate, more enduring than any of her lovers had known.

He made no conscious effort to follow her, so it was almost with a sense of surprise that he found himself beside her on the subway platform. He entered the car behind her. There weren't many seats left and she had taken one of them. He wanted to stand so that he could see her better but his knees went weak and threatened to buckle under him. That was why he squeezed in between the fat man and the old woman with the newspaper.

Now that the game was drawing to a close, his hatred passed and he felt an almost mauldlin affection for Mabel Kent. He wanted to go to her, murmur words of endearment. She seemed to him a beloved child who had to be punished, yet who needed reassurance that the punishment would be quick.

Tears of self-pity burned his eyes. He'd miss her. Miss the long, lonely vigils in the doorway opposite her house. The train jolted to a stop and she got off. There was no reason for him to follow her. There was no place she could go but home. So he might as well stop at the florist shop for the box of roses he needed for his plan.

He couldn't bring himself to leave her, however. There was so little time left. He wanted to spend every minute of it close to her. He trailed her to the door, stood on the sidewalk watching the supple movement of her body, the flick of her legs as she disap-peared up the stairway. Only then did he walk back toward Broadway.

He chose the roses with care, heavy blood-red blossoms, almost black at their throats. This would be his gift to her.

With the roses in his arm, he returned to the block, shambling along slowly like a stranger, pretending to peer at the numbers. He let himself into the foyer, thumbed the bell, and listened to the burr of the automatic release.

When he was halfway up the stairs he heard her door click open and the tap of her heels in the hall. She was peering down at him over the railing but she wouldn't be surprised when she saw the box of flowers. She got them all the time.

She was in her room before he hit the landing but she hadn't bothered to close the door. She'd taken off her dress and put on a loose-fitting housecoat. She was standing before her dresser, fum-bling with her purse, taking out a coin. A tip.

He almost laughed, then his anger came flooding back. But it wasn't a blinding anger, he could see her more clearly than ever before, that what he had to do was right.

He entered the room quietly and heeled the door shut behind him. She looked up at the soft slam of the door and a frown creased her forehead. He approached her, almost apologetically, and held the box out to her. He said, "The man who sent them, he wanted you to look at them, to see if they're okay."

She hesitated, then lifted the lid. The blood-red roses were in front of her. She gave a little gasp of pleasure and her fingers ex-plored for a card. She said wonderingly, "They're gorgeous. But who sent them?"

Harris spoke very softly to her. "I did."

Her glance lifted to his face but her expression was one of con-fusion rather than alarm.

He fought to keep his manner calm, not to frighten her too soon. "Don't you remember me?"

"No," she answered. Then her breath sucked in and fear came to her eyes.

He stayed still. She was looking at him now, he thought, really seeing him for the first time. Her eyes widened in panic. She started to back away from him. He followed her.

She dropped the roses and they spilled across the floor between them. She said, "You're the man this afternoon . . ." Her voice trailed off and he could see she was getting ready to scream. He couldn't permit that.

He threw himself upon her and his hands circled her throat just in time. The scream was cut off almost before it started. It came out as a gurgling murmur.

He bent her backward, his fingers biting deeper and deeper into the soft column of her flesh. She tried to struggle, lashing out at him with her feet, raking at his wrists with her long nails. But her strength was no match for his.

He flung her down on the bed and knelt beside her, the pressure of his fingers growing stronger. She lay still, but still he dared not release his grip. He still had not had satisfaction. He squeezed harder, harder, to produce the burst of emotion that he wanted, and when he could squeeze no more, he suddenly wanted to scream.

It wasn't the way he'd expected it to be!

There was no exultation. Nothing. Only the blindness of despair and the wish to cling to her forever and ever. He lost all sense of time as he crouched beside her. His fingers grew numb and his wrists hurt but still he could not let her go. Finally he fell across her. His face rested on the pillow close to hers, and he shut his eyes.

He had no idea of how long he remained beside her but when he looked up, the room was dark and the windows in the houses across the street showed squares of yellow light. Panic twisted at him, sent him scuttling across the room. He stumbled, grasped a chair and sent it crashing to the floor.

The noise sobered him, brought him back to his senses. He felt along the wall for the switch, flicked it on, and stood trembling in the unexpected brilliance. The roses were a trampled mass at his feet. Automatically he picked one up.

He was acting crazy, he thought. He had to get out fast. He straightened up and forced himself to remain still for a moment. He mustn't flip. He had to relax, play it cool.

He let himself out into the dim hall. He walked rapidly but without stealth, as he'd trained himself to do. The stairs were carpeted. They made no sound beneath his feet. He reached the next landing safely and started along the corridor.

Then the door beside him opened.

A woman stood in the doorway, peering out near-sightedly. She was a short stocky woman with hennaed hair. She wore a dowdy purple dress and her eyes were bright behind the lenses of her glasses. Harris knew her type, a busybody.

He wanted to plunge headlong down the last flight of stairs. But he was paralyzed with terror. The woman stepped into the hall, gave him one swift incurious look and then passed by him to the railing and peered upward.

Her blank gaze had told him all he needed to know. Why did he have to remind himself after all these years of the lesson he'd learned in the drug store? He pulled himself together and kept on walking. At the bend of the stairs, he heard the woman's querulous voice. "Something's going on up there in that Kent woman's apartment."

His head jerked around but she wasn't talking to him. She was speaking over her shoulder to someone in the doorway. She'd forgotten him already. The nagging fury smoldered inside him. He'd like to sink his fingers into the old witch's scrawny neck, make her look at him, the way Kent looked before she died.

Mabel Kent—at least the memory of her staring eyes sent a pleasant tingling sensation through him, even if the strangling hadn't. There was one dame who'd seen him for what he really was, not a nonentity but a killer, a big shot, a guy who'd soon be a legend in crime.

Outside on the street he stopped to light a cigarette. He sucked the smoke deep into his lungs. He felt almost the way he had the time he'd tried a reefer, big, powerful, strong.

But it was only a beginning, and he had to strike again soon—for several reasons. One was to get the feeling of exultation that had eluded him. The other was to make sure people would know.

Maybe the press wouldn't catch on quick that this was a juicy story, just the first of a series of murders. Next time he'd have to leave a trade mark of some kind. His fingers touched the crushed rose in his pocket. It brought a smile to his lips. After this he'd always honor the woman of his choice by bringing a gift of roses.

Excitement plucked at him and he scurried along the street so fast that several times he almost bumped into people. It didn't really matter. After a quick glance of irritation they never gave him a second look.

A night club loomed up ahead. A woman stepped out of a cab and under the lights. She was lush-figured and her hair glowed like silver in the artificial glare. She was a celebrity of some sort because a little knot of people had already formed about her. Harris could hear her laughter and the bright chatter of her voice.

He slid his way into the crowd until he was close beside her. He forgot all about Mabel Kent.

This was the woman, the one for whom he'd really been searching.

AUTHOR'S POSTSCRIPT: I was visiting some friends one afternoon and we fell into a discussion of John Reginald Halliday Christie, London's multiple murderer of women. My friends said that such eerie murders could only happen in the atmosphere of London, a contention which I disputed . . . On the way home, I looked around the crowded New York subway and thought what a strange background it would make for *Mr. Nobody* (the original title for *Anonymous Fame*).

The Glass Bridge

W E were discussing unsolved murders, the Baron de Hirsch, Lieutenant Oliver Baynes of the State Police, and I. At least, de Hirsch was discussing them. Baynes and I were allowed only to listen while the tall, hawk-nosed Hungarian, with scintillating deduction and impeccable logic solved half a dozen famous cases which remain in the files of various police departments, still marked "Open."

De Hirsch can be a very irritating companion. His self assurance is colossal, and his appreciation of his own cleverness is unconcealed. I am always tempted to ask him why, if he's so smart, his shoes always need repairing and his clothes mending. But I never do.

I could see Oliver Baynes getting restless. Baynes is short and dumpy, red-faced, slow-spoken and unimpressive. But he's a good cop—one of the best.

He drained his glass of beer—it was a hot August afternoon—and as he reached for another can, looked across at me.

"Get your friend to solve the case of the blonde blackmailer for us," he said, the sarcasm in the remark hidden behind a completely blank countenance.

De Hirsch paused. His deep-set black eyes glinted; his large, beaked nose flared.

"The case of the blonde blackmailer?" he asked, softly, politely.

"Her name was Marianne Montrose." Baynes used the can opener and got foam on his sleeve. "Last February 13th, between three and four in the afternoon, she walked up twenty-three snow covered steps to a house on a hilltop about thirty miles from here. She went into that house and never came out again."

Baynes poured the beer, slurped the head off his glass.

"Later we searched the house and she wasn't there. There was snow two feet deep all around the house. There wasn't a mark in it to show she had been taken away in any manner. Besides, the owner and only resident is a man with a heart condition, who could be killed by any exertion. So he didn't carry her away or dig a hole and bury her or anything like that. But she wasn't there, and she was seen to enter, and her footsteps went up in the snow on the steps. Went up and never came down again. You tell us what happened to her."

De Hirsch's eyes held steady on Baynes.

"Give me the facts," he said, "and I will."

He didn't say he'd try, he said he would.

"I'll get my dope sheets," I told him, nettled. "It'll be nice to know the truth. Besides, I'll get another article out of it."

Baynes sipped his beer and said nothing, merely looked sleepy. De Hirsch poured himself another generous helping of brandy— my brandy, for we had gathered at my summer cottage. I went to my files and brought back the folder on Marianne Montrose. It was pretty complete. As a true-crime writer for the popular magazines, I kept detailed notes on every case I use. I had already written this one up, giving it the Big Question Mark or "What Happened to Lovely Marianne?" treatment.

"Where do you want to start?" I asked. "Here's the statement of young Danny Gresham, the last person who spoke to Marianne before she went into the house and vanished."

De Hirsch waved away the typescript.

"Read it to me," he said, his manner gracious.

Oliver Baynes made a noise through his nose. He might have been laughing. I glared at him and began to read:

Morgan's Gap, Feb. 3. From statement by Daniel Gresham, 19.

I was in the office of the *Morgan's Gap Weekly Sentinel*, reading proof. It was half past three. The temperature outside was about eight above zero, I guess, maybe six. It was a nice brisk day. I was thinking of calling up my girl, Dolly Hansome, and making a date to go skiing. The snow was nice and deep, with a good crust on it, and some fresh snow on top. While I was thinking about Dolly, a snappy blue coupe pulled to a stop outside.

There was a girl driving. She looked like Dolly Hansome, but taller and better developed—more womanly, that is. She had blonde hair, long, and curly under a red cap and was wearing a red ski suit. She got out and stood looking across the valley and up the slope toward Mr. Mark Hillyer the mystery writer's house. The Eyrie, Mr. Hillyer calls it, that means nest. It's a very good name for it, the way it perches all by itself on top of the ridge.

You might think it was a funny place for a man with a bad heart to live all by himself. In the summer you can drive right around and up to the back of the house where the terrace is, but in the winter the town only cleans the road up to the steps out in front.

That means that Mr. Hillyer never leaves the house after the first big snow, but he doesn't seem to care. In the fall he puts in three thousand gallons of fuel oil and a big stock of canned goods and he's all set. Every day Mrs. Hoff goes up to cook and clean. She doesn't mind the steps and neither does her brother-in-law, Sam. He keeps the steps swept, and clears off the north terrace.

Mr. Hillyer likes to be alone. He doesn't care for people. He's a tall, thin man with a long, disappointed face and a sharp way of saying things. He's written twelve mystery books and has a lot of clippings and reviews. He's especially proud of the ones that mention how clever his plots are. He hasn't written any new books for five years, though. I guess he's discouraged because the ones he did before never sold very well.

Oh, sure, about the girl.

She stood looking up at the house, then turned and came in the office. I jumped up to help her. She smiled and said hello. Her voice was low and husky and sort of gave you a tingly feeling, if you know what I mean. She asked if I was the editor. I said I was the assistant. Then she asked if she could use the phone. I said sure, of course, certainly, and handed it to her. She asked for Mark

Hillyer's number. I couldn't help hearing what she said. Sure I remember the words, just about.

" 'Hello, Mark,' she said, and her voice was different now. 'This is Marianne. I'm phoning from the village. I trust you're expecting me and, Mark, darling—just in case you might have been getting any funny ideas in that clever brain of yours—they know here at the newspaper office I'm coming up to see you. I'll be up in ten minutes.' "

She hung up and smiled at me, and her voice was back again the way it had been.

"Mark Hillyer doesn't like me," she said. "And he's a very, very clever man. I do think he would kill me if he could get away with it. But he can't. Just the same, if I'm not back here in an hour, you'll send the police up to look for me, won't you? I'll stop on my way back, just to let you know I'm all right."

And she smiled at me again and naturally I said sure, of course, I'd get Constable Redman to come up and look for her. I was pretty thrilled; it was sort of like a scene out of one of Mr. Hillyer's books. Of course, I didn't think she really meant what she'd said. But when she drove off, I went to the window to watch her.

She drove away, and a minute later I saw her car starting up the road that winds around to get to Mr. Hillyer's Eyrie. A lot of kids were out on the lower slope with skis and sleds and these new aluminum bowls having a swell time sliding all over the place. I thought of calling Dolly again, but somehow I didn't feel as interested as I had just a couple of minutes earlier.

I saw the convertible reach the turnaround at the foot of the steps to Hillyer's house—the snow plows clear it out. The girl parked the car and got out. She started up that flight of steps. I saw her reach Mr. Hillyer's little front porch. The door opened. She went in and the door closed.

I kept an eye on Mr. Hillyer's house all the rest of the afternoon as I worked, until it got dark. But the girl never came out again.

End of statement by Daniel Gresham

I paused and glanced at de Hirsch. He sat back, his head cradled on the back of the chair, staring upward at my ceiling.

"A most interesting opening for a murder case," he said tolerantly, looking at me. "Naturally, any theory I have at this point must be completely tentative. Please continue."

I read:

Morgan's Gap, Feb. 14. From statement by Constable Harvey Redman.

At about five-thirty yesterday young Danny Gresham came busting into my office, saying a pretty girl had gone up to see Mr. Mark Hillyer and might be in danger. At first I thought it was more of his imagination, but he gave me all the facts and I figured maybe we'd better go see. Anybody who writes books like Hillyer does might just as easy kill someone for real.

I got flashlights and we went in my old car. We got to Hillyer's place just about six. Sure enough, there was Miss Montrose's convertible still parked in the turnaround. And Danny showed me a woman's prints in the drifted snow on the steps.

There was one set of prints going up.

None coming down.

So he was right about her still being there, anyway.

We climbed up, stepping wide of the prints, and knocked. Mr. Hillyer let us in, looking surprised. I told him what the woman had told Danny, and asked where Miss Montrose was. Mr. Hillyer laughed.

"I'm afraid Miss Montrose is having a joke on you and Danny," he said. "She left here an hour ago, just about dark."

"Mr. Hillyer," I told him, "there's a woman's footprints coming up your steps and none going down. Besides, her car is still there."

"By George, that's odd!" Mr. Hillyer said, but he said it as if he were laughing.

"That's what I think," I told him. "That's why I'm asking where the lady is."

"But I don't know where she is," he said, looking me in the eye. "Constable, I'll be frank with you. That girl is a blackmailer.

She came here today to collect a thousand dollars from me. I paid it. Then she left. And that's absolutely all I know. I insist that you search this house to see if you find any trace of her or evidence that I did anything to her. All I want is to be in the clear."

Danny and I searched the house. Mr. Hillyer sat in his chair by the fireplace in his writing den, smoking and waiting.

The house was easy to reach, being only six rooms on one floor. No cellar, no attic. Oil burner's in a little closet. Floors are cement. Walls are double cinder block with insulation in between.

The girl wasn't in the house. No trace she'd ever been there, either. No signs of a struggle, no bloodstains.

Danny and I went outside. There weren't any marks in the snow around the house. The north terrace had been shoveled off, but the snow had drifted right up to it and there was a light sprinkle of snow on the tiles. No marks in it at all. That didn't mean an awful lot, though, because the drifts went all the way down the slope to Harrison's Gully, a quarter mile away almost. There's usually a breeze coming up from the gully and it would lay more snow on the terrace pretty quick.

Danny tried the crust, though, and broke right through, after only a step. Nobody could have gone over that snow without leaving marks. Besides, Mr. Hillyer's heart would have killed him if he'd tried.

So, after we looked in the garage and searched the car and especially the trunk without finding her, we told Mr. Hillyer it looked like Miss Montrose had left all right.

"I'm glad you're satisfied I'm not hiding her, constable," he chuckled. "In spite of the story she gave Danny, and in spite of her footprints coming only toward the house and her car still being there, it's perfectly obvious I couldn't have killed her and hidden her body—unless of course I carried it away over a glass bridge."

I told him I didn't follow that.

"Why, constable," he said, "I guess you don't know your mystery fiction. One of the most famous stories is about a man who's killed by a glass knife. Then the murderer drops the weapon in a pitcher of water and it becomes invisible and nobody can find it. So maybe I killed Miss Montrose and carried her away over a glass bridge— one that's invisible now. Or I have another theory for you. Maybe a flying saucer came down and whisked her away. In fact, the more I think about it the more I imagine that's what must have happened."

"I don't guess you're taking this very serious, Mr. Hillyer," I told him. "But I am and I'm going to call in the State Police.."

So I did. Let them decide where that girl went. I got other things to bother about right now.

End of statement by Constable Harvey Redman.

I stopped reading. My throat was dry. I poured myself some beer. De Hirsch opened his eyes.

"Admirably complete," he said kindly. "You're a good researcher even if you haven't much imagination." He turned to Baynes. "I suppose you took over the case then, Lieutenant?"

"Yeah," Baynes grunted, eyeing him. "But not until Troopers Reynolds and Rivkin had answered the constable's call. They made a search. Same results. Then the case got dumped in my lap. I get all the screwy cases. I went out the next day. But questioning Hillyer was like asking the cat what happened to the canary. He talked about the blackmail angle, though. Said he'd made a slip years ago, and Montrose knew about it. Since then he'd been paying her off a thousand dollars a year. Every year, when she happened to be near, she'd let him know she was coming over in a day or two and he'd get the thousand ready in cash for her.

"I checked with New York. She was in the racket, all right. So his story was probably true. I checked the local bank, too. They'd mailed him ten hundreds, just three days before.

"I looked around the house. Just like the constable and my troopers said. Crusty snow but not strong enough to hold up a man. Even skis left marks. Maybe a toboggan wouldn't.

"Trouble was, he'd never had anything like a toboggan, or even skiis or a sled, in the house. Mrs. Hoff had cleaned that morning and even gone into the garage to get her cleaning things. She'd have seen anything as big as a toboggan, and she swore the whole idea was just a pipe dream. And he couldn't have ordered one special by phone because it would have to be delivered and nobody had delivered anything but food or mail there for weeks. I checked.

"I didn't have anything to take its place, though. The girl had to go somewhere! I got four troopers who could ski, and set them to covering all the region around the house. They covered everything within a quarter of a mile, including a couple of small dips and gullies, and didn't find a trace of her or of any tracks in the snow. Then it started snowing again and I had to call the search off. But I'd made sure she wasn't any place where she could be found.

"Hillyer enjoyed every minute of it. He enjoyed giving interviews and he posed for pictures. He passed out autographed copies of his books to the feature writers. He looked ten years younger all of a sudden; he was having so much fun.

"He passed out plenty of double talk about the mystery of it all. He quoted this guy Charles Fort, who wrote about mysterious disappearances. He talked about spontaneous vanishment, and warps in the space-time continuum, and abduction by little green men in flying saucers. He had the time of his life.

"So, finally, we had to table the case. Absolutely all we really knew was what we knew to begin with. A girl walked up those steps into his house and just vanished. So we sat back to wait for new developments. Then came June."

Oliver Baynes paused to finish his beer.

De Hirsch nodded his great, Roman head. "And in June," he said, "the body was found."

Baynes looked at him in surprise.

"Yes," he agreed. "In June, Marianne Montrose stopped being one kind of mystery and became another kind of mystery. You see—"

But de Hirsch had raised a restraining hand.

"Let Bob read it," he suggested. "I know he has it written out, in a fine, dramatic style. And sometimes I find a certain pleasure in his prose."

So I read:

Morgan's Gap, June 3. Based upon statements by Willy Johnson, 11, and Ferdie Pulver, 10.

The two boys stopped beside the deeply blue pool, no more than thirty yards across. They were in a long, narrow depression with almost sheer sides fifty feet high. It ran for three hundred yards to a rocky ledge where a small waterfall emptied into the natural trap and flowed down to make the pool at their feet. The pool in turn emptied out through a narrow throat in the rock, just wide enough for a small boy to negotiate, too narrow to admit an adult.

Willows and alders, green with new leaves, stretched upward toward the sunlight. Redwing blackbirds darted in and out, and high overhead crows soared on black pinions. A chipmunk, unafraid, chattered at the boys from a branch.

They were barefoot, their shoes in their hands, and the water was icy cold. But, entranced by the secret little world of the gully, they hardly noticed the water's temperature.

"Gee!" Ferdie said. "This is swell. Let's bring a gang and play pirates, huh?"

"Pirates!" Willy sniffed. "Fishin' is more fun. C'mon, throw in your hook."

He thrust a reluctant worm onto the hook of a handline and tossed it into the pool. It rippled in the green water and sank from sight. He waited all of thirty seconds, then impatiently jerked it.

"Gosh!" he shouted. "I caught something . . . aw, heck, it's snagged."

He pulled hard. The line came in, slowly, with an almost unyielding dead weight. Ferdie wasn't paying any attention. He was staring up the gully to where a small fragment of something white dangled from a silver green willow.

"What's that?" he asked nervously. "You thinking it's a ghost, huh, Willy?"

"Heck, no." Willy didn't even look. He was gasping as he tugged in his line. "Gee, I got a big branch of somethin' . . ."

Something dark and red surged upward to the surface, and broke the water with a slow swirling motion. Then the awkward mass turned over and a pale, oval face appeared, surrounded by a halo of golden hair that rippled in the water with a life of its own.

"Jeez!" Willy shrilled. "It's a deader! C'mon, Ferdie, let's get out of here!"

Behind them, as their yells died out in the distance, the pale face and golden hair seemed to hesitate for a moment, as if waiting. Then they sank slowly back into the dark, quiet depths from which they had come. . .

"Well," Oliver Baynes took up the narration, as de Hirsch helped himself to more of my brandy—finished the bottle, incidentally, "Willy's parents called the constable and the constable called me. A couple of hours later half a dozen of us got out up at Mark Hillyer's house. The only decent way to reach the gully without doing mountain climbing was to go down through Hillyer's property. He was perfectly agreeable, and when we told him what we were up to he only seemed interested.

" 'If you find her,' he said, 'look in the pocket of her ski suit. She had a thousand dollars of mine when she left and I shall put in a claim for it.'

"We reached the gully, over some very rough ground, and lowered in on ropes. Then we started grappling for the body. We found it inside of twenty minutes. As it came up, Danny Gresham —who was with us—gave a yell.

"That's her! But how'd she get here so far from the house? She might have flown!"

"She looked well preserved—that water was almost ice cold. She had ten hundred dollar bills in her ski suit pocket, too. We grappled some more, and finally came up with her ski cap and one mitten. I left the men grappling, and made a search of the gully myself. Outside of a few old beer bottles and some tin cans, there wasn't a thing that shouldn't have been there.

"We grappled in that pool all day. I was still hoping to find a toboggan or something, but we never did. Nothing. There was the body, a quarter mile from the house, and no clues as to how it got there.

"We lifted the body out and had an autopsy. She'd died of cold and exposure. Stomach was empty—no telling how long after her last meal she'd died. No trace of poison in tissues."

Oliver Baynes looked challengingly at de Hirsch.

"Well," he said, "there's your case of the blonde blackmailer. Now let's hear you explain it without any double-talk about spontaneous vanishment, warps in the space-time continuum, glass bridges and flying saucers."

My Hungarian friend put his finger tips together, making a steeple of his hands.

"I can't," he said blandly. And as a look of guarded triumph appeared on Baynes' red features, de Hirsch added, "without mentioning the glass bridge, the flying saucer, and above all the winding sheet."

"Oh, sure!" Lieutenant Baynes looked disgusted. "Give us some more jabberwocky and admit you don't know what happened to that girl!"

"But I can't do that," de Hirsch objected, giving Baynes a pleasant look. "Because, you see, I know what happened to her. At least, I will know when you add the one item you have left out of your narration."

"Left out?" Baynes blinked.

"The white object Ferdie Pulver thought might be a ghost," de Hirsch said.

"Oh, that!" Baynes shrugged. "That was just an old, tattered bed-sheet tangled in the branches of the willow trees. Had Hillyer's laundrymark. He said it must have blown off the clothes line during a windy spell in the spring. It didn't mean a thing. We had experts go over it, practically thread by thread. Just an old bed-sheet."

"Not a bedsheet," de Hirsch murmured in gentle correction. "A winding sheet. Thus it is as I said—a glass bridge, a flying saucer, and a winding sheet. Don't you see, in the arrogance of his pride in his own intellect, Hillyer told you the truth! He gave you all the clues. At least, he gave them to Constable Redman and they were in the constable's statement. He killed Marianne Montrose, and whisked her away in a flying saucer over a glass bridge to no-where—which is to say, eternity."

Baynes chewed his under lip. He stared at de Hirsch, puzzled. So did I. It was exactly the situation de Hirsch enjoyed most— when he could dispense bafflement in the guise of enlightenment.

Slowly Baynes reached into his pocket. He took out a wallet. From the wallet he took a twenty dollar bill.

"Twenty dollars say you're just double-talking, like Hillyer," he stated flatly.

De Hirsch's eye brightened. Then he sighed and shook his head.

"No," he murmured. "We are both guests of an old and valued friend. It would not be the act of a gentleman to take money from another guest on such a simple matter."

Now Baynes gritted his teeth. He took two more bills from his wallet.

"Fifty dollars say you don't know any more than we do," he snapped.

De Hirsch turned deep, black eyes on me. I hastily computed what I would receive for a true detective article I'd recently fin-ished, and took out my checkbook.

"I'll say a hundred you can't give us the solution," I announced, looking him fixedly in the eye. I knew my Hungarian friend did not have a hundred, did not have fifty, and I doubted if he had five.

The Baron de Hirsch straightened. "You make it impossible for me, as a gentleman, to refuse," he said. "But I'll need some help. ... I'll need a clothespin."

Baynes' open mouth closed. My closed mouth opened.

"In the left hand drawer beside the kitchen sink," I said. "Should be some there. Mrs. Ruggles, the cleaning woman. . ."

Rising with a single lithe motion, de Hirsch had already left the room, taking out a large, immaculate linen handkerchief as he went. And a fountain pen.

I looked at Baynes. He looked at me. Neither of us spoke. De Hirsch was gone about five minutes. I heard a drawer open. I heard a muffled sound that might have been the icebox opening, or the deep freeze. Presently he came back and sat down. He opened the fresh bottle of brandy I silently brought after he had picked up the empty and stared at it in a speculative manner.

"It will take a few minutes," he said amiably. "Meanwhile, we can talk. What do you think of the political situation?"

"The hell with the political situation," Baynes growled. "What about Hillyer and the girl? How did he kill her?"

De Hirsch struck his palm against his head.

"I forgot to ask!" he exclaimed. "Does Hillyer suffer from insomnia?"

Baynes wrinkled his brows. "Yeah," he said. "He does. That was part of the report I got from his doc. But what—"

"Naturally, I assumed it," de Hirsch broke in. "But of course, one must never assume anything. Why, Lieutenant, Hillyer killed her by putting sleeping tablets in a drink. When she was unconscious, he whisked her away and buried her in the deep snow of Harrison's Gully. There, in due time, her body absorbed the sleeping potion. She awoke, nearly frozen. For a brief, mercifully brief time she struggled against the iron bonds that held her. Then the soft sleep that comes to those who freeze took her and in merciful arms carried her down the long dark steps that led to death."

"Very fancy prose," Baynes grunted. "But you haven't said anything. There weren't any bonds of any kind. Not a mark on her. Nothing. Maybe he did knock her out with sleeping tablets. That I figured. But then what?"

The Baron de Hirsch took his time about answering.

"Tell me, Bob—" he turned to me—"would you say Mark Hillyer has achieved a minor form of immortality from this case? The fame that he always sought, and never found?"

"It certainly has," I agreed. "Already there's a big argument among crime fans as to whether he did or didn't kill her. The mystery of how she got into the gully is as tantalizing as the mystery of what happened to the famous Dorothy Arnold. A hundred years from now, Hillyer's name would still be popping up in books as the double-domes of the next century argue about his guilt or innocence. As Baynes said, he's riding high. He has a new book due out, and all his old ones have been reprinted. He's famous, all right, and he'll stay famous as long as the case goes unsolved. In fact, the longer it goes unsolved, the more famous he'll be like. Like Jack the Ripper."

"Ah," de Hirsch said. "And as soon as it is solved, he is merely infamous—a sordid murderer. A shock to an ego—especially to one such as his. But now I think we can discuss the mystery of the glass bridge, the flying saucer and the winding sheet—all of them invisible."

He rose and went to the kitchen. Again I heard the ice box, or the deep freeze, open and shut. He came back carrying something balanced on his hand. It was covered with a napkin so we could not see what it was. He set the object on the polished top of the coffee table.

"Now," he said, his voice suddenly crisp and authoritative, "let us go back to last February. It is a bitterly cold afternoon. Mark Hillyer, bleakly furious, stands at the window, waiting to see a blackmailer's car drive up. We know what else he saw—children at play. Watching them, an idea exploded in his mind, complete and exquisite, like Minerva springing from Jove's forehead. He

could be rid of his blackmailer quite safely, needing only a mini-
mum of luck. If he failed—well, he was a sick man and could
plead provocation. If he succeeded—what a pleasure to watch the
stupid world puzzle over the mystery he had created!

"He acted at once. He got an old bedsheet, the largest he owned,
and spread it flat on the flagstones of the north terrace. He did certain things to it, and went back inside. A few minutes later Montrose arrived. He talked with her, gave her a drink heavy with
sleeping potion. In twenty minutes or so she collapsed, unconscious.

"He tumbled her from her chair to the floor. He nudged her
onto a small rug. No exertion, you see, nothing to strain his bad
heart.

"He slid the rug across the floor and out onto the north terrace.
There he rolled the unconscious woman onto the spread out bedsheet. He arranged her so that she was curled up in the center
of it. . ."

With a theatrical gesture, de Hirsch whipped the napkin off the
object on the table. We saw that it was his linen handkerchief.
Something lay in the center of the handkerchief—a clothespin,
with little eyes and a mouth inked on it, as if if were a woman reduced to scale, and the handkerchief a bedsheet.

To see the clothespin doll, I had to pry up one corner of the
handkerchief. For each of the four corners had been folded into
the center, completely covering the thing, as if in an envelope.
And the handkerchief was stiff and hard.

Then he saw what de Hirsch had done. He had sprinkled water
on the handkerchief and put it into the deep freeze. Like laundry
on a wash line on a winter day, the handkerchief had become stiff,
unbending. Inside it, imprisoned in it, was the clothespin repre-
senting a woman. The whole thing made a neat package several
inches square. If it had been a real bedsheet and a real woman
curled up in the center of it, it would have been no more than
three feet square.

And at last Baynes and I understood all that Mark Hillyer had done. He had sprinkled a large bedsheet with water on a bitterly cold day. He had put an unconscious woman in the center of it, curled up, and then folded the corners over her. The cold had frozen the wet bedsheet into a sort of box as stiff, as hard as board. In a matter of minutes Marianne Montrose, unconscious, was a prisoner inside a frozen shroud that was as formidable as iron bonds. Then he had thrust the broad, flat object off the terrace onto the hard-surfaced snow. Because of the dispersal of weight, it had left no mark. Instead it had slipped away smoothly down the slope, picking up speed, whisking over rough spots, until at last it shot off the edge of the crusty snow and tumbled deep into the clinging drifts of windblown snow within the permanently shadowed depths of the gully.

As if in example, de Hirsch flicked the frozen handkerchief with his finger. It spun across the table and off the edge, dropping into a wastebasket. There, among white sheets of discarded typewriter paper, it suddenly vanished.

"A flying saucer," de Hirsch boomed. "In Danny Gresham's statement, he specifically mentioned the new aluminum bowls some of the children were playing with in the snow. These are metal saucers in which a child sits and whisks down a slope at truly terrifying speed. They ride the surface, scarcely sinking into a crust at all. It was these that Hillyer saw, these from which he gained his idea.

"The glass bridge was already there—a slick, thin coating of ice which covered the drifts from his house to Harrison's Gully. The flying saucer he made from a sheet sprayed with water in the icy air. And it became the girl's winding sheet when he laid her upon it and folded the edges over her and froze them down.

"Off it went, spinning, sliding, skidding. It could not stop. Over the edge, into the gully. A white object in white snow. Invisible to the searching eyes. A little wind-blown snow over it, and it had vanished. To find it one would have had to step on it. Little chance of that.

"Lássd! Or to put it in French, *voila!* A baffling, an impenetrable mystery has been created by the use of an old bedsheet and the natural forces of winter. A woman has been transported a quarter of a mile by means of a seemingly miraculous agency. A sick man has committed the seemingly perfect murder!"

"The rat!" Baynes burst out. "Telling me to my face how he did it, and making me think he was double-talking me! Why, that girl and that sheet probably hung in the branches of that tree until spring. Then when the thaw came, the sheet unfroze, she fell out and was carried along by the brook down into the pool, leaving nothing—no trace, no clue, just an old bedsheet!"

"But if one with imagination sees the bedsheet as a winding sheet—" de Hirsch reached for the money and my check, on the table— "and if one takes the remarks of a clever man at face value, a mystery may become quite commonplace."

"We'll never be able to prove it," Baynes growled.

"Talán!" de Hirsch commented. "Perhaps not. But we can let him know that his mystery is a mystery no longer, and that he will be the subject of no so-clever studies of homicide in the year 2000. I will write him a letter."

He went off to my study and typed for half an hour. He mailed the letter that same afternoon. The next morning Mark Hillyer received it. I don't know what it said, but Oliver Baynes, via the housekeeper, described its reception.

Mrs. Hoff was dusting in the study when the mailman came. She took the letter to Hillyer on the terrace, and he interrupted his writing to open it. He had hardly more than glanced at it when he became deathly pale—so pale Mrs. Hoff turned back in alarm. As he read further, an ugly, mottled flush spread over his features. He scarcely looked at the second page before ripping the letter up and flinging the pieces into a big ash tray. He lit a match with hands that shook so violently he could hardly bring match head to striking surface, and burned the torn pieces.

As if still unable to relieve his rage, he seized the ash tray and flung it furiously down on the tiles. For an instant, he stood looking north toward Harrison's Gully, his hands clenching and unclenching.

Then his breath began to come with difficulty. He turned, reaching for support, but collapsed before he could reach his chair. Clawing at his chest and throat, he gasped, "Medicine—my medicine . . ."

His heart stimulant was not in the medicine cabinet, but on his bedside table. It took Mrs. Hoff two or three minutes to find it. When she hurried back with it, Hillyer was dead.

I admit I was somehow shocked. But de Hirsch accepted Hillyer's death with composure.

"*Utovegre!*" he commented. "Which is to say, it is as good as a confession."

EDITOR'S NOTE: There have not been many MWA anthologies to which Robert Arthur has not contributed. He is a writer in the classic tradition; *The Glass Bridge* is a lovely variation of the "locked room" situation.

ANTHONY GILBERT

Blood Will Tell

THE house stood in a hollow some distance from the road, looking like some immense packing-case someone had jettisoned long
since and forgotten. Only a light in an upper window betrayed
the fact of its occupation; behind the lighted window the fugi-
tives could discern the shadow of a woman silhouetted against the
old-fashioned yellow linen blind. She seemed to be wearing a
bodice that left her arms bare, and she was rubbing them vigor-
ously with a cloth. Her hair was tied up in a handkerchief, with
tweaked ends like the shadow-toy you make for a child.

The two men had come a long way with fear at their heels.
The older and leader might have been eight or nine and thirty, a
tall dark figure with two days' stubble growth on his chin; the
boy was young enough to be his son, slender and fair, with eyes as
blue as the sea and the mind of a child.

When he espied the house, its light gleaming through the lone-
liness of the trees, Maggs said, "This is it, Curly, this is the house
we been looking for. No neighbours, no 'phone and no kids."

"I like kids," said Curly in peaceable tones.

"Not when you're wearing our shoes," was his companion's grim
retort. "Kids yell. We don't want no one to hear . . ."

"Hear what?"

"Anything. Folks ain't always reasonable."

The boy caught the man's arm. "No violence, Maggs," he urged.
"You promised. No violence. Not like last time."

"Have some sense," Maggs told him in an impatient voice.
"This ain't a mail van driver without the brain to know what was
good for him. This is a lady."

"Maybe we shouldn't intrude. Maggs, you got a gun?"

"D'you think guns grow on trees?"

"I didn't know Harry had a gun last time," whimpered the boy.
"I thought that driver was goin' to die."

"Lucky for us he didn't or we'd ha' been on a murder rap. You
can still get the rope for shooting. Now then, Curly, you leave
this to me, see. Unless you aim to go back to that nice cosy little
cell of yours, with the walls so high you can't see nothing beyond
them."

The boy's slender form shook. "No, Maggs, no. If on'y they'd
of put me to work outside somewhere, sweeping leaves, anything.
Even as a kid I couldn't stand being shut in."

"Then you do as I say."

But still he hung back. "Lady can't open the door if she's washing herself," he pleaded.

"She can put on a dressing-gown, can't she? Not that I'd have
any objection. More'n a year since I saw a woman . . ."

He stormed down the path, skirting the dark barn, and ham-
mered on the door.

The woman in the upper room had heard their voices and
peeped through a crack in the blind. Her heart was thudding in
her breast. She had lived too long with a violent man not to know
the folly of expecting them to go away if she paid no heed. No,
they'd smash the place up. She couldn't have that.

She threw down the towel and drew a short coat over her bare
arms; she twitched off the handkerchief and went to stare at herself in the looking-glass square on the cupboard. She saw a thin
haggard face that might once have been beautiful, faded sandy
hair drawn into an economical knot at the back of her head, defiant, suspicious hazel eyes, a thin scornful high-bridged nose, a
mouth that had learned to set as tight as a trap.

The invaders thumped again. "I'll give her one more chance
and then I'll get the door down," swore Maggs.

"The light's gone out," said Curly. "She's coming. Listen."

"I don't hear nothing. You got ears like a bat."

He lifted his great foot to crash it against the panel of the door when suddenly it opened and he almost fell over. The woman set down the lamp in her hand to say harshly, "No sense doing that. Doors cost money. You in a hurry, it seems."

"And seemingly you ain't." He made to enter, but she shut the door against him.

Maggs thrust his foot in the gap. " 'Scuse me, lady, we're coming in."

"We don't buy at the door."

"That's O.K. We ain't got nothing to sell."

"And we don't need no help."

"We ain't looking for work."

"Fancy me thinking that. Who are you, then?"

Curly spoke over the older man's shoulder. "Maggs don't mean no harm, ma'am. We're hungry, we want food and a few shillings if you got it to spare . . ."

"Beggars, eh?"

"I said I'd handle this," said Maggs furiously, stamping on the boy's foot. "He's right, though. We want a change of clobber first thing, and then some food and dough and we'll be saying goodbye."

"And if I ain't got them? Or ain't willing to part?"

Maggs could have hit her, standing there, so defiant and as plain as the back of a taxi-cab. Women with her looks had no right to talk like they were queens. Why, she must be as old as him, and nothing feminine there, for all she wore a wedding-ring.

"It could pay to be co-operative," he said, slurring the last word, which was long for his clumsy tongue.

"Maggs!" The boy pulled at his arm. "You said no violence. You promised."

"You home-sick?" Maggs suggested, and once more the boy shrank back. But from the shadow he spoke again courageously.

"Maybe we shouldn't trouble the lady, seeing she's alone."

"Who said I was alone?" She stood back and Maggs sprang through the entry. "Bellman!"

She hadn't raised her voice but on the word a great crossbred dog bounded towards them.

Maggs stopped dead in his tracks, but Curly came past and stooped to caress the big noble head.

"This sure is a grand dog you got, ma'am," he cried, eagerly. "These cross-strains, you can't better 'em. For folding sheep, say."

"What do you know about folding sheep?"

"Grew up in the country," said Maggs in surly tones.

"That so? Then how come you're going round with this— scum? I know a hoodlum when I see one."

Maggs swung up his great fists, black with rage. "You keep a civil tongue in your head, missis, or it might be worse for you."

The dog growled warningly.

"And call that brute off. He's a killer."

"Reckon that should make you feel at home. What d'you suppose I have him for? He ain't a lapdog. He's here to guard me against fellows like you. Bellman always knows. Blood will tell."

Maggs yanked something out of his pocket that gleamed in the lamplight.

"Maybe it wouldn't do him any harm to lose a little of that blood."

"You said you hadn't got no gun." The boy's voice was yeasty with panic.

"Found it lying around and figured it might come in useful. Now, missis, do you put that dog out or . . .?"

"You can't blame him looking ugly seeing the company I'm keeping to-night," the woman flared.

She took him by the collar and dragged him through into the kitchen, the men following. She thrust him out of the back door, whispering and caressing as she let him go. Maggs pushed past her and turned the key in the lock; then he put the key in his pocket.

"Best that way," he said, patting it.

"Don't try nothing funny," the woman warned him. "Bellman wouldn't make nothing of them windows."

"I'll be waiting for him," Maggs promised her. "Nothing speaks quicker than a gun."

She whipped open a drawer and snatched out a knife. "You hurt a hair of that dog's head and I—I'll carve you into bits."

"God, I pity your husband," Maggs exclaimed.

"Maybe you should change places with him."

"I'd sooner do a life stretch," retorted Maggs, heartily. "Now, missis, you give us what we ask for or else . . ."

"Or else?" she prompted.

"We'd have to help ourselves, wouldn't we? And we might make a bit of a mess, not knowing where everything's kept, see?"

"They should ha' given you a cup of cold pizen instead of a dose of jail," said the woman, contemptuously.

"Who said anything about jail?"

"They got you on the radio—didn't you know? Two men that broke out of Hollerton Jail day afore yesterday, seen heading this way. The bigger of the two, Stanley Maggs, may be dangerous. The boy called you Maggs."

The man turned furiously. "I might have knowed it was plumb crazy making a break with a chap who's no more'n ninepence in the shilling. Bound to louse things up, weren't you?"

"He warn't afraid of a dog anyways," the woman jibed.

"That's enough about the dog. You start finding that clobber, and don't tell me your man ain't got a spare suit, because I wouldn't believe you, see?"

The woman smiled; it was a smile enough to curdle your blood.

"Reckon you don't know my man. He's mean—'bout the meanest thing there is. If he was here he wouldn't say They're on the run, they got to have food and clothes and dough, so let's open up the larder and turn out our pockets. No, sir."

"Then we'd best wait and take the one he's wearing off his back," suggested Maggs.

The woman screamed with laughter. "You're welcome. Mind

you, he's only a little fellow—but tough. The boy now—what's your name?"

"Curly, ma'am."

"Maybe he could wear women's clothes, those blue eyes and all that fair hair. Not like you, Maggs, unless you aim to join a circus —the Bearded Lady. You'd like fine to have folk paying their tanners to take a gawp at you, wouldn't you now?"

"That'll be enough from you."

"You should ha' come earlier, Curly. When I had my pretties, when I was a bride."

"You a bride!" Maggs jeered.

"I ain't so old, Curly." Her voice had softened. It's just life's hard."

"Maybe you'd best do as he says, ma'am," the boy urged. "He don't like being kept waiting and he's got a gun."

"Sometimes you talk like you had sense, same as anyone else," Maggs congratulated him. "Get on with it, missis."

"I told you, we ain't got nothing to fit you." She began to laugh again and turned coaxingly to the boy. "Your mother ever read you that fairy-tale, Curly, where the tailer snipped with magic scissors and wonderful clothes began to fall down on all the company. There was a picture in the book I had—blue and green and gold—satin." She began to stride about the room snipping with a pair of imaginary scissors. "Doublets and hose," she explained. "That's what they wore in them days, doublets and hose."

Maggs turned to his companion. "She's crazy," he said, "and that makes two of you."

"No," contradicted Curly. "She's scairt, that's all. And you wouldn't let her keep her dog."

The woman, overhearing them, turned sharply. "What makes you think I'm scairt of a pair of hoodlums?"

"Maybe it's not us scared you. If you was to give Maggs what he asks, ma'am . . ."

"Reckon you don't understand. I can't give you what I ain't got."

"Maggs, let's be going. It's like the lady says. She can't give you what she ain't got."

Maggs crossed to the window and stared out through the deepening shadows.

"What d'you keep in the barn, missis?"

"Flotsam and jetsam." The words came like a rap of a pistol. "Just flotsam and jetsam."

"There wouldn't be an old jalopy along of the rest?" His voice was sly.

"My man took that along of him this morning. Not that it would help you. Everyone round here knows that jalopy, and everyone knows my man. They wouldn't mistake him for you nor Angel-face here."

"Maybe he could have loaned it to us."

Again the woman screamed with laughter.

"Stop that," said Maggs. "You freeze my blood. Curly, you stop here and get the money and the grub. I'm going down to the barn."

"I tell you, you're wasting your time."

"Ask pretty and you might get it without trouble. But—get it, see?"

"Could I drive the jalopy, Maggs?"

"Reckon you can. Curly's a right nice driver, missis. Come driving for me and my friends one night 'bout a year since. You ask him."

Curly's face darkened. "I didn't know Harry had a gun," he whispered. "You didn't know neither, did you, Maggs?"

"Who's talking about guns? We won't hurt the jalopy, missis, Curly never hurt a car in his life, and we'll leave it somewheres for him to collect."

The woman came to a sudden resolution. "How'd it be if I was to give you money—I tell him I lost it or something—then you could get along to the next town and get some duds, duds that 'ud fit you."

"Yes," broke in Curly, eagerly. "Why shouldn't we do that, Maggs?"

"How far's the nearest town?" demanded Maggs, suspiciously.

"Not fur. Well—six miles, say."

"And while we're trampin' in you put a call through from that phone booth at the cross-roads and we find a depitation waiting for us? I've a mind to put a bullet through you just for luck."

"No, Maggs," screamed the boy.

"O.K., Curly, O.K. I'll be getting down to the barn. Out of the way, missis." Suddenly he grinned. "I know what it is. You got a man there. It ain't the jalopy you're worrying about. Suppose he thinks we're your husband. Shakin' in his shoes, I daresay."

"Nothing to stop him walking out while you're yammering here," said the woman, indifferently.

"Maybe he thinks we won't be long and he's waiting to get what he came for." He took the key from his pocket and fitted it in the lock. "You do your stuff, mind, Curly, and—no double crossing, see? It's a long road a bullet can't find you."

He flung open the door and vanished into the dark, locking it behind him.

Before the sound of his feet had died away the woman turned to Curly.

"Now's your chance," she implored him. "He won't be up right away. You could get along through the front, go hide in the woods. I'll tell him I couldn't hold you and you gone down to the river. You could lie up in the woods till the hunt's moved on."

"Eatin' nuts like a squirrel?" asked Curly, solemnly. "It ain't the right time of year for nuts, ma'am."

"You don't want to be here when the police come," she insisted.

"The police?"

"Bellman's gone for them. If they find you here they'll take you back."

"The police!" The boy brooded. "That's why you let Maggs shoot his mouth off? Making time, like?"

"That's right. That big shot!"

"You're a brave woman, ma'am. Maybe it's you should be making for the woods. He don't like being double-crossed."

"You'll want money," she said, pulling open a drawer. "I'll give you this . . ."

"Well, thanks, ma'am. Maggs 'ull be pleased. That's one thing I done for him."

"Maggs don't come into this. You want to get off before he's back."

"But" he stared, "he don't know about the dog."

"He will."

"I'll have to tell him, ma'am. Him and me's mates."

"Mates? And the lion shall lie down with the lamb. Not that Maggs wouldn't make the lousiest lion. How come you met up with him at all?"

"He give me a job. Driving a car. He said I drove nice. Never took an exam, though."

"L-driver, eh?"

"But not at night. Maggs said best not. Might attract attention, see."

"Was you driving the car that night, when you got nabbed?"

Curly looked nervous. "Just driving, ma'am."

"The radio said a mail van driver got hurted bad."

"Must have been armour-plated Maggs said, not to ha' died. I parked the car in the alley and kept a look-out. Holler if you see police, Harry said—leastways, whistle. Like this." He whistled clear and radiant as a blackbird. "So I whistled, and then I heard the shot—and the car drivin' away."

"Leaving you to hold the baby?"

"Maybe I move slow," Curly apologised.

"How come they got Maggs?"

"He come back for me. He told the police I never set eyes on any of 'em before, and it was true—except for Maggs."

"What did they give you?" asked the woman in harsh tones.

"Three year—because he didn't die, see."

"A child like you! Didn't you have no one to advise you?"

"They asked me did I want to plead unfit, like I was silly, see? But Maggs said that 'ud mean they'd never let me go. Think of it —all my life behind them walls." He looked about him wonderingly. "It don't seem I did much," he said. "Just drove the car." He looked troubled. "Why don't Maggs come? Maybe he met up with your man in the barn?"

"Maybe he did. Or maybe he's trying to get the jalopy to go. It's O.K., Curly. My man ain't coming back to-night. That's what I didn't want Maggs to know. Well, he's got a gun, and all I got are these."

She thrust her hands together and pushed them towards him. Thin and tanned and bitten with work and weather they were. "Look like hide now, don't they?" she said. "But they was white and supple once, afore I was wed. Soft hands, soft heart, that was me. You married, Curly?"

Curly stared. "No, ma'am."

"When you do, you remember a woman don't stop bein' herself because she's your wife. She ain't a piece of stock you look to make a profit; she likes a bit of attention, a bit of loving, that way she stays loving too. How old you, Curly?"

"Nigh twenty, ma'am."

"You could ha' been the son I never had. You got a mother?"

"Not so fur's I know."

"No folks?"

"On'y Maggs."

"He ain't folks."

"He's all I got."

"You want to keep away from his sort. You're not like him. You're—gentle. Women like that in a man. You'd be good to a woman, Curly. You tried to be good to me. There's joy in the

world for them as can find it. You take my share, the share I
missed. And now—go. Go quick. Here. Take this macintosh cape
of my husband's. No, he won't be wanting it. And go now. Not
that way," as he turned towards the kitchen door. "Maggs locked
that. You go out the front."

"Thank you for the money, ma'am. Maggs 'ull be pleased."

"You're going to stick to him? A chap that was born to be
hanged." She could scarcely contain her rage and scorn.

"That's a turr'ble thing to say about any man, ma'am. He's
coming now," he added, simply.

"I don't hear nothing."

But Curly was right. A moment later the key shot into the lock,
the door was flung open, Maggs came in, his face shiny with sweat,
his voice thick as though choked with phlegm.

"You didn't toot the horn, Maggs," Curly accused him. "Wasn't
there no jalopy in the barn?"

"Never mind about the jalopy," said Maggs, breathless and
dishevelled. "We're getting out."

"I got the money, Maggs." He shook the purse triumphantly.

Maggs took it from him and flung it on the table.

"We don't want nothing from this house. What's that you got
on your shoulders? I didn't notice no scarecrow on the way in."

"She said her man wouldn't miss it."

Maggs threw back his head and roared with laughter. "No, he
won't miss it. You ask him if you don't believe me."

"You mean—he's down in the barn?"

"That's right. He's down in the barn. God!" he turned savagely
on the silent woman. "You must ha' hated him. His head's nigh
stove in."

"You been a long time thinking up that story," said the woman.
"Very pretty, ain't it? I go flying down to the barn and when I
come back you've stripped the house. No, we'll wait till the police
come. You can tell your fairy-tale to them."

"Who said the police are coming?"

"It's the dog, Maggs. She sent the dog for them."

Maggs turned; his face was indescribable. "No," he said. "You wouldn't do that, not even a hellion like you. Not with him down there the way he is."

"I don't know what way he is," returned the woman in a wooden sort of voice. "I wasn't in the barn since yesterday. 'Sides, you're forgetting Bellman. He wouldn't let no stranger come nigh the barn, not without I was with him."

"Who said anything about a stranger?" demanded Maggs, sulkily.

Curly was pulling at his coat. "Maggs, you didn't get it. The dog's gone for the police. We got to get out. Quick."

"You're too late," said Maggs coolly. "Hark to that!"

A distant full-throated barking could be heard.

"He'll have found," said the woman in a tone of bitter triumph.

Maggs snatched out the revolver. "This time," he said, "he'll get it right between the eyes. That's the right treatment for a squealer."

In an instant, heedless of her own security, the woman had flung herself upon him.

"Curly, go stop him," she shouted.

"My God, you wildcat, I believe you blinded me," howled Maggs.

"I'll have to cry myself to sleep tonight," she growled.

"I'm going, Maggs," shouted Curly. "I can't go back, not them walls."

Neither heard him; nor did they hear the soft voice saying, "Thanks, son, but not so fast. There's a few questions . . ."

The next instant the room was full of people. Before Maggs was aware, hands had gripped him, his gun was skittering along the floor, and a voice said, "Reckon we'll use them bracelets" and to his rage and shock he found himself handcuffed. Curly, lost and heartbroken, found himself in the guard of a police constable. The third new-comer was a small dapper man in a dark suit and a black trilby, who held Bellman by the collar. The woman stepped back, pushing her disordered hair into place. The dog pulled forward and leaped up against her, as the sergeant stooped and picked up the gun in a hand veiled by a handkerchief.

"Having a bit of trouble, ma'am?" he suggested.

"Who's that you've brought along?" demanded the woman, indicating the stranger, who answered for himself.

"Name of Pryce," he said. "Your dog here stopped my car, so I guessed there was summat wrong and I drove him down to the station. I travel in sardines," he added.

"No wonder Bellman winded you. O.K., boy, we got the police here now."

Curly was wailing softly. "You promised, Maggs, you promised. Now I'll go back . . ."

"Go back?" Pryce looked from one face to another.

"We've been looking for these chaps," the sergeant explained briefly.

"Oh, them two! Quite a haul you made." He stopped to pat the dog.

"Warn't there a reward?" said the woman. "If so I reckon Bellman should have his share."

"What you got in your veins instead of blood?" demanded Maggs. "Ice?"

"That'll do," said the sergeant.

Curly's voice lifted. "Why couldn't it be me in the barn with my head stove in? Oh Maggs, why couldn't it be me?"

"What's that?" exclaimed the sergeant.

"Best ask him." The woman indicated Maggs with a derisive finger. " 'Cording to him, there's a body in the barn."

"As if you didn't know," taunted Maggs.

"I ain't been near the barn to-day. Mind you, it's just a trap to get the house to themselves. I'm not fooled that easy."

The sergeant was staring at Maggs' shoes. "You just come from the barn?"

"That's right."

"It was the jalopy," broke in Curly. "Maggs thought I could drive the jalopy."

For the first time the woman looked uncertain. "It's a joke, ain't it? Ain't it?" she repeated more sharply.

"Not for him it ain't. Though he could be better off that way than living along of her."

The sergeant silenced him effectively. "You Haywood, take a look in the barn," he said. "Mr. Pryce and me'll keep an eye on these two."

Haywood went out. Pryce stood rather self-consciously near the distraught Curly. Bellman crouched at his mistress's feet.

The woman said calmly, "If it's true, sergeant, there ain't been no one near the house all day but these two."

"We come right up to the house," declared Maggs. "That chap was a goner when we came. Why, now I come to recall it, she was cleaning herself when we come. Cleanin' herself this time of day."

"You wouldn't understand cleaning yourself any time of day," retorted the woman in scornful tones.

"The dog would ha' let me know if anyone was there," she added an instant later.

"He's a grand chap," Pryce agreed. "Came right up like as if he could speak. Let me pat him . . ." He looked at his hands and his expression changed. "That's a funny thing."

"What's that?" asked the sergeant with a bark that might have done credit to the dog.

"I dunno. Looks like blood—only—I'm not hurted anywhere. I was petting the dog—that's it. Must be the dog. On'y he never let on he was hurt."

The sergeant dropped down at Bellman's side, touching him like a man who knows dogs like his own garden.

"Good fellow! Easy, boy." The skillful hands explored the dog's coat and legs. Then he rose slowly. "He ain't hurt—but there's blood on his ruff and one foreleg. How did he come by that?"

"I'll tell you how he come by that," shouted Maggs. "Got it in the barn, afore we come. Him and her, they ganged up on the old man. Well, stands to reason. He was here when we come. Ain't that right, Curly?"

"That's so," agreed Curly.

"And if he hadn't of been he'd have chased us off, wouldn't he? But he was right inside the house with her. And afterwards, long afore I shoved open the barn door, he must have been smelling the sardines on this gentleman's coat. So how come he's got blood on him if he wasn't in the barn afore we reached the house? You tell me that, missis, if you can?"

"Don't say anything," said the sergeant, swiftly. And then the door pushed open and Haywood came in.

"I'm sorry, ma'am," he said, not meeting the woman's eyes. "Reckon you'd best not go down. He—ain't pretty."

"That wouldn't be no change," the woman assured them all. "Well, a man that mean must have had enemies."

"Reckon you won't have to look far for this one," jeered Maggs.

"I'll have to ask you to come along to the station," the sergeant continued, paying no attention to the interrupter.

"To make a statement about these hoodlums? I understand."

Those small sharp hazel eyes met his without fear. He knew a wave of reluctant admiration for her; she must know how this was going to end, but she stood as steady as a house built upon the rock.

"Reckon I wouldn't care about staying here alone with him the way he is," she added. "We'll take Bellman along of us."

"We'll see to Bellman," the sergeant promised.

"He's a good lad. Anyone might be proud . . ." For an instant there seemed a chance that she'd waver. Then she cried angrily, "Ain't the rest of you going to get along? I don't recall inviting none of you . . ."

"Leave your address," said the sergeant to Pryce, who was fid-

dling nervously with the hat he'd taken off. "And don't go anywhere we can't reach you. See?"

The man nodded and dived for the door. Curly stook like a
figure of perpetual grief. Beyond speech, beyond reproaches.

"You shud ha' gone while you had the chance," said the woman
in sudden rage. "Now you can hang along of him one of these
days."

"Get the pair of them back to the station," the sergeant told
Haywood sharply. "The lady and me 'ull wait here till the doctor
and the boys come to do their stuff. Ring from the box at the cross-
roads. Maybe you'd like to put a few things together," he added
gently to the woman. "We'll be locking the place up for the time
being."

"Come on, you," said Haywood to the savage Maggs. He came
across and caught him by the arm, but the big fellow wrenched
himself free.

"Don't hustle me," he said. "Where's your manners? I got to say
good-bye to the lady, ain't I? Know what they say, missis, about
women always getting the last word? Reckon you got that all
right; had it a while back, you did, when you said Blood will tell."

AUTHOR'S POSTSCRIPT: Out of the blue there came into my visual
    imagination this ill-assorted couple of jail-birds staring down at a
    lonely house occupied by a woman alone. I don't know when I
    thought of the dog, or when I knew a murder had been committed.
    I was fascinated by the set-up and went after it. Now I could tell
    you what all my people looked like, including the dog, a crossbred
    collie of a type I have never owned.

ANTHONY BOUCHER

A Matter of Scholarship

No scholar can pretend to absolute completeness, but every scholarly work must be as nearly complete as possible; any omission of available data because of carelessness, inadequate research, or (most damning of all) personal motives—such as the support of a theory which the data might contradict—is the blackest sin against scholarship itself . . .

Such were my thoughts as I sat working on my definitive MURDEROUS TENDENCIES IN THE ABNORMALLY GIFTED: A STUDY OF THE HOMICIDES COMMITTED BY ARTISTS AND SCHOLARS. The date was October 21, 1951. The place was my office in Wortley Hall on the campus of the University.

My conclusions seemed unassailable: Murder had been committed by eminent scholars (one need only allude to Professor Webster of Harvard) and by admirable artists (François Villon leaps first to the mind). But in no case had the motivation been connected with the abnormal gift; my study of the relationship between homicidal tendencies and unusual endowments established, in the best scholarly tradition, that no such relationship existed.

It was then that Stuart Danvers entered my office. "Professor Jordan?" he asked. His speech was blurred and he swayed slightly. "I read your piece in the *Atlantic* on Villon [it sounded like *villain*] and I said to myself, 'There's the guy to help you.' " And before I could speak he had placed a large typewritten manuscript on my desk. "Understand," he went on, "I'm no novice at this. I'm a pro. I've sold fact-crime pieces to all the top editors." He hiccuped. "Only now it strikes me it's time for a little hard-cover prestige."

I stared at the title page, which read GENIUS IN GORE, and then began flipping through the book. The theme was my own. The style was lurid, the documentation inadequate. He had taken seriously the pretensions to learning of such frauds as Aram and Rulloff; he had omitted such a key figure as the composer Gesualdo da Venosa. But I had read enough in the field to know that his abominable work was what is called "commercial." He would have no trouble in finding a publisher immediately; and my own book was scheduled by the University Press for, at best, "some time" in 1953.

"Little nip?" he suggested, and as I shook my head he drank from his flask. "Like it? Thought maybe you could help—well, sort of goose it with a couple of footnotes . . . *you* know."

I looked at this drunken, unscholarly lout. I saw myself eclipsed in his shadow, the merest epigone to his attack upon my chosen Thebes. And then he said, "Of course that's just a rough first draft, you understand."

"Do you keep a carbon of first drafts?" I asked idly. And when he shook his addled skull, I split that skull's forehead with my heavy paperweight. He stumbled back against the wall, lurched forward, and then collapsed. His head struck the desk. I tucked the obscene manuscript away, wrapped the paperweight in a handkerchief, carried it down the hall, washed it, flushed the handkerchief down the toilet, returned to my room, and called the police. A stranger had wandered into my office drunk, stumbled, and cracked his head against my desk.

The crime, if such it can be considered, was as nearly perfect as any of which I have knowledge. It is also unique in being the only instance of a crime committed by an eminent scholar which was *motivated* by his scholarship . . .

AUTHOR'S POSTSCRIPT: What really brought the story on was that Ellery Queen said he'd like to see some short-short-shorts. I thought it was an interesting technical challenge. The book in question in the story—that is, the matter of the relation between murder and other talents—is a problem that has long fascinated me. When I thought of using it as a theme, the plot seemed to follow immediately out of it.

HELEN KASSON

Nonie

IT passed for an accident, but it was murder.

It's funny how you can look at some things a hundred times and forget them, and then a momentary glimpse will burn a scene or the look in someone's eyes ineffaceably on your mind so that you can never escape it.

That's the way it is with Nonie's face. I can remember, as if it were yesterday, that day I found her alone with a dead man and one who, with the blood he had in him, might better be dead, and I can see the release in her pale eyes and the gratitude which she could not word.

She stood in the queer high-necked, long-sleeved dress she always wore, her pinched face almost happy, yet not knowing when she would hear a noise and find him, the child, squirming, convulsing, drooling, and then perhaps there'd be two dead. But two dead were better than two alive, or even one alive, if the one happened to be Klaus Klauber, so I left, content in the knowledge that she was free from the man she called husband, and knowing too that her misbegotten child could not harm her yet awhile.

It was strange, all of it—the way Klaus Klauber appeared on May Sonders' farm one day and stayed on, working the fields and feeding the stock, sleeping in the shack behind the barn that had been built for a smokehouse and never used.

Ed Sonders had been like that. He'd build a new corn-crib and then decide the old one was good for another year. So there'd be the new building standing empty and getting weatherbeaten, waiting for the old one to fall down. That was the way with the smokehouse, until Klaus Klauber hired out to May and moved his dark, knotty body onto the cot May set up for him out there.

Ed had been dead two years when Klaus appeared.

If you passed in the evening, you'd see Klaus sitting on a box tilted back against the smokehouse wall, and he'd always be alone. At first our farm hands used to walk over after the chores were done, but he was rude and unfriendly and they soon stopped coming. Perhaps it was his disfigured face which made him reluctant to make friends, perhaps his accent, and perhaps too it was his alienness which aroused their curiosity. (Anyway, they never fully satisfied it.)

No one knows exactly when it was that he moved into the house. The rumor started, grew, and finally the fact existed, was accepted in a sort of abeyant horror which never quite died out, but no one took it upon himself to reprimand May Sonders and May never came to town after that so that the eager righteous didn't get a chance to snub her.

Nonie was thirteen then and, though she had not yet lost the power of speech, she seldom used it. Even when, as children, we ran through the fields together or, like young animals, rolled naked in the hay hardly, at that time, realizing that one body was different from the other, she spoke little. Her flesh was there, and mine, but she held her own part of herself away, shielded it, as if she feared being known even by me who, if she had allowed it, would have been as close to her as it is possible for two people to be.

So, it is not strange that the thing which had been used so seldom, the thing held so tenuously, was what she lost when she saw her mother fall into the combine.

Or, did she see it? Perhaps she had come running when she heard Klaus shout, perhaps she arrived only in time to see what the flailing knives had left, to stand transfixed, knowing already that her voice was gone, watching the wheat still coming out relentlessly, blood-stained and virulent.

How did May happen to fall into the combine? No one ever knew. Nonie shook her head in dumb denial of everything the Sheriff asked her, and there was no other witness but Klaus himself.

Anyway, however it had happened, Nonie accepted the inevitable as, earlier, she must have accepted Klaus. Yet, how had she forced her child eyes even to admit his image—the evil scar running from eye to nose, the heavy lips—how forced her barely-formed body to contact with his? It might have been the hypnotism of the weak by the strong. Perhaps she had stood powerless, mentally impaled on the gleam in his malformed eye, waiting for him to take her.

Or perhaps, one night as she walked through the fields he came up behind her, and turning she saw not the dark foreigner but the gentle man she had dreamed as she mothered her dolls. And then, with the feel of his maleness (for up to that time she could have known no man) and the moon throwing an aura around him, and the awakening of feelings she could not yet understand, perhaps she wanted him.

I can imagine his saying, "Nonie," in that queer, foreign accent, and her, caught motionless in the midst of motion, waiting, frightened, until the smell of the earth and the cattle and that emanant maleness overcame her. No one ever knew, but there was the fact that she was pregnant and that, two months after her mother died, Klaus came to the townspeople who had taken her in and said he wanted to marry her. (He owned the farm by that time; he had papers to prove it.) Nonie didn't object and they knew she was pregnant, so they let her. What else could they do?

Then we began wondering again—not so much about how May died, but why. Had Klaus felt compelled to give his child a name? By his standards, was allowing a nameless child to be born worse than what he had already done? Or was he that conventional—that he needed the head and foot, the framework of the marital bed, established, before the child, illegally conceived, should lie within it?

We wondered. And then, from the hills, came strange rumors. A passing farmer had seen Klaus in high rage, striding the fields at noon, tearing the wheat with a whip, trampling the stalks back into earth with his heavy boots, the fiery scar throbbing, the eye flashing in its malformed socket.

Another had heard unaccountable sounds floating out of the night. "Like the moan of the wind," he said, "but there was no wind." And one day my folks picked up Nonie trudging the road to town and, for the first time, saw her in that high-necked, long-sleeved dress she was to wear for the rest of her life.

"Is the horse lame?" they asked, and she, flushing, nodded.

It was then they noticed a change in Nonie. She was not quiet but unquiet, restless, almost guilty, afraid to meet their eyes, and this toward people whose fathers had worked beside her grandfather and who, themselves, had held her hand to guide the first steps she took.

Strange reports, but strangest the one we had known longest, that Nonie was going to have a child. Inconceivable, that those two people could have mated and conceived, that that dark blood and Nonie's were to commingle in one being—as inconceivable as that there could be offspring of dog and cat, wolf and ewe, ape and woman.

And yet, one night Klaus was in town, riding high on the wagon-truck as if it were a black charger, knocking at Tennent's door with his heavy fist and shouting in his gutteral voice for the doctor.

I remember the first time I saw the child—Joel, they called him —how surprised I was to find him small and delicate. I had expected somehow that the dark blood would submerge the fair— that the strength of Klaus would dominate. Yet, here was an old-young child, like Nonie, belying, to all outward appearance, the father who gave him life.

You would think, with the birth of Joel, that we'd have lost interest in the lives of Klaus and Nonie. When two people marry and have a child, even though their union seemed unbelievable before, the very fact of two becoming three puts the seal of nature on their being together. And perhaps we might have accepted their marriage and thought no more about it, had it not been for the child himself.

At the age of three, he started falling into convulsions—"fits," some called them. So, our curiosity reawakened, we watched the hill farm and discovered that Joel was not a child at all, but, silent and melancholy, he seemed more a dwarfed adult harboring the soul of Klaus in Nonie's body. We'd see him hunched on a pasture fence staring sullenly at the ground, or leaning against a side of the barn scuffing a hole in the dirt with one toe, or walking home from school alone, passing groups of playing children without raising his eyes.

Strangely, his schoolmates never bothered him. Perhaps, like Klaus, he held them at such a distance that they did not dare; or perhaps they had been told about his fits—or had seen him lying rigid on the ground—and feared to tease him lest they bring one on.

At any rate, he never seemed to need companionship. Nor did he need Nonie, after he was independent of her mother-protection. You'd see her looking at him, mutely, tenderly, and there'd be pleading in her eyes—but he never looked at her. Or, she'd put out a hand to touch his head and he'd draw away, repulsing her with every muscle in his body. I felt sometimes that she must welcome even the convulsions when they came, for then she could touch him, hold him close, mother-like.

For awhile I was over there quite often. Father had given me a stallion which, as he grew older, developed a mean streak. I could handle him most of the time, but he'd go wild now and then, rearing and pawing the air with his front feet when I tried to saddle him. At rutting time he was downright crazy, and hardly a day passed that he didn't break loose, galloping across the fields to jump the fence.

Klauber's mare was usually in the far pasture where Fury couldn't get her, but once I arrived to find her scratched and bleeding in the field next to ours, and Klaus after Fury with a whip.

That horse was a killer and shouldn't have been antagonized, but he had lost some of his energy by then and was snorting and plunging in only a half-hearted way. I was afraid Klaus would be angry with me, until I noticed his eyes. They were strangely awakened—eager almost—but there was no anger in them. When he saw me, he stopped short.

"That's a fine horse." His voice was breathless and his accent seemed more foreign than ever as it bumped over his lips.

I said, "Yes," not telling him how fractious Fury was, because when a man owns a horse he never speaks anything but good of it.

"Do you want to sell him?"

"No." Fury was mean but he was my own, and I didn't want Klaus to have anything which had belonged to me.

"If you ever do, let me know."

I managed to keep Fury at home after that, so I didn't have reason to visit their farm. Anyway, it depressed me. The fields were well-tended but the stock, what was left of it, had a woebegone, neglected look. I remember seeing a cow with one eye missing near our pasture fence, and I remember wondering what peculiar accident could have caused that. Even the chickens seemed ragged and submissive. But strangest was the mongrel dog that prowled the fields, his hair off in scarred patches, lame in one leg, one toe missing, a hook in the tail where it had been broken and never set.

Perhaps that was what had frightened the boy, had sent him into those writhing fits. Perhaps at three or younger, he came on his father in the barn, or fell asleep in the hayloft and wakened to a scream below, or peered around the corner of the house to see Klaus—maybe only wringing the neck of a chicken to be eaten later, or killing a pig to smoke the meat for winter, or maybe

—worse. Still, it was the look on Klaus' face which must have done it, the eye caught between scar and brow gleaming, the lips curled back, the cruel nose widening at the warm blood smell. I can imagine him, the child, standing transfixed for a moment, then running to throw himself down in the orchard, there to empty his stomach as if he might rid his mind of the foul picture with the bits of half-digested food.

Then perhaps knowledge unfolded, grew, until finally it found outlet in those recurring fits. I imagined his questioning eyes on Nonie asking, *Does she know?* and answering, *She does! She knows!* then the revulsion growing and his avoiding even her, and the hatred growing too, because she knew and yet continued to live with Klaus, thus accepting his shame and making it hers as well.

But I didn't know all that yet. Where would a hard-bitten New England farmer who worked with animals and earth and nature and knew only the sweet-rotten smell of decaying life—something he could see and touch—where would he learn to recognize the decay that was Klaus? No one but old Doc Tennent, with his reading and medical training, could have known. And I don't think he would ever have told if he hadn't been caught at our farm by one of those sudden spring showers the day he drove out to set my broken wrist after Fury threw me.

The ride had tired him. Perhaps he felt close to death and was afraid to die with the guilt of not telling on his mind. Yet, who would have taken Nonie, mute, the enemy of her own afflicted child?

Lewis was there—it was his mare had excited Fury—and it was he who had brought the doctor. And it was he who brought up the subject of Nonie. He'd seen her as he passed, standing before her house in that queer, long-sleeved, high-necked dress, and it had struck him with its strangeness,

"In this heat," he said.

"There's a reason," the doctor answered, and then he was silent, perhaps ashamed that he had not taken Nonie away from Klaus long ago. Finally, he told us, slowly, as if, having held the secret so long, it had taken root and was difficult to unearth, looking guiltily at his hands the while. But, when he had finished, we understood. We saw Nonie as he had seen her the night he went to help her bear her child and, for a moment, it was as if we stood in the silence of the room where, even at the peak of pain, Nonie uttered no sound.

And then, perhaps, we began to doubt Nonie. Yet, who can draw a line between the allowable and the forbidden, between duty and dereliction? Who can say, "Just so far I will go—no farther. This is my wifely function." It was for Nonie to decide. Klaus filled the place of husband in his way and, in his way, expected her submission.

The horses and cows and chickens diverted a bit of the stream, and it may have been out of some sort of warped kindness Klaus used them or it may have been from a desire to save as long as possible the only human-thing which was his. That normal he may have been—that he preferred woman-flesh to horses.

Horses. It was just about rutting time.

I took Fury over the next morning. Klaus was in the barn when we arrived. I saw him look from my bandaged wrist to Fury's proud, nervous eyes, and I knew he thought he knew why I had come and despised me for it. There was contempt on his face before he looked down again to the harness he was mending. I hated to do it, but I had to.

"He threw me," I said. "I'll sell him."

The deal was closed quickly. Klaus wanted Fury and I wanted Fury to be there. But as I walked away from the barn, leaving them both inside, I felt sick and frightened. I could almost hear a high, raging snort and the crack of splintered wood and the muffled sound of hooves on flesh and bone.

AUTHOR'S POSTSCRIPT: I believe it started with the realization that there are some instants—perhaps only a look flashing across someone's face—that one never forgets. Then as the story grew, I began to think that I had, inadvertently, hit on the perfect crime, in which the murderer presents the victim with the instrument which, in itself, is harmless.

A Decidedly Innocent Man

I LIKE to talk to lawyers," he said, "especially young ones just starting out, before the bloom is worn off. What'll you have?"

He was just a middle-aged man at a bar, possibly a bore, but I felt like talking. I accepted the drink he offered me and studied him. Not tight, I decided, just convivial. Well-dressed in a casual, easy way. Wide, rather than stout, with so little neck that his head seemed to rest on his shoulders. A small beak of a nose punctuated the round featureless face. His eyes were large and round and stared through things. I felt he was looking into me, not at me. He reminded me, I thought, of an owl.

"What's your line?" I asked.

He grinned and I immediately thought of a cat with feathers, a kind of cat-owl, a new species. That was the effect he had on me, and I had had only two drinks.

"That's a lawyer for you," he said. "Begins by asking for information. Never offers any. I own property. I have investments. I live on the results of the intelligent handling of money, my own and other peoples. I'm as honest as I need to be. Sometimes I'm as honest as I can afford to be. The important thing about me is that I'm not a man who insists on doing everything himself. That's the way to an early grave. It's amazing the number of people there are in this world who are willing to pull other people's chestnuts out of the fire. I have learned to let them do it."

He took a long pull at his drink and set down his glass. "I've just made you a present of one of the secrets of success. You ought to be grateful. I learned it the hard way."

"Wrong pupil," I said. "A lawyer *is* a professional chestnut puller. That's what we're paid for."

"Ah yes." He frowned as if I had disturbed his train of thought. "Always tell the truth to your lawyer! Excellent maxim. I always did. I know the law," he added, "as only a man can who has been in its clutches."

I began to think the conversation was a mistake. A man who has lost a case has a perpetual grudge against all lawyers. He is usually long-winded too. But I was drinking his liquor so I thought it just as well to give him the opening he was going to take anyway. "Perhaps your lawyer wasn't to blame. After all . . ."

"To blame? Heavens no, of course he wasn't to blame. He was excellent. And he has reason to be eternally grateful to me. It isn't often a man has a client acquitted on a murder charge."

My spirits rose. There was something vaguely reminiscent of the opening of an O. Henry story in his approach. I realized that he was steering the conversation skillfully. Smiling, I took the bait. "You were tried for murder?"

He nodded. "And remember," he said with sly gratification, "that no matter what people *think* I can never be tried for that murder again."

There was something about the way he said it that shook me. The thought of fantasy had been my own not his. He was telling me the truth. Cat or owl, one thing I knew, this man was no red herring. I realized with dismay that his manner of speaking one sentence had made me believe he was a murderer.

"Knowing that," he went on, "you can hear what I say without fear. I am an innocent man. My acquittal was the official proclamation of my innocence. Let's sit down in the booth over there and I'll tell you about it." He called the bartender for two more and I followed him to the booth.

"The man for whose murder I was tried," he said, "was a thief, a liar, a corrupter of weaker souls, a despoiler and a destroyer. Morally (what a strange word that is) he was a murderer. Two people killed themselves because of him. He deserved to die. The world was better off when he was no longer in it.

"I was not the only one who would have liked to see him dead. Unfortunately they were all cowards. Chet turned his brother,

George, into a servile pander. Poor George, how he hated the man who had made him the weakling he was. First Chet broke up his brother's marriage, then he defrauded him, then he made him a party to his crimes. George was what he was, there was no way out for him, but there was for me.

"As many careful business men do I had placed a good deal of property in my wife's name. Linda was a pretty, rather shallow little thing, but I loved her. I made the foolish mistake of working too hard; I was too busy to give Linda the attention she needed. I was happy when she found amusing friends and stopped complaining. The situation was made to order for Chet Marlow. He seduced her. I don't think it took much trouble; she was romantic and easily impressed. Then he persuaded her that she could make a fortune with the money I had placed in her name. It was so easy. Of course he manipulated things so that her loss was always his gain. The money changed hands so smoothly, she was hardly aware of it.

"When I found out, I lost my head. I said all the things that a man says to a woman at such a moment. And then, I am ashamed to say, I struck her.

"She left me to go to Chet. But first she made a proud little speech telling me exactly where I had failed her. It was a very good speech, the best one she had ever made. I couldn't help feeling proud of her.

"Her love for Chet and her pathetic dignity carried her all the way to his door. But the door was firmly closed in her face. Chet was no longer interested; he had other ideas. She drowned herself.

"The manner of her death distressed me deeply. She had always been afraid of deep water.

"As for George's wife, she drove her car off a cliff. But that murder was different. Chet had not seduced *her*. She was too plain for his tastes. But he got George, who as I have said was a pretty weak character, involved with a cheap, flashy, succulent woman. Then Chet told George's wife about it and convinced her that George was through with her.

"You can say this for Chet, he was worth murdering. Iago was a blundering fool compared to Chet.

"There were others, but as your time is limited, I will ask you to take my word for the fact that Chet was a vicious, destructive man.

"When I buried my poor wife I decided that Chet had to die. I followed him. I threatened him. I wrote to him, listing his crimes and predicting his death. I wanted to frighten him. I succeeded too well.

"One day I received a communication from him warning me that he had deposited with his lawyer one of those protective letters marked, 'To be opened in the event of my death.' From that moment I knew that anything that happened to Chet would be fully investigated. Murder would out. And Chet had been careful to say that he had named me as his future murderer.

"At first, this depressed me. It seemed he had protected himself forever from my justice, and there wasn't anything I could do about it. For a time, I'm afraid I became a drunken bore, talking more than I should, announcing in every bar and night club that Chet was a coward and deserved to die. It was an impotent performance, one that still fills me with shame when I remember it.

"Then one night I decided I had had enough of that sort of thing. I swore rather loudly that I would drink from then on in the privacy of my room.

"It was at this time that I left town on a carefully planned vacation, for I needed a change badly. I told no one I was leaving, or where I was going. I was sick of them all. What did it matter to me if they thought I was swilling whiskey alone in frustrated self-pity?

"The night before I left town, I went for a last fling to the worst night club I knew. George was there, poor fellow. George was always there. He offered me his flabby sympathy and I drank with him, for though I despised George I had nothing against him. It was not his fault he had become what he was.

"A week later Chet was murdered. I heard about it over the radio and returned to the city. I had hardly had time to wash and change before the police came. I learned that Chet's body had been found in a lonely little park near the city limits. He had been stabbed in the back. No weapon was found. The letter Chet had deposited with his lawyer accusing me had been immediately given to the representatives of law and order. And there they were to question me in all their magnificent efficiency.

"They said I had lured Chet to the place of his death with some clever story, that he had gotten out of the car to walk to the rendezvous and I had killed him.

"I said I had done nothing of the kind. I did not volunteer any information and I refused to answer when they asked where I had been at the time of the murder. I was perfectly within my rights, as you know. The burden of the proof was on them.

"Even when they produced the lighter I said little. It had been found near the body and since it had my initials on it I admitted it was mine. It was Linda's first present to me. I carried it as a talisman only, for efficient use I prefer matches. I said that I lost it at least a week before.

"They arrested me and brought me to trial. Naturally I was acquitted. It was a simple matter of an unbreakable alibi. You must admit that mine was absolutely ironclad. My vacation had been spent at a small beach resort about three hours drive from the city. I had been staying with friends. At every hour of the day, I was in the company of honorable, respectable people. Their testimony could not be shaken. Even at night I had not been alone. I had refused the privacy of the guest room, in order to share the cooler, screened-in sleeping porch with their son, an ex-marine, who slept lightly, and was awake if I so much as went for a drink of water. The most clever cross-examination could not shake these people. I had never been alone for more than a few minutes at any time. This was supported by neighbors and friends who had seen me around the house, sunning myself on the lawn or with the family at the beach.

"The efforts to point out that this itself was a suspicious circumstance fell flat. My friends stoutly maintained that I had confessed that I feared I was becoming an alcoholic and had asked them to watch me and give me no chance to sneak off by myself.

"They *had* to acquit me. Since then I have been at peace with myself. I am free. I am innocent. And I have the gratifying knowledge that Chet Marlow has paid for his crimes."

I stared at my companion. But he only smiled and ordered another round.

"Well?" I said.

"Well what?" The repulsive creature was playing with me, enjoying himself.

I took a deep breath. "You said yourself that you cannot be tried again, so you may as well tell me the rest. How did you do it? How did you deceive the people who gave you your alibi? Or did they . . .?"

He reproved me with pursed lips. "They're honest people. They told the truth."

"Then how was it worked? How did you kill him?"

He shook his head sadly as if I had disappointed him. "I thought a clever young lawyer like you . . .

"Chet signed his own death warrant when he so cleverly left that document pointing to me. It was then that I knew he would be killed. That's why I left town and was very careful to be in the company of the right people the whole time. But the night before I left, I made very sure that George knew about that letter and I was very careless with my lighter. It slipped out of my pocket onto the seat beside him. George was a coward; he wouldn't take a risk. But he couldn't resist a sure thing. And George, you must remember, hated Chet as much as I did."

"But . . ." I began and then was silent.

"You are wondering, are you not, he said, "how much guilt I have to bear? None, let me tell you, none. I acted on my knowledge of George and I protected myself that is all."

"And what about George?" I asked. "What happened to him?"

"George was a fool," he said irritably. "When I was acquitted, he shot himself. He may possibly have thought they could trace the lighter to him, but that was ridiculous. He had only to keep quiet. But in that there was also a kind of justice. He had, after all, been a partner, albeit unwillingly, in his brother's crimes."

We sat some time in silence. I wanted to get up and go, but I couldn't think of a line that would get me out.

The man's round eyes held mine, while his face seemed to blur and disintegrate.

Suddenly he rose. "Let me save you the embarrassment," he said sadly. "It's time I was going. It's strange, isn't it, how people always draw back from me even when I tell them the true story? Even the friends who gave me my alibi are not quite sure. I am at peace with myself, but sometimes I am a very lonely man."

"But why?" I said. "Why tell anyone? You must meet many people who don't know. Why do you tell them?"

He drew himself up. "I'm innocent. Why shouldn't I?" His lips twisted oddly. "Besides, it's the one interesting thing about me. The only thing."

AUTHOR'S POSTSCRIPT: Just a glimpse of two men in a bar started it, one buying the drinks and talking, the other listening, and certainly not feeling comfortable about what he heard. Then I remembered the Ancient Mariner. The glittering eye. What I wanted was the trapped, reluctant but fascinated listener—and the equally trapped compulsive talker whose world has shrunk to the one story he must tell and tell again. A quiet self-made hell that never ends.

STUART PALMER

Future Imperfect

THE solitary drinker in dingy tropical whites had been quietly edging his way along the bamboo bar toward Jerry Waite for the past hour. But it was not until most of the others had said their goodnights and departed and the two were alone, except for Pancho the bartender and a couple or so in the far corner, that he actually made his pitch. "Good evening," he said, raising his glass. *"Salud y pesetas."*

"The same to you," Jerry said amiably, still wishing he knew how to get rid of the fellow.

But the older man sat down on the nearest stool. "Rumor has it that you're an author," he pressed.

Jerry nodded. Actually he was an author only in the sense that he made a living writing television scripts in Hollywood. Usually they were about "the Saint," "the Falcon," "The Shadow," or "Bulldog Drummond," but always involving the same Robin Hood, gentleman-crook character skating on thin ice just ahead of Scotland Yard, Centre Street or the Surete. However, he had written a novel or so, as yet unpublished. Writing assignments around the studios had been few and far between of late, and so Jerry's harried agent had told him to take a trip somewhere and not to come back until he had some new, fresh ideas to offer the story-editors.

Somehow he had stopped off here in Mazatlan, on the upper west coast of Mexico and far off the usual tourist trails, staying on because the food here at the Hotel Grande was magnificent if a bit bizarre—there had been iguana stewed in sherry for dinner to-night—and because there was a sloe-eyed senorita called Concepcion who sang lovely Andalusian songs and played the guitar in the dining room every evening.

Ordinarily Jerry Waite would have given this bleary bar-fly a quick brush-off, but tonight he was bored. He had just about exhausted the amusement possibilities of the town, having listened interminably to the street *mariachis* playing "Guadalajara," "El Novillero" and "La Paloma," purchased a brief-case and a riding-crop of half-tanned alligator leather, been photographed with the tame boa-constrictor from the hotel gardens looped across his shoulders, and getting a rather bad burn while deep-sea fishing for swordfish. All this was a complete change from his accustomed haunts, and pleasant enough—all except for the routine with the snake, who was heavy and odorous and a lens-louse, continually waving its foolish, reptilian snout between him and the camera. But not one of these simple pleasurements had inspired any original story ideas.

Not that Jerry anticipated getting anything interesting from this stranger at the bar either, except perhaps a chance to buy some flawed opals or perhaps the map of a supposedly lost gold-mine. In his crew-cut and Palm Springs sport shirt Jerry looked younger than his thirty years; he was becoming accustomed to being taken for an easy mark. This "So you're an author?" approach was a little different, however; it was another gambit. People who scrape up a conversation with a professional writer are always very anxious to find out where he gets his ideas and does he work directly with a typewriter or use a pen, and what name does he write under, or else—

"I've got a story you can write," the little man offered. Jerry knew those stories, they were always long and rambling and based upon pure coincidence. "It's about a perfect murder," the other continued. "*The* perfect murder." He waited hopefully.

"Afraid I'm not really very interested, my friend. But I'll gladly buy you one drink." Jerry snapped his fingers for Pancho, who was drowsing at the other end of the long bar.

"You don't understand, Mr. Waite. The drinks, of course, must be on me." The stranger, who now introduced himself as Thomas M. Baxter, produced a gold-tipped sealskin wallet stuffed with

Mexican and American currency. "Cognac, please," he told the boy in flawless Spanish. "And leave the bottle here."

Jerry might still have made some excuse and pulled out, but he was to some extent obligated by the highball which was now being poured for him. Besides, he still hoped that the lovely and most elusive Concepcion might tonight keep her laughing half-promise to stop in for a nightcap and then let him see her home—or somewhere. He might as well he thought, kill time this way. So he took a good pull at his glass. "I'll tell you, Mr. Baxter, why the perfect murder doesn't exist," Jerry said patronizingly. "In real life there never has been one and never will be, because if anybody knows the secret it spoils the perfection. Oh, I grant you that some murderers get away with it—take Lizzie Borden. But that is just luck, or inefficiency on the part of the law. And in fiction it's a completely threadbare formula. Somebody commits the fool-proof murder, everything goes off like clockwork, and then just as he's gotten away wih it, Bingo! He forgot one little detail or something. . . ."

"I know, I know," interrupted Baxter. "Only in this story I'm telling you, it's different. This fellow, this friend of mine who killed his wife, *didn't* make any mistakes!" He refilled both their glasses, carefully adding a modicum of fizz-water. "You can check up on it if you like, it was in all the newspapers. Happened back in St. Louis, three or four years ago. Sam Durling—that was his name—did away with his bitch of a wife, and it all worked out just as he'd planned—with one or two unimportant exceptions—and nobody ever suspected him at all."

Jerry blinked, and edged away a little. "Then how—"

"How I know about it? Well, we were fellow *norteamericanos* in a foreign land and we got to be close friends. I guess he just had to tell somebody, and he had nothing to lose because he wasn't a fugitive from justice or anything. And I'm sure he wouldn't mind if his achievement got put down on paper by somebody who knows how to juggle words like you do. It's too good to keep. You could change the names and minor details around when you write the story, couldn't you?"

"Why, I guess so. That's the usual thing."

Mr. Baxter nodded approvingly, and then bent his bleary, red-rimmed eyes on the operation of refilling both their glasses again without spilling a single drop. "Durling was—well, he is a very unusual type—a goodlooking but bookish sort of fellow, about my size but five or six years younger and without a gray hair in his head. He'd been holding down various jobs in the publicity and business promotion game, doing pretty well at it too, I gather, when he met this woman. Her name was Martha Mears, and from what he told me she must have been in some ways a very unusual and perhaps even a brilliant woman. When he met her—it was on a summer vacation up at Lake Tahoe—she was running a little shoestring cosmetic company, making and distributing her own line of cosmetics and beauty preparations. She'd been a chorus-girl and model in her earlier days, and she still had a dazzling pink-and-whiteness that was a wonderful walking ad for her products, though I guess she never had to use them or anything else in that line. Some women are like that."

"Not any of the ones I know around Hollywood," Jerry put in.

"Well, anyway," the little man continued, "they were attracted to each other from the first. Sam saw a gold-mine in her and her beauty stuff. She just didn't have the promotional know-how to promote it right, that's all. Of course you've heard of Martha Mears Natural Beauty Aids?"

"I can't say that I have," Jerry Waite admitted, his eye still hopefully on the door.

"Shall I warm that up just a little?" Baxter poured a stiffish slug. "To be brief, Durling got her to form a corporation, with himself as executive vice-president in charge of publicity and promotion. He splurged on national advertising, featuring the fact that all of the Martha Mears products were Natural. No drugs or minerals or synthetics, just the miraculous touch of modern science on the everyday things of the woods and fields and farms and gardens around us. Mostly a gag, of course. But according to Sam, you should have seen how the feminine public fell for the Butternut Skin Cream, the Oak Leaf Rinse, the Cranberry and Raspberry Lipstick. Real cream and butter in the face creams, real flowers for the scent in everything. It went over like a house-afire, I gather. And more or less inevitably Sam and Martha drifted into a partnership which became a twenty-four hour a day thing and eventually they got married."

"So the story has a sex angle, huh? That's indicated."

"Yeah, sure. But like many another man before him, Sam Durling found out that it's awfully easy to make a bad wife out of a good mistress. He soon discovered that Martha hadn't really become Mrs. Durling, he'd become Mr. Mears—and you can spell that in small type. The new plant was booming with prosperity and the orders and the cash were rolling in by the basketful, but instead of gaining more authority around the place, Sam found himself reduced to the ridiculous standing of a prince-consort. And he couldn't do a damn thing about it, for the business was in her name. In fact, the business *was* her name! Oh, he had a small percentage of the stock, but nothing in line with what he should have had because he and he alone had had the ability and the imagination to increase the business a hundred-fold.

"You see, the business was Martha's whole life, it was her family and her children, and she'd gotten incredibly jealous of Sam's importance there. I guess she had the nature of a queen bee, and the only male she could tolerate around her was a drone. After about a year after they were married she kicked Sam upstairs to the post of general manager, which meant nothing at all since she did the managing anyhow, and she hired a handsome young new vice president in charge of sales and promotion to do his old job. She and the new guy began to have what they called business conferences about two evenings a week, and Martha banished Sam to the spare bedroom because she claimed he snored. You see how all this was the beginning of the end, don't you? It was inevitably building up to murder."

"Why didn't the guy get a divorce?" demanded Jerry, who had himself shipped off two wives to Reno.

Baxter shrugged, and clinked the bottle against their glasses again. "I asked Sam the same question, but he said divorce was out. He'd built the whole thing out of peanuts; it was a million dollar enterprise and he wasn't going to be shoved out into the cold with only his few shares of stock and maybe a little settlement, and everybody laughing at him. It was a point of pride with him, and when he found out that Martha was trying to needle him into giving in and letting her divorce him, after he realized that she had drained him dry as a cornhusk and now wanted to toss him aside like—"

"Like a worn out glove?" Jerry was lightly, stealing a glance at his watch. It was almost two o'clock in the morning, and if Concepcion didn't come soon, she wasn't coming at all.

"Exactly," Baxter nodded, continuing in a voice that was only slightly fuzzed. "So Sam dug in his heels and tried to sweat it out. He told me that nobody ever had any idea of what he had to take from that woman. Gone was the big, jolly, laughing playmate who used to tremble with desire when he kissed her and scream with delight when he tickled her. By this time she outweighed him by almost twenty pounds, and she began to take a sort of sadistic delight in pushing him around—only when they were alone, of course; in public they were still the devoted couple. When they first married he had talked her into giving up the pent-house apartment she'd always lived in, and they bought a big house in the suburbs. Servants at the time were difficult to find and harder to keep; according to Sam she never got along with any of them and they were always quitting or being fired. In the gaps between servants, it was Martha's insistence that Sam himself should do the housework; since he was the one that had wanted the big house and he certainly was only in the way around the plant, except for the once-a-month Newsletter he still wrote up, mostly for appearances sake. Martha tightened up on the money, too—and Sam said she even locked up the liquor cabinet too, keeping the key in her handbag."

"Cruel and inhuman treatment," Jerry said sympathetically. "She was really asking for it, wasn't she?"

"Exactly! According to Sam. Of course this is his side of it, but he had no reason to lie to me, and it all adds up. Martha was out to make life so miserable for him that he'd have to give in and take a powder, but like many of us little guys he was stubborn as a mule. We have more pride and self-respect than most people—and besides, there was his rightful share of the business at stake. So having a good deal of free time on his hands, Sam began to read everything he could find on the subject of murder. At first it was sort of just a "let's pretend" game with him, and then it began to solidify into something real. He decided that the extreme situation justified extreme measures. Murder was of course morally wrong, but this was an exception. But he was damn determined not to get caught. He saw that most people who are driven to that extremity fail because they do it in the heat of passion and leave traces all over, or else they try to be too clever, so that their plan topples over of its own weight. The thing had to be simple—as simple as a stage magician's trick when you get it explained.

"His first thought, naturally, was poison. Martha, like many women of her type, was something of a hypochondriac, always dosing herself for some imaginary ill. But according to the books Sam read, nowadays there are always exhumations and autopsies and all that sort of unpleasantness, even years later. A man could never be sure he was really safe.

"Next he thought of simple violence, because there had been a wave of brutal hammer murders and robberies in the city a few months before. But he wisely had little confidence in his ability to stage the thing properly, to jimmy windows and carry out all the other details in a way that would make it look professional to the police. Besides, he was not a bloodthirsty person, and the very idea of bludgeoning or shooting someone to death was repugnant to him. Martha was a very beautiful woman, and he couldn't bring himself to think of spoiling that perfect pink-and-whiteness."

"I see the point," Jerry admitted. The brandy was getting to his head, but the story was beginning to get to him too. "Go on."

"Plus the fact that a scandal would have hurt the value of the business," Baxter went on. "So he finally got rid of all the books on toxicology and legal medicine that he'd been secretly collecting, and turned to the daily newspapers. Has it ever occurred to you how clearly the nation's press reflects the complex dramatic phases of our daily lives, how they mirror the changing kaleidescope of human comedy and tragedy and hold it fast forever? Or at least until the bound back-numbers in the libraries yellow and crumble away?"

"It has," nodded Jerry Waite, who subscribed to several clipping services in hopes of getting new story ideas.

"Everything that has ever happened, everything that will ever happen, is set down somewhere in the columns of the newspapers," Baxter went on. "That was Sam Durling's belief, anyhow. He had plenty of time—he spent weeks and months poring over the bound volumes of back issues in the public library. And eventually he found just what he was looking for—it was Fate, he said. The item was buried in the back pages in the second section of the newspaper, but there was a completely new and original method of committing murder, which required no complicated preparation or equipment, involved no brutality nor spilled any blood, and left absolutely no traces. Its own inventors had used it successfully—though they had had a lovers' quarrel later and spilled the beans out of spite. They fumbled, but Sam knew he wouldn't fumble. . . ."

"Well? Go on, man!" Jerry saw that Concepcion was standing

in the doorway, wearing only sandals and a blazing tropical sarong. And she was smiling. He half rose, motioned her to the booth near the windows, and called out, "Un momentito, darling!" She pouted, but sat down—and he sent Pancho over with a drink.

"You can look it all up for yourself," Baxter was saying. "The only new, the only perfect way of committing murder. It was a United Press dispatch from Chiloe, Chile, dated December 3rd, 1946. Sam had it with him, and showed it to me. It was a honey, and as you can imagine, he lost no time in putting it to the test. By that time, Martha and he had settled into a sort of status quo, a waiting game, each trying to sit the other out. But knowing her one weak spot, Sam started to lay the preparatory groundwork. He took to leaving around the house various magazines containing articles on cardiac trouble, and once or twice when she came down to breakfast he'd remark casually on how flushed she looked. You of course know the old truism about medical students, how they almost always managed to find in themselves the symptoms of any disease they are studying? He even brought home a couple of old medical textbooks that he'd found in a secondhand bookstore, leaving them on the library table. Within a week or so Martha was watching herself for pains in the chest and left shoulder, shortness of breath and tingling of the extremities. She had swallowed the bait.

"Those who seek shall find, and before too long a time she was calling in her doctor and complaining of certain symptoms of heart trouble. He took electrocardiagrams and gave her all sorts of tests and said she probably had nothing to worry about but that she should take things easy, cut out smoking so much, and only take one drink after dinner. And he'd call in a week or ten days, at ten bucks a call—you know how most doctors make a good thing out of a rich patient. So then Martha really began worrying.

"Just at that time the couple were again without a servant, and

Sam was staying home most of the day to keep the house running. Then he'd go down to the plant at night and do what routine work still came to his desk, mostly the Newsletter and various advertisements and promotional stuff.

"The night he chose was a Monday, when Martha rarely made social engagements or held her so-called conferences with her succession of handsome young executive-type vice-presidents. Immediately after dinner she made herself a mild highball and retired to her bed with a book, as was her habit. Sam let himself out of the house and drove down to the cosmetics plant in the family Cadillac. The executive offices were of course deserted, except for the cleaning women who were sweeping up, emptying wastebaskets and ashtrays, and so on. They soon left, leaving no one else in the building except the watchman, and Sam knew that the man would on no account disturb him when the light was on in his office.

"The PBX switchboard was dead, so nobody could reasonably expect him to answer the phone. As soon as the cleaning women had put away their mops and pails and left, Sam left quietly by the side entrance, and walked down the street a few blocks to a neighborhood movie. There were a hundred or so cars parked in the vacant lot behind the theater, the owners practically certain not to need them until the end of the second feature. Sam was prepared to 'hot-wire' the ignition of one of them, but luck was with him and he found a flashy yellow coupe with the keys still in the dash. He drove quietly home, parking the car in the circular driveway. He let himself in and tiptoed upstairs; Martha was asleep as he had expected, dead to the world like the tired, healthy animal she was, with the reading light still on. She must have been a deep sleeper; anyway when she woke up she found herself wrapped up snugly in a canvas which covered her from chin to ankles, and which tied beneath the bed—"

"A restraining-sheet!" Jerry interrupted. "Like they use for alcoholics and psychotic patients."

Baxter smiled and nodded gravely. "Then my friend Sam did what had to be done. The gag slipped a little, but there was nobody to hear her—or so he thought at the time. The whole thing took only a little over two hours. He placed an empty whiskey bottle by the head of the bed, a glass beside it, left all the lights blazing and tiptoed out. Taking the canvas with him, of course."

"But how—?" Jerry cut in. Across the barroom he could see that Concepcion was tapping her little foot angrily, but he blew her a kiss and sent her another drink, turning back to the narrator. He gulped at his drink. "Go on, man!"

"Well, he got into the borrowed coupe and drove back to the parking lot behind the theater, leaving the car almost where he had found it. Then he went on down the street to the plant, let himself in by the side entrance, and sat down at his desk. From a locked file he took an imposing sheaf of neatly-pencilled manuscripts which he put in the Outgoing box for one of the secretaries to transcribe—it was copy for a sixteen-page booklet that was a week overdue, and certainly a good evening's work. He had even provided himself with a lot of spoiled and crumpled sheets to half-fill the wastebasket, and with half a dozen cigar-butts and appropriate ashes and matchstubs to litter the ashtrays and the desk.

"It took him perhaps ten minutes to arrange the office so that anyone in the world would have sworn that he had been burning the midnight oil there all evening. He took a last look around, then turned out the lights and left by the front entrance, saying goodnight to the dozing watchman as he went out. Taking his own car he drove sedately home, where began the last and most difficult phase. But his story was well worked out. He had come home and been surprised to find a light in his wife's room. He had gone in to her, discovered her sad condition, and called an ambulance at once, then her doctor. There wasn't the slightest doubt, the slightest question but that poor Martha had choked to death during a severe cardiac attack. The doctor had been treat-

ing her heart—it was all in the records. He signed the death cer-
tificate without a moment's hesitation."

Baxter beamed, and raised his glass. "Wait a minute," Jerry
Waite protested. "That alibi—"

"That was just the sort of alibi that an innocent man would
have," the other pointed out. "Not that the police ever did more
than make the most routine investigation, a bare formality because of the medical history. Sam confessed that he did have a few
moments of sweating when he learned that a necking couple had
been parked near the house during Martha's last hours. But their
statements helped rather than hindered, for they said that they
had heard the unmistakable sounds of a loud drunken party, of
women shrieking and laughing—"

"*Laughing?*"

"Oh, yes." Baxter nodded. He smiled again, showing almost all
his teeth. "I guess it's time to tell you what was in that clipping
Sam Durling carried so tenderly in his wallet. I can pretty near
quote it from memory. '*Chiloe, Chile (UP) Narciso Quesada and
his married paramour Violeta Manaos Cerpa, confessed yesterday
that they had killed her husband, Manuel Cerpa, by tickling him
to death. The couple tied Cerpa to a table and tickled the soles
of his feet with chicken feathers until he choked to death, police
said, from laughing.*' "

There was a long silence. "I'll be go to hell!" whispered Jerry
Waite, almost reverently. "You mean to say that *that* could kill?"

The other nodded. "Perhaps some people are more ticklish
than others, I don't know. But it worked fine with Manuel Cerpa
and with Sam's wife, the only two times it's been tried. At the in-
quest the coroner and his jury decided that while Sam was faith-
fully slaving away at the cosmetics factory his wife Martha had
been carrying on with some unknown lover who drove a yellow
coupe—the petting couple had noticed the car in the driveway,
of course. The carousing and love-making had brought on a heart
attack, maybe while the boyfriend was still there. It was hardly

surprising that he never came forward. Sam, of course, was duti-fully crushed and heart-broken at the funeral and after. Martha hadn't made a will, so he inherited the business and everything. After a decent interval he sold it out for something over a mil-lion dollars after taxes, and started to make preparations for a trip abroad to forget his great sorrow. . . ."

Concepcion, her bright-swathed hips swinging with feminine fury, went suddenly out of the bar, but Jerry Waite did not even notice her leaving. "And that's all there is to it?" he demanded, still awed.

"Almost all," said Baxter quietly. "When you write the story you ought to end it there, probably." He was speaking with la-borious precision, and had to grip the edge of the bar with both hands to steady himself. "Until one night—the last night Sam was ever to spend in that big house. He was peacefully asleep about four o'clock in the morning when there came a heavy hammering on the front door. Finally he got up and put on a dressing gown and went downstairs, to admit the police."

"The police! But I thought you said—"

"Wait. In spite of anything he could say or do they took him away with them. They put him in a back room in an outlying station house and beat him with a rubber-hose off and on for forty-eight hours."

Jerry's face went blank, and his eyes narrowed. "But then it isn't the perfect murder!"

"Just a minute. He finally confessed, of course. A full con-fession. He repudiated it at the trial, and hired the best lawyers he could get, but the jury found him guilty without a recom-mendation for mercy, the judge pronounced the death sentence and off he went to State's prison. The appeals failed and he sat in Death Row for what seemed like an eternity, and then one morn-ing they came and got him and slit his trousers and shaved his head and dragged him down the hall to a Little Green Door. . . ."

"And then?" Jerry prompted breathlessly.

"And then he woke up, of course—in his own bed at home. All of it had been a nightmare, after the time he dreamed he woke up and heard that hammering on the door. Call it conscience, call it what you will. But he told me he'd dreamed it several other times since then, with only minor variations on the theme. Once or twice he's actually got as far as the electric chair itself, but he's always awakened in time. Devilish real it was, though—at least as he described it." Baxter shuddered. "So there's the story of The Perfect Murder, my young friend. Shall we have another bottle of cognac?"

Jerry Waite thought he had had enough. "Perhaps we both have," the other agreed. They went upstairs together, with Jerry steadying the other man. It turned out that Baxter's suite was only a few doors down from Jerry's, at the far end of the corridor. "How about coming in for a nightcap?" the older man asked hopefully.

Jerry thanked him and said no.

"We could even play some gin-rummy maybe? Or some chess?"

"Not tonight, thanks." Jerry turned toward his own room, but over his shoulder he could see Baxter struggling with his key, shoulders slumped. Jerry locked his door, slipped out of his clothes and threw himself raw on the bed, letting the softness of the little breeze from the Pacific cool his body. "Perfect murder my eye," he finally decided. "I don't believe it. The old guy was lonesome and he just wanted somebody to talk to and an excuse to stay up and drink himself blotto. But he was good—he almost had me believing it for awhile." Jerry turned over and was asleep in five minutes.

Something jerked him awake just before daylight, and he sat up in bed and cursed the parrots until he realized that this voice was no jungle-fowl greeting the new day. It was a man somewhere here in the hotel, screaming as if he were being torn to pieces by the redhot pincers of Torquemada's inquisitors. It is usually a good idea to mind one's own business in a foreign hotel at night, especially if like Jerry Waite you can speak only a few words of the language, but there are sounds no human ear can long endure.

He grabbed up a robe and ran out into the hall, joining the other guests who were excitedly gathering there. They moved uncertainly down the length of the hall, toward the door from behind which the hellish screams were coming. Finally the manager appeared, a big blond Mexican with black trousers over his nightshirt, and after some fumbling with a ring of keys the door was opened and they went in and woke up "Mr. Baxter" and he stopped screaming.

Jerry was foolishly reminded of the line in the Katzenjammer Kids comic strip—"Rollo, you brought it on yourself!" He couldn't help wondering what would happen if someday the dream went on past the point where the executioner reached for the switch, but probably Baxter-Durling would always wake up just in time. That was the hell of it. Anyway, from one point of view you could still call it The Perfect Murder.

AUTHOR'S POSTSCRIPT: The hotel bar, the señorita and the crashing bore who tied himself to the famous visiting writer are all real. Or were once. The gimmick—the press clipping of a murder by tickling is genuine. And it seemed to me that a man, not basically the murderer type, might be punished by his subconscious so that he received the punishment which the law missed. Sort of a deathwish thing. The New England Conscience.

LAWRENCE G. BLOCHMAN

The Girl with the Burgundy Lips

MARSHALL T. CUSTER
VILLA MISLAID HORIZON
HOLLYWOOD CALIF

YOUR FICTIONAL DETECTIVES ARE ALWAYS SMARTER THAN THE POLICE DICKS AND YOUR BEST SELLER QUOTE MYSTERY OF THE MADCAP MODEL UNQUOTE BEARS RESEMBLANCE TO MURDER OF OLIVIA BRENN CURRENTLY BAFFLING NEW YORK COPS. AS OLIVIA WAS SAN FRANCISCO GIRL PAPERS HERE WANT COMPLETEST COVERAGE. WILL YOU FLY EAST AND SOLVE MURDER FOR THOUSAND PER WEEK PLUS EXPENSES MAXIMUM FOUR WEEKS

CARP, MAN ED
ALLIANCE

BENJAMIN CARP
MANAGING EDITOR
FAR WEST NEWSPAPER ALLIANCE
SAN FRANCISCO CALIF

YOU HAVE BOUGHT SOLUTION OLIVIA BRENN MURDER BUT FOUR WEEKS NEEDLESS AND EXTRAVAGANT. SUGGEST ONE WEEK PLUS TWO THOUSAND BONUS UPON CRACKING MYSTERY. FLYING EAST TONIGHT SEND CHECK CARE MYSTERY WRITERS OF AMERICA 228 WEST 24TH ST NEW YORK

MARSHALL T. CUSTER

New York, May 15

Mr. Ben Carp, Man. Ed.,
Far West Newspaper Alliance,
San Francisco, Calif.

Dear Carp:

Filed my first story Night Press Rate Collect last night and I
trust you've given it a proper play on page one. I must apologize
for slight delay. But it took that half-wit lawyer so long to get me
out of jail that I thought he'd carried the case to the Supreme
Court in Washington. Naturally I did not wire all details but am
air-mailing same so you can send $500 to Joseph Kittle, attorney
at law, as his retainer.

First let me veto the New York cops' theory that Olivia Brenn
was murdered by Ruby Loring, her roommate. True, Ruby disappeared and has not been seen since Olivia's body was discovered, but I don't see her as the killer. I'll begin at the beginning.

Olivia Brenn had been living for six months in a little two-
room apartment at 7½ Minetta Lane, which is an alley in Green-
wich Village just south of Washington Square. As all the world
knows by now, Olivia was an artist's model. She was small, slim
and shapely. She wore her sleek dark hair boyishly short. She
posed in the nude. About two months ago when the posing sea-
son was slack and the pickings slimmer than a nine-day diet, she
took in Ruby to share the rent. Ruby modeled, too, but not in
the nude. She was about the same size as Olivia, except she had
more chest expansion. She also had long blonde hair. And whereas
Olivia wore severe suits and blouses, Ruby went in for girly-
girly-fluffs and flounces. She was fine for modeling big picture
hats and full sleeves and filmy furbelows.

Well, the cops think Ruby and Olivia got along like a couple
of alley cats eyeing the same fish-head. Nobody ever saw them together. Apparently they never went places together—specifically
not to the studio of an artist named Henry Pallett on Washington Square, South, although they both posed for Pallett. Ruby
posed for magazine covers, which he painted for his ham and

eggs, and Olivia posed for the arty art which he painted for fame and posterity. The cops have been making faces at Pallett, hoping he'd admit that the two gals were fighting over him, but he says no, his interest in Ruby and Olivia was purely artistic, his senti- mental nature being completely absorbed by a tomato named Jeanne Woods.

Of course it wouldn't occur to a cop that maybe Jeanne was jealous of the way Olivia posed in the nude, and expressed her jealousy through homicide. Or that the blonde Ruby had maybe been doing a little extracurricular posing with Pallett herself and did a quick fade-out when she found what happened to Olivia. I don't say I've adopted this theory myself, but I put it down here just for the record.

When I got to New York yesterday, I sauntered over to the scene of the crime. I walked up the rickety stairway to the third floor of 7½ Minetta Lane. The door to the late Olivia's apart- ment wasn't locked, so I went in. A meek-looking little guy with his hat on was sitting on a studio couch, reading a book which I recognized immediately as The Mystery of the Madcap Model. I congratulated him on his literary taste.

"Who the hell are you?" this guy wanted to know.

"I'm the author of that book you're reading," I said, "and I'll be glad to autograph it for you."

"Not for me, you won't," the little guy said. "I don't go for this tripe. This happens to belong to the former tenant of this apartment and—"

"I know, don't prompt me," I said. "You find a similarity with the Olivia Brenn murder and you're looking through the book for clues."

"I got all the clues I need," said the little guy. Then he intro- duced himself: Kenneth Kilkenny, detective first grade, Homicide Squad. He looked more like a shipping clerk than a police dick. New York's finest must be pretty hard up for detectives if they have to take on runts.

"Don't be so dogmatic," I told Kilkenny. "Let's not approach this case from the orthodox police point of view. Are you positive, for instance, that Olivia Brenn was strangled?"

Kilkenny just grunted. He was deep in the book again. I could see he was gripped by it. I went on:

"I mean the effects of some poisons resemble the effects of strangulation. You know—purple face. The neurotoxins. Take cyanide—"

"*You* take cyanide," Kilkenny interrupted, still not looking at me.

"What does the medical examiner's office say about the possibility of poison?" I said.

"Look," Kilkenny retorted. "Why don't you go write another book? You're not invited to this murder."

"Sure I am. The Far West Newspaper Alliance invited me at great expense." I opened a closet door. I saw a couple of suits that must have belonged to Olivia, and five or six fluffy dresses that would have been Ruby Loring's. There were Cuban heels and tight little felt cloches to match one, and high French heels and floppy hats to go with the other. Detective Kilkenny looked up from the book.

"You do look a little like a storybook sleuth with that canary shirt and emerald-green tie," he said, "but your pearl-gray featherweight felt hat should be pulled down a little more over one eye. And where's your beautiful blonde secretary? I thought you guys never went out on a case except with a starry-eyed dame who gets waylaid by thugs so you can rescue her."

"My blonde amanuensis ran away to be a bareback rider in the circus," I told him. "I now rely exclusively on my faithful hip flask and my little gray cells."

"Go find yourself a big desk to put your feet on, so you can think hard and analyze clues," Kilkenny said. "You can't stay here."

"Sure I can," I said. "You can't throttle the freedom of the press, Kilkenny. I stand on my constitutional rights."

Kilkenny closed the book and a bookmark fell out. It was a sales check from Hoffman's. I could read *Silk slip $35,* but I pretended I didn't see it. I went over to the dressing table and looked at the cosmetics. There was Burgundy lipstick, sun-tan powder and dark rouge for Olivia. The tangerine lipstick and light-colored powder must have been Ruby's. I strolled into the bathroom.

"You'd look more authentic if you had a few teeth knocked out, a black eye, and one arm in a sling," Kilkenny said. "Why don't you go find yourself a drunken brawl, so I'll know for sure you're a shamus?"

"I'm not a brawler, Kilkenny. I'm the cerebral type. I collect orchids and rare jade. And I like it fine right here."

"I'm warning you, Custer," Kilkenny said. "If you don't scram I'll have to jug you for obstructing justice."

"I'm not obstructing anything," I said. "I'm merely giving you the benefit of my trained deductive brain. For instance, while the evidence shows Ruby left this apartment in a hurry, it also indicates she did not expect to go far or stay away long: she left her dresses behind in the closet. She did expect to be gone overnight, however. Did you notice she took her toothbrush with her? There's only one toothbrush in the bathroom and one brush and comb on the dresser. Did you notice?"

"I do my own noticing," Kilkenny said, very tough. "Get out."

He had come up behind me, and somehow I got the idea he was going to sock me. Turning abruptly, I put up my arm to guard my chin, and I knocked his hat off. He was as bald as a Chihuahua. I laughed. I don't know why the idea of a bald-headed detective should strike me so funny, but it always does. I couldn't stop laughing—until Kilkenny snapped the handcuffs on me.

"Since you know so much about this case," he said, "I'm going to hold you as a material witness."

Well, you can score an error against me for not guessing that Kilkenny had no sense of humor. Anyhow, I was in the clink for three hours before I could get hold of this lawyer Kittle, and he took another six hours to get me out.

And now I must get to work and dig up the murderer of Olivia Brenn for you. Keep clean, Carp.

Yours in crime,
Marshall T. Custer

New York, May 16.

Dear Carp:

I just filed my second story on the Brenn case, and as you can see I am making progress.

Today I went back to 7½ Minetta Lane, which is a very old building, obviously erected before the invention of fresh air. It is three stories high and half a story wide and is wedged in between the corner delicatessen and a modern apartment house. It would probably have been torn down a century ago, only there isn't room to build anything on the site except maybe an elevator shaft. Besides, it's historic. Two famous poets and a famous etcher starved to death on the premises.

The modern tenants are also slightly tainted with Art, not only the two models who occupied the third-floor cells—the late Olivia and the missing Ruby—but also Pierre Duval, who lives just under them. Duval is an unemployed winetaster who is also a part-time painter. Every Sunday he goes to Washington Square and paints the arch.

The apartment under Duval, the ground-floor mole run, is the habitat of a sausage-and-pickle-juggler named Franz Ziegler who operates the delicatessen next door. Ziegler took over the shop five years ago and ran it with his wife until she died last year. He now carries on with a one-eyed lame-brained pumpernickel slicer and puts in a fourteen-hour day among his beloved cheeses and salami.

I had spotted this delicatessen yesterday, and while I was languishing in the poky, I figured it would be just the place to go for odd bits of information about Olivia and Ruby. There are two reasons: *A,* when a widower of one year, still in the prime of life,

starts thinking about the opposite sex in a tender way, his attention is going to be focused pretty close to home if he spends fourteen hours a day behind the counter; and *B*, two chicks who get
their feed money from such a whimsical trade as modeling are
apt to be on good terms with a guy who could stake them to a
pastrami sandwich when their professional posing wasn't paying off.

When I dropped in on Ziegler, he was smacking his lips and
unpacking a lot of imported beer and Limburger cheese. He was
pushing forty, but there wasn't a gray hair in his sandy crew cut.
He had a round face with two dimples and blue eyes.

"I understand Olivia Brenn ran up quite an unpaid bill with
you," I said, taking out my wallet. "If you'll tell me the total—"

"Miss Brenn never came near this place," Ziegler said. "I guess
it wasn't good enough for her. She never spoke to me."

"What about Ruby Loring?" I asked.

His face changed and I knew I'd hit pay dirt. He growled: "I
got nothing more to say. I told the police everything."

I explained that I was a writer, not a cop, and that I didn't
share the police theory that Ruby had killed Olivia. I said: "You
haven't heard from Ruby since the murder, have you?"

He said he hadn't. He had no idea where she might be. He
looked at me strangely as he said this.

I thought I saw tears in his eyes, so I said, "You were pretty
sweet on Ruby, weren't you?"

"I was crazy about her," he said. "I still am. We're going to
be married as soon as her divorce is final."

I asked him where her ex-husband was. He didn't know. Ruby
hadn't heard in ages. He didn't send her any alimony.

"So you've been taking care of her?" I asked.

"Not really. She worked, you know. A model. But when things
were tough she used to come in here to eat."

"And you gave her little presents now and then?" I remembered the sales check. "Maybe a slip from Hoffman's?"

"Oh, that," Ziegler said. "Yes, I gave her little presents once in a while. Don't get the wrong idea, though. There was nothing between us. She was very strict about that. Nothing until her divorce was final and we could get married."

Then he told me about the last time he saw her. On the evening of the murder Ziegler and Ruby had dinner together—on a small roast squab, some cucumber salad, Gruyère cheese and beer, and fresh raspberry tarts. They ate in the third-floor apartment, because Olivia was out. And Ziegler had a little present for Ruby—the new silk slip from Hoffman's.

"She was crazy about the slip," Ziegler said. "It was handmade, with little red lip-prints embroidered here and there on the front. She tried it on right away and said it looked fine."

"Did she kiss you to thank you?" I asked.

"Don't go getting wrong ideas," Ziegler said. "She just kissed me, that's all. There's nothing wrong about that."

After dinner Ruby went out to meet some man who had promised her a photographic job for some dress account. She told Ziegler she'd stop by for a glass of beer when she came home, but she never did. He hasn't seen her since, he says.

It was a rainy night and business was slow, so Ziegler closed his delicatessen shortly after eleven. He went to his apartment, took off his shoes, and settled down with a book to wait for Ruby. He didn't read much, because of the infernal racket in the apartment just above—the apartment of Pierre Duval, the unemployed winetaster. The noise was loud and bacchanalian— shrieks of female laughter, a strong alcoholic baritone, thumping on the floor, and the crashing of glass.

By midnight Ziegler had absorbed more decibels than he could stand. He climbed one flight and banged on Duval's door. No response. Duval continued singing, with a shrill obbligato of woman's laughter. Ziegler tried the door. It was unlocked, so he opened it.

The place was a shambles. There were several empty bottles on the floor, and a half-empty gallon jug of red wine on the table.

There was a pair of woman's shoes on the mantelpiece, a woman's blouse draped over the floor lamp, and a skirt hanging from Duval's Sunday easel.

Duval was sprawled in an armchair with his hair in his eyes, wine stains on his shirt, and Olivia Brenn on his lap. Olivia was half undressed.

"I was so mad," Ziegler said, "I told them if they didn't stop their racket, I was going to call the police."

The party calmed down immediately. Ziegler went back to his book and fell asleep. He woke up a little before one. He thought Ruby might have come by while he dozed and that he hadn't heard her knock.

He went up to the third floor to see if she was home. The apartment door was ajar, he says, and the light was on, so he looked inside. Ruby wasn't there, but Olivia Brenn was.

Olivia was lying on the floor. At first Ziegler thought she was just drunk, but a second look told him she was dead. Her face was blue and her eyes were bulging.

Ziegler rushed back to his own place to call the police, and that was the end of the story so far as he was concerned.

I haven't got Duval's version yet, as apparently he's unemployed no longer. I'll catch him tonight.

Button up well, Carp.

Yours in crime,
Marshall T. Custer

Dear Carp:

New York, May 17.

Was that story I filed last night full of heart interest? It should have been, because as Aeschylus said, "Bronze is the mirror of the form; wine, of the heart." And I tell you confidentially, Carp, that following my talk with Pierre Duval last night I was full of both wine and Aeschylus. Duval is a generous man with both potation and quotation.

I intercepted Duval coming into Minetta Lane with his arms

full of bottles. He is a tall, dark guy with droopy eyes, droopy nose and droopy mustache. To those who like mustaches, he is probably handsome. When I said I understood he was a wine-taster, he corrected me: "I am an oenologist, sir. An oenologist."

He confirmed that he was no longer an unemployed oenologist. He has been retained by a big keg-to-bottle firm. He is testing wines for acidity, specific gravity, etc., to determine which blend will best hold bubbles of carbon dioxide for synthetic sparkle.

Duval was carrying several bottles of homework, as well as a few little vintage items from France which he had noticed around the shop and on which somebody might want his opinion. One of these was a bottle of Château Margaux which was opened simultaneously with our interview. You will be delighted to hear, Carp, that it was the best Bordeaux I ever tasted.

Well, as we sat there surrounding the Château Margaux and surrounded by Duval's paintings of the Washington Square arch on Sunday, I asked about the orgy on the night of the murder.

"Orgy, my eye!" Duval said. "We were just having a little wine for the stomach's sake. I was celebrating my new job, and Olivia just dropped in to sample the raw materials I was working with."

"Do people usually disrobe when they sample the raw materials of your trade?" I asked.

"Olivia didn't really disrobe," Duval said. "She spilled some wine on her blouse and skirt, and you know how red wine stains if you don't get it out right away. She took off her things to wash out the spots and hung them to dry while we went on sampling. She wasn't undressed, actually. She had her slip on."

"Ziegler says she was sitting in your lap," I reminded Duval. "Was she in love with you or vice versa?"

"We were very good friends," Duval admitted.

Duval said Olivia left him about half past midnight and he fell asleep immediately. He was awakened a little after one by Ziegler running down the stairs, yelling for the police.

Duvall said he knew Pallett, the artist. He didn't know if
Pallett had been making passes at Olivia beyond the call of artistic duty. He thought not. But Jeanne Woods, Pallett's girl, could
have been jealous of the model anyhow—maybe murderously
jealous. And Duval quoted at me from the Song of Solomon:
"Love is strong as death; jealousy is cruel as the grave."

As for the missing Ruby Loring. Duval said he scarcely knew
her. She wasn't his type. She drank beer.

"I don't think Ruby strangled Olivia," he said. "It was a man's
job. The finger marks were still on the poor gal's throat when I
saw her—big fingers. Ruby was a small girl, like Olivia."

Duval was just pulling the cork out of a tall, tapering bottle of
French Rhine when there was a knock on the door. It was Detective Kenneth Kilkenny, Homicide Squad.

"Hello, Kilkenny," I said. "I was over to West Twentieth Street
today to have a look at the Homicide Squad in its native habitat.
I didn't see you anywhere around."

"I was at the morgue," Kilkenny said. "How come we don't see
you at the morgue, Custer?"

"The Custer method involves the study of live characters, not
dead ones," I told him. "Incidentally, Duval says there were finger marks on Olivia's throat. You wouldn't hold out on me,
would you, Kilkenny?"

"You mentioned poison the other night," Kilkenny said. "Do
you know the autopsy showed small subcutaneous hemorrhages
in Olivia's scalp?"

"That sounds like strangulation," I said. "What else did the
autopsy show?"

"The medical examiner's not finished yet," Kilkenny said.

"Not yet? After almost a week? Where I come from we finish
an autopsy in an hour."

"I'll bet," Kilkenny said. "We take a month sometimes. By the
way, I turned Pallett and his girl friend loose today.

"Well, well. Exonerated?"

"Not exactly. But he's having a one-man show in his studio to-morrow. Invitations went out three weeks ago, so we'll let the show go on. Too bad you're not invited, Custer. You could sleuth your head off among all the free liquor and freewheeling Village dames."

"I'll be there," I said. "Early."

Duval poured a glass of wine. "How about a beaker of dragon's blood, Minion of the Law?" he said.

"Not while I'm working," Kilkenny said. "Well, good night, all you lovely people. See you in jail."

After Kilkenny left, Duval and I had a few more whiffs of the grape. Just as Duvall seemed about to burst into song, I asked him if he had a key to Olivia's apartment. He said no, but the no was partially concealed by a slight eructation, so I said: "In these old houses, I'll bet any key will open all the doors. Let's try."

We tried, and—surprise, surprise! Duval's key did open the late Olivia's door. Duval wouldn't come inside the apartment with me, though. He said he'd wait outside to warn me in case Kilkenny should start gumshoeing up the stairs while I was there.

I just took a quick look around the bathroom. The lone tooth-brush was still in the glass over the washstand. I took the brush, popped it into an envelope, and slipped it into my pocket.

I had one more stirrup cup with Duval, then sank my spurs into shanks' mare and galloped home to bed.

Good night to you, dear Carp, and don't forget to take your vitamins.

> Yours in crime,
> Marshall T. Custer

New York, May 18.

Dear Carp:

Better get that $2,000 bonus check ready and certified. The Olivia Brenn case is in the bag, but Kilkenny threatens to lock me up again if we print the latest before he gives the word, so please consider these details of Pallett's studio party as top secret until I flash you.

The *vernissage,* as we artists call it, was scheduled for five in the afternoon. There was a preview for the press at four thirty, on account of the news value of the pictures modeled by the murdered Olivia and the missing Ruby. So I dropped in at four o'clock sharp to cast an eye over Pallett and his jealous tomato.

Kilkenny was there first, of course—with his hat on. Franz Ziegler was also there, stacking sandwiches like cordwood. One table, devoted to whiskey and sausage for the working press and noncommercial artists, was Ziegler's department. A second table, featuring a mosaic of midget cakes around a brass samovar, was for critics and connoisseurs. A third table offered microscopic hors d'oeuvres for dilettantes and possible buyers.

Ziegler had unveiled his *smörgåsbord,* stowed his several reams of waxed paper and other debris in the kitchenette, and departed while I was making friends with Pallett. I didn't even try to get through Jeanne Woods's painted war mask and supplementary hostile grimaces. For my money, her Nile-green hostess pajamas could have been made of cast iron.

Pallett was wearing his artist's uniform of midnight-blue corduroy and Windsor tie. He followed me around while I looked at his canvases. They had a decided blue tone, like Picasso in his Blue Period.

The Brenn nudes were painted with bold, coarse strokes, obviously with the flat of a dry, broad brush. The Ruby Loring magazine covers were done with a fine, glossy finish, every hair in place. But despite the difference in style, the features of the two girls looked pretty much alike—the work of an artist who has struck a vein some art editor likes.

"Free yourself from commercial art, Pallett," I said. "You have talent, but you're in a rut. Everything you paint looks like a cover girl."

"I'll make the break someday," Pallett said.

"You're not getting any younger," I said. "Tempera fugits."

About this time the flash bulbs and whiskey corks began popping all over the place. One corner of my jaundiced eye caught Kilkenny sneaking off to the kitchenette. I followed.

The kitchenette was a little bigger than a phone booth. I guess the girl friend didn't do much home cooking for Pallett. The pots and pans had an inch of dust on them. So did the little gas range. Kilkenny opened the oven and I noticed that the roaster inside didn't seem dusty at all. Kilkenny noticed it, too. He lifted the cover off the roaster and took out a tightly wadded bundle of silk.

When he unwadded the silk, a strand of coarse blonde hair fell out. The silk was a lady's slip with little red lips embroidered on the front of it. On the back was a deep red stain as big as a man's hand.

"Looks like blood, Kilkenny," I said. "Let's rush it over to my room. I've got the chemicals to make a quick benzidine test."

"You!" Kilkenny snorted. "If you print one word of this before the murderer is under lock and key, I'll toss you right back in the clink. Go out there and mingle with the guests."

I went out and mingled like a percentage girl with the rent due. I watched artists talking about the pictures with their thumbs. I saw Pierre Duval come in and consume at least 3,000 calories. I saw Kilkenny go out with his evidence in a brown paper bag. Then I sneaked out myself—to write this letter and clean up a few little odds and ends. I am now going back to Pallett's studio.

I expect to file my final story tonight. It should catch the late-afternoon editions. Say your prayers regularly, Carp, and brush your teeth twice a day.

Yours in crime,
Marshall T. Custer

New York, May 19.

Dear Carp:

Received your wire of congratulations, but noted no tele-graphic money order attached. Thanks anyhow.

Well, here's how it all happened: About ten last night Duval and I were sitting among the Duval collection of Washington Square arches on Sunday, testing various methods of dimming the glow we had contracted at Pallett's studio party. We had just about decided on a bottle of rainwater Madeira that Duval had found in some old cellar, when Kilkenny came barging in like six atoms in search of a chain reaction.

Kilkenny waved a yellow teletype message under my nose and yelled: "Damn you, Custer, you go right back to jail. Listen to this: San Francisco Gazette headline—'Gazette Reporter Cracks N. Y. Mystery. Writer Captures Model's Killer Singlehanded.' I told you—"

"You told me not to break the story until the murderer was under lock and key. Well, he is. Right here."

"Nuts, Custer. Duval's not the guy."

"Stop being so mysterious, Kilkenny," I said. "Everybody knows by now that Franz Ziegler killed Olivia. Modulate your voice."

Kilkenny didn't modulate anything. He kept yelling I'd tipped off Ziegler by breaking confidence, and how Ziegler disappeared from his delicatessen three hours ago.

"I've had these buildings surrounded for two days," he shouted. "I don't know how he got through. But I got three hundred men combing the city for him."

"They're combing the wrong places," I said. "Ziegler didn't leave the building. He is now locked in Mr. Duval's genuine antique pre-Revolutionary bathroom. Have a look."

While Duval was unlocking the bathroom, I told Kilkenny how we slipped Ziegler a Mickey. I got Ziegler to come upstairs to taste some genuine Hochheimer and to identify some dime-store earrings I said I thought might be Ruby's. I put a few drops of choral hydrate in his wine, and when he passed out we laid him in the bathtub.

When we opened the door, Ziegler was still reclining peacefully in the tub, a little damp behind the ears and above the eyes because the leaky shower was dripping on his head. Kilkenny put the cuffs on Ziegler and jumped for the telephone.

"You can tell your side-kicks, Kilkenny," I said, "that they can stop looking for Ruby Loring. Ruby and Olivia were the same person."

"All right, Sherlock Holmes," Kilkenny said when he had hung up. "How did you discover the masquerade?"

I told him it was easy, once I had a good look at the toothbrush. It had traces of two lipsticks on it—Burgundy and tangerine.

"Even in the improbable event that both girls used the same brush," I said, "we must remember that few women brush their teeth while wearing makeup. One exception, yes. But two, living together and using the same toothbrush, is beyond the realm of plausibility. Therefore, Olivia and Ruby were one. The fact that they were never seen together bears this out. So does the striking resemblance of their features in Pallett's paintings.

"I assume that Olivia created the character of Ruby in order to get more work—double work with Pallett, for instance. The anatomical differential, both hair and build, was obviously synthetic, as borne out by the fact that Ruby never posed in the nude. The masquerade started out as a business proposition, but I guess Olivia got carried away by the spirit of the thing and decided to create a private life for each of her incarnations. As the blonde Ruby she was practically living off Ziegler, although she played coy and held him off at arm's length. At the same time she was having fun and games—as Olivia—with Duval.

"After she dined with Ziegler on the night of the murder, the synthetic Ruby took off her blonde wig and her falsies and went down to drink with Duval, as Olivia. But she apparently did not take off the new silk slip which Ziegler had given her. So when Ziegler stormed into Duval's at midnight, he must have recognized Ruby's slip on Olivia, and realized the truth. He then later obviously went upstairs, confronted Olivia with the facts, and killed her in a jealous rage. He took away the slip, the wig and the falsies to prolong the legend of the two separate individuals, and to cast suspicion on the mythical Ruby. By the way, Kilkenny, why don't you look for the wig and falsies?"

"We found 'em the day after the murder," Kilkenny said, "in an ash can in Washington Square."

"Very clever," I said. "So you went on talking about Ruby to give the killer a sense of security. And by keeping the heat on Pallett and his tomato, you trapped Ziegler into planting the silk slip in Pallett's oven when he delivered the sandwiches today. Am I right, Kilkenny? What do you think of the Custer method now?"

Kilkenny admitted it was okay for fiction, but that my deductions weren't backed by proof that would stand up in court. The police, he said, had scientific basis for the same conclusions. For instance, an analysis of stomach contents during the autopsy showed traces of wine—which Olivia drank—and also cucumber and raspberry seeds, which matched the menu Ziegler said he fed to Ruby. Therefore Ruby was Olivia. And the clincher was the red stain on the slip which turned up at Pallett's. The medical examiner's chemist said it was wine.

"I am dying of curiosity," Kilkenny said, "to know how the Custer method put the finger on Ziegler."

"Why, it just stands to reason," I said. "Pure logic and deduction. Given the set of circumstances and character relationships, it couldn't possibly be anybody else."

"Sure, for a book," Kilkenny said. "But for a jury, you got to have evidence. If I could get a conviction on pure logic and deduction, I would have grabbed Ziegler six days ago. But I had to wait until he furnished me with proof, which he did this afternoon. He left a beautiful set of fingerprints on Henry Pallett's roaster, and on the silk slip. I guess he didn't know we can develop prints off cloth with nitrates and iodine vapor."

So you see, Carp, how unimaginative and uninspired police methods are.

"Furthermore," Kilkenny went on, "since this Ziegler seems to have a jealous and murderous nature, we're going to exhume the late Mrs. Ziegler tomorrow. We may find poison."

"Speaking of poison," Duval interrupted, "how about a drop of this excellent rainwater, Minion of the Law?"

"Rainwater hell," said Kilkenny. "I've finished the job. Pour me a glass of wine."

I'm seeing Joseph Kittle today, and if the learned counselor has got his fee from you and can clear me with the law, I'll see you tomorrow.

Keep your fountain pen filled, Carp, and your checkbook handy.

Yours in crime,
Marshall T. Custer

EDITOR'S POSTSCRIPT. *The Girl with the Burgundy Lips* started as an assigned story, to be done with errors in matters all the way "from potations to quotations." It ended up appearing without errors in *Colliers* and with errors in *Ellery Queen Mystery Magazine*, for the detection of which prizes were awarded to the readers.

We have reprinted here the version without prizes.

ANDREW GARVE

The Man Who Wasn't Scared

IT was in September 1957, shortly before my retirement as Chief Constable of Downshire, that the man who was soon to become notorious as the "Downshire Terror" first showed his hand. A chap named John Iles, a driving instructor employed by the Excelsior School of motoring in Donchester, had been to the pictures after work and had left his car parked in a quiet run-in beside the School's premises, as he usually did. When he went to collect it just before ten o'clock he found that someone had torn off a headlamp, forced a door and slashed the upholstery. On the driver's seat there was a cutting from the *Donchester Herald* reporting a court case in which Iles had recently been involved—one of his pupils had panicked during a lesson and mounted the pavement before the dual control could be used, slightly injuring a woman. Pinned to the cutting was a sheet of paper on which the wrecker had pencilled in block capitals: FIFTEEN KILLED AND 112 INJURED IN ROAD ACCIDENTS IN DOWNSHIRE LAST MONTH! NO WONDER, WITH MEN LIKE YOU IN CHARGE OF NEW DRIVERS! WHY DON'T YOU PAY ATTENTION WHEN YOU'RE ON THE JOB? IF IT HAPPENS AGAIN, YOU'LL BE FOR IT!

It was an ugly little incident, and we did all we could to discover who was responsible. But there wasn't much to go on. The job must have been done after dark, for no one had seen anyone near the car. The wrecker had evidently worn gloves, for there were no useful fingerprints. The paper on which the message had been written was common typing paper, un-watermarked, and could have been bought at any stationer's. The message itself afforded no clue, except that it pointed to a reasonably literate person. We interviewed a number of people who might conceivably have had a private grudge against Iles, including the woman who had been knocked down by the School car, the pupil who had mounted the pavement, and several others who had failed to pass their driving test after tuition—but we got nowhere. Iles himself was very upset by the incident, and the School had to give him some sick leave.

We were still working on the case when, a few days later, the first murder was committed. A young man named Jocelyn Wade, a member of a well-to-do county family, had been up to London for the day in his fast sports car, and on his way back had dropped into a quiet country pub, the Dog and Feathers, about five miles beyond Donchester. He had left the pub just before ten —and at ten-thirty his body had been found lying beside his car in the car park. His skull had been crushed by two blows from a heavy instrument, possibly a spanner, delivered by someone who must have crept up behind him. On the car seat, the murderer had left a sheet of typing paper, with the pencilled words: THIS MAN DROVE THROUGH DONCHESTER HIGH STREET AT 42 M.P.H. THIS EVENING. WATCH OUT, YOU DOWNSHIRE SPEED FIENDS! IT MAY BE YOUR TURN NEXT! Once again, there were no fingerprints, no material clues. Once again, the assault had taken place in darkness, and the assailant had got clear away.

We knew now that there was a maniac in our midst—a man with his own crazy notion of a road safety campaign. Next morning the activities of the "Downshire Terror" were the chief topic of conversation all over the country. The popular newspapers were full of him. Hordes of reporters arrived in Donchester, virtually taking over the County Hotel. They wanted to know not merely what we were doing about the Wade murder, but how we proposed to prevent any more deaths. On that point, it wasn't very easy to be reassuring. The peculiar grimness of all these multiple-murder cases, where sudden attacks are made out-of-doors after dark and no personal motive links the murderer and victim, is that the police usually have to wait for further attacks before they can close their net. What I did say was that one of the best safeguards might well be for everyone to drive with exceptional care in Downshire until the Terror was apprehended.

It seemed certain that we should need outside help in our task, and I had already asked for a conference at the Home Office to concert plans. But before it could be held, there was a second murder. This time the victim was a woman, a Mrs. Fray. She had been visiting friends in Donchester and had set off home in her car soon after nine o'clock. At ten she had been found lying beside the car on a grass verge, not far from her house, with her head battered in. The usual piece of paper on the driving seat said: THIS WOMAN FAILED TO STOP AT THE HALT SIGN IN DONCHESTER THIS AFTERNOON. The front near-side tyre of her car was flat, but there was no puncture—the valve cap had been removed and the valve loosened. It seemed probable that the Terror had marked her down during the day, followed her to her friend's house, loosened the valve in the street after dark, and assaulted her on the road home when the flat tyre had forced her to stop.

The new murder gave even greater urgency to the conference at the Home Office. It was attended by several experienced officers from the Yard and by the Chief Constables of the counties adjoining Downshire. They were all short-handed, for like Downshire their territories lay between London and the sea and at this time of year the crowded state of the roads and the frequent accidents were a heavy strain on police manpower. However, they agreed that reinforcements for Downshire were essential. The best hope seemed to lie in greatly strengthened night patrols, so that even if the next murder couldn't be prevented we should at least have early information on which to act. The Terror, after his butchering excursions, must have a lot of blood on him, and his first need would be to rush off to some quiet retreat where he could remove all traces. Our aim must be to intercept him. Our counter-measures included dividing the county up into sections with a system of road checks that could be brought instantly into operation. We also fixed up a decoy plan, by which plain clothes men in private cars would drive around the built-up areas of the county at more than the legal limit in the hope that the Terror would eventually follow one of them.

For a week after the conference, nothing happened. Then the Terror suddenly struck again—and this time it was in broad daylight! A lorry driver named Albert Stokes had stopped his vehicle in a lay-by some ten miles outside the county boundary, and after lunch had stretched out in his cab for a nap. He was found there in the middle of the afternoon, dead from multiple head injuries. The message on the seat said: THIS MAN PASSED ME IN DONCHESTER AT 32 M.P.H. HIS LEGAL LIMIT IS 20 M.P.H.

It was now clear that the Terror, though still concentrating on what happened in Downshire, was prepared to pursue his victim outside the county if necessary. That meant that every driver who passed through was taking a risk, unless he drove impeccably. The odds against any one person being picked on were, of course, considerable, but by now the word "Downshire" had become synonymous in the public mind with sudden, violent death, and most people preferred not to take chances. There was no great falling off in the amount of traffic, but there was a marked improvement in road behaviour and an impressive observance of all speed limits. At this rate, the Terror would soon be short of victims.

Another week went by—a week of unremitting inquiry into the earlier incidents and of ceaseless vigilance by the road patrols. By now, a huge force of police had been drafted into the area. As one quiet day followed another, I began to think that the Terror had abandoned his campaign. Any sane person would certainly have been deterred by our preparations. But, late one night, he killed again. His victim, a man named Lever, was found with the usual head injuries only a short time after the assault.

His car was in a ditch in an unfrequented lane, and it looked as though he had driven it there himself. The message on the seat said: THIS MAN WAS DRUNK IN CHARGE! Within seconds of the discovery, our machinery went smoothly into action, and we must have missed the escaping murderer by the narrowest of margins.

We brought in yet more police and increased the patrols. For nearly a fortnight, Downshire waited in a state of mounting tension. Then, suddenly—and in a way I hadn't foreseen—the end came.

I was driving home one night, very tired after a late conference at the station. I had just turned into the High Street when a small black car passed me. For a moment I could hardly believe my eyes, for it was doing over 40 m.p.h. in a restricted area—and drivers in Downshire simply didn't do that sort of thing any longer! Then I decided that it must be one of my decoys. I put on speed until I could read the number. I knew all the decoy numbers, and it wasn't one of them. I stepped hard on the accelerator, and so did the chap in front. Two other police cars swung in from side turnings and joined in the chase. We raced through the town at sixty miles an hour, and I passed the black car at sixty-five. Its brakes squealed as I slowed down in front of it, there was a crash as it hit me, and then it swerved off the road through a garden fence. As it stopped the driver jumped out and began to run. I gave chase, and so did half a dozen other officers, and we caught him in less than fifty yards.

It was the driving instructor, John Iles! He was wearing a long, plastic raincoat, and there was blood all over it. He'd just done his last job!

We found out afterwards that he'd been spending his "sick leave" in a caravan, parked beside a stream in a lonely spot in the next county. After each murder, he'd gone straight back there to clean up. He told us he felt that his mission in Downshire was now pretty well accomplished and that he'd intended to return to work on the following day. So if he hadn't been the one man in Downshire who wasn't scared of the Terror, he might have got away with it.

He was hopelessly mad, of course. If his deeds hadn't made that clear, his attitude in court would have done. According to him, he was a public benefactor and should have had a medal. He admitted he'd killed five people, but he pointed out that in the month in which he'd been operating, road casualties in Downshire had fallen from 15 dead and 112 injured to 7 dead and 43 injured, solely on account of him—a net saving of 8 lives and much useless suffering. The judge said grimly that this was the arithmetic of bedlam, and had him bundled off to Broadmoor without any more fuss.

There was exuberant relief throughout Downshire when it was realized that sanity had returned to the county and that the danger was over. The next month's road casualty figures were an all-time record at 20 killed and 133 injured.

AUTHOR'S POSTSCRIPT: It's always seemed to me quite crazy that we should kill five thousand people a year on our roads and think practically nothing of it. The wry idea of *The Man Who Wasn't Scared* came to me one day when I was driving on our weekend battlefield.

Theresa

Go on, Miss Pontois. Just say anything that comes into your mind."

Miss Pontois pressed her thin lips together and shut her eyes against panic. Today it had not been difficult to talk. Up until this very minute the sentences had seemed to bubble up in her. Then, without warning, the name had been there, each familiar letter clawing at her thoughts like tentacles.

"Say anything at all. It doesn't matter how unimportant it may seem."

Theresa.

Miss Pontois felt the cold, electric prick of fear. Then, suddenly, it was all right, because she felt herself suspended several feet above the couch, looking down at herself, looking down at Dr. Wagner with his gold pencil poised over the notebook, looking at the situation as though she were not part of it.

". . . perhaps we've had enough for one day."

Miss Pontois recognized the reprieve and lost no time gathering up her heavy purse and frayed fur jacket. Hurrying from the building, she felt herself pursued by some terrible, undefined danger. The fact that it had already grown dark increased her sense of apprehension.

At the corner of Madison Avenue, she paused for a moment, debating whether or not to take a cab. She was still undecided when a bus pulled up. Impulsively, Miss Pontois boarded it, reminding herself that, after all, she and Phyllis had to watch their money more closely now.

Not that they had to pinch pennies. Phyllis had a good job at an advertising agency and Miss Pontois was able to contribute toward expenses with her alteration business. Nevertheless, they couldn't afford unnecessary extravagances.

The bus was crowded and overheated. As Miss Pontois pushed her way to the back, she told herself for the hundredth time that these visits to Dr. Wagner certainly came under the heading of unnecessary extravagance. She had said so from the very beginning. But Phyllis had insisted.

Why?

The unexpected question startled Miss Pontois, Instinctively, she began marshalling her thoughts against the insidious, subconscious attack. Phyllis was only doing it for her good. Phyllis was trying to help her over this period of—well, nervousness. There was nothing her child wouldn't do for her.

"But Phyllis is *not* your child, Miss Pontois." Dr. Wagner's voice filtered through the muffled sounds of traffic. "It's true you took care of her most of her life, but you undertook to care for her in the capacity of governess. Naturally the relationship changed and developed through the years. Now she is your friend. But she is not your child. She doesn't belong to you." The gold pencil tapped out a dull rhythm on the notebook. "You must begin to face things, Miss Pontois. Any situation can be handled once you face it."

Miss Pontois felt the heat rise up in her face. She wasn't going back to Dr. Wagner any more. Phyllis couldn't make her. Oh, she knew very well the child would try. Phyllis had a stubborn streak in her. Sometimes she could be almost as stubborn as Theresa.

It seemed to Miss Pontois that the bus lurched suddenly, as she again thought of Phyllis' sister. She felt her purse slip from under her arm, but managed to retrieve it immediately. Balancing herself against the post near the exit, she dipped her hand quickly inside. Reassurance came as she touched the cool metal of the 12-inch shears. Miss Pontois had taken to slipping the shears into her purse shortly after she and Phyllis had moved. Not that the new apartment wasn't pleasant enough. True, the building itself had a run-down look, indicative of a landlord grappling with rent control. But even so, Miss Pontois found it quite acceptable.

Her single objection was the fact that it was too far east. After dark, the last long crosstown blocks with their closed shops and ominous doorways filled her with dread. And this particular evening, the last two long blocks seemed even more ominous than usual. She found herself taking a firm grip on her purse as she hurried past the darkened antique shop, past the small butcher shop where, invariably, a solitary chicken hung by its neck in the dirt streaked window.

At the corner of Second Avenue she paused for breath, watching almost gratefully the stream of southbound headlights. Then she crossed the street and started down the final stretch of darkness. Ahead of her were six brownstone houses in varying stages of neglect. The windows of the last house had been boarded up. Which was no doubt why the lurking figure caught her attention.

Later, Miss Pontois realized that terror had come before recognition. For it was only when she was in full flight, her fur jacket thumping crazily against her sides, that Miss Pontois identified the shadowy form as Theresa.

Once inside the apartment, she leaned exhausted against the front door, trying to shut out the terrible pursuing image.

"Ponte, is that you?" Phyllis' voice called from the bedroom.

"I . . . I'm home," Miss Pontois managed finally. And she knew she wouldn't have gotten the words out at all if it weren't for Phyllis' picture. From the foyer table the well loved photograph looked back at her with deep, wondering expression, so like Phillip . . .

"Ponte, what's the matter? You're white as a sheet."

Her glance swung from the picture to Phyllis herself. The dark eyes were filled with puzzled concern. Suddenly, Miss Pontois found herself probing behind the concern. Did Phyllis know? And if so, how long had she been concealing the knowledge that Theresa was back?

Once again Miss Pontois experienced a sense of shock as the

unframed, unwanted questions stabbed at her convictions. But this was inconceivable. Phyllis wouldn't hide anything from her. Phyllis always told her everything. Besides, she knew her child so well that she could catch and identify even the most subtle shadings of emotion. Surely if Theresa had been in touch with Phyllis, she would know it at once and with certainty.

Why, from the very beginning, from the time she had come to take care of the two girls, she had always been able to detect Theresa's influence on Phyllis. In fact, within a matter of months she had even been able to anticipate it and to prevent it. And it was due to her constant vigilance that Theresa's ruthlessness had never taken root in Phyllis' personality.

"I just had the strangest experience," Miss Pontois began, tentatively.

"What happened?"

Wasn't the question a shade too urgent? A shade too tense? Miss Pontois hesitated and covered her hesitation by hanging her coat in the guest closet. When she turned back to Phyllis, her decision had been made. She was not going to mention Theresa . . . not yet.

Her glance slid away from the girl's alert, waiting expression. Change the subject, she told herself. Get Phyllis thinking about something else.

"You know, Phyllis, these sessions with Dr. Wagner are really quite unnecessary."

"Now, Ponte," Phyllis began placatingly, "it's rough, of course. It *will* be for a while. But you've got to stick with it. You've *got* to." This time the urgency was unmistakable.

"Why? I'm not sick."

"You know you haven't been the same since . . . since Dad died."

Well, that much at least was true. Part of the world gets cut away and the edges grow back again and you find yourself in a different world. But that doesn't mean you're sick.

"He can help you," Phyllis said. "He's such a wonderful doctor."

Miss Pontois sniffed sarcastically and went on back to her own room. Relieved that Phyllis hadn't followed her, she gently closed the door. Doctors! What good were doctors. Doctors couldn't bring Phillip back. And all those years ago, when Miss Pontois had been a girl, when she had been known by her own name, Eugénie (not affectionately as Ponte, or mistakenly as Miss Pon*tiss*—but Eugénie) all those years ago doctors had also not been able to bring back the young man she was going to marry.

She had watched him struggle in the gray waters of the lake. And there was nothing she could do, nothing but hang onto the overturned canoe and watch. Only she seemed to be seeing everything from somewhere above the water . . . watching him and watching herself, too.

This was the first time Miss Pontois experienced the curious, suspended feeling. The second time had been a year ago, driving away from the hospital . . . driving away from Phillip. She remembered clearly the way she had felt, as though she were hanging above the East River Drive, watching herself in the ugly green taxicab.

It had all happened so suddenly . . . the headache, the sleep that wasn't sleep with the eyes open and rolling, unseeing . . . the ambulance. And yet they had been watching for death. But not for the father—for the mother, for Terry. Terry had been dying for over two years. The Mister had never been sick a day in his life.

For this reason, Miss Pontois had never been able to shake off the feeling, unreasonable as it was, that Terry had planned it that way—*a Terry Carroll creation*. The hated phrase slipped back into her mind and she saw Terry at the peak of her career as a designer, presenting her newest and sleekest gown to the enormously wealthy and invariably too stout customer.

A Terry Carroll creation. There was truth in the phrase. And in time Miss Pontois found that it applied to much more than Terry's genius for fashion. It encompassed her power over people and situations. The woman had an almost diabolic ability to make things come out her way. And her way would certainly have demanded Phillip's death before her own. She would never have left Phillip to Miss Pontois.

It was this fact that gave Miss Pontois the irrational yet persistent feeling that Terry had directed the sequence of events, including the ironic detail that Terry herself was spared the terrible knowledge of what had happened. Already lost in the advanced stages of senility, she was protected even from the awareness of her own impending death.

However, Miss Pontois was forced to take into consideration the one discordant note belying any such pre-arrangement. Terry's illness and the timing of Phillip's death could not possibly have been a Terry Carroll creation for one simple reason— never would this proud and aggressive woman have chosen for herself the slobbering helplessness of senility.

"It's all a matter of the supply of blood to the brain," the doctor had said as kindly as possible. "There is nothing that can be done. It's a matter of time." Time. Time enough for Phillip to have died first.

Miss Pontois eased out of the impractical and expensive black slip which Phillip had bought her five years ago. Every few months she went over the lace border, carefully mending the places where the lace sometimes pulled loose.

There was a light tapping on her door. Miss Pontois slipped into one of the freshly starched swirl aprons she usually wore around the apartment. "Come in, dear." Her voice was casual. For a moment she had almost forgotten the frantic flight down the dark street.

Phyllis pushed open the door, but she didn't enter the room. "Ponte, I'll be home early . . . by the time you've had your bath and watched some TV."

She remembered now. Phyllis had phoned in the early afternoon to tell her she wouldn't be home for dinner.

"Don't worry about me, Phyllis," she said sincerely. "Just have a good time." The girl threw her a quick kiss, her nose crinkling up into Phillip's smile.

It wasn't until she heard the front door slam that Miss Pontois realized Phyllis hadn't told her whom she was going to meet. Her thoughts careened back to the conversation on the telephone. She was certain of it. Phyllis hadn't mentioned meeting anyone.

Miss Pontois ran from the bedroom. Frantically, she pulled at the front door.

"Phyllis . . ." The girl turned, startled, as the elevator door slid open. She was meeting a few of the girls from the office, Phyllis said, in answer to Miss Pontois' question. It sounded quite natural, except that Miss Pontois saw the girl's right hand fly forward in a little gesture of confusion. She saw the good navy suit and the mink stole caught up smartly the way Miss Pontois had taught her to wear it. And just as Phyllis stepped into the elevator, she saw the gold earrings. Phyllis was wearing Terry's earrings.

Back in the apartment, Miss Pontois' cold fingers circled the black wrought iron railing which separated the foyer from the sunken living room. She stood, swaying for a moment, like a bewildered actress who has forgotten her lines. Then she walked down the three steps onto the oriental carpet. *Her* carpet. She and Phillip had chosen it together because Terry, naturally, had been too busy to spare the time. Together they had picked out the blue Chippendale sofa and the rest of the furniture—*her* furniture.

Miss Pontois lifted her chin defiantly, as if she were answering an accusation. She could almost hear Dr. Wagner's precise syllables. ". . . but it's not *your* furniture, Miss Pontois. It doesn't belong to you."

Belonging. It was a curious word, a word that eluded the probing of the gold pencil. Miss Pontois smiled a secret, crafty smile. To which woman had Phillip really belonged? Dr. Wagner would never be able to answer that question because Miss Pontois was never going to supply the necessary information. She would never tell him what had happened the night Terry had left on a business trip. Nobody knew about that night. Nobody except, perhaps, Theresa.

Miss Pontois sank to her knees on the bright patterned carpet. She rested her head against the blue velvet pillow of the couch. That night both girls had gone out. But Theresa had returned early to the silent apartment, to the locked bedroom door.

The frightening thing was that Theresa had never said anything. At first Miss Pontois was terrorized by the girl's refusal to admit what she knew. It gave her the feeling that Theresa was biding her time, waiting for the ultimate, the vulnerable moment.

However, Miss Pontois soon discovered that her new relationship with Phillip took care of her fear, transforming it, inevitably, into a growing sense of triumph. Before long it even became possible for her to ignore Theresa. In fact, the disassociation became so complete that when Theresa finally moved away, the girl's actual physical absence tended to make very little difference in Miss Pontois' life.

Abruptly lifting her head from the blue pillow, Miss Pontois tried to remember the reasons Theresa had given for leaving home. Why was it she seemed to get these blank spots lately? Firmly, but without conviction, she told herself that Theresa had joined the Red Cross. In the 1940's so many girls were joining the Red Cross. Miss Pontois pressed the back of her hand against her forehead. After all, she hadn't paid too much attention to the surface explanation for Theresa's departure, because deep down was the triumphant knowledge of the real reason.

And when the war was over and Theresa still didn't return, Miss Pontois continued to enjoy her private sense of triumph. Eventually, she grew quite proficient at ignoring the occasional twisting fear that some day there would be a reckoning . . . some day Theresa would come back.

Miss Pontois shivered. Suddenly the living room seemed alien to her, as if Theresa had already invaded it. She got up slowly and went into her bedroom. It was the one room Theresa had rarely entered. And, even now, in this new apartment, Miss Pontois experienced the old sense of relief as she closed the bedroom door.

Sitting on the white wing chair, which had once been in the living room, she began reviewing the events of the past few hours. So much had happened so quickly. First there had been the name and the way the name had come to her in Dr. Wagner's office. That's when it had started.

And yet not really then. She began to understand that the name had come only because the atmosphere of Theresa had already begun to envelop her again. She wondered, vaguely, how long Theresa had been back. But that wasn't important. She mustn't waste time on unimportant speculations. The fact remained that Theresa was here and that Phyllis had gone to meet her. Of so much she was certain. Only the presence of Theresa could adequately explain Phyllis' strange reticence. Only Theresa could have induced her to wear the earrings.

"I don't believe in false sentimentality," Phyllis had said when Miss Pontois suggested that she keep something of her mother's. "I didn't feel close to my mother when she was alive. I don't feel close to her now." Nevertheless, at Miss Pontois' insistence, Phyllis had chosen at random from the pathetically few remaining possessions. Packed away in the familiar striped dress box, ornately lettered T. Carroll, were a pair of multi-colored summer shoes, a red quilted robe, a box of tarnished costume jewelry—and the earrings.

The first time Miss Pontois had seen her, Terry had been wearing them—the gold earrings and the inevitable red dress that dramatized her shining black hair. It was the Mister, however, whom Miss Pontois met first. Seated in the show room, opposite the mirrored wall, he began asking her the routine questions.

Miss Pontois liked to think of those first moments with Phillip, not as an interview, but as a conversation of discovery—a conversation which was interrupted by the arrival of Terry. She had appeared before them reflected in the mirrored wall.

It seemed significant to Miss Pontois that the first time she was exposed to Terry it was to a reflection of her. For it appeared that her life was to become surrounded by reflections of this intense, neurotic woman.

"Terry . . ." Phillip turned to his wife and Miss Pontois had the curious sensation that a part of his personality had vanished, absorbed in the supercharged atmosphere. "Terry—this young lady is answering our ad."

Terry. Miss Pontois rejected the nickname immediately. This woman wasn't the type for nicknames. It was like finding a nickname for a black panther.

"This is Miss Pontois," the Mister said.

"Miss *Pontiss*," Terry repeated mistakenly, and the husky voice with the peculiar rasping quality made the mispronunciation even more irritating. Miss Pontois had never been able to determine whether or not the error was deliberate. But from that moment on she was rarely to be called by her correct name.

Terry pushed at the strands of straight hair escaping the not quite invisible net. "It will be far from an easy job, Miss Pontiss."

"Yet she's such a lovable girl," the Mister interrupted. He had been talking about Phyllis, of course. And his wife had been talking about Theresa.

The Mister gave her cab fare and jotted down the address. It was uptown in the nineties. When she arrived at the apartment, it was Theresa who greeted her, throwing a small wooden block at her. Miss Pontois ducked, but not soon enough. The blood spurted from her cheek and Phyllis started to cry. She picked the little girl up in her arms and began comforting her.

"Phil," she said, "little Phil." She relished but failed to identify the delicious sensation that came to her as she spoke the name. "Don't cry like that, darling. After all, you didn't do it. It was Theresa."

Her feeling of guilt, because she'd placed the blame as she had, was almost immediate. However, her conscience was somewhat soothed by the fact that Theresa had vanished. Nevertheless, she sensed that the child was hiding somewhere, watching her. And now Theresa was back again. From somewhere in the city she was watching—waiting for the opportunity to strike.

On the other hand, this time Miss Pontois had been given an opportunity to anticipate the attack and, consequently, to defend herself. Of course, she would need to have a more definite idea of what Theresa was up to. For this, Miss Pontois knew she would have to rely on her ingenuity and watchfulness. She would have to recognize each unrelated, misshapen piece of the puzzle as it presented itself.

Relaxed, somewhat, by the very orderliness of her thoughts, Miss Pontois began to prepare for bed. Her immediate problem, she realized, was one of self control. She mustn't tip her hand. If Phyllis should find out that she knew about Theresa, her important advantage would be lost. From now on, she must be careful not to react to the changes in Phyllis' behavior, however difficult this might be.

Miss Pontois soon discovered, however, that it was equally difficult to control her reactions when Phyllis' behavior followed the accustomed pattern. Because she was now geared for change, the usual unnerved her almost as much as the unusual.

For instance, all the following morning and afternoon she waited for Phyllis to call and give some excuse for not being home to dinner. But Phyllis didn't call. Instead she came home at the accustomed time.

Seated across from Phyllis at the dinette table, Miss Pontois found herself hard pressed to meet this challenge of the ordinary. She resorted, finally to a barrage of chatter.

"I spent all afternoon on Mrs. Hadley's dinner dress. I simply can't keep up with her dieting. I no sooner get her alterations finished than she loses ten pounds . . . or gains them. Have you an idea what ten pounds does to a figure?"

She watched Phyllis push the food around on her plate. "Ponte . . . if you really wanted to, you could build up a business for yourself—not just alterations. After all, once I was grown up and out of your hair, you spent all those years working with Dad and Mother." Now Phyllis looked at her eagerly. "Why, I remember lots of times your suggestions were even better than Mother's."

"No!" Denial was fierce and instinctive. Years ago Miss Pontois had learned the price of offering a better suggestion than Terry's. She could still hear the husky voice, shrill enough to penetrate the fitting rooms—"I didn't ask for your opinion, Miss Pontois. There are times when you are too quick to forget that you are a paid servant." Later, of course, there were always the tears, the apologies, the inevitable lavish gift with which Terry tried to make up for her outbursts.

Phyllis had stopped eating. Miss Pontois sipped at her water and tried to rid her mind of the sharp thrust of memory.

"Building the business up again would take some doing," she said, finally. "You know perfectly well, Phyllis, that things had been going down hill for a long time. All those rich old women were dying off . . ."

"But they have daughters . . . and granddaughters. You could start building something again if you wanted to do it." Phyllis paused, and Miss Pontois found herself waiting with a sudden and peculiar sense of dread. "The trouble is, you don't seem to want anything. You're too caught up in the past."

"How can you say that!" Miss Pontois' voice sounded high and strange in her own ears. "I'm doing very well with the alteration business. We've moved to a new apartment . . ."

"Yes!" There was a raw, scraping sound as Phyllis pushed back her chair. "*We* moved . . . us . . . we. That's what I mean. You're too dependent on me."

Phyllis paused and Miss Pontois became aware of an unnatural
silence, as if the low, steady hum of living had been abruptly cut
off. She stood up and began clearing the table, conscious that
Phyllis was trailing after her into the kitchen.

"Suppose you let me take over the dishes tonight," Miss Pontois spoke into the dead, echoless vacuum. She needed to be alone.
She needed to examine what Phyllis had said. Somewhere in the
protest, in the veiled accusation, there must be another piece of
the ugly jigsaw puzzle.

"Thanks for the reprieve, Ponte." Phyllis was smiling self-consciously. "As a matter of fact, I want to wash my hair."

Almost before she realized she was speaking, the familiar warning was out. "You'll catch cold!" Miss Pontois said. And then,
more hesitantly, almost apologetically, "It'll never dry before you
go to bed. You always get those sore throats."

"I won't get a sore throat. Honestly, Ponte, when are you going
to stop treating me like a baby?"

Phyllis was still smiling, but something was wrong. Once again
Miss Pontois had the curious sensation they were talking into an
echoless void.

Phyllis left the kitchen and Miss Pontois turned the hot water
on full force, as though the very sound of it could penetrate the
inward sense of silence. Slowly, she began turning over the things
Phyllis had said, examining each word for its hidden meaning,
its revealing clue. "You're too dependent on me." There was an
insistence about the phrase and she returned to it again and
again.

Suppose she *was* dependent on Phyllis. What was so terrible
about *that?* Miss Pontois turned off the water and began slipping
dishes into the foam. There had been a time when it was the
other way around. All those years when Miss Pontois had been a
kind of buffer, softening the impact of the constant jarring con-
flicts between Phyllis and her mother. "I hate her, Ponte!" Phyllis
would say. And Miss Pontois would find herself reciting all the

right objections to such an attitude, controlling as best she could the strange, warm feeling of security she found in the girl's reaction to her mother.

Miss Pontois set the last dish to drain in the rubber rack. She was getting nowhere. She was going around in circles. But she mustn't panic. Perhaps if she kept busy . . . She decided to spend a few hours working on Mrs. Hadley's dinner dress. She might even be able to finish it tonight. Besides, she could think better when she was busy in "the workroom."

"The workroom," a fairly large back room—and the main reason for taking the apartment—was adequately equipped with objects salvaged when T. Carroll, Incorporated had collapsed. There was an overhead fluorescent light, a large work table, two antiquated yet surprisingly efficient sewing machines, and a group of headless, stout dressmaking figures.

These stood huddled in a corner as if they had suddenly taken refuge from a common terror. Most of the figures belonged to customers who had vanished years before. Some of them, as Miss Pontois had pointed out to Phyllis, had simply died off. Others had literally been driven away by Terry. At first the Mister had been unable, and later unwilling to explain the increasingly irrational outbursts which were to vent themselves, finally, in the tiny room with the barred window.

However, it wasn't the barred window that was to haunt Miss Pontois for the rest of her life. It was the door—the door with the little round hole conveniently carved out at eye level. More than once she had waked up in the middle of the night, cold with terror, having dreamed that she was locked up and at the mercy of the watching, faceless eye. Involuntarily, she would reach out to the remembered door, seeing again, with sickening vividness, the gouged out pattern made by angry, clawing hands.

Miss Pontois rubbed at her eyes. She had always hated the dead, unnatural glare of fluorescent lighting. Directly in front of her stood Mrs. Hadley's headless figure draped in the red taffeta dinner dress. Suddenly Miss Pontois was conscious of a pain in her right temple. It passed almost at once, leaving Miss Pontois suspended slightly above herself. She was looking down at Mrs. Hadley's macabre, red-draped form. She was watching her own hand as it picked up the sheers. Once she even imagined that she cried out. But the small, throaty sound in no way impeded the downward, slashing action.

"My goodness! What happened!" Phyllis' voice brought Miss Pontois abruptly back to herself. The girl stood in the doorway, a turkish towel wrapped around her head.

"I decided to take some of the fullness out of the skirt," Miss Pontois lied. She reached out her hand and the red fabric seemed to moan under her fingers.

Phyllis came into the room and sat down on the high wooden stool near the work table.

"There's something I want to say to you." The towel slipped onto her shoulders and the brown hair, darker now because it was wet, tumbled in all directions over her forehead. Miss Pontois, looking at the wet-black hair, found herself thinking of Terry. "It's kind of hard to put it into words," Phyllis said.

"Not for you, Phyllis. Words were never hard for you. Remember the poem you wrote in the fourth grade . . ."

"Ponte, stop it! Stop dragging in the past!"

Miss Pontois turned away from the angry girl. When Phyllis was this way, she began to lose all resemblance to her father.

"There's something you must understand." Phyllis was speaking quietly now. Too quietly. "I'm doing my best to help you, but I've got to help myself first."

Miss Pontois felt her body tensing against the unknown threat. When Phyllis spoke again, it was with a strange, new emphasis.

"I think it would be better to have my own apartment. At least for awhile."

Miss Pontois managed not to make a single motion. She even

stopped breathing, knowing that the slightest disturbance—even so much as a breath, would shatter the world.

"Ponte!"

The alarm in Phyllis' voice released her. Suddenly her mind was moving—taking the measure of the situation. Theresa wanted to take Phyllis away from her. That much was clear. That much she could have anticipated if she had been given a little more time. Another day, even. But Theresa had always moved swiftly. Well, she was still ahead of her. She still had the advantage of knowing Theresa was back. And she must keep that advantage. Because Theresa wasn't through yet. All her instincts told Miss Pontois that taking Phyllis away was just another fragment. She wasn't being permitted to see the whole, ugly pattern. Not yet. Therefore she must play it smart.

"Well," Miss Pontois said, carefully, "maybe it *would* be a good idea. I'm not exactly the best company in the world."

"It isn't that. You mustn't think . . ." For a moment she was afraid Phyllis was going to cry. "We'll see each other often," Phyllis managed finally.

Looking at the girl's distraught expression, Miss Pontois momentarily forgot her concern with herself. Poor child. She must remember that Phyllis, too, was an instrument of Theresa's evil will. And it was unfair that Phyllis should be made to suffer any more than was necessary. This thing was between herself and Theresa.

Miss Pontois put her arm around the girl. "We'll start looking for a place tomorrow."

She saw the slow flush spread over Phyllis' cheeks. "I've found a place, Ponte."

After that there wasn't much more to say. It seemed the apartment consisted of one room which was already furnished. Therefore only her clothes would have to be moved. And Phyllis thought perhaps tomorrow morning . . . Since she wasn't too busy at the office, she would take the day off.

Of course. It would **have** to be tomorrow. Trust Theresa to see that the break was quick and clean.

Because Miss Pontois was already steeling herself to the fact that she would not see Phyllis again for some time, she was startled when the girl suggested showing her the apartment the following afternoon. Phyllis even insisted on calling for her. But it wasn't until they were on the bus, heading uptown, that Miss Pontois realized she didn't know where they were going. She had neglected to ask the address. It came as a shock, therefore, when they got off the bus at Ninetieth Street. It was so close to the old neighborhood.

The building was a gray stone mansion which even now seemed impressive, in spite of appalling signs of disrepair.

"It's one flight up, to the front," Phyllis said, as they entered the cavernous and dimly lit vestibule. However, it wasn't the encompassing gloom, nor the wide and treacherously uncarpeted stairway that affected Miss Pontois. These were, after all, impersonal symptoms of neglect. It was when she stepped into the high ceilinged apartment that the intimate, choking sense of evil rose up at her.

Instinctively, her eyes searched the room. There was an absurdly large fireplace, two conventional, overstuffed chairs, two studio couches.

Her glance swung away and swung back again. Two couches! Two chests of drawers. Two people could live in this room.

Of course. The truth was so simple, she wondered why she hadn't realized it immediately—last night when Phyllis first told her about the apartment. What better way for Theresa to keep Phyllis within the area of her influence than to share an apartment with her? Miss Pontois felt almost giddy as she walked toward one of the studio couches. She wondered if it was Theresa's. Perhaps it was still warm from the pressure of Theresa's body.

"Are you all right, Ponte?"

"Of course I'm all right."

"I'll put on some tea. Look!" Phyllis said and triumphantly raised a venetian blind revealing a compact pullman kitchen.

"No. No I really can't stay." She had to get out of here. It was possible that Theresa had planned this visit and that she had walked into a trap. Theresa might appear at any moment, before Miss Pontois had fitted all the pieces together, before she understood the whole terrible plan.

"Nonsense," Phyllis was saying. "You've got to initiate the place. Tea you must have. As a matter of fact, I could use some myself." She rubbed her hand over her throat. "You were right after all. Washing my hair wasn't such a good idea."

Miss Pontois ignored the implied apology for last night's outburst of anger. Then a curious thing happened. For a brief second her mind seemed to go blank. She remembered watching Phyllis as she held a kettle under the cold water tap. And the next thing she knew, Miss Pontois found herself standing at the coffee table looking down at the earrings.

"I've got to have them adjusted." Phyllis' voice was startlingly close. "They're too tight." Miss Pontois watched the hand pick up the earrings and deposit them in one of the chests.

"There are so few things left that belonged to her," Phyllis was saying. Again there must have been that strange jump in time, because now Miss Pontois was seated in one of the overstuffed chairs and Phyllis was sitting on the coffee table.

"You know, Ponte, it's a curious thing when someone dies. You begin to see them differently."

Miss Pontois flicked her tongue over her dry lips. So now Phyllis was white-washing her mother—Phyllis, who hated false sentimentality. If Miss Pontois had ever doubted Theresa's return, here was proof. In fact Theresa must have been back longer than she suspected, to have worked such a change in Phyllis.

"Oh, I admit Mother was a very difficult person," Phyllis was saying, as if in answer to the unspoken accusation. "It's only that I'm beginning to see what made her difficult. Ponte, do you realize what she did? She came here as a child . . . with nothing . . . she couldn't even speak the language. She *had* to be aggressive. She had to be single minded. And Dad was a wonderful person . . . but he was a dreamer . . ."

Suddenly Miss Pontois was on her feet. The misguided defense of the mother was bad enough, but now this . . . this subtle attack on Phillip.

"Theresa is back!" She heard her own voice, almost unrecognizable. Her throat hurt, and she couldn't seem to hold her lips together. She saw Phyllis' white face suspended over the coffee table.

"You haven't mentioned Theresa in years."

"She's back. You didn't think I knew."

In the high-ceilinged room the shadows stirred. Miss Pontois turned and ran.

When she got home, the phone was ringing. She picked up the receiver. "Hello," the familiar voice said into her ear. "Hello . . ." the two husky-shrill syllables snaked through the wire. Trembling, Miss Pontois pressed down the cradle with her finger. Fear of the remembered voice was nothing compared with the terror of the reality. She listened again. There was a monotonous humming. The connection had been broken.

Carefully, she sat the receiver next to the phone. She wasn't going to expose herself to that voice again. Aware of the sudden weakness in her legs, she sank down on the steps leading to the living room.

She had done it. She had tipped her hand. Phyllis would have told Theresa, of course. Her advantage was gone.

Well then, there was only one thing to do. She must take the initiative. She must face Theresa. *Any situation can be handled once you face it.* The unexpected application of Dr. Wagner's words gave her a surprising sense of excitement. After all, she had always been able to cope with Theresa in the past. She had even succeeded in driving Theresa out of their lives. She would do it again, for the Mister's sake, if for no other reason. Because look what was happening to his little girl. Look what was happening to Phyllis. She must protect Phyllis from the evil of Theresa.

Now that she had arrived at a decision, she felt energy and control flooding back through her. She even replaced the receiver on the hook and derived a certain satisfaction from the fact that she could ignore the intermittent ringing. She had won a small victory over the telephone. And it represented, in a way, a victory over Theresa.

She went to bed and slept soundly. The next morning she found that her feeling of confidence not only persisted, but was stronger than ever. Her thoughts were clicking off unhesitatingly, dictating quick, decisive action.

She called Dr. Wagner's office and cancelled her appointment for that afternoon, aware of how well she was handling the conversation with the nurse. She was being just casual enough, just firm enough. It was as if her whole body were a sensitive machine which could be counted upon to respond smoothly to given impulses. And for this reason she was without even the slightest sense of fear or apprehension. Her main function had become a purely responsive one. Consequently, she felt relieved of the necessity of planning ahead in any great detail. She was convinced that once she confronted Theresa, once she forced her to reveal whatever monstrous scheme she was so cleverly engaged in plotting, her own course of action would inevitably present itself.

At exactly three o'clock she left for the apartment uptown. The conviction that this was Theresa's apartment and that she would find Theresa there had taken such complete possession of her that she felt almost as if an appointment had been made. Any stirrings of doubt were immediately put to rest by the swift, logical clicking away of her thoughts. For example, she told herself that if Theresa happened to be out, she had only to choose a strategic spot and await her return. Since Phyllis was working, it was only logical that Theresa would get home ahead of Phyllis.

Busy with, and even comforted by such thoughts, Miss Pontois walked swiftly west. So great was her preoccupation that it left her completely unaware of the violent change that had taken place in the weather. In fact she felt unusually warm, even though her thin neck was exposed to the damp, penetrating cold of the dull November afternoon.

Her immediate objective was to take the Madison Avenue trolley uptown. But when she arrived at Madison and 57th Street, Miss Pontois received quite a shock. The trolley tracks weren't there.

White with this surprising realization, she allowed two buses to pass her by. It's because of going uptown, she told herself, by way of rationalizing the error she had made. It's because of going back where we used to live. For a moment, Miss Pontois let herself imagine the sound of the street cars the way she used to hear them from her bed at night. But of course the street cars had been discontinued many years ago.

The trip uptown was slower than she had anticipated. But she was glad of the opportunity to collect herself. And by the time she arrived at her destination, the feeling of control and energy had returned. She even managed to smile a bit over what she was beginning to think of as her "flightiness."

Again, acting on an impulse that seemed to be coming from outside herself, she crossed the street and looked up at the gray stone building. The windows on the second floor stared back at her blindly. The drapes were drawn. Miss Pontois felt the thumping of her own heart. If the drapes were drawn, then someone was inside. Even as the thought formed itself in her mind, she saw a hand reach out and pull the window up a crack. The drapes parted for an instant and then fell together again—but not before Miss Pontois had seen the loose red sleeve of a robe.

The next thing she knew, she was standing in the half open door of the apartment. She didn't remember pressing the buzzer. She didn't remember passing through the huge, gloomy vestibule. Instead it seemed to Miss Pontois that the hated red of the robe had dissolved without a noticeable passage of time into the hot, flickering light in front of her. For a moment Miss Pontois thought that the heat and the dizzying sense of motion were coming from her own body. But then she saw that a fire was going in the fireplace. And then she saw Theresa.

"I tried to reach you last night." The husky voice wasn't as shrill as it had been on the phone, but there was a grating edge to it. It was so like her, so like Theresa to dispense with preliminaries, to talk as if she had never been away. But of course she hadn't been away, not really. Because the threat of her return had always been there, like a presence, waiting for this moment.

"What are you staring at?" Theresa gave the door an impatient shove and it crashed shut.

"You always *could* wear her colors . . ."

Theresa drew the robe closer with a defiant gesture and walked toward the studio couch. "I was lying down. I have a cold."

A pillow had been pulled from under the cheap chenille spread and the whiteness of the case seemed to keep its intensity even in the darkened room. Theresa sat on the edge of the couch and swung her feet up.

"You still hate my mother," she said, and Miss Pontois sensed the mockery behind the malice.

"Don't you think I have ample reason?" She was determined to match Theresa statement for statement.

But the husky voice came back at her—slow, deliberate. "The real reason, of course, is because you feel guilty . . . because of my father." Here it was finally—the admission, concealed for so long, growing a dark network of roots that threatened to undermine the very foundations of Miss Pontois' life. "That's why you hate her . . . have to hate her . . . even though she's dead."

"But she *isn't* dead." Across the red shadows their eyes held. Miss Pontois felt herself pulled forward by the strange connecting force between them. She *isn't* dead. She's alive . . . in you."

Theresa half rose. "Dr. Wagner is right. You're sick, dangerously sick!" For a moment Miss Pontois stood swaying on the edge of understanding. And then knowledge exploded inside her. So this was what Theresa had been plotting. This was the total picture in all its viciousness . . . in all its logically conceived horror. She was to be put where Terry had been . . . behind the same locked door with the little round hole, and the clawed marks converging on the hole.

There was a hoarse, penetrating cry—like no sound she had ever heard. Miss Pontois watched the long shears flash and flash again. She watched herself as she looked down at the dark, hated red. It was moving now with a life of its own, staining the white pillow.

The strange sense of detachment, the peculiar suspended feeling, remained with Miss Pontois until she returned to her own apartment. It was when she switched on the lamp in the foyer that release came in the form of a new and deeper shock. On the foyer table, Theresa's picture stared up at her from a pool of yellow light.

Somebody had been there. Somebody had switched photographs. Where then, was the other one? Miss Pontois pulled at the shallow drawer in the foyer table. The drawer fell to the floor spilling a deck of cards, a pair of glasses, a green stub of pencil. But Phyllis' picture wasn't there.

Where was Phyllis?

Without bothering to peel off her fabric gloves, Miss Pontois moved through the rooms in a frenzy of motion—switching on lights, spilling the contents of bureau drawers here and there, and on knobs and light switches, leaving a dark red sain.

AUTHOR'S POSTSCRIPT: My point of departure: I believe it was a deep emotional experience, so deep in fact, that it has not spent itself in the story but is, presently, overflowing into a novel. I guess the "gimmick" came next, a natural consequence of the fact that this particular emotion could only be expressed in the "peculiar" form of the suspense story.

LAWRENCE TREAT

Justice Magnifique

FROM the crest of the hill where Paul Slater lounged, looking down on the picturesque Breton valley, he saw the murder unfold.

He was not aware, at first, that it would be murder or that he'd be drawn into it. He merely saw the man and woman—in black, peasant dress—enter the valley and take the path that led upward, towards the cliff, saw them without paying too much attention to them.

Slater was near the end of a week's sketching trip, and it had been productive. Tomorrow he'd be with Bettina, his chic, French wife, and she'd have to admit he could get along fine without speaking a word of the language. And his victory would be sweet.

"How will you eat?" she'd asked him, when he'd suggested the expedition.

"Easy. When I want chicken I'll flap my wings. Like this." He crooked his long arms and wobbled his elbows.

"And you'll get an omelet," she said, laughing.

"When I want an omelet," he remarked, aware that laughter enhanced his wife's loveliness, "I'll make like one."

She surveyed him with soft, deep eyes. "You look more like a string-bean to me," she said.

She kissed him good-by fiercely, as if she feared she'd never see him again. "Maybe I should come, too," she said. "Ask me, Paul."

He shook his head. "You're beautiful, but you'll keep. And besides your family wants this week with you."

"I'll worry so," she said tenderly. "Paul, think of all the things that can happen, and you can't even speak French."

"Look, darling, I don't paint in French, and we'll meet in Brittany, as agreed, and have a hell of a time together."

"That does sound grand," she said. "Our meeting in Brittany —that part of it."

So he'd left gaily. After the grind of commercial art in a New York advertising agency, he craved a summer of serious painting, and this was it. He drove a tiny yellow car along the French roads, hunched over the steering wheel like an anchovy surrounding a caper, and thought good thoughts. When he felt like it, he parked the car and wandered off. With a sketch pad under his arm. Getting into the back country through fields hidden by high, earth ramparts. Like now.

He studied the shape of the secluded valley spread out below him. The stream tumbled into it noisily, past sharp cliffs and over a stony bed, then meandered through softer land. His eyes took in the patterns of greens and the play of light and shadow. He returned to the two figures, and with a start realized something was wrong.

The man, big and powerful, towered over the woman, who retreated in fear. She kept arguing and raising her arms to protect herself, and every time he approached her, she leapt back. Suddenly, he bore down on her and grabbed her. She fell to her knees, and he began dragging her by an arm.

To Slater, the situation was obvious. The man wanted to haul the woman to the cliff and push her over. The realization of what was happening, together with his powerlessness to prevent it, made Slater gasp with horror. Then he did the only possible thing. He stood up and yelled.

Maybe the man and woman were too absorbed in their struggle, maybe the rush of the stream drowned out all other sound. In any case, Slater's shouts had no effect. The big peasant had lifted the woman and was carrying her; she fought back savagely, scratching and kicking. Her wooden shoe caught the man in the groin and he dropped her abruptly. As she tried to scramble off, he pulled something from his belt and struck brutally at her head. She sagged and lay still.

Paul Slater, standing on the hillock, felt his muscles tighten and grab. He had a cramped, sick feeling in his stomach. Trancelike, with a sense of living through a nightmare, he watched the peasant wipe blood from his face, pick up the woman and trudge for the rock.

"He'll throw her over the cliff," Slater thought. "He'll claim she fell. How could he guess I saw the whole thing?"

The peasant, however, advanced only a few steps. He halted, lifted his head and studied the landscape. Suddenly detecting Slater, the peasant lowered the body of the woman, and stared.

Despite the size of the peasant and the fact that he was armed with a weapon of some sort, he was a good hundred yards below Slater, and wearing heavy, wooden sabots. Still, because the terrain he had to cover was less rocky, he could probably beat Slater to the ridge where the little yellow car was parked. Therefore Slater decided to go the other way.

It was impossible for him to see the peasant's expression, or for the peasant to distinguish anything besides Slater's general appearance. The big farmer would merely be aware of a spare, tallish man with light hair, wearing the clothes of a foreigner. Nevertheless, despite the distance, the two men locked glances, and the hostility of each established a bond between them.

"I have to get help and accuse him," Slater thought, "and he has to kill me before I manage to do it. He's shrewd and he's familiar with the countryside, whereas I—maybe Bettina was right. A strange land, strange people, strange language. I'm in a vacuum."

The two men turned simultaneously, and both began running. Slater knew he was cut off from the car, and that if he approached it he'd have to deal with a giant for whom he was no physical match. And the peasant doubtless knew he had to act fast. But he had no idea of his tremendous advantage, that Slater lacked a knowledge of the French language.

At the highway, Slater headed downhill. He'd enter the first house he came to. He'd have protection, and his need for an English interpreter would be obvious. Conveying his news might be a slow and awkward process, but at least he'd be out of danger.

He kept running at top speed, breathed a sigh of relief when he saw the house.

It was a two-story structure of stone, with brick window sills that gave it a mild, architectural pretense. The home of a well-to-do farmer, probably, who felt himself a cut or so above his neighbors. Slater shoved open the gate and saw the neat, colorful flower garden, bisected by a muddy, clay path. As he walked up the path and turned momentarily, he was horrified to see the small, yellow car coasting down the hill.

He ran to the door. It was unlocked, and he opened it and slammed it shut behind him. When he heard a baby crying upstairs, he relaxed.

"Hello?" he called out. Nobody answered.

He entered the first room off the central corridor and noticed the carved, Breton chest and the sturdy, oak table. He strode to the window and peered through the curtains. Outside, the peasant had parked the yellow car and stepped out. Slater left the room and raced for the kitchen and the back door. It was locked. He turned at once and ran to a room upstairs. From the window, he saw the peasant sitting in the garden as if this were his home. Obviously, he had no idea that Slater was trapped inside.

The baby cried again, and Slater saw it lying in a cradle alongside a bed. "It's a French baby," he told himself, "so don't talk to it in English. Besides, if you open your mouth, friend murderer's going to hear, and he'll come up and beat your brains out. So sit tight."

The baby apparently disagreed about the need for silence. It began screaming. If that kept up, Slater reflected, the peasant would come upstairs. Then Slater spotted the pile of clean diapers, and he leaned over the crib and felt the baby.

He'd had experience with a niece, and so he was adept. He folded the diaper in three parts, as his sister had taught him to, and removed the dirty diaper and slipped the baby into another one. A big, healthy boy, Slater observed, and he pinned him up expertly and returned him to the crib. The infant stopped crying and Slater stepped back proudly. When he turned, he saw the big peasant blocking the doorway. He'd removed his sabots and was wearing slippers.

Slater froze and stared at the round, reddish face. The scratch on the cheek was caked with dirt, and the dark, shrewd, peasant eyes glittered with satisfaction. A peasant is the better man, they seemed to say. Everything the peasant had done thus far was right; everything Slater had done was wrong.

Slater had the impression of reading the peasant's mind, and of agreeing that Slater had been a fool. Naturally, the nearest house belonged to the farmer, and naturally the crying baby belonged to him and his wife. Now there remained only the comparatively easy job of attending to Slater.

Slater could jump through the window, and take the risk of getting cut by glass or breaking a leg. Or stand his ground. Either way, his chances were not good.

After awhile he grew aware that the peasant had not moved. The man still blocked the door, his gimlet eyes holding onto a look of cunning triumph.

The baby made an awkward, meaningless motion, coughed once and fell asleep. Slater saw the dirty diaper; he saw women's clothing spread out on the bed. The woman must have been dressing when her husband had told her to come out to the fields.

Slater wondered why the peasant remained there, rooted, expressionless, in the doorway. And then he edged towards the window. The peasant immediately advanced the same distance. When Slater reached for the casement, the big farmer growled and made a threatening gesture. Slater withdrew his hand.

The sweat came out on Slater's forehead; his knees were weak. He thought of Bettina, of the dead woman in the valley. Time—measured by the slow, steady tick of a clock—dragged.

Outside, a car went by. Somebody called from the road; a bicycle bell jangled; a motorcycle spluttered. Shakily, stiff-legged, Slater inched away from the window and along the side of the room. The peasant stepped clear of the doorway for the first time.

Why? Slater asked himself. Why? Because I'm supposed to do something, fall into a worse trap. Except that nothing's worse than this, menaced by a great, hulking body and its sly, animal brain.

He slid cautiously along the wall, and the peasant circled correspondingly. When Slater had gone halfway around the room, the peasant had made the same arc, and the two men were equally distant from the doorway. Incredulous, Slater said to himself, "He's going to let me out. But why?"

With his eyes glued to the peasant's, Slater took a tentative step forward, curious as to what his reaction would be. The peasant let out an oath and lunged at Slater. Though Slater tried to side-step the charge, a giant arm pushed him off-balance and sent him spinning against the door jamb. Staggering, he recovered his footing and lurched into the corridor. He scuttled downstairs.

The yellow car was still parked in front of the gate and Slater ran to it and climbed in breathlessly. And as he turned on the ignition and started the motor he wondered why he hadn't been pursued. He drove off jerkily, still puzzled by the relative ease of his escape. A half mile beyond he stopped and looked in the back of the car, because the thought had come to him that the peasant had let him go, after having put the body of the dead woman in the car, to link him with the murder. But on the floor behind him lay a bloody wrench.

Slater studied the weapon without touching it. Now he could guess the peasant's scheme, and it was a good one. A stranger stops at a house in which there is a woman alone with a baby. The car in all likelihood has been seen there. The stranger will admit having entered the house and having gone into the valley, where the body of the woman will be found. He has the murder weapon. The logical inference is that he assaulted the woman, that she escaped and ran to the valley, where he overtook her and killed her lest she accuse him of the assault.

In rebuttal would be Slater's simple word. And his story would be incredible, no matter how skillfully he told it. Add the problem of language and a local suspicion of strangers, and what chance did he have? He'd be in jail tomorrow, the day Bettina was due on the four-thirteen train. When he didn't meet her, she'd panic and worry, and eventually she'd have to take the brunt of the whole situation. If she could.

He repeated the words, if she could. Then the full force of his predicament hit him. No alibi, no person he'd spoken to since breakfast. He hadn't even flopped his arms for an omelette. He was nobody, doubly a nobody because he couldn't speak the language of the country. To seek out the police would be suicide.

And the alternative? Slater frowned. To guess what the peasant would do next, to follow the workings of his mind and wait for his mistake. To pit his own intelligence against an individual who was on his home grounds and had every advantage.

Stated that way, the alternative sounded foolhardy. And yet, Slater had no choice. And besides, he had to show Bettina that, French or no French, he could take care of himself. He'd boasted about it often enough, and had to make good.

He tapped the steering wheel. "Facts," he said. "Here's a big brute of a peasant living in a landowner's house, instead of in one of those stone cottages that are half-house and half-barn, with a manure pile at the front door. So the guy probably married a rich woman and then decided to get rid of her. With a baby to take care of, he probably has another woman in mind, but he'll avoid her like the plague for the next week or two. No hope there. What I need is time, and a friend to help me out. Because the murderer is undoubtedly figuring on my going straight to the police with my story, and my getting accused before I know what it's all about."

Slater started the car and drove on towards the town of Lannion, where Bettina was due to meet him. Beyond the outskirts he found a field concealed by the typical high, earth fences surmounted by a hedge, and he drove the car inside and hid it in the bushes. He took overnight things from his bag, and trudged into town.

He arrived at four o'clock, found the station and waited for the four-thirteen to arrive from Paris. Then, as if he had come by train, he walked to a small hotel and took a room for the night.

To the proprietor, who spoke a few words of English, Slater made it known that he wished an interpreter for a day or so. A half-hour later, a delicate young man with small, anxious features introduced himself as Monsieur Bayon, a school teacher.

Slater shook hands formally. "I need company," he said, "and I'd like to learn something about the life of a French town. Tell me the gossip and be my friend for a day. Since this is vacation time you're free, aren't you?"

"Yes, Monsieur. It can arrange itself."

"Good. Have dinner with me, and make your own terms."

Bayon, distant at first, reacted to a good bottle of wine and poured out his heart. He was engaged to be married, but marriage is expensive, and he and his Katrine were saving their money. In five years, perhaps, the great event would take place.

"Do it now," Slater said amiably. "Love should never wait."

"But the father and mother of Katrine, they do not consent, unless."

"Are you marrying Katrine or her parents?" Slater asked.

Bayon looked startled. "Her father," he said with awe and respect, "is a man of authority. He is Monsieur the Judge."

As they ate the cheese and fruit, a stir started in the restaurant, and Bayon rose and went to another table at which there was vehement conversation. He returned with the news.

"There has been murder," he said excitedly. "The wife of Claude Ferrou, he find her in the fields. Her head is crushed, pouf! And there is talk of a man in a small yellow car."

"This Ferrou," said Slater. "What's he like?"

"An ox of a man. He marry the daughter of a landowner, she is a little ugly but very rich. I see him in the café many time, when he come to sell the cows. They have the small baby."

"And the yellow car?"

"Several people notice the license number that end in seventy-five, which is from Paris. And a small yellow car from Paris, that is easy for the police, they have the organization. They will find."

Oh, no they won't, thought Slater, not until I'm ready. Aloud he said, "And Ferrou—will he marry again?"

"It is to be seen."

Slater ordered another bottle of wine. "What will happen to the baby?" he asked.

"The family of Ferrou, they are peasant, they live near. There is always someone to care for the small baby."

Slater filled both glasses. "Find out all you can," he said, "and tell me about it tomorrow. The thing interests me."

In the morning Bayon arrived with the latest bulletins. The police had questioned Ferrou at length; they had made a thorough examination. Yesterday afternoon Ferrou had been in the fields at some distance from the valley, and had had trouble with a small bull, which had gashed his cheek. When he had returned to the house, his wife was absent and had gone looking for her. He had almost stumbled over the body.

The house told its own story. In the garden were the footprints of a stranger, clearly evident because he wore shoes instead of sabots. He must have found Madame Ferrou alone. The upset furniture and a broken bottle of wine showed there had been a struggle. Probably the stranger had tried to assault or rob her, and she had resisted and escaped to the valley. He'd overtaken her, and the ground showed where a second and fatal struggle had taken place. It was here that the stranger had smashed her skull with a weapon, probably of iron.

Neither the stranger nor the weapon had been found, yet. The yellow car was still missing, but several more people had seen it parked in front of the Ferrou house. A neighbor, seeing the car, had called out to the Ferrous and received no answer, proving the house was empty at the time. As for Ferrou, he had been released.

"The police," Slater remarked, "can make mistakes, and often do. And after all, Ferrou only married her for her money."

"Why not?" Bayon demanded. "Many tried, he had the success. Is there something of evil in money, when you marry?"

"Skip it," said Slater. "But he's the sort of man who would kill, isn't he?"

"Ferrou? Impossible. He always live here; everybody know him." Bayon spoke with annoyance. "It is the stranger who kill."

"Where's Ferrou now?"

Bayon answered coldly. "At the Café de la Place. With friends. He take the glass or two of wine, and then go home."

"Good. We'll go down the road and wait for him, at a point between the café and his home."

"Which road?" Bayon asked, as he had suddenly become wary.

"Show me. You know where he lives."

"In this direction," Bayon said, pointing north.

Slater shook his head. "I think it's in the opposite direction." He pointed south, whence he had come yesterday. "Anyhow, that's where we're going. You've an idea about me that's bothering you. Am I right?"

"I walk badly," said Bayon, ignoring the question. "I have an evil of the feet."

Slater took him by the arm. "Come with me," he said sternly. "And don't worry; we're friends."

Bayon hesitated and glanced up the street, as if looking for help. Then, dominated by Slater, he shrugged and yielded.

Without speaking, they walked along the highway. Traffic was sparse, a few cars and trucks, an assortment of scooters and bicycles, a two-wheeled cart drawn by a pair of horses in tandem.

When Slater reached the field in which the yellow car was parked, he halted.

Let's sit here and wait," he said. "I've been too inquisitive about Ferrou, haven't I?"

Bayon gulped uncomfortably. "It is but natural."

"No," said Slater. "I think you guessed, and so I'll tell you what happened. I saw Ferrou kill his wife, but I have to prove it. And the only person who can help me is Ferrou himself."

"You are mad."

Slater shook his head. "Criminals usually convict themselves, in one way or another. I'll let Ferrou choose his own way. I've got a little scheme."

"Monsieur," Bayon said anxiously, "it is best that you give yourself to the police. And in my company, so that Katrine's father will hear of my bravery."

"The hell with you," Slater exclaimed. "Fight your own battles, and I'll fight mine."

"Yes, Monsieur," said Bayon, thoroughly cowed.

They waited until the black Citroen came down the road. Ferrou was driving, and at sight of Slater, the peasant stopped. He growled something in French, and Bayon answered in a quick, nervous voice. Then the giant stepped out of the car and approached menacingly.

Slater stood his ground and pointed to town. Bayon spoke again, pleadingly, but Ferrou paid no attention. He strode up to Slater and grabbed him by the jacket. Slater wrenched free and called out, "Bayon—get help—the police!"

Then Ferrou was on him and Slater went down, with the heavy body crushing him. He hit Ferrou on the jaw, but Ferrou merely tightened his grip. Then Ferrou's hands clamped on Slater's throat. Choking, gasping, Slater worked at the fingers that were throttling him. He bent one of them back double, and Ferrou loosened his grip and rolled over in pain, but he still clung to Slater. Slater pounded with short hooks to Ferrou's body, until a truck stopped and two men jumped out and pinioned him. Slater nodded a grateful surrender.

The interrogation of Slater took place in a large, somewhat dirty room, furnished with a few tables and a number of wooden chairs. A half dozen armed police stood guard while the chief, a long-nosed man with a black mustache and quick, incisive gestures, sat in the center. His sharp eyes seemed to accuse Slater before the questioning even started. Bayon sat next to Slater and acted as interpreter, and Ferrou, opposite, dwarfed the table on which he leaned.

Slater gave his story in detail, and gave it argumentatively. He told where he'd hidden his car, and why, and he pointed out that though the murder weapon was in the car, his own automobile wrench lay unused, in the trunk.

"Tell the chief," Slater said to Bayon, "that her nails will have bits of blood imbedded in them. And Ferrou's face is scratched, not mine."

Bayon translated meekly, without energy, and listened respectfully to the chief's reply. Then he said, "She claw the earth. The earth is in her nails. If there is blood it is lost; there is so little."

"Tell him to look," Slater said irritably. "With a microscope."

Bayon merely compressed his lips. His main interest seemed to be to ingratiate himself with the authorities, so that Katrine's father would hear well of him. *My friend,* Slater thought sarcastically. *I had to go get myself saddled with him.*

Ferrou, catching the drift of the questioning, sat back smugly. The police chief studied Slater with cold suspicion, as if probing for a weak spot. He spoke to Bayon in rapid French; then resumed his scrutiny of Slater.

"Monsieur le Chef," Bayon said obediently, "he ask what you do upstairs, when you see the baby."

"I diapered him," Slater said. "He needed it."

"Diaper?"

"The cloth," said Slater. "Around the legs. He was wet."

"Ah," said Bayon. He spoke to the chief, who grinned broadly and turned to shout an order. For a few minutes nobody paid any attention to Slater.

"Tell him," said Slater, "that Ferrou made up the story about the bull, that he smashed his own furniture in order to frame me, and that he drove my car and his fingerprints are on it somewhere. Tell the chief to investigate, instead of accusing me."

Bayon said nothing.

"Tell him," Slater demanded angrily, "to have a doctor examine Ferrou and me for day-old bruises and scratches, from yesterday."

Bayon licked his lips, and the door opened and a woman came in with a baby. "Monsieur le Chef," said Bayon, "ask you should change the baby."

"At last," said Slater. Apparently the chief wanted to see if Slater knew how, in order to substantiate his account. Slater stood up eagerly, and with a practiced hand he folded the diaper and made the change. The baby cooed. The chief looked interested, and the mother shook her head and began objecting. When Slater had finished, she took her infant and tore off the diaper as if it had been contaminated. Angrily, erupting in a flood of words, she refolded it in a triangle and pinned it in place.

The chief and his staff had a spirited argument, but Slater saw he'd won an important point. They folded their diapers in triangles here; his technique of diapering the Ferrou baby had been noticed and it proved that he had handled the infant yesterday afternoon. There was hardly need for Bayon to transmit the information.

"Good," Slater said. "I guess the chief realized I'm telling the truth. He's a smart guy, after all."

"He say," Bayon observed, "that criminals do the things strange, but you are the first who change the baby before you attack the mother."

"Nuts!" Slater said furiously. "He's crazy. He doesn't know

what he's talking about. But tell him it's late and I have to meet my wife at the station, and I have something important for him, first."

"Yes, Monsieur."

Slater leaned forward and spoke earnestly. He'd gone through all the preliminaries, done his best to plant doubts. Now, before Bettina arrived, was the time to ask the question that Ferrou couldn't answer.

"Listen carefully," Slater said. "Ferrou claims he was chasing a bull when his wife was killed, doesn't he? Ferrou claims he was somewhere else all afternoon. Get that clear first, will you?"

Bayon translated, the chief nodded attentively, and Slater said, "Good. Now I'll show you how Ferrou convicted himself. Ask him how he was able to identify me on the road a little while ago, if he never saw me before." And Slater leaned back triumphantly. "I took you along Bayon, so that I could have a witness that that was what happened."

Bayon licked his lips. "He identify you because I tell him who you are, when he stop the car. It is unfortunate, Monsieur, that you do not understand the French.

Slater said, "Oh." Bayon, the fool. Bayon had gummed up the works. Bettina wouldn't be much help, after this.

Slater spoke icily. "Would you send someone to the station to meet my wife?"

"But yes," said Bayon, "if you will describe her."

Slater gritted his teeth. "She's the most beautiful woman there, and I want her quick."

Bayon translated and the chief gave an order to one of his subordinates, who left the room. For the next fifteen minutes Slater sat in glum silence, martialing the arguments that Bettina could give. Then the door opened and she swept in.

Slater jumped up, and she ran to him and clung tight.

"What happened?" she asked, finally. "Oh, my darling, what happened?"

He held her hand and grimaced. "Betts," he said, "tell this goof I didn't kill anybody, will you?"

Her hand tightened in his, and she squeezed it nervously while she spoke to the chief for all of five minutes. At last, the chief stood up and bowed. Then he said something that caused Bettina to break into smiles and look up happily.

"Paul, he says you'll have to make a signed statement and that there will be certain formalities, but you're free."

He gave her a dazed look. "Betts, what magic did you use? I gave him all the logic in the world and he wouldn't believe me, and then you come along and in a few minutes it's all over. What did you tell him, anyhow?"

"Nothing, really," she said. "I just talked about us. And he said I'm young and beautiful and in love with you, so how could you possibly assault anyone as ugly as Madame Ferrou? He said it speaks for itself."

Slater grinned. "French," he said. "Why bother learning it, when all you need is the right wife?"

AUTHOR'S POSTSCRIPT: Last summer we spent a week in St. Briac, Brittany . . . One day I'd put in a harrowing time at nearby Dinard getting our car greased and struggling with minor repairs and major delays. My French has definite limitations, and I came home exhausted. Under the circumstances, being sick was out of the question, but I gave a fairly good imitation of it for a half hour or so. Lying down on a cot, I felt miserable and thoroughly sorry for myself. I could hear French voices, mostly children's, and they sounded strange, with the words blurred by distance and filtered through the walls. I seemed not to belong here, and I wondered at the madness of people speaking different languages and unable to communicate. The ordeal of the stranger who is sick, and is cut off completely and can't make himself understood sifted through my mind and my mood. Now suppose, I thought—just suppose . . .

JAMES A. KIRCH

The Stranger on Horseback

HE was careful about the way he moved his feet, the way he held his body. He took short, restraining steps. He tried to pace himself by the sound of other heels clicking against the pavement. He knew that he was all right so long as he held with the ebb and flow of the street, but that he could not allow himself to break the tempo. He had to hold himself back, inside the breaking point. He was dimly aware that that might be the only real escape offered him, to break wildly into the open and run, until finally someone put a stop to his running. He was like the drinker who knows that one more tilt of the bottle will bring oblivion. That much was left to him, that he could refuse that escape.

He turned left when the flow of the crowd seemed to swerve, but he didn't change his pace. He walked as he had been walking, until he felt the harsh hand on his shoulder.

He didn't turn around. He heard himself say, "It's all right," but he wasn't sure what he meant when he said it. He wasn't sure of anything except that now that his movement had been broken his hold on himself had been broken with it.

The hand pulled him relentlessly and he let himself be drawn backward. The thought struck him that maybe this was better, better than running through the streets, better than forcing his body forever to take slow, measured steps; and then he heard a voice say. "You might have been killed, bud," and he realized that the hand and his being stopped had nothing to do with him, nothing to do with what had happened to him. He had stepped off the curb into traffic, and a stranger, a man to whom he was no one, had caught his shoulder, holding him back. It might have happened to anyone, even to the man who had held him. Its happening to him had no significance.

Except that it *had* happened. Except that there would always be someone to reach out and grab his shoulder, to destroy the pattern he had set for himself. He knew that there were too many for him, that there would always be too many. He knew that in walking through the streets in the only way he could, he was running —because of what had happened.

He lifted the man's hand from his shoulder, and he started back. He walked faster, returning. He could do that, now, even jostle others aside if it became necessary. Now that he was going back, it no longer mattered who took notice of him. He chose the same streets he had walked along before, even though there was a shorter way, through the park. He seemed to be undoing what he had already done by retracing it. When he reached the brownstone apartment, the childishness of this struck him, and he let himself in by the front door, although he had left by the rear. He ran the first half flight, until he remembered what he was running *to,* and not *away from,* and then he walked the remaining flights, his thin hand gripping the rail.

The telephone was just inside the door. There was a large oval mirror against the wall, behind the telephone table, and he remembered how Alice had hung it there so she could watch the shadowy play of emotion as she talked, laughing with delight at her quicksilver loveliness. He studied his own reflection as he dialed. It was a thin, white face, with plain features. It wasn't a face like Alice's, that could be switched and changed as she pleased. He could freeze it to a fixed, set mask that told nothing of the turmoil within him, but he could not vary the mask.

His voice was better. He could control the words and hold some part of the fear out of the tone. When his call went through, he said carefully, "This is Carter R. Rowe." He gave the address and then he waited until the man at the other end had written it down. "You'd better send someone out here," he explained. "Maybe more than one. You'd know about those things. It's my wife, Alice. She's been murdered."

They sent three men: a small, thin man who introduced himself as Lieutenant Cross; a heavy, bull-like detective, Sergeant Hannigan; and a policeman in uniform. At first, Rowe directed his words to the uniform, but gradually the realization took shape in his mind that this was beyond the traffic violation stage, beyond the point where an ordinary policeman could distinguish right from wrong. It was the men in street clothes who asked the questions and who went into the bedroom together and closed the door, leaving the uniformed policeman watching him disinterestedly. It was the uniformed one who drew the notebook from his pocket and sat down, his legs crossed, resting the book on his thigh, as the others came back from the bedroom. For a moment the thought struck Rowe that he could talk to these men as he would discuss an accounting problem with Mr. Jeffers, the head of the firm. He would show his figures and balances and they would listen respectfully, keeping to the issue at hand. He watched Lieutenant Cross dial the telephone, and when the lieutenant had completed his call and spun to face him with dull, disinterested eyes, he knew that this was not a problem on which he could work together with these men.

"All right, Mr. Rowe," Cross said. "Let's hear your story."

"I came home—" he began.

"Just a minute," Cross said. "Let's have the background first. Where do you work?"

"Jeffers, Lynn and Holbrook," he said. "I'm chief accountant. I've been with them seven years."

"Married how long?"

"Ten years," he said. Ten years and two months. The two months wouldn't matter to them.

"Age?"

"Thirty-seven."

Cross looked at the bedroom door. "And the—?"

"Twenty-eight," he said. That was right. It was twenty-eight, almost to the day.

"All right," Cross said. "Now, in ten years, problems come up between a couple. I'm a married man. I know. You got any of those you'd like to tell us about?"

Rowe shook his head. There were no problems, no problems at all. Everything had ended the moment—the second—he had opened the bedroom door. "No," he said. "Nothing at all."

"Friends?" Cross suggested.

Rowe gave him a list. Hall and Elsie Simmonds. Jerry Bancroft. The Redmonds. Clark Hammond. "Mostly people I met in business," he explained.

"Nobody else?" Cross said, watching him. "No special friend of yours?"

"No," he said.

"Look," said Cross. "Ten years is a long time. In ten years, a man might make friends his wife doesn't know about. Just a friend, maybe, that he sees off and on. Some girl who gives him a build-up when he's low. If there's anyone like that, it'd be better if you told us about her now."

"There's no one like that," he said, flatly.

Cross nodded. "Maybe it's the other way around. Some guy a girl tries to be nice to, and he gets ideas. Maybe she finds out her husband suspects her, and tells the boy friend off."

"There was nothing like that," he said. "There was just Alice and me. There was always just the two of us."

Cross studied him a moment, shrugged. "All right," he said. "Let's have the rest of it. What happened today?"

He told them how he had rung the bell, the way he always did, to let Alice know he was coming, and how he had opened the door with his key. He had stood in the hallway a moment, waiting for her, and then he had dropped his hat on the chair in the corner and knocked on the bedroom door. He had knocked three times, and then he had opened the door and seen her.

"You called the police?" Cross asked.

"Yes," he said. "I called the police."

"I guess that covers it." You can go in now, Mr. Rowe."

He sat still, not moving.

Cross said again, "You can go in. You'll have to identify the body."

"I know her," he said slowly. "I know who it is. It's my wife. I don't want to go in there."

The heavy-set one, Sergeant Hannigan, said, "It's a formality, Rowe. Makes it simpler." The sergeant dropped his feet from the rung of the chair opposite and stood up. "Come on."

Rowe didn't move. He said, "I can tell you how she is. She's half crumpled across the pillows. Her legs are drawn up as if she were trying to push something away from her. She has the knuckles of her left hand in her mouth."

Hannigan said, from the doorway, "She couldn't have fought much."

"She didn't fight," he said. "She never fought—anything." He said it to himself more than to Hannigan, knowing that the detective had no way of understanding how important that part of Alice was to the whole. "Her name is Alice Lee Rowe. Mrs. Carter R. Rowe. My wife." He felt that there was more he should say, but he didn't know what it was. "She was stabbed. There was a towel wrapped around a knife handle, and then she was stabbed with it."

"A quick end," Hannigan said. "The knife was rammed home hard, and then pulled out halfway."

He remembered that. The knife had seemed to go almost through her. He hadn't been sure but what it was through her, pinioning her to the bed.

"I did that," he said. "I drew it out a little. It seemed to go right through her."

"I see," Lieutenant Cross said. He said it as though he didn't see, as though he didn't understand why Rowe had had to draw it out a little, in case she were pinned to the bed. Now that Rowe thought of it himself, he realized that it had made no difference to her. But at the time, while he had been standing over her, it had seemed important, and he had grasped the end of the towel and drawn the knife out a little.

The knock at the door drew his mind from it. "Doc West," Cross said. "Or the lab boys." He nodded to the uniformed policeman to open the door.

It was both. The medical examiner was a square chunk of a man; the laboratory men were quick, thin-faced boys who might have been part of Rowe's own staff of accountants. The medical examiner nodded brusquely to Cross as he passed him on his way into the bedroom. The others lagged a moment in the doorway, exchanging greetings. The older one spied Hannigan and grinned. "You here?" he said. "Thought you'd been pastured."

"Next week," Hannigan told him. "Six more days and a life of ease."

Cross had opened the door to the little study off the living room. "You can wait in here, Mr. Rowe," said. "And if you don't mind, I'd like the jacket you're wearing." The lieutenant turned to the lab men. "There's a towel around the knife," he explained. "When you check it, you might want that coat."

"*He* do it?" the younger one asked.

Cross scowled. "The way he tells it, nobody did it. Nobody at all. Unless it was a stranger who passed by on horseback."

Hannigan led Rowe by the arm to the bedroom. "Let's get this over with," the detective said. "You can close your eyes, for all I care. Just tell me who she is. It'll save us all trouble."

He didn't look at her. He looked beyond her at the window, at the little ring dangling from the shade. He said, "She's my wife, Alice." He stood there, keeping his eyes on the curtain ring, until Hannigan turned him gently and guided him to the door of the study.

He wondered what they would do to her. He had read somewhere that they were callous in their work, but he knew that she was still beautiful, even in death, and he hoped that her beauty would make them handle her tenderly. Lines of Thomas Hood came back to him, and he felt the urge inside him to recite them aloud:

"Take her up tenderly,
Lift her with care;
Fashioned so slenderly,
Young, and so fair!"

He rose to his feet as though to leave the study, and the uniformed policeman stirred in his chair. Rowe checked himself and stepped to his desk, rummaging for cigarettes. He found a crumpled package and lighted one, and then, remembering, held the package out. The policeman leaned forward, caught himself, and leaned back. He was on duty. He couldn't smoke. But Rowe could smoke. *He* was free to do what he wished. He could open the bottom drawer of his desk and have a drink of the Scotch they'd been saving for Christmas. He could take off his shoes, or his tie. There was a policeman in the room watching him, and yet he could do whatever he might wish, and the policeman could not prevent him. Suddenly he understood what there was that he could not do, what they meant to keep him from doing, and the policeman made sense to him. There was a reason for him just as there was a reason for everything.

"I'm not going to kill myself," Rowe said.

He watched the policeman whip out his notebook and write, "I'm not going to kill myself"; and after that he didn't say anything else. He just sat there, smoking the cigarettes and staring at nothing, until he heard Cross call from the other room and Hannigan opened the door.

Lieutenant Cross was leaning against the telephone table, his hands braced behind his back, as though he were getting ready to push away from it. "All right, Rowe," he said. "We've got a lot of it. It was a nice idea. It would have been hard to prove that you'd come in twice today. But you were seen the second time. Why was it *twice*, Rowe? Why did you leave, and then come back? And why didn't you tell us about the first time?"

Rowe shook his head. He had forgotten that part of it. It was something he *hadn't* done; what he might have done instead of calling the police. When the man's hand had caught his shoulder in the street he had known there was no place to go but back. The two times were one in his mind.

Cross pushed himself away from the table. He picked up the gray felt hat from the chair in the corner. "Here's where you slipped, Rowe," he said. "You might have pulled it. Husband comes home from work and finds his wife murdered. But when you left this morning, you were wearing a hat. This hat. We checked with your office. You wore it at lunch. When you were seen coming home, you were bareheaded, but your hat was inside the apartment. Why, Rowe? Why did you kill her?"

"No," he said. "It wasn't the way you—"

Cross crumpled the gray felt in his hands. "The hat, Rowe," he said patiently. "Who brought it home? Who put it inside? This guy you dreamed up? The stranger on horseback?"

"No," he said. "It's my hat. It has my initials in it. I wore it today."

Cross loosened his grip, dropping the fedora to the floor. He kicked it once. "Okay," he said. "That's what I figured. Let's go."

He heard the clang of the outer door and the ring of footsteps down the corridor the way he heard all sounds now, with the knowledge that these things, the opening and closing of doors, the sound of footsteps, the brittleness of voices, were the slender links that connected him with the world outside. They were audible evidences that the universe had not shrunk, by some strange inversion, to the grilled door and the three plain walls that housed him.

It was Hannigan. Rowe said, "I'm glad to see you, Sergeant," and he meant the words as he said them. It was a moment in his life now to see even this stocky detective who came in with the outdoor rain on his topcoat and an air of damp freshness about him.

Hannigan sat down heavily on the edge of the bunk, spreading the wet tails of his coat behind him. "It's 'Mister' now. Just plain Joė Hannigan."

Rowe felt that that was supposed to make a difference between them, that Hannigan was no longer part of the law, but the law and the people outside had become fused in his mind. There was himself and what had happened to him, and then everyone else outside and apart from him. He took the cigarette Hannigan offered without saying anything.

Hannigan said, "How's your lawyer, Rowe?"

"All right," he said. "Mr. Jeffers sent him. His name is Rangold."

"Ed Rangold." Hannigan accepted him verbally. "You talk to him?"

"He knows what happened," he said. "You all know what happened."

"Yeah," Hannigan said. "Sure. We got your story, But that's not enough."

Ed Rangold had told Rowe that it wasn't enough. There was nothing for the jury to sink its teeth into. "Reasonable doubt," Rangold had said. "But, man, it has to be *tangible* doubt. There has to be a dark alley somewhere in the picture, some other way it *could* have happened.

"I told him what happened," Rowe said.

"You ran," Hannigan said, slowly. "You came in and found her that way and ran. Why? There has to be a reason for that, Rowe."

It came back to that, to the one point where his decision had been wrong. That was something he could not explain, any more than he had been able to explain drawing the knife out of her side.

"I was upset," he told Hannigan. "I wasn't thinking."

"Why?" Hannigan repeated. "Don't you see, Rowe? That's not a normal reaction. You weren't afraid of *her,* were you, Rowe?"

He didn't answer, but Hannigan found his own answer. "If

you'd been afraid of her, you couldn't have touched the knife."
Hannigan leaned forward, resting his elbows on his knees. "It's
things like that, Rowe, little things, that I can't figure. They
worry me, Rowe. A guy like you, if he'd killed his wife, giving
her a clean book, like you did. That doesn't make sense. A man
planning a murder like it shapes up as you did—leaving himself
without even an out." Hannigan inched over on the bed, talking
earnestly. He seemed to have forgotten anyone was with him, to
be going over to himself the things that had come up in his mind.
"Like you saying you always rang the bell before you opened the
door. If a woman is as scary as that, she's not going to let a
stranger in when she's only half dressed. But you *gave* us that,
Rowe, for free." Hannigan stopped a moment, weighing a
thought. "That could be it," he said. "You might figure as long as
she's gone, your life is over. You might be asking for this, Rowe."

"No," he said. "I don't want to die, Hannigan."

"Nuts," Hannigan said. He got up, pulling his coat around
him. "Look, Rowe," he said, "I'm not on this any more. I'm a free
man. I'm heading for Florida. I've got twenty years behind me
and I never yet worked on a case that went sour. I never had a
backfire after we sent a man up. I've got a nice clean slate, and I
want to keep it that way."

He understood now what Hannigan wanted. He felt a flash of
bitterness toward this man who could balance a life against his
own peace of mind, but there was no strength to the feeling. He
saw that circumstances had made him and what happened to him
a part of Hannigan, and that Hannigan had come to him asking
for help. He was aware that he could give that help, by a word or
gesture, without affecting the case against himself. But he couldn't
give it.

One thing remained to him: the end of their marriage. Not a
culmination of years of fighting, of hate, fear and deceit. He had
a right to that, to the honesty of his love for her. His eyes met
Hannigan's steadily. "I didn't kill her," he said.

His thoughts stayed with Hannigan in the endless chain of hours that time had become to him. It gave him something to do with his mind, to force it to analyze this man about whom he knew nothing, to attempt to measure the strength of Hannigan's motive. He knew that Hannigan's interest in him was a selfish interest and he knew vaguely that this fact lent force to it. He considered Hannigan as a man apart from himself, as someone who had become entangled by accident in his life. It was not until the third visit, until the day Hannigan laid the pictures of the knife on the bunk between them, that the feeling of uneasiness took hold of him.

"The police never traced it," Hannigan said. "They figured they didn't need it, so they let it slide. It's not easy to tie a knife to the person who bought it."

Rowe's lawyer had explained that, as a point in his favor; and Rowe had understood that it was a weak point, a straw on the water, but that there was that one slight thing in his favor.

"I may try it," Hannigan said. "I want this thing clean, Rowe. Wrapped up neat. And the knife could do it."

It was then that the uncertainty had been born inside him and he had forced his face to its fixed, set mask. It was at that point that he stopped considering Hannigan as someone apart from himself, and understood that the crossing of their lives had enwebbed them both. After that visit, after Hannigan had left, he became aware that the outcome no longer rested with his lawyer or with the mood of the jury, but upon the efforts of this man to whom he was nothing. He was suddenly, sharply afraid of this man whose life had been forced into his own.

He knew when they came to release him from jail that in some way Hannigan was responsible for his freedom. He accepted the sympathy of the others, the apologies for the errors that might have been made, and he let his lawyer lead him on a triumphal march to the street, but his mind was on Hannigan and his eyes sought him in the corridors and on the sidewalk. When he saw the bull-like figure in the doorway of a bar opposite, he knew he was being given a choice. He could go along with the others, or he could face this man who had broken his pretenses and saved his life doing it. He shook free from the lawyer's hand and crossed the street to the bar, following the ex-detective to a table.

He looked across the table at Hannigan. He knew that this man understood him now, that Hannigan knew the reasons underlying all of his actions. He was aware that his life, the ten years he had guarded, was open to Hannigan as it had been open to no man in the past. He didn't know what Hannigan thought of him, or how Hannigan judged his actions, but he felt close to him with the knowledge that here for the first time was a man who knew his life for what it had been. He said, "She couldn't help it, Hannigan."

Hannigan said, "It must have been a hell of a life for you, Rowe."

He didn't answer that. There was no answer to it. It had been his life, and she had been his wife and he had loved her. In her way, she had loved him. He was certain of that. It was why he was still there, always, when the others had gone. "She couldn't help it, Hannigan," he said again.

"I wouldn't know," Hannigan said. "But you'd have burned for it, Rowe. That I can tell you."

It had not been fear of that that had sent him into the streets when he first had found her. This thing had happened to her, a thing for which his forgiveness was useless, his understanding meant nothing. It had not occurred to him, at first, that he might be accused of the murder. He had seen the veil torn from their lives—her warmness, her weakness, held up to public laughter. He had been running from himself, and not from the police. He had been unsure of himself, wondering whether he might not, during the trial, scream the truth to the world. He had told Hannigan that.

"It would have been too late," Hannigan said. "That's why I

tried to show you. You couldn't have waited until you were half-way to the chair, and then shouted accusations at a dead woman. You'd have just cinched it, that way."

He couldn't have done it the other way, either. When Lieutenant Cross had asked the names of "special friends," he couldn't have handed him a list of men and said: It might have been any of these; they're the ones you mean. He felt it was important that Hannigan, who understood him and what he had done should understand the reason for doing it. He said again, "She couldn't help it, Hannigan."

"*He* didn't know that," Hannigan said. "He thought she'd divorce you and marry him. When he found out he was wrong, he killed her." His thick fingers drummed the table top. "It was Bancroft," Hannigan said. "Jerry Bancroft, in case you didn't know."

He hadn't known. He wondered now how Hannigan had known, how this man apart from their lives had plucked the name Bancroft out of nothing and said: This one here, he did it. He was the one. The feeling of closeness became stronger in him as Hannigan picked up the thread of his thoughts.

"I was looking for a man," Hannigan said. "The way I saw it, if you hadn't killed her, there had to be another man in her life." He hesitated, as if he were wondering how he could say it. He said it honestly, finally, the way it had happened. "I found too many men."

It was out. The wall Rowe had spent ten years building was down. He kept his eyes on the glass-topped table between them, not looking at Hannigan. He knew that Hannigan was winding it up for him, closing the book, and that Hannigan would go on now until it was finished. He waited it out.

"The rest was routine," Hannigan said. "It was a question of checking where each one had been the day of the murder, of whittling it down. The knife was the clincher. When I traced the knife to him, I had it."

It had been as simple as that. One of them had used the knife, so one of them had bought it.

"For the record," Hannigan said, "it was just one of those things. A man makes a play for a married woman and she gives him the brush-off. So he kills her. The rest doesn't matter. The papers'll give it the once-over-lightly. There's no meat in the story. Cross had it tagged, right from the start, only he didn't know it. For the book, this Bancroft was the stranger on horse-back."

Rowe said slowly, "I owe my life to you." He knew as he said it that the feeling that should have been in the words was missing. He wanted to say more, to praise Hannigan's work, but he felt the need to be away from this man against whom he was defense-less. He pushed back his chair and rose to his feet. "My friends are waiting," he said.

"Sure," Hannigan said. "Well, I'll be seeing you, Rowe."

His nod accepted the lie, but he knew that Hannigan was not deceived by the gesture. There was hatred inside him for this man from whose final prying he had failed to protect her. The hatred would be in his eyes for Hannigan to read. He could say again: She couldn't help it, Hannigan; but Hannigan would shrug and say: I wouldn't know about that.

Rowe turned swiftly and walked to the street. He did not look back. When he joined Ed Rangold and old Mr. Jeffers on the cor-ner, his face was a still, fixed mask. "Sorry," he apologized for breaking away. "I had to see that man. I owe him a lot." He steeled himself for the rest of it, the lie that would rebuild the wall. "Because of Alice," he said quietly. "Even more than myself."

AUTHOR'S POSTSCRIPT (FREELY TRANSLATED FROM THE ORIGINAL TELEPHONIC): The origin of the story is a patchwork of what one knows about people and what one thinks he knows, but can't say surely to be so. A man seems to be in love with his wife and she with him, and yet she, shall we say, digresses. He knows it, but will not, cannot admit it. I looked at the situation from the rear, as it were, assumed murder as the force to compel revelation, and watched the stranger on horseback ride away.

The Night the Stair Creaked

AT day's end, watching the audience file in unnatural silence from the courtroom, Nathaniel Fogg looked old and tired, and he was both. He knew with the certainty of a perceptive man and a lifetime lawyer that his client was innocent of murder, as charged. But he knew that as things now stood he had lost the case. The summaries tomorrow would be no more than formalities.

A man would be found guilty and sentenced to death.

A woman already dead would be considered avenged.

The State in demanding a life for a life would reaffirm its strength as an institution, and a square-jawed young prosecutor with his face radiating a Galahad righteousness would better his chances for the nomination to the state legislature.

With the courtroom nearly emptied now, the prosecutor approached the older lawyer in a spirit of conciliation. He beamed his vote-getting voice at him. "No hard feelings, Nate?"

Young Barlow, they called the prosecutor. "The smartest county attorney who ever came out of the woods . . ." He didn't like to be called young Barlow, and he didn't like his smooth and unlined face. Insecurity made him stiff and brash sometimes—callous about other people's feelings. People wanted to like him better than they did, sensing there was nothing the matter with him that a few more years on his husky shoulders wouldn't fix.

A meager smile set on Nathaniel Fogg's face as he looked at young Barlow briefly. "No hard feelings," he replied, and it was true to an extent: he felt as well disposed toward the ambitious prosecutor as he would have toward anybody who played with a man's life as though it were table stakes in a poker game.

Nathaniel's smile always tended to make young Barlow nervous. Seeing it now, he rubbed restless fingers over his cleft chin,

mindful of the old lawyer's reputation in the county for pulling
live kicking rabbits from very battered courtroom hats.

But scarcely this battered a hat!

There were, of course, other men who could have come in
Debora Hobson's bedroom and in the heat of anger or twisted
passion, struck that killing blow. Spectators at the murder trial
could have named a good many of them. The evidence, however,
pointed straight to Otis, the husband. Young Barlow had made
the most of this circumstantial evidence. In the questioning he
had chalked up one damning admission after the other . . . Otis
and his wife had been drinking, they had quarreled, he had hit
her hard enough to knock her down—

"But not hard enough to make that depressed fracture on the
skull the coroner keeps talking about," in tight-faced defiance
Otis had insisted. "There wasn't any mark on her head, or not
much. Not then. She got right up and socked me back. I was fed
up. I been fed up for a long time. I walked out on her."

He claimed he had left the rooming house a good two hours
before the time set by the coroner's jury as the murder time. He
had gone down to Hadley's Cove and just walked around in the
wind from the ocean he said. It was dark and he hadn't met anybody. He had been trying to make up his mind whether to go
back or not—whether to ever go back.

With circumstances dovetailed against Otis, everyone had expected Nathaniel Fogg to plead guilty and cite enough provocation to get a manslaughter charge. But the old lawyer hadn't.
This phase of it occasioned young Barlow some slight uneasy
wonder. It did at first. Not now.

Some defendants, in spite of evidence against them, make a
good impression on the stand. They do naturally. Otis Hobson
didn't. He was too sullenly resentful, scared, bewildered, or de-
spairing. Add to this the fact that he had no standing in Rock
Haven to begin with. A drunk and ne'er-do-well . . . for weary
years before the murder it had been common gossip that he quar-

reled often and violently with his wife because of her over-friendliness with other men.

"Over-friendliness" was young Barlow's sarcastically delicate phrasing. Now with the courtroom empty of everyone except old Codfish Hargrove who was poking around with his push brush and bucket of green sweeping compound, young Barlow wasn't so delicate.

"The woman was a tramp and everyone knows it," he said to Nathaniel Fogg. "I don't like to press for a death sentence in a case like this. Now why don't you quit betting into a pat hand and plead your man guilty? A few years on a manslaughter charge, and—"

"No."

"In the name of common sense, Nate, why?"

"Because he's not guilty."

"What's that got to do with it? The evidence is going to convict him."

"Maybe. I talked it over with Otis. We decided to fight it."

Young Barlow shook his head in honest bewilderment, and the older man said, "Something I don't know if you've found out yet, son. A murder trial's something more'n a game. It's got people in it—"

"All right, all right. Small solace your moralizing's going to be for Otis when the hanging verdict comes in against him to-morrow—"

Young Barlow stopped talking because he saw that Nathaniel Fogg's capacious mouth had opened in a wide yawn. Young Barlow remarked testily, "It's a good way to catch fish."

Nathaniel Fogg clacked his jaws shut. "What's that last you said?"

"Save that act for the courtroom, Nate. You heard me."

"Look, bub—" Nathaniel Fogg grinned, wryly or slyly, young Barlow couldn't tell which—"that yawn meant no disrespect. It came from sleepy necessity. I've had a hard and frustrating day in court, as you well know."

It was not, young Barlow, felt, a dignified admission. "Then you *will* enter a guilty plea," he said flatly.

"No."

"But it's your only chance!"

"I might have been inclined to think so—but you've just given me an idea."

Young Barlow was sure now that the grin had been a sly one. It made him nervous, even knowing he had the case sewed up. He said with a small, tight show of anger on his smooth face, "You haven't got the *creak* of a chance."

That last was a dig. The way things now stood it was the creak of a board that was going to fetch Otis Hobson the death penalty —rather it was the absence of that creak. His landlady hadn't heard it.

She could have alibied Otis. Enough anyway to plant a reasonable doubt in the mind of the jury. But she was a God-fearing, Christian woman, she testified, and she could not, in conscience, admit to hearing what she had not heard.

"But you *must* have heard it!" Otis Hobson had cried at her on the night they had picked him up slogging around by himself at Hadley's Cove, and brought him back to the rooming house before jailing him. "I went out of the house two hours before the coroner says—*it* happened. This heavy carpet on the stairs—you might not heard me coming down, but you *had* to hear that bottom step. It creaks. It *always* creaks. Loud! You know how you always make a joke about it when you get a new tenant—"

"Even if she did hear you going out, Otis," the constable holding him pointed out in as reasonable a voice as he could, "who's to say you didn't come back again, maybe through the side door, and—"

"I left enough tracks down at the Cove," Otis had cried again, "to show I was there's long as I said."

"Maybe. If the tide's left anything—"

"Anyhow, I didn't hear him going out," his landlady had insisted again. The pale lips on the spare face had pressed tight as she looked at Otis. "I'm sorry. You—you always paid your rent. And I—your wife certainly would of tried the patience of a saint, Mr. Hobson. Maybe it's like you say and you went out, though, before *it* happened. But if you did, *I* didn't hear you."

Otis tried once more, pleadingly. "But you had to! Look. Your back was toward me, but you were sitting just inside the parlor door. You'd been reading, I guess. I could see your hand just putting the book down on the table. Your other hand was rubbing at your eyes or patting at your mouth or something; I could see your elbow moving. And the stair creaked under my foot. Loud, like it always does. You *had* to hear it."

Nathaniel Fogg had tried to the last to reap some advantage for his client on this issue.

"Do you admit," he had bullied the landlady on the stand, "the step creaks?"

"Course it creaks, the pesky thing."

"And you were close enough to hear it?"

"Yes—if there'd been any creak to hear."

Nathaniel Fogg had turned and strode slowly past the jury box. The floor boards creaked under his step, and he bent his ears to their sound. In the 38 years he had practiced as a country lawyer in this courtroom he had come to know every protesting sound in the bare boards. They were old and worn and flint-dry, like himself.

Before the jury box he had paused, a lanky, oddly mournful figure in a high stiff collar and salt-and-pepper suit that looked as though it had come out of somebody's attic. He stood there, gently teetering.

"Can you hear that?" he questioned the landlady.

"That flood board creakin' under your foot? Course I can.

There's nothin' the matter with my hearin', Nathaniel Fogg, if that's what you're insinuatin'.''

"But you do admit you put the book on the table at about the time Mr. Hobson says he came downstairs and saw you from the doorway?"

"Yes. It was a draggy book and I was getting sleepy. I remember I got up and poked the fireplace and made myself a cup of tea from the kettle. That perked me up and I read for about another two hours—till I went upstairs and saw through the open door like I've already testified, and called the police."

Nathaniel Fogg permitted himself the meager smile that always made young Barlow nervous, even knowing he had everything going his way . . .

Now in the silent courtroom young Barlow moved with Nathaniel Fogg along the aisle to the door. They had to pass the old sweep-up man, Codfish Hargrove. Mindful that Codfish's vote, if it came to that, was as good as any man's, young Barlow said cheerfully, "Good evening, Mr. Hargrove."

Codfish Hargrove didn't answer, just kept pushing his broom, and Nathaniel Fogg screwed his long face up and gave him a wink.

The two lawyers moved on out of the courthouse together then, down the worn gray granite steps and onto the black tar sidewalk of Water Street. A harbor wind pushed up the street between the Customs House wharf and the sagging warehouse of the Turk's Island Salt Co. It brought a tang of sea-weed iodine and smoky herring . . . but then a more modern tang took its place as a stripped-down, hood-off car slammed past so close to the narrow sidewalk that they could feel its hot-rod breath from the noisy exhaust.

A tow-headed youngster at the wheel looked back, waving and grinning. "I missed you that time, Nate," he shouted.

"Ought to rule that clap-trap abomination off the public streets," young Barlow fumed. "That kid, what's his name—"

"Vinal Harrington."

"He's been going to fix that exhaust all summer. I don't think he wants it fixed. I think he likes it noisy."

"I think you've given me another idea," Nathaniel Fogg said. "Come on with me to the Cove House. I'll buy you a drink."

"I do not indulge in public drinking," young Barlow said.

Nathaniel Fogg smiled benignly. "Maybe that's what's the matter. You've been out of school long enough now to quit getting your law so much out of books. Maybe you ought to mix around with people more—"

He stopped because young Barlow was already moving away in the assured manner of a young man going some place. Where he was going was to the bowling alley. He didn't enjoy bowling, but he thought it kept him in shape.

Nathaniel Fogg stood there, liking the feel of the wind beating at his great shock of gray hair. As soon as young Barlow was out of earshot, Codfish Hargrove came shuffling down the granite steps. "*Mr.* Hargrove," he mimicked. "Never did trust a man thet called me mister." He dropped his voice until it had almost a conspiratorial tone. "Whut was it you winkin' to me about, Nate?"

"Put it this way, Codfish: I always liked your singin'. Ain't heard you sing for a long time."

Codfish gave him a grin that showed a black and empty tooth space. "I'm talkin' a sight closer to the truth'n you are, when I mention the reason you ain't heard me sing for a long time is I ain't had a bottle for a long time."

"Thought that might have something to do with it. I'll be glad to provide the, uh—stimulation."

Codfish Hargrove's cheeks were white and flabby. They shook as his big jaws chomped in anticipation. "When?"

"Later tonight—on one condition."

"Whut's thet?"

"You round up Jim and Howard and take the bottle over in the barber shop doorway to do your harmonizin'."

Codfish sensed that he was in a bargaining position. "Only one bottle for the three of us?"

"If you get to soundin' like you're runnin' dry, there just might happen to be someone drop by with another."

Codfish sighed pleasurably. "Sounds's though't might run into a right musical evenin', Nate. Only one thing; we got a constable'n Rock Haven not much appreciatin' the finer things. You mind whut happened the last time? You had to put up to git me out of the calaboose."

"I'll speak to the constable, Codfish. It's my considered opinion he likes music better'n he used to."

Codfish nodded. "Only one thing; who drops by with the first bottle?"

"Just possible I will. I got a fair bass when I'm hoarse from talkin', like today. We might make it a quartet to start . . . And now if you indulge in *public* drinking, Codfish, come on over with me to the Cove House for a binder on the deal."

"I'd take to that right kindly, Nate." Codfish Hargrove's hand slapped at his bagging coat pocket where the handle of a monkey wrench poked out. "Was goin' down there anyhow. Wind's freshenin' and Mr. Hood wants me to climb up'n tighten the bolts on his blasted sign—one out in front says Cove House. Rain's washed out the back-valley roads so bad a lot of the out-of-town jurymen are stayin' there. At the Cove House. Claim the sign squeaks all night'n they can't sleep."

"Thet so?" Nathaniel Fogg shook his head. "Hot-rod cars and *un*creakin' signs, and sardine boats putting a diesel smudge over the harbor where sailin' vessels used to be—this town is sure modernizin', Codfish."

"Ain't she? But some folks bothers easy, don't they? I had a room in back of the barber shop for 20 years now, and I never noticed the sign creakin' p'tic'ly."

Nathaniel Fogg said, "Funny, the things folks don't notice sometimes right under their noses." His hand reached out and transferred the monkey wrench from Codfish's bagging coat pocket to his own. If Codfish noticed, he didn't say anything about it.

After leaving Codfish, Nathaniel Fogg climbed the granite hill in his gangling stride to Harrington's Hilltop Garage on Pine Street. He stopped near the grease-smeared youngster who was taking down the engine of an A-model Ford.

"You fix the exhaust yet in that hot-rod of yours, Vinal?"

"No, but I'm goin' to, Mr. Fogg—"

"Don't be in too much hurry about it," Nathaniel Fogg told him, and when the youngster looked up, curious, he continued, "Could I make it worth your while, Vinal, to stay up all night to-night—and keep your mouth closed about it for at least a day or two?"

"Might be. What else I have to do?"

"Once an hour, on the hour, you take that hot-rod abomination of yours out of the garage and run her past the Cove House."

"That all?"

"Unless you could get a couple of your automotive friends to snort around with you—make it a kind of parade."

"I could do that."

The unguarded talk of the jurymen filing into the courtroom the next morning was all on the same complaining level:

"Damndest night I ever spent. Somebody made a racetrack around the hotel all night long—"

"Bunch of drunks in the barber-shop singin'. Three o'clock before the constable shut 'em off—"

"Sign creaked and cranked all night outside my window—"

"Outside *my* window, from the sound of it—"

Young Barlow observed with interest. The boys, it would seem, had experienced a bad night in their rooms at the Cove House. Well, it was all grist to the prosecutor's mill. There'd be no horsing around the juryroom now. Disgruntled and sleepy, they'd be inclined to settle the case quickly, on the evidence—get it over with and get home.

Young Barlow assumed his Galahad stance and looked across at his jousting opponent. Nathaniel Fogg looked sleepy too—and quite unattuned to the jury's mood. No doubt about it, old Nate was slipping. Well, a lifetime in a courtroom took it out of you, he supposed . . .

Young Barlow in his summary made an excellent impression on the spectators and jury both. The twelve-good-men-and-true looked afterwards a little self-consciously breathless as realization set hard upon them that they would today go down in Neebago County history as a hanging jury. They still called it that, even though the State had long since substituted the electric chair for the seven-times-around hangman's knot.

When he sat down young Barlow had only one small worry left. He knew that a defense lawyer, lacking evidence to build a case on, could sometimes in the closing moments of a trial sell his personality to the jury in the interests of his client.

Young Barlow's worry was short-lived. With the first words of Nathaniel Fogg's summary it was evident he was not attempting this evasive tactic. He seemed, in fact, to be drearily aware that the race was run. He appeared just an old beaten man going through some motions, saying the obvious, the ineffectual things: that there were other avenues of exploration in this case, other people with motives and with opportunities . . .

Nathaniel Fogg was not even bothering to confront the jury closely. Instead, he was standing off to one side in a manner so apologetic that young Barlow felt almost sorry for him.

As his summarizing droned on, Codfish Hargrove down in the front row yawned cavernously. His big jaws took all the slack out of his flabby cheeks with that uninhibited yawn.

The yawn was infectious. One of the jurymen fought the inclination, then lifted his hand in an instinctive mouth-covering gesture as he enjoyed a deep yawn of his own.

At that instant Nathaniel Fogg shifted his lean weight. Energy flowed to his drooping body as he snapped himself erect. His arm came up. A bony finger sought out the yawning juryman accusingly.

His voice drove hard. "Did you hear that?"

"Hear what?" the surprised juryman blurted.

"You mean you didn't hear anything?"

"No—nothin' special."

Nathaniel Fogg's finger prodded at another juryman. "Do *you* know what I'm talking about?"

"I didn't hear anything— Unless—you mean that board creaking under your foot a moment ago?"

"That's precisely what I *do* mean. How many of the rest of you heard it? Raise your hands?"

Most all of the jurymen raised their hands.

Young Barlow swapped a nervous glance at the judge, and he was half out of his chair to protest this unorthodox questioning of the jury before he remembered the advice of an old-horse political councilor: "Be charitable to your enemy when you have nothing to lose." He eased himself back in his chair.

A tired smile touched the lugubrious face of Nathaniel Fogg as he moved to confront the jury closely. "And now, gentlemen, I rest my case. Most of you heard the board creak under my foot. One of you, specifically, did not. Now I make no exaggerated claims. I do not say this established the innocence of Otis Hobson conclusively. But I am about to show that it does establish a reasonable doubt as to his guilt. Now I could bring medical practitioners and biological scientists into this court to assert that when the eustachian tubes of the inner ear are closed off by a pronounced stretching of the jaw, as in the act of yawning, an appreciable or complete blockage in hearing occurs . . . That is what I submit could have—almost certainly *did* happen—in the case of Otis Hobson's landlady. She has testified that her book was dull, she was putting it down, she was growing sleepy at the time Mr. Hobson testified he came down the stairs. She did not hear the bottom step creak because, like the gentleman in the jury just now, she yawned— Like this—" Nathaniel Fogg opened his own considerable jaws to demonstrate. A few of the jurymen grinned; more of them yawned luxuriantly back.

The tardy voice of young Barlow cut across the courtroom. "I object! This whole irregular procedure, Your Honor . . . irresponsible inference—"

"Objection sustained," the Judge ruled. "Irregular it is. But I would remind the attorney—and the jury—that all circumstantial evidence is inference. As for this particular inference being irresponsible—" he turned a measured glance upon the jury—"that is your particular responsibility, gentlemen, to decide."

That evening young Barlow reappraised his way of life and self-consciously but resolutely repaired to the tap room of the Cove House to indulge in a little public drinking. There he sought out Nathaniel Fogg, and the talk built up fast: a post-mortem on the decision on the Hobson case.

"Twarn't anything remarkable that turned the decision my way," Nathaniel Fogg declared modestly. "I just prepared my case right down to the last minute, that's all, leaving nothing to luck—"

"Luck!" young Barlow protested dourly. "You had more court-room luck today than a man could rightly expect in a lifetime. Even making your talk dull, the way it appears you deliberately did, couldn't have assured that juryman's yawn at the precise psychological moment to let you make that point about the creaking step. Even if you planted old Codfish down there in front and primed him to open that big mouth of his— You couldn't be *sure*. It was luck—"

"There'll likely be gossip around to the contrary, son," Nathaniel Fogg interrupted. He yawned, and favored young Barlow with his meager smile.

"No hard feelings?" Young Barlow was braced to hear it. But Nathaniel Fogg didn't say it. Young Barlow allowed that

Nathaniel must be conversant with the same old saw about being charitable when you have nothing to lose. He still had to learn that some people are just charitable naturally.

EDITOR'S POSTSCRIPT: In the absence of comment on his story by Mr. Johnson, I provoked a friend's comment on Mr. Johnson, of whom he said: a very lovable man, whose life seems to be a marvelous chain of digressive discoveries. Once in a Maine village, he went on an errand with Ryerson, a simple mission, to pick up a coffee pot for a picnic. But on the way they found sea shells of "purest ray serene," explored a sea-wrecked shanty, visited a custom's man at home since he wasn't on duty to inspect them, and did fetch back the coffee pot in time for the picnic. Well, in time for some picnic.

Snap Shot

THE really terrifying thing about Lampeter was that he was so ordinary. Neither large nor small, neither intellectual nor brutish. Running decently to fat, as a man may at forty-five. Wearing glasses for reading. The only really surprising thing about him was that he was still a bachelor. You would have thought some woman would have picked him up and popped him in her pocket long ago.

And whatever dragons lived inside his head, whatever dread familiar stood at his elbow whispering commands that could not be disobeyed, whatever worlds he created and whatever worlds he destroyed, they left no mark at all upon his placid face. No single ripple distorted the surface of the dark lake to give warning of the creature that laired in the depths.

How Mr. Robinson and Mr. Smith found out the truth about Lampeter is a mystery. The Robinsons and the Smiths know everything. They live by knowledge. Almost the first time they saw him, Mr. Robinson (who spoke five languages) said to Mr. Smith in one of them, "Here is our man." And Mr. Smith said, "I believe you are right."

"There's going to be an all-time record scrum," said "Tabs" Milligan. "Every paper in the land's here."

"Of course there's a scrum," said "Polly" Flinders. He was first photographer for the *Trumpet*, and conscious of the prestige this conferred. "It's not an itsy-bitsy little film star, Tabs. It's Paraman. He *is* news."

There's old Cummins, looking like a constipated crab. Clever with outdoor work, though. Lots of faces I don't recognize."

"If they don't get a move on it's going to be too dark to take proper photographs," said Polly. "And this is one we don't want to miss, isn't it? Prime Minister of England shaking hands with Paraman. Think of that!"

"It is a sign of the new age," said a small, dark man with a beard.

"It's a bloody miracle," said Polly. "And, boy, here she comes."

The four-engined airliner swung in a majestic curve across the airport, headed into the wind, centered itself on some invisible mark, and came down as firm and straight as if it had been ruled on paper. The pilot picked up the eighty tons of metal and laid it down on the runway as lightly as a feather.

Lines of men in blue began running.

"They've got as many police here as the Coronation and May Day put together," panted Milligan. He was trotting forward with the other newspapermen.

It was superbly organized.

One minute the landing strip was empty. The next minute there was a thin but unbroken blue line round the airliner, fifty yards from it. Unbroken on three sides. Through the fourth, in three well-regimented platoons, each with its roped approach way, came the Deputation of Welcome (morning dress and smiles), the Security Detachment (bowler hats and frowns) and the forty or fifty photographers, in every variety of dress and with no time at all to bother what they looked like.

Landing steps were quickly run out.

But someone had miscalculated. Insufficient frontage had been allowed for the photographers to form a single line. Normally this might not have mattered a great deal, but this was by no means a normal occasion.

The line shifted and spread. Two policemen tried to hold back the ends. They might as well have tried to grasp quicksilver. The policemen were evaded, their protests unheeded, as the line elongated, then swept round in a half circle, until the right-hand end rested almost under the shadow of the great airplane.

Down the gangway walked two large men, in brown coats and

black hats. They saw the stretching line of photographers, and frowned. But events were moving too fast for them, too.

For, behind them at that moment, appeared the world-famous figure photographed a hundred thousand times, but until then never seen in the flesh in the Western world. The small beard, the face, almost startlingly brown, the graying hair, the smiling tired eyes. The eyes that had seen everything and forgotten nothing.

The battery of newsreel cameras on the parked vans started to purr in grateful unison. The flashlights of the photographers winked almost simultaneously.

The Prime Minister stepped forward with an impulsive gesture of boyish charm (rehearsed behind locked doors until it had achieved a polished spontaneity), and thrust out his hand. Paraman grasped it, and said something with a broad smile.

The Prime Minister looked round for the interpreter—and in that very moment it happened.

Paraman pulled has hand away and laid it over his heart. A look of wonder came into his eyes. It was as though a question, often asked, had surprisingly been answered.

Then his knees folded under him and he dropped, quietly and without fuss, onto his face on the concrete runway.

"For a moment," said the Prime Minister, "I thought he'd had a heart attack. That would have been bad enough. Then I saw the blood on his hand."

"Yes, sir," said Commander Elfe.

"Even then I couldn't grasp it. Murder!"

"Extraordinary timing," agreed the Commander. His own head was loose on his shoulders at that moment, and none knew it better than he. "We do appreciate the importance of clearing this up quickly."

They were standing in the magnificent Privy Council room in Whitehall. The Prime Minister moved over to the bow window and stared across at the waters of St. James's Park.

He had, in fact, and quite cold-bloodedly, considered whether or not he should sack the head of the Special Branch, and had come to the conclusion that for the time being he had better support him.

"I don't want to exaggerate this," he said, "nor, God knows, to minimize it. I don't think it will mean war. Their radio's been white hot, of course, but the world's outgrown the Sarajevo days. On the other hand, if we don't catch the man, and prove that he did it, and why he did it, and clear the whole thing up, why, it'll leave a legacy of distrust for ten years—in just that part of the world where we most need trust."

He came back into the room. The Commander was not quite certain whether the Prime Minister added, "And it will certainly lose us the next election." Spoken or not, the thought was there.

"I'm sure you'll do your best," the Prime Minister concluded, shaking hands almost formally with Commander Elfe.

"Like a doctor," said the Commander to Superintendent Bliss, "who has just pronounced sentence of death with a hope, a very faint hope, of reprieve. How are you getting on with those bloody photographers?"

"There are exactly forty-five of them," said the Superintendent, "and they are all precisely what they said they were, if you follow me."

"Yes."

"About two-thirds of them were from newspapers. Some old and tried hands. Some new boys. In every case the newspaper concerned says they were absolutely reliable."

"Of course."

"The other third were from private news agencies, large and small. But since there's nothing to stop anyone forming a news agency—it only needs a man, a boy, and a back office near Fleet Street—"

"Quite so," said Elfe. "I suppose we're concentrating on the smaller agencies. Was it a camera gun?"

"I think so. It would be the obvious way, wouldn't it?"

"Have the experts made anything out of the weapon you found on the runway?"

"It's a small air pistol of a very powerful new type. The pressure's too high for ordinary loading methods. It's fired with a compressed air capsule which, incidentally, gives it a higher muzzle velocity than a .38."

"And therefore higher accuracy."

"Yes. A real murder weapon. Two other points about it. It's got no sighting apparatus of any sort, and the exterior of the muzzle is screw-threaded an inch from the end."

"That sounds conclusive to me," said Elfe. "It was specially made to screw into the socket of a camera. And it was calibrated to the camera sights. Right? When the cross wire of the camera view finder was over the victim's heart, the murderer simply pressed the button. All right. You've got all the cameras. It shouldn't be difficult to see which one's been tampered with."

"It shouldn't," agreed the Superintendent. "But it is. Most of the cameras are made to be taken apart, and all of them, except the very smallest, could have been used to hide a gun. But none of them has actually got a socket that fits the screw threads on the gun we found. Of course, we're not dealing with fools. It would have been quite easy to make the thing in two parts, with an outer metal bush that fits into the camera and is screw-threaded in the center to take the gun."

"I'm afraid that's right, too." Elfe thought it out slowly. His mind was not working with its usual calm precision, and that wasn't only because he had been up for two nights. For the first time he was beginning to weigh the odds against them. "I take it that as soon as he'd fired, the assassin would unscrew gun and bush—quite a natural sort of gesture—if anyone did spare him a second glance they'd think he was removing an exposed plate or something. Drops the gun down his trouser leg and onto the ground. Puts the bush in his pocket. Just an ordinary small piece of metal. By the way, they were searched pretty thoroughly, weren't they? Was anything of the sort found?"

"No. But by that time they'd crossed two hundred yards of grass field, and been standing about for half an hour. It could easily have been trodden into the ground. Or dropped down a drain."

"All the same, we'd better search for it," said Elfe. "And find it. We can't hold forty-five photographers on suspicion, even in a case like this."

There was a great deal to do, but, unfortunately for Elfe's peace of mind, very little that he could do himself.

There were forty-five men, with forty-five backgrounds that needed checking. There were forty-five cameras and one gun that needed a laboratory going-over; and thirty editors and fifteen agencies who had to be told why they couldn't have the photographs their men had taken of the biggest news event of the century.

("As long as *no one* gets a photograph, I don't mind," said the editor of the largest paper of all, quite genially. "But you release a single one to anyone ahead of anyone else and you'll raise a head of steam which will blow you out of Scotland Yard.")

Much of this could be attended to by the regular organization. But there were other matters, more subtle, less objective, which could be attended to only by Elfe's own department. The motives behind the killing. Known terrorist organizations. Pressure groups. The dim politics of the half world of secret agents, official and unofficial, of military attachés who had never been in any army and of trade delegates who dealt with anything but trade.

It was not at all plain, for example, to whose advantage the killing of Paraman, at such a time and place, might have been. To his successors? Yet it seemed clear from their reactions that it had come as a bigger surprise to them than to anyone else. To those who wished to increase the tension between England and Paraman's country, and might profit from such tension? Elfe was

not a great believer in the figure of the world financier who man-
ufactures wars and revolutions for his own enrichment. Most of
the big financiers he knew were timid men who liked a thirty per
cent margin of security for their money.

The really frightening thought was that the killing was probably quite illogical. There were at least three groups in England
who would kill merely for killing's sake. Imaginary grievances,
sterile causes, which were rooted in terror and flourished in the
occasional sensational stroke.

"When we get to the bottom of the matter," Elfe said to Bliss,
"we shall find that Paraman was killed because his predecessor
had someone's aunt flogged in Poland twenty years ago."

"Doesn't matter who it is," said Bliss, "as long as we catch
them. Did you see the *Trumpet* headline today?"

"I never read the papers," said Elfe.

Nevertheless, the writing was on the wall. In forty-eight hours
at the most the Foreign Secretary was going to be on his feet
answering the questions of a critical House; and unless he had
some answers to give, public opinion was going to demand a
scapegoat. And Commander Elfe had no delusions as to who
would be cast for that role.

Early that evening he left his office and walked slowly down
Parade Street, into the Park, past the south end of the Palace, and
out into Buckingham Gate. In a lesser figure, his method of progress might almost have been described as furtive. He paused in
front of the modest building which houses the Director of Public
Prosecutions, and then, almost as if it were an afterthought, went
inside.

The Commissionaire saluted as Elfe said, "Has Mr. Hughes
gone home yet?"

"I don't think so, sir. Shall I tell him you're here?"

"I'll announce myself," said Elfe. He walked up one flight of
steps and stopped outside a door marked *Deputy Director,* and
underneath that, *Gladwyn Hughes,* and underneath both, *KEEP
OUT!*

He opened the door without knocking and a white-faced black-jowled man, who was plotting something on a large sheet of graph paper pinned to the table, roared, "Get out," and then, looking up, "Come in. I thought it was that fool Langley. You don't happen to know a function of seven that combines with itself to produce either nought or infinity?"

"Not being a mathematician or a magician, no."

Gladwyn Hughes was both a mathematician and a magician. He completed the *Times* crossword puzzle every morning between Woking and Surbiton, had played contract bridge for England, and was capable of thinking in three different planes simultaneously. He had come to the D.P.P.'s office via the Legal branch of Scotland Yard and would one day head the C.I.D.

"You're worried about the Paraman case?"

"I'd like your help," said Elfe.

"Of course. Anything I can do. What do you want?"

Elfe sat down in the shabby armchair. It was very comfortable. "What we really need," he said, "is a fresh mind on the problem."

"Do my best," said Hughes. "I've read about it, of course. Tell it from the beginning to end. It'll help you as well as me."

The long hand had gone right round the old-fashioned clock on the mantelshelf before Elfe had finished.

"It's a stinker," said Hughes. "If we were a totalitarian country we'd have all those cameramen in cells now, giving them Number One treatment, and the first to break down would be awarded the starring role in the forthcoming trial, and everybody else would be covered with coats of whitewash."

"Except me," said Elfe.

"Well, yes. I expect you'd have been shot already. *Pour encourager les autres.*" Hughes looked curiously at Elfe. As a psychologist, it always interested him to see how his superiors and colleagues reacted under pressure. He thought Elfe was doing quite well. A little tight round the mouth, but plenty in reserve still.

"Could I see the films?"

"Now?" said Elfe. "Yes. I expect so. If I telephone from here they could have them ready by the time we get there."

In the basement of Scotland Yard there is a tiny private cinema, at which very odd films are sometimes shown. The two men settled into their seats, and the white fanlight of the projector cut across the darkness.

"This is the longest version," said Elfe. "Unfortunately, the focus is on the Prime Minister and Paraman. You can see the photographers, but they're a bit blurred."

"Again," said Hughes a little later. And still later, "Again." The second time he had a stop watch in his hand. The third time he made notes.

As they came out of the projection room Hughes said to Elfe, "I want to get hold of one of those newsreel cameramen. A reliable one. Can you do that? I've got the glimmering of an idea. If it comes to anything, where can I find you?"

"At my flat," said Elfe. "I don't suppose I shall go to bed."

It was two o'clock in the morning when Hughes arrived. His eye was bright, and he said "No" regretfully to the whiskey that Elfe pushed across. "I've been drinking with an Irishman called Milligan. I survived, but only just. Now, I'm going to strike a bargain with you."

Elfe cocked an eye at him.

"If I give you the idea that leads to the man you want, will you let me stay in on the case until the end?"

Elfe hesitated barely a second, then said, "Yes, of course."

"All right. Then here it is. All you've got to do to locate your chap is to develop *all the films and plates* in their cameras."

"There are about three hundred of them."

"It doesn't matter if there are three thousand. What my cameraman told me—and, remember, they see dozens of receptions every week—was this. The normal drill at an airport is that the photographers are marshalled up, in a sort of column. They're not allowed to dodge all over the place. The ones in front take their shots and then it's an understood thing that they then stand aside and the next lot take theirs—and so on. It works quite well normally, because if you've got a lot of agency boys there, they don't all want the *same* picture. One lot will take the exit from the plane, the next will snap the walk across the tarmac, the next the ceremonial handshake, and so on. You follow me?"

"Yes, but—"

"Wait. Unfortunately, in this case, it didn't work that way. The occasion was unique. Everyone was impatient. Instead of staying put and doing the thing in an orderly way, the photographers behaved like a lot of bobby soxers, dodged the police, and strung out *in a single line* across the runway."

"Yes. The film showed all that, but—"

"Wait again. That meant they all had an equal chance of taking a photograph. And I've no doubt at all that they all did. *Except one.* He couldn't. He had a gun in his camera. Remember?"

Elfe breathed out slowly.

Then he mumbled, "I said it needed a fresh mind. Keep in touch."

At eleven o'clock the next morning the red telephone on Mr. Hughes's desk sounded off and the voice of Elfe said, "Bull's-eye, Gladwyn. It's a Mr. Lampeter. Works for the Multum in Parvo Agency in Shoe Lane. Founded three months ago. Directors Mr. Smith and Mr. Robinson."

"What are you going to do?"

"We shall try some shock treatment," said Elfe. "Stay where I can reach you."

Lampeter was worried. He had done just what he had been told, both at the time and afterward.

"Afterward is important," Mr. Smith had said. "Just behave quite normally. They'll confiscate your camera, of course, but it won't tell them anything. You've got another. Go out and get on with the job."

So, for two days and the beginning of a third, Mr. Lampeter

had sat in the backroom office, with the deaf and dumb girl, and had sallied forth to photograph two weddings, a presentation of athletic trophies, and the birth of triplets.

But he wished that They would get in touch with him. They had told him it would be soon—but three days! And then the incident of that morning. It had upset him.

The dumb girl made a mooing noise to attract his attention and he looked up. The red light was showing above the side door —the one which led by the emergency staircase to the back entrance in Pepys Court.

He jumped to his feet and unlocked the door. Mr. Smith and Mr. Robinson came in, and something in their faces chilled the welcome from Mr. Lampeter's lips.

"What is it?" he said. "What's happened? Is something wrong?"

"I don't know," said Mr. Robinson. "What happened to you this morning?"

"At the wedding?"

"Yes."

"It was all a mistake. A big man bumped into me in the crowd. He apologized. Somehow I lost my wallet. It was found later in the corner of the room. I suppose I must have dropped it there."

"Was there anything in it?"

"Just some money. And my commutation ticket. How did you know about it? Were you there?"

"We were there," said Mr. Smith. He did not think it necessary to explain that Lampeter had not been out of their sight since he left the airport.

"The man who bumped into you. Did you know he was a detective?"

"A detective! Are you sure?"

"Of course, I'm sure. His name is Sergeant Hibley. And he is in the Special Branch."

"But why?"

"I should think it's quite plain," said Mr. Robinson brutally. "They wouldn't pick your pocket for love."

There was silence in the tiny dusty office. The deaf and dumb girl broke it by pushing an envelope into her typewriter and addressing it noisily. She disliked the shape of Mr. Robinson's mouth, and Mr. Smith's eyes frightened her.

"You remember," said Mr. Lampeter, breathlessly. "You promised that if anything went wrong you would look after me."

"Of course," said Mr. Smith. "We said it and we meant it. The car's outside. Get your hat and coat."

Mr. Robinson wrote on a piece of paper, "We shan't be back today. Lock up when you go," and pushed it in front of the girl who looked at it indifferently. Men, with their comings and goings and self-importance, meant little in her private world.

"The car's outside," said Mr. Smith. He looked at his watch and made a calculation. It was five o'clock on an early summer evening. They had almost four hours of daylight ahead of them. It should be enough.

"I've always wanted to see how you manage this part," said Gladwyn. He sank into the back seat of the car. "When do we sight them?"

Elfe nodded absently. He was busy with a roll of large scale maps. Beside the driver a young police wireless operator with black eyes and a cheerful, gipsy face twiddled the dial of the set.

"We flushed them ten minutes ago," said Elfe. "Shoe Lane, up Ludgate Hill, along Cannon Street, over London Bridge. New Kent Road. Old Kent Road."

"If you're not following him," said Hughes, "who is?"

"No one, really. That isn't how it works at all. This is the first part of Operation Network." He demonstrated on the map. "There are a limited number of places you *must* go past when you leave London. If he breaks Southeast, I give the codeword and about twenty-five posts are manned—each with a wireless— easy, really . . . Has he got past New Cross, Illingworth?"

"Coming up to it now, sir."

"Right or left?"

There was a moment's pause, then the set crackled. "Left, sir."

"Looks like A.2."

"What happens when he gets out in the open country?"

"You'll see," said Elfe.

The car slid on through the warm summer evening.

"A.2 it is, sir," said the operator. "We're going to air control now."

"Do you mean to say you do it with airplanes?"

"One airplane, way up, to coordinate. The real work is done by helicopters. They are the ideal answer to a car in open country. Keep above a closed car and a bit behind it, and ten to one the people inside don't even know it's there. The real limitation is speed. If the controlling aircraft sees that the helicopter is getting left behind it whistles up another from in front."

"I see," said Hughes. "Have you any idea where those characters are taking Lampeter? Or what they're going to do with him?"

"Bypassing Dartford," said the operator. "On Rochester Road."

Elfe marked the location on his map and said, "I could guess the answer to the second question."

Mr. Robinson was an expert driver, and he drove his car hard. Lampeter sat in the back with Mr. Smith.

Once, as the milestones showed Rochester approaching, he said, "Where are we going?"

"To the coast," said Mr. Smith. "We'll have to hide you until we can get you out of the country."

"I see," said Lampeter. He shivered a little, and Mr. Smith looked down at him curiously. "There's nothing to be frightened of."

"I'm not frightened," said Lampeter. "I had a feeling that I'd been asleep for a long time, and was just waking up."

"Perfect," said Mr. Smith. "We turn off here, I think."

The car threaded a network of byroads, which degenerated into country lanes. Ahead of them lay the sea. Lampeter could sense it.

"Down here. It doesn't look like much of a track, but it'll take the car."

Suddenly they were out of the close country and on the marsh. A short, straight, sandy track, pointing out like a finger to a tumbledown house and barn.

"Is this where I hide?"

"This is where you stop," agreed Mr. Smith.

The car came to a halt. Mr. Robinson cut the engine and they climbed out.

In the silence they could hear the birds at evensong, the distant complaints of the marsh cattle, and the buzzing of a million insects.

Lampeter pushed open the door of the old house and went inside. A few minutes later he came out, a puzzled look on his face.

"There's nothing there," he said. "Nothing for cooking, no bed—"

He stopped. Mr. Robinson had come round from the back of the car. He carried a spade. Mr. Smith was taking something from his pocket.

For a fattish man in bad training Lampeter moved quickly. And he moved in the one direction which gave him a chance— between Mr. Smith and Mr. Robinson.

Mr. Robinson swiped at him with the spade and missed. Lampeter ran with the speed of fear. Then there was a sharp crack, and a curious sound like the clapping of soft hands as the air opened and shut over his right shoulder. Then it was as if steel fingers had gripped him by the arm. The force of it almost spun him round, but he kept on running. There was a gate ahead and a line of bushes. And through the bushes something winked suddenly, in the sun. It was the windshield of a car, moving.

"Help," croaked Lampeter, through dry lips. Then something caught him full in the back and the earth rose up at him and the red globe of the sun swung round full circle and he was diving into merciful blackness.

As he went down he seemed to hear, far off, two more shots. . . .

Elfe looked down at the three men. Mr. Smith and Mr. Robinson were dead.

"That's always the way of it," he said to Gladwyn Hughes. "If things go right, they're terrific. If things go wrong, they destroy themselves. In their code, it's the only answer to failure."

"Is Lampeter dead?"

"Three parts. But I think we'll be able to pull him back."

"Why bother?" said Hughes. He looked at the spade and mattock. "Wouldn't it be easiest to finish the job, and bury them all?"

"My dear Gladwyn," said Elfe. "You can't be serious. Our job is to patch the little man up, then put him in the dock and deal with him according to law. Right? Right."

AUTHOR'S POSTSCRIPT: When walking on a quiet summer evening through the Queen Anne period streets which lie to the south of Buckingham Place, I found myself opposite the door of the Director of Public Prosecutions office, which was a charming building in Buckingham Gate. The door opened and a middle aged, white faced, black-haired man, wearing a black homburg hat walked slowly out. He was evidently deep in thought, and I could not help wondering what criminal's life might be affected by the outcome of his meditation. Finally, he drew from his pocket a copy of the *Times* newspaper, and with great satisfaction inserted a word in the bottom right hand corner crossword. This was the beginning of the story.